A FLAME UNDER THE MOON

MONICA AMORE

Cover design by MiblArt. All stock photos licensed appropriately.

Editor: Rachel Bunner

Instagram username: @rachels.top.edits

Proofreader: Chelsey Brand

Character Artist: Clint A.

Instagram username: @clintcreates

Visit my website for more books, merch, character art prints & more.

www.authormonicaamore.com

Digital Edition ISBN: 979-8-9889334-0-3

Paperback Edition ISBN: 979-8-9889334-1-0

Hardback Edition ISBN:979-8-9889334-2-7

DEDICATION

FOR THOSE WHO WERE LEFT IN THE DARK,
AND FORCED TO CALL IT A HOME,
LET THE LIGHT WITHIN YOU BE AN INFERNO.

CONTENTS

TRIGGER WARNINGS

Grief and loss
Sexually explicit
Consensual Sex
Explicit language
Blood and gore
Extreme violence
Sacrifice
Torture
Trauma
Loss of a family member
Threat of sexual assault (not by MMC)

Author's Note

Warning to the reader: This book contains mature language, graphic violence, explicit content, and subject material that may be disturbing or upsetting. It is intended for readers who are 18 and over.

PROLOGUE
The Captor

Her voice carries me through an open field where the air is warm. The grass is high enough to brush against those perfect fingertips as she walks toward a raging sea. The sun is setting, soft strokes of orange and purple fill the sky between the hands I long to touch. Her back is to me while she stares at the ominous waves crashing against the shore. Her hands are gently splayed at her sides, the air is charged, and I know she is powerful. She's clad in silver armor with a sword strapped to her back. My eyes trail down its blood-stained, leather sheath to hips that spark more of my curiosity. I inhale the briny air of sea and sage, standing on the brink, hoping that I can somehow smell her, that I can touch the very hands that have brushed against my soul. Every night I've dreamt of her, a soft, light voice that carries so much rage and sorrow. This all feels so real. I don't know what this means for me, but I cherish these moments with this dark-haired stranger. She becomes a remedy in all my hollow spaces that are waiting patiently in the dark. She's the reason I seek to dream, because every night, I see a little more of this beauty. It's not enough, it will never be enough. Even if I'm nothing but a particle of dust floating in the wind, I long to be caught in her storm. As I reach for her, something takes hold. I'm swept up in a whirlwind.

"No." I shoot up from the bed so fast, the blankets go flying in a purple blur. My eyes widen at the sight of my dream slipping through a chasm in my room. It's disappearing through the early dawn in swirls of golden light floating across my bed. As I stand here watching it churn like stars, my heart slams against my chest.

This has never happened before.

Before I can catch my next breath, someone bursts through the door. The Seer stands in the doorway with his eyes narrowing in on the last pieces of my dream drifting out the balcony on a light gust of wind. Time seems to stop with the remnants of shadows left in its wake. He sees it, which means I'm not crazy. Then he looks at me, eyes narrowing in, traveling further down my stomach. He smirks. I feel the cool morning air brush across my legs.

"What are you doing here?" I demand while dragging a purple sheet off the bed to cover my crotch. His amber eyes are flaring and churning like some far galaxy, a reminder that he is more than just a man, and if he's bursting into my room unannounced, it's important.

The blue markings on his body peek out as he adjusts his robe. The ageless, magical prick now stands casually in the doorway, returning to that curious stare as he clasps his hands behind his back.

"I had a vision last night. Time to sheathe your sword, soldier. You have a job to do. The king requests that you meet him in the Great Hall," he says. His eyes trail down to my chest as though he can see my heart beating. He grins before turning to wait outside.

The sheet drops to the ground. It only takes a few moments to put my armor on. As I step into the hall, he leans forward. "You'll want to hear what I have to say before you meet with the king."

THE TASTE OF TRUTH AND BETRAYAL

PART I

CHAPTER I

VIONA

DREAMS FADE FASTER THAN a shooting star ascending through the skies. Memories begin to burn until they turn to ash, becoming so delicate, one touch could ruin them all. If you could get one more moment, one more glimpse inside a memory fragment, knowing it would be the last time, would you do it? I've tried ever so desperately to hold on to her last memories, keeping them sealed in the back of my mind, away from any wind or current that could blow them out of reach. That is where her laughter hides, the sound of her voice still echoes through the halls, and the smell of her hair drifts in the air. If I fall too deep, I will burn.

Yet that doesn't seem like it would be so bad.

I should have jumped into the pyre that day. If only I knew what was to become of me, if only I knew what would happen to us, I would have burned upon the flames with the only one who ever loved me. I remember staring at her body through the fire, her lean frame shrouded in white as the smell of her scorched flesh filled the air—a scent that I will never forget. I stood there until her body turned to ash, until the last few embers winnowed what remained. Seeing the last pieces of her float away to a place so far from reach was the end of me. For the longest time, I've known it was the beginning of something far more potent than I could ever grasp–something she made me promise to never talk about.

A faint voice is now calling me from beyond the waves, hidden between the earth and sky. A beacon for the darkness living inside me. It has slept for years in this hollow space where memories are alive and burning. Now it blooms, growing stronger by the day. What once lurked in the shadows in every corner of my dreams wants to break free.

I look out from my balcony. The early mornings no longer offer hope as they once did. They are now a cold, desolate place. My only company is the sound of the waves crashing against the cliffs and the cool morning air that greets me.

I glance over to a mourning dove as it sits on a ledge nearby, keeping its distance. I close my eyes, listening to its soft coo, falling into a somber silence, but the whisper grows louder. My hands grip tightly around the stone banister until my skin is on fire. The back of my throat burns. Tears shroud my vision. I scream as I abruptly pull away from the balustrade, the palms of my hands scraping against the rough stone. I curse under my breath. The little dove flies away, taking its cries with it, while I'm left rubbing my hands to soothe the pain.

I try to keep it together, but I want to burn the world down and take everyone with me. There is no point in watching the sun rise in a place that feels so empty without her. Especially tomorrow, my birthday. The day I turn twenty, only to spend another year without her. A reminder of how unforgiving life can be.

There is a gentle knock at my door, pulling me from thought. So faint, the sound barely registers.

"What is it?" I yell, still feeling the heat on my skin from the burn.

On the other side of the door, someone is fumbling with keys. I exhale sharply and roll my eyes. I flounce toward the door and swing it open with such force, the poor girl stumbles back in fear. I'm heated with rage as I stand here, still in my white nightgown. My black hair is messy from yet another restless night. My chest heaves as aggravation rises, waiting for her to speak. Her blue eyes widen. She swallows the lump in her throat while trying to keep her composure.

"Prin—"

"Do. Not. Call. Me. That," I reply, every word clipped.

Her hands tremble. She takes a few steps back and nervously bows. "I'm sorry, Miss, please forgive me. I am new."

"Clearly," I scoff. My eyes sweep over her. This girl wears the clothes of a cook, so why would she be here at my door? I cross my arms over my chest and lift a brow. "What do you want?"

She flinches at my tone. I can see her mind whirling as she carefully formulates her words, but her silence is starting to irritate me.

"May I come in, miss?" Her voice shakes. She turns her attention down the hall, looking anxiously to her left and right. I sigh, step to the side, and motion for her to come in while glaring daggers as she enters my room. Her eyes skim over my chambers.

"Are you alone, miss?" She moves with haste, closing the door behind her.

"Of course I am." She clears her throat and slowly pulls something wrapped in cloth from her apron. "This is for you, for your birthday."

My brow lifts. At first, I think it must be some sort of special pastry, seeing as she is from the kitchen. But when she places it in my hands, the shape quickly takes form in my grip. I look at her with curiosity before unraveling it. The cloth drops to the floor. "Why are you giving me a dagger?" My tone slightly softens as my thumb trails along the hilt of the weapon.

"This is not from me, miss. It's from Alyce."

My brows furrow, and my head cocks to the side. "Alyce?"

She isn't known for gifting, and she certainly isn't this kind. So what is the old bitch up to now? Before I can ask this girl any more questions, she starts making her way toward the door.

"I'm sorry. I cannot be here any longer," she says nervously. "Keep it hidden, and do not speak of this again, not even to Alyce."

Confusion spreads across my face as I watch her leave, no, basically run out the door. Her footsteps echo down the hall. I look at the dagger and examine it—such a simplistic blade, but it hums at my touch.

Suddenly, I feel the light beaming in through the balcony, casting a soft glow around my body and the dagger. I stare at the curious blade for a moment longer before remembering I cannot be late.

I STAND SECOND IN LINE among the royal guards. My body tenses hearing the bustling of life beyond the doors to the throne room.

Glassware chimes together, and laughter fills the room. It is far too early for these types of festivities. I glance at the two guards standing on each end of the door, but their expressions remain stone-cold.

I look back at the guard behind me as we wait for the doors to open. He is a man I've known for many years, yet he's barely ever spoken more than a few sentences to me. I expected him to have some sort of reaction to the sounds coming from the throne room, but of course, he doesn't notice. His expression doesn't change. My head peeks further down the line. They all wear the same expression—all but two. A part of me has always felt only a few of them actually have a pulse.

The doors swing wide open, pulling my attention forward.

All eyes are on me as we enter the throne room. Most people fear me, but not because I am the daughter of the king of Sao. My right to the throne has long been forgotten. They fear me for the darkness that shadows my every step. Every time I walk into a room, oh, how the energy shifts. I bring something they all recognize, I am death whispering into their ears. The crowd parts. Words don't have to flow from their lips for me to know what they're thinking. I can feel it as silence enshrouds the room.

I'm clad in silver armor among the royal Blood Moon Knights with a sword sheathed at my back. The dagger is kept hidden against my thigh, thanks to Alyce. My armor bears the kingdom's crest—a full moon—embedded into the shoulder blade. The same crest adorns our banners along with a sword and leafing. They hang between each tall stone pillar filling this vast space.

I glance toward our flag hanging on a wall above the throne. Below sits my father, not even taking notice of my arrival as he sifts through a stack of papers. I don't expect anything more from him. A smile tips the corner of his mouth as he engages with a man with dark blond hair sitting beside him on the dais. I can't fully see who it is due to the height difference between myself and the guard before me, but the man's presence alone is enough to make my jaw tick. He hasn't had anyone beside him on the throne since . . . I swallow the lump in my throat and take a deep breath, pushing those thoughts as far away as possible.

Another smile stretches across my father's face—the kind of smile that tells me he's up to something. His black and gold attire is far more elaborate than usual. A white tunic ruffles out from the chest and cuffs of his coat, secured by a form-fitted vest adorned with gold embellishments. He waves around his glass of red wine, laughing at a remark from that stranger next to him. His shoulder-length hair is tied back, but a few thick, black strands have fallen over the side of his face. That tells me he's about five drinks in. He usually can't stand having his hair look a mess when he's sober. He's clad in ego, but he looks absolutely ridiculous to me.

I glance around the room and start piecing things together. Many familiar faces fill the crowd, mostly council members, but there's something more here. I cannot place it just yet, but I *feel* it hanging in the air. My breath hitches as my veins thrum against my darkness, setting me on high alert. New and unfamiliar faces fill the crowd, whispering while they stare at me with curiosity. I'm used to eyes searing down my back. What's a few more? None of these bastards deserve to be here, but my father feels otherwise for some reason.

A young man's voice pulls me from thought. He stands out; he's surrounded by elders whose faces are marred by war, their weapons sheathed at their sides. Judging by their sullen expressions, they have no choice but to listen to him boast about his latest achievements. There's a woman locked onto his left arm. Her brown hair is pinned up, and her deep blue eyes watch him as she pretends to hang on every one of his words. Her gown tells me she let him spend every penny he had to be his little trophy for this event. Good for her. Use the bastard. He's just another arrogant prick who likes to run his mouth. As I walk past him, I feel his eyes rake down my body.

"A pair of tits in the Royal Guard? How appetizing," he groans.

It stops me in my tracks. Eyes still facing forward, the rest of the knights step out and walk around me to their posts. My pulse rises to a raging speed. I let his insult carry over the crowd. Everyone's head turns, and all chatter comes to a sudden halt. I turn to face him. My eyes darken. My upper lip twitches in disdain as I look him up and down. The insult came from a man who looks like he has to pay just to feel a woman's touch. He's repulsive. His eyes lock with mine, realizing who stands before him. His cheeks flush. Those dark brown eyes stare back as he nervously tugs on the collar of his coat.

The men around him slowly step away. His lady follows the others, putting more distance between us.

His last words are barely a whisper as metal slices through the air.

In one quick motion, blood sprays across the crowd as his head goes rolling. Everyone backs away, trying to avoid the blood mist, not realizing they have already been caught in it. His head plops against his woman's boot, landing face up with his mouth agape. Her fancy dress is painted red.

Such a pity.

My sword is slick with his blood. All the color in her face drains as shock seizes everything but her eyes. They bounce between me and what used to be her man. When his body slumps over, the crowd erupts in chaos. It is the sweet melody of justice. They move about the room, putting distance between themselves and the carcass, and me.

The king sits emotionless, watching me with a calm, trained eye as screams fill the room. For a moment, I think things might be changing between us, for the smile I thought he cast my way, but that little sliver of hope wanes rapidly as the mysterious guest comes into view. The king leans over to the dark-blond-haired man and whispers in his ear. Time stops, as my breathing stills.

Solas. Pirate of the Western Seas.

A betrayer of our kingdom.

All the memories come flooding in from the time when he and his shadow-wielding men brought the clamor of war to our kingdom. My eyes search the crowd. It's easy to depict who his men are now. They stand frozen on each side of the room, garbed in dark, leather pants and long-sleeve tunics with weapons strapped across their bodies. They look as if they haven't showered in weeks. They keep me in their lines of sight, stalking me like prey. My grip tightens on the hilt, keeping it raised at my side. As I lock eyes with them, I feel the trickle of blood dripping down its blade, seeping between the cracks of my fingers. I'm ready to remind them why they should have never crossed blades with us.

The rest of the Blood Moon Knights remain at their posts, keeping their hands on the pommels of their weapons. They might not always treat me with the respect I deserve, but they know where the real enemy stands.

Tension hangs in the air, forcing my father to rise from his throne. "It's always interesting to witness the moment former enemies lock eyes. Battle scars open up, reminding us where we once stood. There is still much animosity between us. There was a time when we stood upon the edge of the blades. Now we will unite and strengthen our alliances. If you value your heads, I suggest both sides stand down so we can move on with our day."

His voice bounces off the walls. The rest of the council and other nobles in the room look around in confusion as unease still trickles at their core.

"*NOW!*" My father's voice thunders across the throne room. There are faint whispers among the crowd as everyone moves back into place.

Solas stands with a smirk and begins speaking to his men and the rest of the guests he brought. He wears rings on every finger, his hair neatly tied back, and his white, long-sleeve tunic is tucked into a pair of black, form-fitting breeches. I imagine choking him with the very cloth that's nicely tucked around his neck. This room appears to be easily charmed by him, but I can see past his façade. He is a monster in the guise of good manners and a dapper appearance. Behind his dark green eyes, there's nothing more than a cold, ruthless criminal. I inch closer to him, trying to hear what he is saying to the guests.

"Well, it appears as though loose lips will sink ships. I can assure you, no one else from our company will behave as poorly." Solas points over to the pool of blood where the decapitated male and his carcass rest. He turns to his men. "I expect you to be on your best behavior while we are guests at King Mal Tarvas' castle." Solas picks up his wine, those thick rings chiming against the glass. A chill goes down my spine when his cold eyes look my way. "Shall we continue? The rest of us would like to leave with our heads intact if it is okay with you, *princess.*" He facetiously bows with a smirk.

I let my words die on my tongue out of respect for my father. I lift my head, and my back straightens. It takes everything in me to lower my sword and not end Solas' life right here in this very throne room. I glance over at my father, who has clearly sobered up. For the first time in years, he really stares into my eyes. I see nothing but the consequences that will soon follow.

The festivities resume per his orders. I look around the room, seeing some of the highest of the court and some of the newfound faces adorned in blood splatter.

I step out of sight and go back to my post.

It's true what they say.

I am the forgotten Princess of Sao. Let my darkness be their warning.

I might have a pulse–cut me, and I'll bleed–but I died a long fucking time ago.

CHAPTER 2

AS SOON AS THE festivities conclude, I storm out of the throne room. I can feel the relief lifting off some of the council and other guests at my exit.

Fucking assholes.

Solas and his men have always been our enemy. They've killed our men, they've robbed the people of our kingdom. Now they're staying in our castle, and I can't do a damn thing about it.

Today, wine flowed freely, and it will continue to do so until they leave. My father and Solas celebrated their alliance for reasons unbeknownst to me, but I know something nefarious is up my father's sleeve. Maybe my father wanted to expand his wealth and struck a deal with the pirate king to own a part of the seas in exchange for their new residence on our land. All I have are assumptions.

Not everyone on his council seemed thrilled. I might be a part of the royal guard, but I have no clue what goes on within the council.

I pick up my pace, making my way down the dark corridor. Normally, this place has light beaming in from every glass-stained window, but today, the weather has other plans. Ominous clouds loom above the castle, and thunder rolls in the distance. I can feel the rain coming; it has always made my joints ache.

Suddenly, a hand wraps around my arm, grabbing me at a weak spot of my armor by my elbow. I can tell by the sharpness of those boney fingers who they belong to. They feel like daggers digging into my skin.

"Alyce, what's gotten into you?" I hiss, almost stumbling into her with the way she yanks me to her side. She might be an old, petite woman, but she still has plenty of force. I can tell by her grip alone, she isn't pleased.

"My gosh, Viona, do you always have to be so dramatic?" she whispers, quickly looking over her shoulder. A few of her salt-and-pepper curls bounce around her face.

"Dramatic?" My head tips back as I erupt in laughter. My voice echoes down the hall, causing a few people to look our way. She tugs me again. Though she's being serious, my eyes warm when I look at her. I can't help but smile at her sudden visit. My voice lowers. "That asshole disrespected me."

"So you decided decapitation was the answer?" she retorts in a loud whisper. If looks could kill . . . Those deep brown eyes have a way of penetrating my soul.

A couple walks past us, arm in arm. Alyce straightens her posture, shaking the curls away from her face, and smiles at them. I look straight ahead, not even giving them notice as we wait for them to pass. The sound of the woman's heels clacks against the stone floors, filling the silence between us until they are gone.

"Speaking of the deceased, can you please replace the dress his date wore? Buy her several, and give her enough coin so she can find other lodgings if she wishes. It's not her fault he was an asshole. "

She nods as another couple walks past us. "Do you know what the king could do to you?" she asks.

I scoff, "Doing something to me would mean he'd have to actually acknowledge me. You and I both know he would do no such thing," I remind her.

It's clear she knows I speak the truth with the way she glances sideways at me. Still, her eyes roll. We turn the corner and look up the flight of stairs. She sighs.

"I'm getting too old for this, girly."

She gathers her skirt at her side, mustering the strength to go up the endless incline. I know better than to tell her she doesn't need to go with me. She will only take it as an insult. While she gets a firmer grip around my arm, I look down at her withered hands. Her fragility has started to peek through more every time I see her. She grows weaker, a little smaller than before, but her spirit has remained as fierce as any knight's.

"You know, I could have used your assistance in there today. You could have been my accomplice as we slayed the rest of Solas' men," I tease. We begin ascending. "You'd look lovely in a bloody shade of red. And with these fists? I bet you still pack a punch." I gently pat her hand.

She scoffs under her breath, keeping a steady eye on her footing, but then she looks at me. Her eyes warm, and she stops in her tracks. The memories we shared long ago have started to fade from her mind, but as we stand here midstep, I see a little piece of the old her returning. She looks up at me with a tenderness I have been longing to see. A warm smile stretches across her face, her age showing at the corners of her mouth and under her eyes. Laughter finally breaks free as I watch her mind flash back to a time where things were vastly different between us.

"Bold, just like your mother. I remember a time when she and I were on the battlefield together, long before she was a queen. You were born with her fight in you. As soon as you could walk, you had a wooden sword in your hands."

A smile stretches across my face, knowing she remembers. "And you still never let me beat you." I snicker.

We continue the walk up, and I begin reliving the memories of sword fighting in the gardens. My mind drifts to a time where she was remarkably agile, when her hair was as black as the night sky, and every muscle in her body was just as threatening as her beauty. She was my mother's personal guard and best friend. She would have been my guard too, if she hadn't been taken from me. Though she has stepped down from the Royal Guard and is now in charge of the household, at least she is still around.

"It's funny how violence was always the end game for you, girly. That hasn't changed much, but I'm afraid I'm too old for sword fights nowadays."

The stairway grows dim. Rain begins to patter against the windows. I keep my eyes on her feet and hover my hand behind her back. She tightens her hold of my arm to maintain her balance. I help her up the last few steps. When we enter the long, dark hallway that leads to my room, she exhales.

"I suppose a good game of chess will suffice?" I smile in an attempt to hide my sorrow. I know there will come a time when she won't be able to sneak up here anymore. I feel that time is approaching too quickly.

She pretends like she doesn't hear me. That's her way of telling me the answer. Every time I try to get close, she pulls back. After all these years, I still try not to let it hurt, but today, it just stings a little more.

"Happy birthday, Viona," she whispers, her voice masked, and it's her way of changing the subject. I look at her, nodding my head, and I pat my thigh to show her where the dagger is hidden. She nods, then looks forward. "It was your mother's."

Those words stop me in my tracks. My heart plummets to the ground. Suddenly, I feel the shape of the dagger pressing against my skin. It explains the warmth I felt when I first held it in my hands and why I continue to feel it hum. I turn to look at Alyce. I shake my head as tears enshroud my vision. Gifting me anything, especially something so sentimental, is unlike her. My pulse begins to race. Her eyes grow wide. She tugs me along before I have any more time to react.

"This seems like a perfect time to take extra precaution." Her tone returns to the iciness she treats me with when my father is around.

We enter my chambers. There's a young girl changing the sheets on my bed, and she jumps at our entrance.

"Wait for me down the hall," Alyce orders. The girl bows and takes her leave. When she closes the doors, Alyce seems to freeze.

"Why is Solas here?" I ask, but my question is lost.

Her back straightens as her eyes sweep over my room. I can see her mind flashing back to the last time she was in here, but she remains stoically poised. I hate how this space is a reminder of what was lost. Sometimes, I blame myself for what happened. She walks past me toward one of my desks, and I freeze. Her hands trail over the scattered papers.

"You've always been so curious," she says with a sadness matching my own. She picks one up and begins to skim through my notes. "The White Forest? Interesting choice of study. If someone were to ever see th—"

"It's nothing!" I lie, taking a few steps forward. I lift my chin and still my breath, trying to hide the fact that my heart is beating out of my chest. I cannot deny what has been calling to me. A place forbidden for as long as I can remember. Every day, my curiosity grows deeper.

She places the paper down and walks over to me. She reaches up. Her warm, frail hands cup the sides of my face. My eyes swell with tears at her touch, remembering her smell of orange blossoms. The only soap that doesn't irritate her skin.

"Such a beautiful girl to have so much untamed rage. Do not worry, they are just notes to me." She winks. I exhale with a faint smile. "Your blue eyes carry more flame than fire itself," she says.

I stifle a laugh. "You're one to talk," I softly scoff.

She smiles warily and begins to leave. "Things will always change, girly." She pauses by the door, holding on to the knob. She looks at me in a way that has me concerned. "It's the never-ending curse of time. Remember who you are. You must always keep your strength and your wits about you."

Before I can say anything, the doors close behind her. I touch the sides of my face. The strangled sob lodged in my throat finally breaks free. I suck in a shaky breath, regretting that I didn't beg her to stay. The last thing I want to do is spend another birthday alone.

I wake to the cool breeze of the summer's night air drifting in through the balcony. I lift my head from the desk, pressing my fingers to the sides of my temples. Staring at the scattered pages of old literature, I realize I've made little progress. It's going to take a lifetime to bind it back together, but this book is special and worth the frustration. I've had it since I was a child. It's about a man who travels the seas in search of adventure. I stand, sweeping my gaze over the stack of pages, trying to find where I left off, but my eyes fix on one of the notes about the White Forest with a map showing its precise location. Though it's marred with age, it's the only map I have. The mysterious forest lies east of here, in the very center of our continent, Vendrelle.

A few months ago, I began writing down every piece of information I could find. They say a demon in the guise of a beautiful woman guards the White Forest. Most have never seen her and lived, and those who have returned were never the same. They say monsters can be heard in the woods, beasts that bend to her whim. Some find it to be lore, meant to keep curious children out of the cold, harsh elements. I've seen one man return, only his mind seemed to have stayed behind. The white haze is just as alluring as the stories. Behind these notes are my hidden journal entries of the dreams I've had. Dreams of a place I've never been, yet somehow, I have walked through its snowy terrain my entire life. I feel as though I know it like the back of my hand. Each dream ends with a longing that follows me into my waking state.

I sense something shift in the air. It sends my pulse to a racing speed, and suddenly, I feel as though I'm being watched. Adrenaline kicks in. I glance over to another table, looking for my sword. A labradorite stone I mostly use for a paperweight glints in the faint light.

There it is, right next to the stone.

I quietly retrieve my weapon while keeping my eyes on the balcony. The sheer curtains billow in the breeze. Metal slices in the air as I unsheathe my sword to scout the balcony. My eyes squint, adjusting to the night. A strong gust of wind kicks up, and I hear the sounds of waves crashing against the shore in the distance. The smell of sea air and sage drift in. When I find no one, I head back inside.

A few moments pass. I place my sword onto the edge of the desk and go back to my studies. Minutes later, the door slowly opens, and I feel who steps through. It's a presence that sends a chill down my spine. Even though my heart begins to race once more, I don't move.

"Making friends with the enemy, clever but predictable," I hiss. My back is still turned while I pretend to sift through my papers on the desk, but I'm frantically trying to cover the notes and all my journal entries. I hear the door shut behind me. I almost flinch at the sound, but I keep my composure.

"There she is, the girl who never knows when to keep her mouth shut," my father mutters icily.

"The girl." I scoff under my breath.

My father takes another step forward. I quickly turn around. My eyes lock with his, stopping him in his tracks. This is the first time we have been within ten feet of each other in years. Now he is here, looking at me as if I were a ghost. One that's haunted him his whole life while he refuses to refer to me as his own daughter.

There's a glint of mourning behind his eyes. One that comes and goes so quickly, I think maybe I imagined it. I watch as it is replaced with something dark and sinister. His jaw ticks. He studies me for a moment, noticing my hands resting on the edges of the papers. He crosses his arms over his chest. The fabric of his fine clothing tightens around his elbows and shoulders as he scratches his shadowed jawline. I had forgotten about the speckles in his dark brown eyes and how I used to count them as a little girl. Memories that have been locked in time. It's strange how easily they break free.

Now, all I want is for him to leave because his presence makes me sick. All the hurt and pain come flooding back in, like waves pushing me up against the side of a cliff. I suddenly feel cornered by emotions I do not want to face today. I glare at him as all these feelings tighten around my throat, a pain that can only be soothed with fire.

"Have you come to congratulate me on making such a great impression on your newly found ally?" I can't help but let words fly.

He scoffs, closing the space between us just a little more. My heart speeds up, but I lift my chin and keep my poise. "Do you realize what you could have done?" His upper lip twitches. "Another war could have broken out because of your reckless behavior." The more words that flow off his lips, the more anger rises within me. "I came to tell you myself that I will *NOT* tolerate such embarrassment."

"He insulted me!" I challenge him, raising my voice higher, remembering the man's words as he tried to degrade me in front of an entire room full of people.

"I DON'T CARE! NOBODY DOES!"

His words cut me like knives. I am angry at myself for still allowing him to affect me this way. A searing pain grabs my heart as the truth to his words sinks in. He's right. Nobody does, and nobody ever will. As the days stretch longer, I feel it. I've always been alone, and nothing will change.

"Tell me, Father, have your knees suddenly gone weak?" I hiss, glaring up at him. "I never thought I'd see the day where a *king* would drop to his knees to please his enemy. You—"

My vision goes white. A sharp, prickling pain splays across my face. I stumble back into the desk. Papers go flying. He shakes his hand, soothing out the sting from slapping me.

Tears threaten to break free, but I refuse to give him the pleasure of seeing me break. My chest heaves. My fists clench until my fingernails are digging into my skin. All the years he has spent barely speaking to me, treating me like I was nothing more than a guard. The reality chokes the air around me. He came in here, not to see if I was okay, but to remind me of who wears the crown. He catches something in my eye. Suddenly, he grabs my wrist and yanks me toward him. My body slams against his chest, hard enough to make me wince. My skin grows hot from anger.

The veins on the side of his temple pulse. His jaw ticks. Those eyes widen, as if he's piecing together the very thing that makes my nerves unravel.

"Your powers . . . are they awakening?" his voice snaps, breath potent with wine.

"I have nothing," I lie, holding back a shaky breath as I try to pull myself free from his grip.

"Do you value your solitude so much that you fear the potential of what you can be? The kingdom of Sao was named after a god's moon. We can be the most powerful kingdom in all of Vendrelle." His mouth turns up into a threatening grin, but those words, *his words*, mean nothing to me.

"Let go of me," I warn, gritting through my teeth, hoping he lets go before he feels anything else seep through. His eyes bore into mine. His stark black hair falls in his face. Moments stretch on as he studies the truth of my words. I worry he will see right through me the way he'd see right through my mother when she'd lie. When he finds nothing, he lets go.

I take a few steps back until I feel my body hit the edge of the desk. I swallow the lump in my throat. He combs a hand through his disheveled hair, suddenly realizing his leather tie has fallen off.

It's strange how a person can still know someone years after they've been gone. Vanity has always been his demise. He begins searching the ground. I rub my wrist, soothing the pain from his grip. The black leather tie falls into my line of sight. I take a quick step forward, covering it with my foot. When he realizes he can't find it, he angles his shoulders and clears his throat. Silence stretches on. He takes one long look at me before he leaves. I remain in place until I no longer hear his footsteps.

In a blinded rage, an angry cry rips from my throat as I turn around, dragging my hands over my desk and spilling all my work onto the ground. I'm beside myself that, after all this time, his words still cut me so deeply. Papers float into the air and scatter all around me. Black ink plummets to the floor. I slump back into my chair, as my eyes focus on the dust that has settled over the handle of one of my drawers. A chipped and faded cyan crescent moon is painted above.

I stare at the shape until my breathing stills, not wanting to remember the last time I opened this drawer, but I reach out and pull on its handle. A necklace lies atop a blue, silk cloth inside. The small, silver crescent moon with a broken chain glints in the candlelight. It's been years since I've been able to wear this. As I hold it against my chest and close my eyes, memories begin to flash.

My mother kneels down in front of me. Her hazel eyes sparkle in the morning light as she clasps the necklace around my neck. I see her lips moving, but as time keeps pressing forward, her words begin to fade. I look down at the necklace, holding it in my tiny hands. The corner of my mouth tips up as I gaze at it shimmering in the sunlight. She looks up at me through her long lashes, smiling brightly. My stars, she is beautiful. Prisms of light shine through her light-brown hair. Every part of her held the good in me. She was my hiding place.

I blink back the memories. All the good that once thrived is now buried in ash. She was the last ember of my life. When she died, everything dimmed. We were left with the darkest parts of ourselves.

I place the necklace down on top of the desk and get ready for bed. Her voice is but an echo now.

"The world will see you, they will know you, and you will be glorious."

CHAPTER 3

I AWAKEN TO THE coolness of the night air licking my skin. I can't keep my eyes from rolling into the back of my head. My body is being carried somewhere in the arms of a rider. All I can see are flashes of the night sky and a faceless man cloaked by shadows, holding my weightless body. Whoever he is, he has taken me against my will.

How did I get here? How did I go from dreaming to being in his arms?

I can't speak, can't move, but as we ride faster into the night, I'm becoming more aware of the magic he has cast over me. I feel it thrumming in my head as it lulls me back into a resting state.

The horse gallops in a rhythm of haste. Its hooves striking loudly against the cobblestone streets. A force of energy moves through me—the man's power reverberates around us. An explosive sound follows. Guards begin yelling, and a bell rings in the air. It's a sound I've only heard in the past when our enemies have breached the castle walls, confirming he just blasted his way through the metal gate.

He rides faster into the open fields. My stomach takes a dip, tightening when I realize we are heading toward the White Forest.

Is he mad? He's taking us to our deaths.

Though I have thought about mine countless times, I never thought my life would end like this.

Screams are held inside me along with the frustration of being unable to fight my way out. I am motionless in his arms. Though my eyes are weighted, my will is strong. He holds me firmly against his body, and I'm close enough to smell his scent. Cedar and campfire smoke taints my skin as my head rests unwillingly against the curve of his neck. I want nothing more than to end his life, look him in the eyes and watch him take his last breath, but I remain powerless under his compulsion.

As the ringing in my ears begins to fade, I hear men on horseback flanking our sides. The sound of their weapons clanking against their armor becomes clearer. My head falls to the side, catching a glimpse of a guard bearing my kingdom's crest. Metal slices through the air as the guard unsheathes his sword. He gains speed, inching closer to the cloaked man who has me in his arms. He raises his weapon, commanding the others to ride faster. Just as he's within arm's reach, his scream is snatched from him as the sound of his body hits the ground. I know then that his end was delivered by the blade of my captor.

We ride hard, moving with the landscape as it curves around the hills. More guards follow on this never-ending chase, lit by the glow of the moon. My father's guards are no match for him; he ends them so effortlessly. These men have spent their entire lives dedicating themselves to the king, to fighting, to war—and their lives are gone within a blink of an eye. My senses are slowly starting to come back to me, laced with rage.

Warm, thick liquid sprays across my body. I'm no stranger to what this is, I've felt it many times before on the battlefield. Its metallic scent assaults my nose, and my heart becomes a catalyst of my need for revenge. My hate for this man now runs wild and free. Every time I hear the sound of his blade slicing through flesh, it fills my blood with the need for revenge.

Up ahead, a cluster of birch trees comes into view, stretching for miles on each end and surrounded by a thick, white haze. I was right, he's mad. We are heading straight for it, and there is nothing I can do.

I know as soon as we enter the White Forest, their chase will end, and I will be lost. I fear what is to come. It is dangerous as much as it is treasonous. Clearly, he doesn't give a damn.

Without hesitation, the horse takes flight into the haze. There is no time to brace myself as it swallows us quicker than I can manage to hold my breath. The air thickens, the cold burning my lungs. Everything around us falls silent. The snow glows with a radiance, as if neither the moon nor the night exists.

The horse we ride is as white as our surroundings, and its mane falls to the side. I watch its head motion idly as our pace slows to a trot. It is as if the horse knows there is no more threat, no more chase to lead.

I mumble, struggling to form the words to tell this man how I am going to enjoy killing him, but he presses his fingertips against the side of my temple. I'm being lulled away into that empty space of sleep. My vision blurs. The White Forest starts to feel further and further away. He leans down to the shell of my ear. His cool, minty breath fans across my neck, sending a wave of chills down my body.

"Do not fear me, Princess," he says in a deep, sultry voice. "I just came to collect what's mine."

CHAPTER 4

M Y EYES SLOWLY DRIFT open to the sound of crackling fire. It's warm and inviting. For a moment, I think I'm back in my room under a thick, wool blanket. The heat envelops my body as I lie on my side. My hand is flat against the ground in front of my chest, but there's a sharp pain in my palm. Grogginess fades, and my senses rise, allowing me to realize where I truly am. The ground is cold and the blanket draped over me starts to feel like an icy cage.

A figure comes into view on the other side of the fire. I freeze, my heart races, slamming against my chest. I watch my captor through the flames as they snap and bite the bitter cold air. They illuminate his body, casting a soft glow against the morning light. He has removed his hooded cloak, giving me a perfect view of his face. Hair as dark as night, draping down in soft waves framing a well-defined face and resting atop his broad shoulders. His sun-kissed skin tells me he spends most of his time outdoors, which means he isn't from the White Forest—we are just passing through. Judging by his shadowed jawline, he's been riding for a few days. My eyes scan the area. His sword lies nestled between the protruding roots of a birch tree.

He hasn't noticed I'm awake. Now, if I can only move quickly enough to grab his weapon, swing around, and pierce his heart, then I can be on my way.

I quietly exhale, trying to steady my breathing, but rage is fueling my adrenaline. I inch my way into a better position so I can push myself up.

One more exhale.

I jump to my feet, kicking off the blanket and swiftly reaching for his sword, but his speed is unmatched. He sidesteps me, blocking my path. I raise my head, noting the vast difference in height. His presence is intimidating as he stands before me, clad in black. A pair of piercing, green eyes glare down at me. His chest heaves, it's clear I just pissed him off, but his lips curve into a grin when he sees my stance.

"Do you really think you're skilled enough to take my own weapon from me?" he asks in a condescending tone. His hands rest casually at his sides.

"Fuck you," I growl, taking a step back to create distance between us.

He smirks with a brow raised, clearly not seeing me as a threat. He was skilled enough to take me from my home, but now that I'm awake, he's going to regret ever laying his hands on me. He won't be holding me hostage for long, and that is a fact. I'm going to wipe that arrogant smirk off his face, and if I have time, I might cut that fucking brow off too.

"So you're a *feisty* princess," he purrs. "With such an impeccable mouth." His eyes linger over my lips far longer than I want.

My head cocks to the side, my brows knitting together.

Is this asshole flirting with me?

"I am not a princess," I retort. Not that it matters what he sees me as.

"What are you then?" he asks, taking a step forward.

I take one back. "I'm nobody."

He laughs, baring his straight, white teeth. "Well, if you're nobody, then that means no one will ever come looking for you." His eyes darken. He takes another step forward, but I stand in place.

"Viona," I reply.

He stops. For a moment, the distraction gives me hope, but it only widens his smile. I just need him to get a little closer.

"Viona . . . " he repeats my name. It rolls off his lips so smoothly, it's just as distracting as it is infuriating.

"Do you always wake up angry . . . Princess?" He calls me by that name once more, taking that last step forward.

This asshole is done talking.

I drop to the ground, landing on my hands with precision. I push off with momentum, swinging my leg to the side, making a full circle, pivoting my heel and sweeping his legs out from under him. His body flies into the air, landing with a hard, heavy thud against the ground. I run for his sword, grinning and grabbing it with both hands. I am quicker than he gave me credit for.

He stands, putting his full height on display again, glaring at me with a grimacing smile. With quick strides, he's behind me, moving faster than I can turn or counter. His large hand wraps around both of mine while I hold on to the hilt of his sword. His grip tightens, warning me to cease any further attempts. Pressure builds between my grip. The tighter he squeezes, the more my knuckles squish together. Pain rises through my fingers, and I grunt through my teeth. Clearly, he's trying to show dominance, but I will not yield to this asshole.

"Is it customary for princesses to wield swords, or do you just like playing with big things?" he taunts. I hear the smile in his words as his minty breath fans over the top of my head.

I thrust my body back, hard enough for him to loosen his grip. The moment one hand slips free, I jab my elbow into his stomach. He bends forward, grunting, releasing me from his grip. I slip out, turning around to face him with his sword still in my hands.

It gives me great pleasure seeing the wind knocked out of him. He looks up at me, eyes flaring with anger as they peek through his hair. A bitter laugh rumbles from his chest, finding amusement rather than pain as he tries to catch his breath.

In a blind, heated rage, I lunge forward. He dodges my move, taking me down with a leg sweep, mirroring the same maneuver I used moments ago. I lose my balance, falling backward, as his sword goes crashing to the ground. Just as I think my body will follow, he catches me.

We stand frozen in midair with one of his hands pressed against the small of my back and the other wrapped around my wrist. Seconds stretch on as I continue heaving. My eyes wander to his high cheekbones, strong jaw line, and full lips. The white of my sleeve catches my eye. It's only now that I realize I'm wearing the tunic and trousers I was taken in. The chill begins to drift through the thin fabric. He sinfully grins. It's almost like he can see my thoughts forming.

Does he think this is some sort of game?

"Let me go," I seethe in a low tone.

He is an incredibly handsome prick. His jaw ticks while studying me with those piercing, green eyes as they linger over my face for far too long. With one hard yank, he steadies me back onto my feet, pulling my body flush against his. I think I might have yelped at the motion.

Cedar, mint, and his musk envelop me once more. This time, I am in full control over my body, yet I don't step away. I've never been this close to a man before, close enough to feel his body heat radiating against mine. The feel of his hand on my back warms my skin. We are mere inches from one another, standing in the middle of a place that has been forbidden for centuries. Something blooms inside me. I inhale a sharp breath as his eyes hover over my lips. I swallow hard, pushing my thoughts far from reach.

"Let me go." My final warning comes out as a faint growl with simmering rage. He complies. I take a step back, quickly turning my head to the side. My hands run down my thin tunic and trousers, trying to fix a wrinkle that isn't there, as if the action will smother the awkwardness that hangs in the air. I cross my arms over my chest to block him from seeing anything further. He turns away, giving me space. Being taken against my will in the middle of the night was the furthest thing from my mind before I went to bed last night.

As the adrenaline wanes, I feel the climate settle deep in my bones. I run my hands up and down my arms.

"Here." He throws a black cloak in my direction. I catch it in midair, holding it against my chest.

"Offering me your cloak?" I scoff, throwing it back at him. "I *refuse* to have anything else of yours touching my body."

His face contorts into a scowl, and he throws the cloak right back. "If you don't put this on, you'll freeze," he retorts, baring his teeth. "Besides, I'm not that generous. Mine is over there," he says, pointing over toward the fire where his cloak sits nicely folded on a rock. "This one was made just for you," he continues. "I was instructed to bring it."

"Instructed?"

Interesting.

He just turns around, muttering something under his breath.

The numbness in my toes pulls my attention back to the cloak, and something catches my eye. I hold it out in front of me, taking in the intricacy of its design and tracing my fingers along the embroidery. Black roses with thorns line the hood with small stars weaving around them. The design flows all the way down to the front. The little stars cast a silver shine. Around the black roses, there's a faint aura. It seems to glow at my touch as I run my hands across it. I feel my captor's eyes prying, watching me examine the cloak.

"Who made this?" I demand.

"You'll meet her once we get through this gods-damned forest."

Her.

"You speak as if I don't have a choice."

"That's because you *don't*. You're coming with me." He loses that suave tone while tightening the string on his bag with emphasis. I clench my teeth, loathing the finality in his words.

Furiously, I drape the cloak over myself, fastening it with haste. As soon as it touches my body, to my surprise, magic envelops me, chasing away the bitter cold. I exhale deeply, letting the warmth seep into my skin. It feels like a stone has been lifted off my chest as the magic thrums against me. Then I remember I have a much bigger stone to lift. He's staring right at me.

My brows knit, glaring at him long and hard. Wearing this cloak by no means indicates that I'll comply with his demands.

"I'm not going," I remind him.

"*Yes*, you are."

"No."

He sighs heavily, taking a step forward. "Not many people tell me no, Princess," he seethes in a low, throaty growl. There's darkness forming in his eyes as green tendrils of smoke drift over his irises.

"And not many people treat me with such disrespect without losing their head," I shoot back.

He snarls, moving so fast that I don't have time to react. He strides toward me until my back hits the trunk of a tree, stopping me in place. He towers over me, chest heaving. I can see how his stature could be intimidating, but I've conquered worse. Suddenly, the haze in the forest thickens around us as if it's going to swallow us whole.

He leans down, lips brushing up against the shell of my ear.

"Get on the horse, or I will force you to sleep for so long, you'll be dancing with all the monsters lurking inside that pretty little head of yours." He growls every word like a promise.

I almost stop breathing. How could he know something so personal? I refrain from reacting, but the air tightens in my lungs regardless. He speaks so invasively, intruding the most intimate parts of my mind—burdens I do not share with anyone else.

"Be careful how you threaten me, captor. If it's monsters you see, imagine what they'd do to you if I let them out."

"Are you asking me to dance, Princess?" he taunts.

Silence hangs in the air. My breathing quickens, noticing the way his eyes trail down to my lips. He grins when they slide back up to meet my glare. I rein back my snarl, letting the harsh features in my face wane. Instead, I smirk.

As he's transfixed on whatever fantasy he's made up in his head, I grab him by the hips and shove my knee up into his groin. A full, deliberate assault to his crotch. His eyes go wide, and he drops to his knees with one hand on his groin while bracing the other against the tree.

"I don't dance, asshole. Enjoy your pain," I seethe.

I run past the fire, grabbing his sword before disappearing back into the thickened haze. An angry howl rips from his throat. I swear I hear a laugh as his voice echoes throughout the woods. Hearing him groan in pain gives me great pleasure. He got exactly what he deserved.

I keep running through the snowy forest. The trees are sparse, but the fog is growing thicker. Every step feels sacred. I let the connection I've always felt in dreams guide me. A strange sensation grazes down my spine, and I quickly look back, expecting to see him at my heels, waiting to hear the weight of his boots crunching upon the snow. The mist is growing so thick, it's hard to see what's in front of me. I jump over a root protruding from the ground, but my foot loses traction, causing me to slip. Pain shoots up my spine as I land hard on my ass—the snow is anything but soft. I keep going, but the further I get from him, the more something pulls me to go back.

Am I already losing my mind?

The sooner I'm out of the White Forest, the sooner I can get back home and find out why that bastard traveled from the other side of Vendrelle to take me.

THE MAGIC HAS NOT WANED from this cloak. It is woven through every fiber, every thread, shielding me from the cold, harsh elements of the White Forest. Its creator likely would have never guessed it would aid my escape.

Everything here is frozen, cold, and desolate, unforgiving in a way that could bring madness to anyone lost within these woods. It has all started to become a blur, blending together as one big, white cloud. The haze grows thicker by the second, hindering my ability to escape.

The connection to this place is like the flicker of a flame. Unpredictable, unsteady, one sudden shift in the wind, and it could unfurl. There's a still presence within the fog following me through it; I sense it at my heels. I finally see why this place has been forbidden: It's clearly cursed. Anyone who steps forth into this frozen chasm would surely meet their end. If I stay here any longer, I fear I will meet mine too.

I lean against a tree to catch my breath. My lungs burn, and my cheeks feel flushed. My eyes squint as I attempt to examine the land. Still on guard, I look both ways, ducking low to the ground, and make my way over to a large, fallen log. From what I know from lore, there could be far worse things hidden here besides the man who hunts me. I sit on the log, and some of the tension in my back releases. I sigh, drifting my eyes toward the ground.

"Shit . . . " I mutter, looking at the soft, satin slippers that are still covering my feet. My captor couldn't have grabbed my boots on his way out with me? I pierce the ground in front of me with the tip of the sword to keep its hilt off the ground, wondering if the cloak has also protected my feet from frostbite. I pull the slippers off and thoroughly inspect them, running my hands over the soles of my feet. Warm to the touch. I sigh, relieved to discover I have been unscathed by this climate. My confidence in the cloak is restored.

"Thank the gods," I whisper under my breath.

Something cold lands on my cheek, then another on my eyelash. I look up to see snow falling from the sky, reminding me of a book my mother read to me long ago. *"Snowflakes are a winter's kiss from the past."* Remembering useless literature won't help me right now.

My eyes skim over the land once more. Visibility is vital, and right now, it isn't on my side. I can't see anything past the haze.

I press my fingers over the bridge of my nose, trying to soothe the tension behind my eyes.

"What's mine."

My captor's voice taints my thoughts. He gave no name, no mention of where he was from. No intentions other than the obvious, which was to take me through the forest. One thing I know for sure is that there was power coursing through him. I can't explain it, but I felt it grab onto me each time he touched me.

I have the ability to sense when others have powers, but I don't have any of my own. Not yet, at least. Today, I am damning myself for it. Maybe if my powers had awakened when they should have, I could have defended myself better.

When I was born, a Seer told my parents that, one day, my powers would bring the beginning of a new era. My mother warned me the world would either see me as a blessing or as something to be feared. My father's eyes filled with greed, looking past the heart of his daughter, seeing me as nothing more than a weapon, something to give him an advantage. He had waited for my powers to awaken so I could take the throne. A life I was destined to have, but one I never wanted. When he realized I could offer nothing, I became useless to him.

A light catches off the blade of my sword where it sticks up from the ground. I stare at my reflection, my silhouette faint and blurred. Long, jet-black hair and a pair of bright-blue eyes stare back. I'm the depiction of a curse, and though I see features I shared with my mother, they are also a constant reminder of what was lost. My mother was my beacon of strength. The one who loved me despite my father's disappointment.

She always said—magic or not—if I could wield a sword, I would bring my enemies to their knees. She made me promise to learn how to fight just in case anything happened to her, and if my powers were to awaken, she advised me to tell no one. The world we lived in was damned, and my beauty would bring all the darkness to me. She often talked about her absence like it was imminent—as if it was her destiny. It came to her in dreams she shared only with me and no one else. Losing her when I was ten years old was the catalyst of my training.

When I told my father I wanted to be a warrior right after she died, he agreed. He thought becoming one might awaken the powers that hid within me. It also worked out to be a good distraction, relieving him from feeling obligated to spend time with me. I trained for years, almost every day, working my way up in ranks. Not to please him, it was for my mother. Though he did get one thing right: I am a weapon. Being a skilled fighter is where I find my power.

Ten years of training later, I still take a piece of her with me each time I face an enemy. Each time I unsheathe my weapon, it is for her. I can feel her surging through my veins with every swing of my blade. Her death and our lost time fuels every attack. I am always ravenous, and facing me is often fatal. I began to relish being bathed in my enemy's blood, craving that release, just like I do now. There's something calling to whatever lies dormant inside of me, and now it's starting to listen, like a shadow growing larger by the day.

There's a stillness to the air, and I feel something shift beyond the frozen brush behind me. My breath stills, all my deepest thoughts come to a halt as a soft breeze runs along my face. The haze begins to clear, receding back into the forest like a snake retreating from a predator. My chest tightens, and all the hairs on the back of my neck rise.

A woman's voice faintly whispers in the wind, humming a song that carries a slow, melodic tune. My eyes dart forward, using the reflection of the blade to look behind me. As I peer into its silvery light, I squint my eyes, no longer seeing my face. A woman's silhouette takes shape. Her flowing, black hair drapes down over her face. Eyes as dark as night stare back. My heart pounds against my chest, low and heavy as a chill breaches the security of the cloak. I quickly rise, pulling the blade from the ground. Our eyes meet, stealing all the air from my lungs. The humming stops. Her almond-shaped eyes narrow in on me. Wind drifts between us, whipping our hair around our faces.

I know who stands before me, a demon in the guise of beauty, the one who guards the White Forest.

CHAPTER 5

THE ETHOS OF HER power is palpable. I should be running right now, yet I remain in place with my sword raised at my side. It seems as though time has stopped. Only the wind drifts between us, causing her thin, white dress to cling to her form. I feel her powers thrumming against my skin, as a tethered pull draws me toward her—one I can't seem to understand. Her eyes hold lifetimes of secrecy. The chaos storming behind them is evident, reckless even. No wonder few men have survived. I can only imagine what she did to them once they stepped inside her storm, caught in delirium. Though the stories about this woman are haunting, I find them powerful. I can now see why men would throw themselves off the highest cliff to be with her. I'm almost tempted to do so myself, not for the same reasons they do, but just to feel an inkling of that power beneath my fingertips. As I continue to stare, I know every second she leaves me alive is a blessing. But something tells me she has no intention of hurting me. She isn't a threat, so I lower my weapon.

The wind whistles through the canopy of the trees like a distant song, moving closer until its soft, cold breeze breaks through the warmth of my cloak, toying with the hem. My eyes lower to the sound of movement around my feet as the foliage begins crackling. Suddenly, all the frozen leaves break from the shackles of the solid ground, rising into the air as her hands will them to.

"What is your name?" I ask.

Moments stretch on. She smiles in a way that's hauntingly beautiful.

"My name is Adnama," she says, dipping her chin and keeping her eyes fixed on me. Her voice is soft, gentle, and ethereal. I've never heard a name like hers before. It sounds ancient, beautiful and powerful.

"My name is V—"

"I know who you are, Viona."

Blood drains from my face hearing my name leave her lips. She drifts forward, floating inches off the ground as the leaves are still floating idly around us.

"Are you the one people fear? The reason why the White Forest is cursed?" I'm unsure if I really want that answered.

She scoffs, coming closer and smirking humorously. Lavender, sage, and sea fill the air, reminding me of the shores of home. Her long, white fingernails lightly drag across my collarbone, sending prickles of unease across my skin. My heart beats rapidly against my chest at the thought of her nails being sharp enough to cut through flesh. Her head slightly tilts to the side. Under her curious stare, my palms grow clammy.

"Do you believe everything you hear?" Adnama whispers, brushing the loose strand of hair away from my face and tucking it behind my ear. She's cold to the touch. I swallow the lump in my throat.

"No. Of course not," I reply. My back stiffens as I feel her drift behind me. "It has been told by so many over the years. Monsters, flesh-eating demons, witches, and darkness dwell here. Not many enter and leave alive, and it has been forbidden to even try." I realize I sound like I am defending stories I never truly believed myself.

"Yet here you are, standing on two feet, very much alive and well. How do you explain that then?" She laughs, her eyes sparkle with amusement as if she already knows. My mind flashes back to the memory of my captor so effortlessly breaking through the cursed haze to enter the forest. The thought of him brings the blood back into my face, and I feel my cheeks flush with warmth.

She continues, "There *is* a little bit of truth to the whispers of your ignorant people, Viona. Darkness does dwell here . . . that is true. Beasts do lurk here, if I will them to. But something far worse sleeps just beneath your feet. Depending on what set of eyes you use, perception can always be misconceived. This place is not cursed. It is being,"—she pauses, looking up toward the trees, choosing her words very carefully—"preserved." She grins. There is an unsettling glint in her eyes.

"What do you mean 'preserved?' And they are not *my* people," I say, becoming defensive. "They serve my father, King Tarvas."

She lifts a brow and then tips her head back in a loud laugh that escapes with such force, it's sent echoing through the trees. I look around, expecting wildlife to emerge from their hidden burrows, but the space remains empty.

"You are destined to take the throne of Sao, are you not? So they are, and will be, your people." A sinister smile forms on her face as a strand of her black hair falls loose. "Once your powers have awakened, that is." She pauses.

My pulse rises to an unsettling speed. Words evade me.

Her smile doesn't fade. "I feel it coursing through you. It haunts your dreams. It is slowly starting to wake from its two decades of slumber. As of recently, it calls to you in your waking state. Like a slow melody, synchronizing with the beat of your heart. Pulling you down so deep, you feel like you are drowning." Tendrils of her energy dance along my skin, looking for any fissure to slip inside. The devastating truth to her words cut me like shards of glass.

She continues, "Something you have not shared with the king." Her voice lifts.

She drifts closer. As her bony fingers wrap around my arm, I feel her calling me. Of all the shadows that lurk in every corner of my mind, one is hers, stepping into the light. Her eyes begin to change color. That rich mahogany disappears, buried beneath a sea of black. Like stone to flint, something ignites. I suck in a sharp breath. The sound of her heartbeat reverberates around me, low and faint. I release a frothy breath of air, feeling her snake through every vessel of my veins. She smiles, tilting her head to the side once more.

Adnama drawls a chilling whisper. "You have so much chaos inside."

How can she feel this? How can she know?

My heart is beating like a war drum.

"Let go," I warn in a shaky breath, feeling the sudden heat flaring beneath my skin. She relents, drifting back. The darkness recedes from her eyes, returning to the rich brown I saw moments ago.

"Your secrets are my very own." Adnama grins. She turns to face the forest, running her hand down the bark of a birch tree. "There *is* one monster. The one you call your father as he sits on your throne in the kingdom of Sao. The one who feeds you and your people nothing but lies." She turns to look at me with a stone-cold glare. "A *deceiver*."

Confusion spreads across my face, and though she spoke the truth about me, this doesn't make any sense.

"What are you talking about?" I snap.

"King Mal Tarvas . . . " She whispers his name like a hissing snake.

A darkness looms over me with a heaviness pressing against my chest. My nostrils flare, I grit my teeth at hearing another insult leave her lips. The air grows thick. Instinctively, my grip tightens around the hilt of the sword until my knuckles turn white. Asshole or not, he's still our king, and one I have fought to protect every time enemies were at our gates. He is the one my mother loved long ago.

"You have no right to accuse King Tarvas of such things." I glare, meeting the intensity in her eyes.

She takes notice of where my hand is placed. She stoically smiles, wind bellows at the hem of her shrouded, white dress. She stands tall with confidence and seems unaffected by the rage rising inside me

"I am not the enemy here. I came to warn you. You're giving your trust to the wrong people. What you have inside of you is special. It is a gift, not an omen. But it is untamed, Viona, just like the rage I see before me. If you aren't careful, the darkness will consume you in the wrong ways, and it will be strong enough to destroy you and all the lands with it."

She drifts back. The wind picks up around us, sending another wave of lavender in the air and bringing the shock of bitter cold with it. She ascends higher, leaving me in the whirlwind she created. The sound grows louder as it whips around me. I hold my hand up to my face to shield it from the swirling snow. I am losing sight of her.

"You will be glorious in the light but will suffer a calamitous defeat if darkness is the guide to your decisions," her voice echoes.

Then she is gone. The winds stop. Every particle that was swept up by the whirlwind drops to the ground as if nothing happened. Here I am again, by myself, enshrouded within the silence of this forest. The world around me fades to black, and I know her words will haunt me.

CHAPTER 6

M Y EYES SLOWLY FLUTTER open to see a fresh dusting of snow shimmering on the ground and on top of my body. Soft orange and pink hues of light illuminate the haze. My chest tightens, realizing how long I've slept. I don't remember anything after Adnama left. I must have passed out.

"How is this possible?" My breath hits the cold air, leaving a frothy mist in its wake. In desperation, I search for the sword, sliding my hands under the new layer of snow until I feel the sword's frigid hilt. The brush is becoming more dense as I make my way through the forest. Treading through it discreetly is nearly impossible. I duck beneath a large, protruding tree limb, shuddering at the sound of snow crunching beneath my feet, and carefully maneuver the rest of the way through the branches and undergrowth.

"Finally," I exhale, relieved to see a clearing up ahead. I draw in my lower lip as I survey the land. The atmosphere is dry and I'm parched. I've been in this forest for too damn long. I'm fighting the feeling of hunger and the weight of this sword.

I spot a path on the other side of the clearing with snow barely cresting its surface. A vast green forest expands. Birds chirp in the canopy of the trees, the first sounds of life. Their calm demeanor tells me there's no danger nearby. I risk exposing myself to the enemy, but I have no choice if I plan on leaving the White Forest. My eyes sweep over the clearing one more time before I run as fast as my legs will carry me across the way. Already, the air is shifting the further away I get from the White Forest. The air becomes warm, and rich as earthy aromas fill the air. A small victory to claim, knowing I have made it out unscathed.

A thick layer of trees bow above, darkening my trail and preserving the light dusting of snow on the ground. Something bright catches my eye further down the path. I run to it and kneel, examining the snowy imprint. My eyes widen. A fresh set of footprints lead off the trail, disappearing into the brush.

How could this be?

"Shit!" I murmur, whipping my head up and looking all around me.

Suddenly, the forest feels as though it is tightening, as if every branch is closing in on me.

Before I can discern my thoughts, a hand cups over my mouth and pulls me off the trail. A large arm wraps around my waist, pinning both arms at my sides. I thrust my body violently, growling and thrashing against the attacker, holding on to the hilt of the sword. My heels drag against the ground as we move deeper into the forest. One of my slippers falls off. Twigs snap under his boots as he struggles to keep me in his grip, but his strength overpowers mine. The more I try to scream, the tighter his hand clamps against my mouth. My cloak snags against the brush.

The attacker drags me through hanging vines and into a cave ten feet high. We're now cloaked in darkness in this space. His scent of cedar envelops me. I know that scent. I know *exactly* who this asshole is. I begin thrusting harder in his grip.

"If they find us, they will kill us both, Princess," he whispers in my ear. His minty breath fans down the side of my face. "You wouldn't want them ruining all the fun now, would you?"

I grunt and mumble in response, sensing his smirk.

"Shh . . . Look straight ahead, and you'll see," he whispers, loosening his grip over my mouth just enough for me to take a deep breath.

I stop struggling, hearing heavy footsteps treading closer, reverberating through the ground below us. The forest goes silent. The clamor of metal fills the air, ceasing my movements.

Several giant, hideous, man-like creatures come into view. All weapons are drawn as they move with stealth past the cave. Steam curls off their singed skin. Their hair varies in length, lying slick against their scalps. Their stench hits us like a wave, and the smell of rotten flesh fills the air. I swallow and clench my teeth as I steady my breathing. Even though my captor has both my arms pinned down at my sides, my grip tightens around the hilt of his sword. I eye each one who stalks past the cave, searching for weaknesses within their mismatched armor. A low growl rumbles up from one of them, gurgling in the depths of his throat. The sound is jarring. The creature suddenly stops in his tracks with his chin slightly raised to the sky, smelling the air and exposing the soft flesh under his chin. The kill shot. My adrenaline rises, and I wonder if my captor will fight with me if we are discovered. Sweat forms above my brow. As his chest presses against my back, I feel his breathing deepen.

Another creature pushes through the pack, striking the one who stopped in the back of the head. "What are you doing you idiot? Keep going! He gave us very little time to find her," he commands, deep and throaty. His teeth are as sharp as blades and heavily rotted.

The other responds with a sound that makes my skin crawl. Saliva drips from his pointed fangs. The two stare each other down for a moment before proceeding forward.

The group continues to advance. I remain motionless with my back pressed against my captor's body. We stand quietly in the dark until their footsteps fade deep into the forest.

He releases me from his grip, and I create space between us, leaning over as my lungs beg for fresh air, still holding his sword idly at my side.

"What the fuck were those things?" I heave. I've never seen creatures like that in my entire life.

He rushes me, grabs my wrist, and rips his sword free from my hand. His eyes remain fixed on me as he tosses the blade aside.

"Larkins," he says, watching my every move like a wolf who's cornered its prey.

"I thought she said no monsters lurk in the White Forest," I murmur, wondering if these beasts roam the area.

"If you are referring to the lore, then no. Larkins do not wander into the White Forest. They wouldn't survive the cold."

"Then where are we now?" I ask in a scathing tone.

"Southeast, on the outer rim of it," he confirms.

Which means we are on the other side of the forest, far from home. I make a mental map in my head.

"Who is this *she* you speak of?" he questions, arching a dark brow.

"That doesn't matter," I scoff. At some point or another, I will cut that brow off his damn face for being so curious.

He extends his hand out to help me back up, but I smack it away. "Who exactly are these *larkins*?" I ask. Silence hangs in the air, and something catches me off guard: His eyes seem to glow. I'm not sure what I should think about that. "Tell me," I demand, pretending I don't notice how the corner of his lips perk up as I take a step forward.

"Some say they aren't of this world. They're nomads, traveling in groups. Some say they hold an alliance to a darker force, a dark lord, but they are also willing to do the dirty work for anyone who wants to keep their own hands clean." There's something hidden behind his eyes, as if his mind is drifting to a memory that seems to haunt him. "They're extremely dangerous killers," he warns.

I huff out a laugh, glancing out toward the entrance of the cave.

"Is that what you are, too? A cheap hire? Someone who takes people in the middle of the night against their will?" My eyes flick back to his, stabbing a finger into his hardened chest. He snarls at the motion, glaring down at the tip of my finger before his eyes trail up the length of my arm to find the look of disdain on my face. "Seems like you have something in common with them. You should all be friends," I sneer.

A growl rumbles in his chest as his nostrils flare. "I am *nothing* like them," he says, gritting through his teeth. "I had no other choice but to take you. Right now, we can only assume they're out here looking for you, too." He points a finger back at me. His tone is almost convincing, but it isn't good enough.

"Right. Now all of a sudden, everyone wants me," I mock. "I'm of no importance to anyone," I say, but it's more of a reminder to myself. I've spent my entire life carrying that feeling around.

He tilts his head, looking out the mouth of the cave. In these few seconds, my eyes rake down his body, noticing how well-defined his arms are. Then something catches in the faint light. I take notice of the dagger sheathed at his side. I quickly grab it and hold the blade up against his throat.

"So are you going to tell me how you found me? Or am I going to have to make you bleed to get what I want?" I seethe.

He responds with a cocky grin. "You don't have to make me bleed to get what you want, Princess." That sultry voice returns. "If it soothes your curiosity, finding you was easy. You're quite messy when angry. I followed the trail of destruction you left in your deranged state while making your way out of the forest. I could assume where you were headed, so I went ahead and waited." He looks at me with prowling, sated eyes. I don't know what he's searching for in my face, but then they drift to my lips, I press the blade harder against his skin in response.

"And your mouth still runs with insults while my blade is at your throat. You're either a fool or have no fear," I retort.

He lifts a brow, grinning. "Correction, that is *my* weapon you hold in those greedy little hands of yours."

How dare he correct me? Even though we both know it's true, the last thing I'll do is admit it.

"Let me remind you of how I got away." I go to knee him in the groin, but this time, he blocks me with his thigh, moving it between my legs.

"Naughty girl," he purrs. "Is that all you think about?" His eyes bore into mine, challenging me, while he firmly holds his hand around my free wrist, pinning it against the wall. I still have the knife to his throat. My stomach dips, feeling the top of his thigh press between my legs. My cheeks flush, remembering how sheer the fabric of my tunic is—the only fabric between his chest and mine.

His eyes darken with a smoldering look that spreads across his face.

"Let me remind you again, this weapon you hold is *mine*," he says the last word like a sinful promise. He ever so slightly nudges his thigh a little higher between my legs. I suck in a sharp breath at the sudden pressure. I swallow, not sure if we're talking about weapons anymore.

The corner of his mouth curls into a grin as he wraps his hand around my other wrist that holds the blade. He pushes it away from his neck until it's at my side. I try not to react to the heat pooling between my thighs. I feel like I've been put under a looking glass and lit on fire. Seconds stretch on. His piercing, green eyes bore into mine. I swallow hard, exhaling a shaky breath, feeling crazy that, for even just a second, the urge to rock myself against his thigh was strong.

What the fuck is wrong with me?

"If you want to keep what's between your legs, then I highly suggest you step away from me right now," I warn.

The tension hangs in the air. His jaw flexes as he searches my face.

"As you wish, Princess." He lets go and backs away.

"If it is wishes you're granting, then I wish for you to get out of my way so I can leave."

He ignores me, directing his attention to the mouth of the cave once more.

"They sense your presence here," my captor says with a tone of foreboding. "If they're looking for you, then we need to keep a low profile for a while so we won't run into any more of those larkins." He observes my attire. "You need new clothes, and we need to eat." He looks down at my feet, grunting humorously.

My eyes dart to the floor to see what he finds so amusing. One foot is exposed.

"I would still have my slipper if you hadn't dragged me backward through the forest." I quickly move my bare foot, placing it behind my other, trying to block him from looking at it any longer.

"I have a pair of boots for you too." Humor rumbles in his chest as he crosses his arms.

As much as I hate to admit it, he's right. I can't keep running without food, water, and a missing slipper. The cloak can only do so much. For stars' sake, I'm still in my sleep attire with someone else's blood splattered across it. Whatever clothes he has to spare would be better suited for what's to come.

"Alright, give them to me now," I demand as if they will magically appear in his hands. He has the power to put me to sleep, so this simple task shouldn't be too daunting.

He laughs. A loose strand of hair breaks free and dangles down the side of his face. "Very pushy. I have to retrieve them from Cirrus. He's lying low not too far from this cave."

My brows knit. "Cirrus?" My tone goes flat as I deadpan.

"Do you not name the horses you ride in your kingdom?" he replies, making his way out before I can answer. He stops at the mouth of the cave, holding the vines to the side, and turns to look at me. "I will be back shortly, Viona." He tries to sound reassuring.

I scoff under my breath and turn away, avoiding eye contact and staring into the darkened cave, but give him a tight nod. I feel him study me for a moment before leaving.

Once his footsteps fade, I exhale deeply and find somewhere to sit with the bit of light in the cave. Though he's gone, my heart is racing. The way he said my name sounded so sultry and smooth. When it rolled off his lips, it did things to me I don't want to consider. I lock them away because thinking of them will pull me off course. I gnaw on my bottom lip, feeling the tension make roots in every fiber of my core. There are no training sessions to drown myself in. No books I can try to sew back together. I'm far from home, in a land I was raised to fear, with someone I don't know. Someone who uses magic so effortlessly, and possibly does quite more to me. I don't want to know what else he's capable of.

There's very little time to think of a plan. I can take the items he gives me and try to fight him off until I break free again. Or skip the small talk and kill him when he steps back into the cave. I could also just take a chance and run right now. His sword remains on the ground. He's either dumb or doesn't want to leave me defenseless against those creatures in case they come back. A part of me feels it's the latter.

Leaning against the cool, stone wall, my eyes grow heavy. I picture the cloak over my body more like a thick, warm blanket surrounding me in heat. The comfort reminds me of my bed. Before I can even decide what to do, sleep claims me.

CHAPTER 7

J UDGING BY THE SMALL amount of light still in the cave, it's not long before my captor comes back. My eyes slowly open, watching him lace up a pair of black boots. There's tension in his jaw as he occasionally glances toward the mouth of the cave. Seems like those fucking larkins have us equally on edge. Faint light shines in, illuminating every muscle in his arms. They flex and bulge as he weaves the lace in and out of each eyelet. I enjoy the view for a few moments, admiring the intensity in his eyes and how chiseled his jawline is until he slightly shifts. I notice not one but two daggers tucked into his boots. I'm reminded that pretty things still bite, and he could easily use those against me. I hate admitting this, but the asshole is skilled, so I make a mental note to remember where those daggers are.

I sit up slowly.

He immediately lifts a brow and looks at me. "You're finally up."

Without saying anything, I turn my attention to the mouth of the cave.

"Larkins are intimidating at first," he says. "I remember the first time I saw one. I had that same look when—"

"Do you mind?" I snap, whipping my head in his direction. "I'd rather not think about it."

He looks amused by my response. I can feel his emerald stare prying into my space, but I have no interest in making small talk with someone who abducted me. His eyes linger for a moment, but he doesn't press further.

"I wondered if I would have to wake you up and risk your wrath. You're quite the little flame."

I give him a side eye. His mouth curves into a grin as he pulls the lace through and loosens the top edge of the boot.

"Here," he says, leaning forward and sliding them over to me.

Why would he lace these for me?

"They're for you. I certainly don't have dainty little feet." He winks.

I give him an eye roll and take the boots.

"Everything you need is over there," he says, pointing to my right. He brought back a stack of clothes, a water skin, and a small bag with a strap, which I assume holds food because the aroma instantly hits the air the moment I move the bag.

My stomach begins to rumble. I pull the sack of food and place it over my lap. I unravel the cloth, conjuring my primal hunger. A piece of bread, cheese, and salted meat are all individually wrapped. I immediately go for the bread, breaking off a corner and shoving it into my mouth. My eyes close, swimming in bliss, tasting the soft, moist roll melting on my tongue. I've never had bread with such a pleasant taste before. My head tilts back against the wall. A groan rumbles in my chest while my tongue dances with the flavors.

"You keep making sounds like that, and we are going to have a completely different problem," he purrs. My eyes flick open to a sight that reminds me of a wolf longing for a taste of its prey.

I should find that appalling, but my stomach takes a dip. I can feel my cheeks turning red. "Get out," I retort, my face still stuffed with bread. It's the only thing I can say to squash the butterflies wanting to flutter.

He raises his hands in surrender, smiling widely. Light glints off his perfect, straight teeth. "Alright, I apologize," he says, staring into my steel-blue glare. "You are quite beautiful even when you're angry. Don't stone me because I find your moans absolutely breathtaking."

Fuck him for making my heart sink even further. Is this asshole playing games? I've never had a man speak to me like this, let alone someone as handsome as him, but he has me flustered in so many ways. I reach over to the water skin, grabbing it with force, not taking my eyes off of him. My lips curve up into a snarl before taking a big pull of my drink.

Humor flashes in his smile, but he finally leaves me be, reaching for his bag. He pulls out a cloth with bread. Any beast can be distracted if presented with food, even men.

I take another long pull of my water. It's the perfect combination to wash down the bread. The salted meat is just as good, with a savory flavor that leaves me craving more. I save the rest and pack it away to conserve my little resources. I take the stack of clothes and set them on my lap, curious to see what else he brought.

I hold the dark, long-sleeve fabric out in front of me. It has the same floral and stardust design as my hooded cloak down the plunging neckline. It's so low that it would end just below my breasts on my sternum. My brow lifts, wondering if this was his idea, but he doesn't look like he'd know how to make something like this. The black trousers are made from a thick material I've never seen before. Despite the fancy designs and high quality, it's an elaborate version of something I'd wear back in Sao.

"This is extraordinary clothing. I wouldn't think a criminal like you would have access to things like this," I mock, breaking the silence between us.

"You can compliment the woman who made those in person when we arrive at my home in Callisto," he replies.

I place the clothes back down on my lap with emphasis and glare at him. "I have no interest in seeing the dungeon of a hole you crawled out of."

"You don't have a choice," he quickly snaps back.

"Who are you to give me orders? You're not my king. You're nothing but a criminal who's taken me captive. You've killed our men and taken me from my home in the middle of the night."

The anger in me unfurls. Visions of red flood my thoughts, as I relive the moments his blade sliced through each guard. Seeing their now-dried blood sprawled across a part of my night tunic is a constant reminder. The amusement drains from his face, and something glints in his eyes. I'm unsure if it's regret, but it is gone before I can analyze it. He slightly cocks his head to the side.

"He really must have kept you living under a rock. You don't even know who or *what* you are," he counters, leaving me no room to speak while his words sear my insides. Not knowing who I am or what remains dormant is a struggle he has no right to talk about.

He goes to speak but then cuts himself off. Instead, he stands, brushing the breadcrumbs off his lap, and points a finger at me. "You have five minutes to put your clothes on, then we're leaving," he orders before strolling out of the cave.

He keeps watch outside the entrance, leaning against the wall facing the forest.

I grab the pants off the pile, cursing while I slip them over my legs. *Prick. Who does he think he is, ordering me around?*

Five minutes to put my clothes on. I scoff.

His words pierce harder than they should. He's right. I've just existed while my father has brushed me aside day after day until it's become years, and I've become nothing more than a guard to him and everyone else. No conversation has ever gone beyond my oath to the crown, until he finally entered my room that night just to remind me where my allegiance should be.

As I pull the tunic over my arms and body, I realize, though I might not have all the answers to my current situation, I know who I was before all of this. I was a warrior. I *am* a warrior. And it's about time I remind my captor not *what* he has taken but *who*. My eyes dart over to the sword he left.

I fasten my cloak and strap the small bag over my shoulder. With precision, I stalk toward the cave entrance. Adrenaline kicks in, drawing out the edge of anticipation and vengeance unfurling in my veins. I lick my lower lip, allowing the darkness to run wild. I charge the last few steps, swinging the sword in an uppercut motion. He moves just in time. A curse leaves his lips, followed by a deep seething growl. My blade strikes into the stone wall where he stood, igniting a spark as the blow reverberates through my hands and arms.

"Fuck!" I yell, using all my weight to free the blade, but it won't budge.

There is no time. I can feel his next move as if our thoughts are in a synchronized entanglement. His arms extend out. He's inches from grabbing me, but I refuse to allow him to restrain me again. Before he can get my arms, I turn, dropping to the ground. I yank one of his daggers from his boot, roll, then rise to my feet, standing directly behind him. He quickly turns to match my stance and pulls his sword from the wall effortlessly. The sound of metal slices through the air, echoing through the forest. The sun bounces off the blade, obstructing my vision for a moment.

"I'm *not* going with you!" I remind him, tightening my grip on the dagger.

His eyes darken. "Like I said, Princess, you don't have a choice."

"You don't get to decide for me," I hiss, taking a step back to size him up. He's obviously bigger and stronger than I am. Size has always been seen as a disadvantage in every fight I've been in. One look at me, and the enemy was already claiming victory. I fed off their arrogance, just like I am now, staring into the eyes of my captor. I've brought men down to their knees countless times before taking their lives. Men twice, three times my size. With my captive being bigger than most of the men I've fought, this victory is about to be another one I can claim under my belt. He's only moments from being another lifeless body I'll leave on the ground for nature and starved creatures to claim. His weapon outweighs mine, so I must rely on close combat to win.

Somehow, it seems he has the same thoughts, because he eyes my weapon and smirks.

"I do believe my blade is bigger than yours. Do you think you can handle it?" He grins. Those eyes flare in cynical darkness like looking into a mirror—the look of chaos teetering on the edge, just waiting for a release. The only difference is he finds this humorous, while I find his amorous behavior repulsive.

Or at least, that's what I'm going to keep telling myself.

I move into my sideways stance with the dagger parallel to my shoulder, waiting for him to make the first move. And he does just that—such a typical male. If I had time to roll my eyes, I would.

He strikes down violently, but I catch his wrist midway above me. I advance forward, kicking him in the stomach. His body staggers back, and his shoulder-length hair thrusts forward as all the air gets knocked out of his lungs. A choking laugh erupts from his throat, but I give him no time to recover. I lunge forward, aiming for his torso, but the bastard blocks me, kicking me with his foot. I stumble back, falling onto the ground. A primal grunt escapes me. He swings at me again, striking down with his sword, but I quickly recover, pivoting his move. I'm too agile for him. I swing my leg into the air, making contact with his wrist to block his strike. His arm flies back, sending his weapon crashing against the gravel. I grin, relishing the sight of seeing him empty-handed. That gratifying sound fuels my next attack. I use his open stance to my advantage, kicking him again in the stomach, using all the force in my hip to strike that blow and silently thanking Alyce for teaching me that move long ago. His shoulders push forward. A deep guttural sound escapes him. My fist meets his face. I'm not sure what's more gratifying, watching him drop to his knees, or seeing his blood mist the air. Probably both.

He shakes his head, flinging hair away from his face, splashing blood on both of us.

I grab him by the throat and hold the dagger against his neck. We glare at each other, trying to catch our breath.

The sunlight flickers between the canopy of the trees, beaming across his face. I watch that light dance in his irises as he humorously grins with blood glinting off his teeth. We are mere inches apart. There's something else hiding behind those eyes. A part of me wants to give chase, to seek what he hides, but time is fleeting.

"Such curious eyes for a little flame," he says. The corner of his mouth twitches up. I can smell mint on his breath mixed with a metallic scent. No anger filling his eyes like before when we were in the White Forest. No promises of his threats to make me sleep with the monsters lurking inside my head. His shallow breaths almost feel familiar. I blink back. For a moment, a pang of guilt strikes me, seeing the small trickle of blood drip down the side of his mouth. What if this is his game, mind manipulation, baiting me?

Not this time. I refuse to be his victim. I shake my head and push the blade harder against his neck, nicking his skin. He hisses in pain.

My lips curve into a smile, relishing the sight of him kneeling before me and admiring this disastrous beauty. "It almost feels like a sin to kill such a beautiful man," I whisper.

"Beautiful," he echoes in a soft exhale.

Before he can speak any further, I plunge the dagger deep into his chest.

A gurgling sound ruptures in his throat. The dagger slides out, now slick with his blood. His body falls to the ground before I take off running.

Flashes of our fight replay in my mind as I make my way through the vast forest while maneuvering over gnarled logs heavy with rot. I yank my cloak back so it won't get caught on any protruding brush. While skimming the terrain, I'm searching for the edges of the forest, but all I can see are glimpses of his emerald eyes as the sun danced across his face. Guilt keeps making roots and wrapping around me like thorny vines. It's already too late. There is nothing more to think about because I am free.

Free . . .

When it comes down to it, I've never really felt that way my entire life. It is a luxury I was never meant to have. There is always something holding me underwater. It's impossible to find peace within the somber silence. Right now, though, I have nothing but the little contents in this bag, a cloak to keep me warm, and a weapon in my hand. This is insanely freeing.

I might have escaped my captor, but why is there something trying to convince me to go back? This inexplicable tethered pull feels more like a chain wrapping around my throat because all I want to do right now is get away from him.

"Stay focused, Viona, before you—"

My body runs right into something hard, dark, and solid. I fly back, landing against the ground so violently, the air punches out of my lungs. My bag goes flying along with the dagger. A giant shadow hovers over me, eclipsing the sun.

"I thought I smelled something pretty." The smell of rotten flesh is so potent, I want to hurl. It only takes a few seconds for my vision to come back into focus. My mouth gapes open. Chills creep down my spine, I'm terrified by what towers over me.

A larkin.

Fear seizes all sounds that want to escape my lips. He grabs me by the neck, lifting me off the ground.

I can't breathe.

A wave of panic washes over me.

He suspends me in the air like a rag doll. My eyes burn, and my heart is sent racing. I try fighting back, fighting for air, fighting for my life, but it only makes his grip tighter. The larkin is feeding off my fear and enjoying every moment of it.

"My king will be very pleased when he sees what I've found." A look of pleasure beams off his face, exposing his rotten teeth. His golden, amber eyes flare with delight. I'm powerless against him as my lungs beg for air. My chest is moments from bursting. Darkness must finally be coming because everything around me is fading.

Just as I'm face-to-face with death, something blooms inside me. Deep within my core, my soul cracks, causing the ground to shake and rumble beneath us. The sudden movement catches the larkin off guard just enough to throw him off balance and loosen his grip around my neck. Desperately, I gasp for air, sucking in as much as possible while he steadies himself.

Crimson light illuminates our faces. His eyes dart down to my chest. That distant shadow in the depths of my body unfurls a dark energy in waves of heat. As it courses through my veins, I somehow remain unscathed by its force.

The larkin's eyes widen. "What are you?" he snarls, saliva glinting off his rotten teeth.

Voices call my name in faint whispers. The power coursing through me rises to the surface until I'm compelled to repeat their words in my head, in a language unknown. Suddenly, my body releases a violent wave of energy, striking him in the chest. He drops me on impact. I slam against the ground, landing on my side. I gasp for air, glancing up momentarily to see the larkin wobbling back, clenching his heart before falling to the ground.

Someone comes up from behind me, placing a hand on my back. I know who it is as soon as I feel his touch. The captor's sword falls from his grip. He's on his knees, pulling me into his chest.

"Are you hurt?" He looks down at me with deeply knit brows. The pad of his thumb gently brushes away the hair lying slick against my cheeks.

In a ragged breath, I mumble something. His jaw tightens, unsatisfied with my inaudible response. His eyes grow dark as they dart over to the larkin, whose body still lies on the ground not far from where we are.

My captor slowly helps me to my feet, but my legs are like jelly beneath me. I press my hand against his blood-stained chest to hold myself up. He wraps his arm around my waist and swings my other arm around his neck.

"I've got you," he says. A few moments later, I stand on my own. My captor lets go, still keeping a watchful eye as if I'm something delicate and fragile. I'm not sure if I find it endearing or frustrating.

"How," I rasp out, still catching my breath. "How can you be alive when I killed you?"

"It would take a lot more to kill me, little flame."

"What?" I curse under my breath, choking out the word. He looks me over again, extending his hand out, but I wave him away. "I'm fine," I retort, looking over to the larkin who's now barely moving.

I pick up the sword and aim it at my captor's chest. "You owe me an explanation later."

I stalk over to the beast, dragging the tip of the blade across the ground. I peer down at the massive beast, watching him cling to life while he still pathetically clenches his dying heart. He groans in agony, in unbearable pain, and I relish the sound.

My captor walks past me to the larkin and presses his boot down against his chest. The beast's lips pull back into a painful snarl, exposing his fangs. I position the sword against the larkin's stomach, holding back the urge to pierce his singed skin and watch him bleed out. I need to extract more information.

"You said your king sent you. Tell me who it is so I can send him your head, and tell him you failed miserably," I grit through my teeth.

The larkin chokes out a humorless laugh. "You stupid bitch. You deserve all he has in store for you," he curses.

My captor's fists tighten, and a low growl rumbles in his chest. "Tell the pretty woman who sent you, or I will make you suffer more than she already has," he promises, glaring down at the beast, putting more pressure against his chest.

The silence angers me. If this larkin wants to play games, I'll show him what kind of games *I* like to play. I slowly push the tip of the blade into his stomach, slow enough so he can feel every inch sliding its way through his flesh. He responds with an agonizing cry.

"Do I have your attention now, *beast*?" I seethe, allowing the blade to go even deeper. Blood oozes out from the sides of his wound.

"Tell me who sent you," I repeat myself.

"*King . . . Tarvas*," he sputters under his breath.

My stomach turns as my blood runs cold. My mind reels back to when one of them said *"our king."*

Our. I blink back, tightening my grip on the pommel as a whirlwind of emotions rises. My heart is now pounding in my ears. How many more alliances is my father going to make with the enemy?

"*What* does he have in store for me?" I ask.

The fucker smiles. "He has a special cell for someone like you. He said we can do what we want with you as long as you're brought back *somewhat* alive." A throaty growl rumbles in his chest as he struggles to breathe. Blood trickles over the sides of his mouth.

Somewhat alive.

A cell.

Feeling nauseated and disgraced, my mind begins reeling through all the gruesome details of what the larkin could mean, those words strike me harder than any blade ever has. I take a step back, trying to catch my breath.

You're giving your trust to the wrong people. The words of Adnama are heard like an echo floating on a whisper in the wind.

The larkin gurgles out a laugh. "He has an eye for power, and now"—he pauses—"now I know why he wants you. What you've done to me . . . I feel it burning my insides. What is surging through you is from . . . " A look of clarity forms on his face. Before I can torture him for more answers, his eyes go glossy. Then, he is gone.

Haunted by his words, I freeze, staring down at the beast's now-lifeless body. Why? Why would my father put me in this position? To be hunted by these larkins, not caring of the condition I'm brought back in just to throw me in a fucking cage. What does he want with my powers?

I look up at the canopy of the forest as everything becomes a blur. The darkness inside me returns with the affirmation, snaking through my veins, and it's latching onto my emotions as they run wild. My hands tighten around the hilt of the sword. All I can do is shake my head in disbelief.

"Why would my father do this?" I rasp, feeling the back of my throat burn and trying to blink back the tears, but it's useless. A few slip down my face.

My captor looks around with urgency. "That is something we will have to figure out later. We must leave now. The rest of them will be here any minute." He takes a step toward me. I point the sword at his chest. Trust is earned, not given.

"There is no *WE*." I tighten my grip around the pommel.

Frustrated, he runs a hand through his hair, but it falls to the front again.

I always knew my father was an asshole, but this is salt on my wounds. I never thought he would do something like this. Now I'm looking at a dead larkin, a captor who wants to take me, what else is going to happen?

"We need to go," he repeats himself with growing concern.

I'm being torn in half between two worlds, barely keeping myself together.

"Viona!" His voice snaps me from thought. He takes another step forward, despite the blade being pointed at him.

"You said you came to '*claim what's yours,*'" I seethe, reminding him of what he has done to me. "You used your magic to lull me to sleep. You abducted me. I cannot trust you. What if you plan on doing the same thing my father wants to do to me?"

His fists clench together. "Fuck," he grunts. I can hear the regret and frustration in his voice. "You have every reason not to trust me. But right now, we are about to get swarmed by the rest of those larkins if we stay here. They won't stop until they have you. I cannot protect you if you keep running from me."

I scoff, "Protect *me*? Clearly, I don't need your help there. I was doing fine on my own."

"You don't have control over your abilities right now. You *clearly* almost got yourself killed!" he yells, the veins in his neck bulging. "*I* can help you."

My jaw clenches shut. Maybe he can help, or perhaps this is just another lie told by another man.

He sighs, taking another step closer to me, lowering his voice this time. "Know this, I will not let anyone harm you. It's a promise I don't deserve to make you right now, but I hope I can earn it in time," he says, sincerity filling his voice. He grabs the tip of the sword and angles it between his sternum. "If it is me who harms you, then I will *give* you my life to take, willingly." Those words leave his lips like a vow, forcing my skepticism to pause. I lock eyes with him in sheer wonder as he leaves me breathless. He gently pushes away the blade, closing the distance between us. His features soften. "We will find out these answers together."

I look down at the motion of his hand extending toward mine—a peace offering from my enemy.

That invisible tether pull returns, but it isn't wrapping itself around my throat this time. It's a soft brush of wind against the palm of my hand, gently nudging me to take his. A coolness settles over my body, holding back the waves of heat licking beneath my skin until it recedes far from reach.

This is a risk I have to take. I know I need time to think about what to do, but I can't do it here in hiding. If my powers are awakening and my destiny is true, maybe someone can help me. I remind myself I've been a skilled fighter long before this. I can handle anything that comes my way, and if my captor decides to turn, I will end his life. And this time, I won't miss.

"Okay," I agree, reaching for his hand. "Let's get out of here."

He blinks, clearly shocked at my willingness to comply as he takes my hand with a firm, tight grip and leads me through the thickened forest. I let go once I find my footing. We run for a few minutes, ducking under tree limbs, keeping a low profile, until we find a clearing.

"To your right," he calls out. I continue through the jagged path until I see his horse up ahead. The pure ivory form contrasts against the bold, lush forest. The horse is quietly grazing on some grass, looking serene. There's no time to hesitate as I approach him. I hoist myself onto his back, praying to the stars he won't be startled and rear up, but he casually looks back as if he remembers me. I gently run my hand along the side of his neck and give him a little scratch behind his ear. His demeanor remains calm under my touch. Looking deep into his dark eyes, he seems to smooth out all the panic and fear warring inside me.

My captor mounts Cirrus, adjusting himself behind me. "I see you've made a new friend," he says as I hand him the reins.

"He's a lot nicer than you," I reply, reaching forward to give Cirrus another pat. Cirrus snorts in response and swishes his tail.

"Hold on," my captor warns, and we ride as fast as Cirrus can carry us.

CHAPTER 8

E VERY TIME MY EYES drift shut, the larkin returns with that malicious glare I know will continue to haunt me. The power in his grip was unwavering. They roam these lands? Bile wants to work its way back up. I wonder what other forces the king has at his disposal.

Back home, any magic is forbidden unless one is born of nobility or has a high rank, while commoners are forced to keep it hidden. My father has killed anyone who practiced, and he used every opportunity to remind me of my lack of ability. Once again, I repeat the mantra that my power is in my fight, agility, and strength, and not in the prophecy my birth was cursed with.

A faint smile quirks my lips, hearing Alyce's voice echo, reminding me I can also use my beauty as a weapon. She does lie quite well, I'm far from beautiful, but I still appreciate her enthusiasm.

Though, a few years ago, I was tempted once to try it on the Prince of Corsal before they became our enemies. Back then, my father wanted me to get information about the prince's homeland. The kingdom of Corsal to the south has a smaller presence on the battlefield, but they make up for it with immense power. My father wanted to gain the knowledge of their source, claiming it was hidden somewhere in the desert ruins, the territory that lies between our kingdoms. It was information we never retrieved because I backed out at the last moment.

The larkin's face flashes before my eyes again, pulling me from thought. Before I let my mind go back to that snarling face, I focus on Cirrus trotting through the terrain, allowing the steady rhythm of his hooves to calm me. I focus on the landscape and its abundance of lush trees. It's like a mirage in the middle of desert ruins, it feels unreal, except it stretches on for miles. This place is buzzing with life as if magic is cast on each blade of grass. The slight breeze is cool and gentle. I unhook my cloak and place it between my thighs to cushion my palms while I lean forward to release some tension in my back.

Cirrus slows his pace. I can tell he needs rest too.

My captor finally breaks the silence. "Is that how you normally fold your clothing? Because I can assure you, the children in town might think you have a ball for them to play with."

I click my tongue and roll my eyes, irritated that he has ruined a peaceful moment. I was perfectly content without having to engage with him. "Do you mind? I said I'd go with you, but that doesn't mean I will speak with you along the way. Besides, I don't mind if my cloak has a few wrinkles. I'm not trying to impress anyone, especially where we're going," I retort. "But if answering you means you'll stop talking, then yes. My back is sore, and I need something to lean on."

"You can always rest against me, Princess. I won't bite," he says. I can feel the smirk stretching across his face. "Callian," he continues.

"What?" I slightly turn, flicking my eyes to his. I swallow the lump in my throat. I didn't realize how close I would be; he's mere inches from my face. He doesn't respond, but his eyes speak as they trail down to the curve of my lips. My cheeks grow hot. I quickly turn away, looking straight on as my heart flutters uncontrollably. I can feel him smiling as if I have eyes in the back of my head.

"My name is Callian."

Callian . . . My mouth quirks up into a little grin.

"How kind of you to tell me your name," I scoff. "Am I now supposed to suddenly lean back and rest against you?" I throw my hands into the air and scoot forward, creating more distance between us, even if only a few inches.

"I take it you've never shared a horse with anyone before," he surmises. I look back again. Callian's brow is raised, and a smile tips the corner of those perfect lips. His eyes glint, acknowledging the unexpected gaze we shared moments ago. "Does that mean I'm your first?"

I growl.

Briefly, I think about the others he's possibly shared a horse with. Not that it matters, really. Before my thoughts grow too ridiculous, I snip them.

"How much further do we have to go?" I ask, clearing my throat, hoping that by changing the subject, we can leave the awkwardness behind.

"We will reach the kingdom of Callisto by tomorrow afternoon. We can find a place to rest in the Sebina Mountains for the night and start back up at dawn."

Not long after he speaks, we leave the open meadows and ride west with the sun at our backs. The forest thickens the higher we ascend. The last bit of sunlight touches the treetops and filters through like shimmering beams of gold. The cold of dusk drifts in. I'm uneasy about spending another night out in the open, worried the larkins will be able to track us down. I nervously rub my hands together while soothing out how sore they feel.

"We will be safe up here for the night," he reassures me, reading my mind. "Remember what I told you? They don't do well in colder climates. We'll be fine."

"I hope you're right." I unclasp my hands, resting them on my awkwardly folded cloak.

"I'm always right, Princess."

A laugh escapes me. "You're such a fool," I say in a tone much softer than I intended. A smile lingers on my face as I stare ahead, taking in the last bit of light.

Though I want to keep going, I know this is for the best. Cirrus needs rest, and the thought of eating the remaining food in my satchel is making my stomach rumble. I need to get off this horse as soon as possible. If I continue being in such close contact with Callian, I will only grow to regret it.

SOMETHING IS OUT THERE. A darkness moves among the shadows, cloaking itself in nightfall. It leaves me with an unsettling knot twisting in my stomach. I glance along the outer rim where the light from the small fire fades into the forest. Despite what Callian said, we are still exposed to the elements. I'm putting faith in the words of someone I barely know, but what other choice do I have?

None. I keep telling myself.

I take a deep breath, close my eyes, and try to focus on the sounds around me. My thoughts drift to a million places at once. I'm tired and weary. My bones ache from the long ride. My facade is waning, but Callian has already seen enough of it today. He doesn't need to know about all the things that plague me. The sound of the firewood crackles from behind, pushing my looming thoughts far from reach. I'm glad I'm not alone and left to bear the cold in this unknown territory by myself. In some fucked up way, his presence is a small comfort.

I turn around and walk back to the fire, watching Callian throw in another log before he sits back down. I sit across from him on the other side. Flames and smoke curl into the cool, night air, just high enough for me to get a glimpse of the way he tucks a wild strand of hair behind his ear. The heat of the fire warms my face. When the flames settle, he stares at me from across the way, his thick brow raised with curiosity. Fire dances in his emerald eyes. I sense he is slowly trying to peel away the intricate layers I've placed around myself. If he looks close enough, he might find the darkness sleeping within, something I'd rather keep hidden for now. But the silence becomes tantalizing. Hours earlier, I wanted nothing more than for him to stop talking. As his gaze deepens, his stare does things to me that I don't want to admit.

I rise to my feet to stretch my legs, walking away again until the campfire glow is at my back. I stand on the edge of darkness, peering out into the forest with my arms crossed over my body. The serenity of the moonlight beams in through the trees, but it still isn't enough to calm my nerves. Faint sounds of insects chirping their night songs doesn't help either.

Something shifts in the air, causing the hairs on the back of my neck to rise. The chirping stops, the forest grows silent. I must have stopped breathing too, because my body goes on full alert. The eerie silence looms. Wind bellows in the distance, growing in strength as it nears me, rustling the leaves and causing the branches to creak as if they're responding to what's coming. My feet grow heavy as though

I'm sinking into the ground. My eyes close, surrendering to the lure of this chasm. My head tilts back, and somehow, I slip into the dark.

A resounding swell of crashing waves charges the air. My eyes flutter open. My arms fly out, trying to keep my balance on the ledge the moment I realize I'm standing on a high cliffside. I stumble back. It takes a moment to find my footing, but the heavy, ominous clouds that roll and rumble in the distance grab my attention. Another relentless wave slams against the cliff, and I'm drawn back to look at the jagged rocks below. I suck in a sharp breath, beguiled by the sea's roaring beauty, yet I'm frozen in terror. My heart begins to race. Every thud reverberates throughout my body. The wind blows my hair in all directions and across my face. Between the dark strands, I see a crimson glow burning beneath the waves. The center of my chest illuminates the same crimson light. The sound increases, every pulse growing in strength until it's all I hear. I place my hand over my chest, feeling my powers hum beneath my palm. With every beat, they become synchronized with my heart. I'm entranced by the ruby glow as it floats idly beneath the waves like a beacon. I'm teetering on the ledge, wanting to give into the pull. Without a second thought, I step off the cliff.

A firm hand grabs my arm, pulling me back through the hollow space I was in.

My vision becomes obscured. The ocean disappears, and a chill sweeps down my body. The night air is frigid against my skin, but it doesn't stop the sheen of sweat above my brow from forming. Callian's warm, calloused touch affirms where I truly am. Back in the forest under the night sky.

"What happened?" Callian growls, a predatory glare spreading across his face as he looks me over for injury. He seems relieved when he finds none. He diverts his attention to the outer rim of the forest as his jaw ticks.

I rub my temples, trying to soothe the sharp pain. "I'm fine," I lie, although it's clear I'm not.

He loosens his grip, though he remains in my personal space. "I was calling out to you. You just stood there, frozen, staring off into the distance as if you were somewhere else. I got up, and when I touched your arm, you jolted back into me."

I hesitate for a moment before speaking, trying to form another lie, but one never reaches my lips. The adrenaline still roams free. My balance is off. My legs are like jelly. I don't even notice I've lost my footing until Callian springs into action by wrapping an arm around my waist. He helps me walk back toward the fire.

"Sometimes, I see . . . " Hesitation fills my voice as my words trail off, unsure what I'm about to say.

"Visions?" he finishes my sentence. There's a foreboding look on his face.

"What do you know about my . . . visions?" I ask, struck by the notion of him possibly knowing about something I've always kept so hidden.

He helps me sit back down. "Let your body recover before we answer each other's questions."

I nod, finding my place on a log by the fire.

He sits beside me and hands me my waterskin. "Here, drink this."

We no longer have the fire separating us. His scent envelopes me—cedar, mint, and musk. He combs a hand back through his long hair, but it just falls around his face again. Deep in thought, he watches the flames as he laces his fingers together and rests his elbows on his knees. I can tell he wants to comfort me, but he gives me my space.

I realize my powers are growing. Visions appear not only in my dreams now, but in my waking state—an unfamiliarity to me. I remember what I did to the larkin. This is just an inkling of its capacity. It will only grow, abiding in this cursed vessel I call my body.

I decide to be honest, as hard as it is. "That was more than a vision." I break the silence, holding back the slight tremor in my palms as I clasp them together. Those have grown over time, from war and being ordered to do things I wish I could undo. My cheeks flush, hoping he doesn't notice.

I take a deep breath.

Callian shifts his body. His thick lashes drift to my hands and then to my face. "It's okay if you don't want to tell me," he says in an unexpectedly gentle tone.

I swallow the lump in my throat. "I was on a cliff. An ember was glowing beneath the waves, and it was calling out to me. At that moment, I wanted nothing more than to go to it, even if it meant to jump. I was so willing, it was inescapable. The risk would have been worth it all." My voice rasps against the rawness in my tone. My heart is racing, unaccustomed to sharing my intimate thoughts. Am I a fool for oversharing? I turn my head, meeting his intense stare. "I've had dreams like this my entire life, but never visions when I'm awake."

Callian's brows pinch while he runs a hand along his shadowed jawline. "I think you've had these visions in your waking state longer than you realize."

I blink back a few times, confused. "What do you mean?"

There's an uneasiness in his demeanor as he rubs the back of his neck. "The night I took you, you were not in your bed when I slipped into your room. You were on the far balcony, standing on the ledge, looking toward the ocean. I didn't want to startle you, fearing you would fall to your death. I used magic to lull you to sleep. I have many powers, but persuasion is one I don't ever use. At that moment, I had no choice." He searches my eyes, waiting for a reaction, but my body is too numb for words. "For that, I apologize," he continues.

"That night, I did hear a voice. I remember being on the balcony but nothing more." I pause, still spent, and listen to the fire crackle. "How much do you know of my visions?" I ask.

"There is a prophecy, but one so shrouded in mystery that we can only infer the real meaning. I don't remember it much. I've only heard it a few times in my life." He looks forward, brows still knit together with concern. "It has been said that a leader will emerge from ash. This person will bring unity, but only if they wield their powers for good. All this time, we had no idea who this person would be or when they would be born . . . until our Seer recently had another vision. He saw you." Callian turns to me, our eyes locking as if something unclear has just pieced itself together. "Clear as azure skies. The princess of Sao."

A chill rushes down my body, listening to his deep, sultry voice. That tethered feeling pulls taut around me. Something glints in his eyes, but he clears his throat and looks away before I can see what it was. Silence fills the air.

"A princess belonging to a king who is rumored to be full of darkness. The White Forest has separated us for centuries. Yet, we have always had a watchful eye on the borders. To our surprise, he never started a war with us. He grew silent in the shadows of his kingdom. Now, as you sit before me, it seems more likely he was trying to keep you hidden," Callian surmises.

"Some of the darkest parts of the ocean never see light," I whisper.

"Hmm?" He gives me a sideways glance.

I faintly smile. "It's what my mother used to say." The mention of her almost steals my breath, but somehow, talking with him doesn't make it so heavy. I look at the fire, focusing on the tips of the flames as they brush the cool, night air.

"A diamond in the rough," Callian chimes in, pulling my gaze from the fire. Now it is I looking at him in confusion. He hums, smiling at me, "A rare beauty with lots of sharp edges."

I scoff, but the corner of my mouth curves into a smirk, and I look down at the tips of my boots. "Well, that is the most insulting compliment I've ever received."

His emerald stare brushes against the side of my face. "I could give you more if you wish," he says with a grin.

"Insults or compliments?" I humor him.

"Either or both . . . but, quite frankly"—he leans in a little closer—"whichever will make you smile again."

My heart skips a beat. My cheeks flush. I pick up a small branch from the ground and begin poking at the fire to keep the embers aflame.

"Such a daring game to play with me. I suppose if you feel this stick protruding from your eye socket, you'll know I took it as an insult," I tease, but honestly, either would be fun.

Callian's head tips back, and a loud laugh escapes him. The sound rumbles deep in his chest and it echoes through the woods. "I like the way you think," he says, following my move by picking up a stick. He begins to stir some of the wood in the fire.

After some time, he says, "I saw how you handled yourself today. Though you wear the weight of darkness on your shoulders, you are resilient. Don't ever think of yourself as anything less."

The warmth of his smile reaches me. It is soft and endearing. He looks at me a few moments longer before getting up to tend to Cirrus, leaving me with a warmth in my chest. I admire his positivity toward my situation, even though my future still feels bleak.

Callian pulls an apple from his bag to feed Cirrus then settles him in for the night. Cirrus neighs while Callian scratches behind his ears. His tail swings freely, swaying side to side. Then, the unexpected happens. Cirrus lowers his head so that Callian can press his forehead against it. It makes me wonder if this is their nightly ritual. Callian laughs, that radiant smile reaches me, warming my heart once more. Their bond seems strong, and it's evident they mean a great deal to one another.

Callian comes back with a stack of items in his hands, one of the items being my satchel. He sits beside me and pulls the remaining food out of his bag, indicating we should eat before resting for the night. We do just that, listening to cicadas and crickets hum their night song.

Once my belly is as full as it can be, I take a long drink from my waterskin and place it back into my satchel. I lean my body against a small boulder behind the log we sit upon, hoping it will ease the tension in my back. While staring at the onyx sky, my eyes grow heavier by the minute. Callian begins unraveling a thick, fur blanket. He lays it out, keeping it a safe distance from the flames. My eyes flick to his, the expression on my face likely legible.

"Your back will thank me in the morning after sleeping on this," he says, trying to assure me, but that brings no comfort. He sets my cloak down on top of it.

"Where will you be sleeping?" I ask as I raise both my brows, because I only see one blanket.

"Right beside you." He smirks.

"You are foolish if you think I will let you sleep beside me," I retort.

"Have you not shared the same sleeping quarters with anyone else before? Or am I going to be able to claim another first?" he taunts with that damn smile tipping the corner of his mouth. It infuriates me to see how humorous he finds all of this.

"*That* is none of your business," I seethe, walking over to retrieve my cloak. I hold it against my chest as if shielding my clothed body would help.

Callian sits on the blanket with his knee bent upward and an arm resting on it. Then he pats the empty space next to him in a cocky, seductive way. "It's nice and warm," he drawls in a smooth, deep voice that does things to me I refuse to think about.

"I'll be fine right here," I reply, stubbornly leaning on the boulder and nestling against this little nook. I turn my back to him, draping the cloak over my body. I close my eyes, hoping he won't speak to me. Minutes pass, and I can feel him watching with amusement while I try repositioning myself, but the hardness of the log under my fucking ass is already making it really difficult.

I hear him moving around to get comfortable, letting out a deep sigh with so much emphasis, as if he's so relaxed—the damn prick.

"There is nothing wrong with sleeping beside someone. I promise you, my hands won't wander." He almost sounds irritated by his own words.

I turn around. "If you were truly a gentleman, you would switch places with me while *I* sleep on that nice, soft blanket!" I hiss, before turning back around to cover my body again. Thoughts of his hands wandering start to take over. A warm sensation forms low in the pit of my stomach.

"We have a long ride ahead of us tomorrow. It would be foolish for only one of us to be fully rested. We both need to be in good standing," he presses.

I ignore his final plea as I try to get comfortable. All in all, he's right. My body is screaming at me to listen to the prick. I curse under my breath as I lie down beside him, putting as much distance as possible between us. With my arms crossed under my head, my eyes remain on the night sky. From the corner of my eye, I see him smiling as if he has won this battle.

"You know, I sleep naked sometimes," he teases.

I huff, rolling my eyes. "Please don't give me nightmares."

He laughs, shifting to his back and lacing his fingers behind his head. He stares up at the sky, looking at the moon's luminosity. Even in the dark, his white teeth glint in its light.

"The more you smile, the more I fantasize about cutting that grin off your fucking face," I warn.

"Is that a promise?" His expression doesn't change as he challenges me.

I accept. I twist my body toward him. Less than a second later, I'm straddling him, with a handful of his tunic in my grip. I lean down, chest heaving with rage. We're mere inches apart.

"It's more than a promise, asshole. I will rip your soul from your body and feed it to my demons," I vow.

He grunts. "I'm starting to like it when you're like this."

"Like what?" I say, each word clipped, baring my teeth and gripping his tunic tighter.

"When you're so angry, you can't decide whether you want to kiss me or plunge that dagger into my chest. Again." His green eyes bore into mine, studying me with an intense, smoldering look. Fuck him for being so infuriatingly handsome and annoyingly accurate.

"I would never kiss you," I reply.

"Your lies are as sharp as the tip of that blade that's so sinfully sheathed to your thigh." Callian flicks the leather strap with his finger. "I'd be careful if I were you," he warns. His touch rubs against my thighs as he wraps his big hand around the hilt, reminding me of how close we are. He lifts his head. So close, any sudden movement might tumble me onto his lips. "Keep tempting me, Princess. I just might like it." He smiles with a malicious grin.

He has me, with his weapon and the upper hand. I give him one last glare before releasing him from my grip, and return to my side of the blanket.

ASSHOLE.

I lie on my back, letting the cold chase away the heat I feel coursing through my veins. It's like running a hand through a field of wheat, feeling little shards of the leaves pricking my skin.

"You're insane." A little too late for a retort, but I can't seem to help myself.

He grins. "Am I? You're the one who decided to travel with a stranger."

I want to turn my back so I won't have to fall asleep facing him, but trust is still a fickle bitch right now. Handsome or not, this was the deal

I made with the enemy. I face him, but soon, my eyes lower. I don't respond any further.

CHAPTER 9

The forest hums with wildlife, and the sun filters in between the leaves, shining warmth across my face. The fire must have died out at some time through the night, as I no longer hear the crackling of its flames. It was a comforting sound to fall asleep to, something I wasn't used to back home, because most nights are hot. I hope to enjoy this newly discovered comfort someday when my life doesn't feel like it's being turned upside down. The palm of my hand moves up and down in place. Long, heated breaths fan across the top of my head. The scent of cedar and misted musk fill the air. I slowly open my eyes to see my hand on Callian's hard, muscular chest. Even worse, my greedy fingers slipped through the drawstring of his tunic while I slept. My heart descends into the pit of my stomach.

What am I going to do?

He faintly groans in his sleep, tightening his arm around my waist, warm and claiming. My legs are so comfortably intertwined with his. Every muscle in my body freezes at the sight. My ears grow hot.

How the fuck am I going to get myself out of this mess?

I'm afraid to move and terrified he'll feel my heart thundering in my chest, but his breaths remain slow and heavy, affirming he's in a deep sleep. I've never lain this close to anyone before. I feel so small nestled against his large frame. I'm petite, only reaching five feet three inches, but my legs are shapely under a layer of hard muscle. His thighs are the size of my waist. I fell asleep last night with the fear of having another vision. Yet, lying in his arms, I realize I haven't slept this well in . . . actually . . . a very long time, but this is insane. How can I find comfort in the arms of the enemy?

My mind begins reeling, telling me all the reasons to deny him, but my body melts beneath his touch.

"Good morning, Princess," he says, that smooth, sultry voice rumbling in his chest. Though I didn't think my cheeks could get any hotter, they do.

I remain silent.

Maybe if I pretend I'm still aslee–

"As much as I'd love to lie here and express how I've enjoyed you *finally* warming up to me, I have to relieve myself of my morning duties." I sense the smile spreading across his face.

"Warming up to you?" I instantly shoot up, leaning my weight on one elbow. "Listen to me *captor*, warming up to you is the *LAST* thing I will ever do. Believe me when I say this."

"So we are back to calling me 'captor' again? You wound me." He purrs the last three words, pursing his lips. His emerald eyes glimmer in the morning light. His dark hair is sprawled across the blanket, exposing all the hard lines of his shadowed jawline. His lips slightly part into a smirk as he wraps his large hand around mine. I realize I still haven't moved it away from his chest. His heart beats calmly and steadily beneath my palm. "Do you truly mean that? Or is it your way of showing how much you like me?"

I want to kiss him. I want to taste the lips of my enemy, my captor. I want to know what it's like to brush my lips across the side of his mouth until my tongue slides across his perfect, white teeth before kissing him, something I've thought about quite a few times. Damn the fucking stars. A soft exhale leaves those perfect lips that continue to tempt me. His grin fades to lust as if he's hearing my every thought. I grab a fist full of his tunic, clenching it tightly, and glare, even though the rest of my body is a traitor.

"I mean every word I say," I retort.

His eyes trail over my face once more, studying every curve from my brows to my full lips.

"You lie so beautifully, little flame," he coos.

I exhale at the sound of his voice. Silence hangs in the air as I try to place the heat coiling between us. That invisible, tethered pull returns, plucking that string of curiosity. It's rising faster than my heart can catch up. There's no denying it. My body is thrumming.

"Why don't you show me just how much you hate me, if that lie comforts you," he challenges me, running his hand along the side of my waist. My body hums beneath the warmth of his touch as his fingertips trail up, stopping just below my ribcage. His restraint is beginning to falter.

Sucking in a sharp breath, my legs clamp tightly around his. My anger is melting into palpable lust by the second while his hand is left wandering my body. I loosen my grip on his tunic, losing all sense of sanity, enjoying how he challenges me. My power unfurls inside me, hidden amidst desire as it snakes its way through my body, fueling me with confidence.

"Is that what you want? For me to lie to you?" I whisper. A smirk tips my mouth. My voice is smooth and taunting as I pull myself from his hold and sit on top of him, both legs straddling his hips. His hands grip my waist, holding me firmly. I lean in slowly, so close, until my lips graze against his ear while something else is coming to fruition. "You want me to lie? To tell you that I don't want to know what it would feel like to have your lips on mine?" A darkness purrs, curling its sway on every word. Words that do not feel like my own. "That I don't want to know what it's like to belong to you and only you?" I continue.

His hands move up my sides with desire. He throbs beneath me, pressing up against my bundle of nerves, and damn, our clothing is the only thing separating us right now. I close my eyes, lick my lips, and tilt my head back. A soft moan escapes me. The sound of my voice seems to seep into him like a remedy.

"Fuck," he groans, throbbing beneath me once more.

I let the confidence ignite and take over. I can't stop myself from what I want, from what the darkness in me searches for. I welcome all the desire to come through. I look back down at him while my eyes trail over his body. "Is that what you want, *captor*?"

His eyes are drowning in so much need and want. Leaning down, my hands press against his chest, but I wince from a sudden, sharp pain in my temples. My mind is clouded. I close my eyes, trying to push it back down, but it's a battle slipping from my reach. My eyes flutter to the back of my skull. My head suddenly feels too heavy to lift. The darkness snaking through my body leaks into my eyes—a sharp, piercing pain inflicting them. Suddenly, they fling wide open. My head flies back, and a bright flash of light makes everything around me disappear.

Dark, ominous clouds roll across the sky, the voices come rushing in like waves. The sun no longer beams through the treetops. They bleed fire. Every tree and bush in sight is being burnt to ash. Thick, heavy plumes of smoke enshroud the sky. Embers rain down over the landscape. A wave of terror washes over me when I look past the roaring, swirling infernos.

It's me, standing on a small hill with a power swirling out of control. I scream, but no sound comes out. I frantically place my hand over my throat, trying to speak again, but my voice is gone. Determined, I get up and start running toward myself, trying to stop the world from burning. That version of me turns, staring with a stone-cold gaze. For a moment, I think she's reaching for me, but her power grabs me by the throat, stopping me from going any further. My airway is constricted. I can't breathe. She appears directly in front of me with eyes the shade of onyx. As I struggle for air, I stare into the eyes of someone who is no longer there. She is the birth of my destruction.

"Please stop," I say in the back of my mind, but she only stares back. She's nothing but an empty vessel. My body feels weighted, but I fight against being oppressed by the same darkness. I use all my strength to lift my hand. I grab her by the wrist. On contact, another burst of white light explodes around us. Everything disappears.

My hands go to my throat as I gasp for air. Callian's eyes are wide with confusion and shock.

"Viona?" He sits up, placing his hands over my arms. "Are you alright?" He cups my face, lifting my head to look at him. "Say something!" he repeats himself. I'm too drained to speak. I manage a nod to give him some sign that I'm okay, and he exhales heavily with relief.

I place a hand over my temple, trying to soothe the pain. My skin is hot, a little too hot, as more heat spreads across my chest.

"I saw myself standing on a hill, but it wasn't me. There was fire . . . " I pause, taking another deep breath. The back of my throat burns.

I look at him as tears swell in my eyes, and a tight line forms between his brows. "It was me, but it was like my soul wasn't inside anymore. I was gone . . ."

I remain sitting on Callian's lap. He sits quietly while I continue explaining everything I saw from beginning to end, even though it only lasted a few moments. I explain how I felt something reach for him moments before it began. His lips press into a thin line.

In the back of my mind, so much anger and shame threaten to overwhelm me for what we were doing. This time, I let it fester to punish myself. A defense I am so good at because I hate feeling so exposed. How many times is he going to watch me fall apart?

Yet, I notice his hands never moved away from me amidst my talking. I didn't flinch at his touch when he started rubbing small circles on my lower back. Callian didn't make me feel like the monster I always felt I was. There is no disgust or regret in his eyes for thinking of me in a lustful way only moments ago. He gently squeezes my hand when he notices a tear slip down my cheek.

For the first time since my mother died, I have someone to sit with me in the dark. It's a kindness from him I didn't expect. Even though I barely know him, this is a comfort I didn't think I needed until he came along. I'm also reminded of the necklace my mother gave me long ago. I look down at the now-empty space where my chain once hung on my chest, realizing it was left in my room the night I was taken. Last I saw, it was on the side of my desk.

He smiles, touching the loose strand of hair that dangles in front of my face and tucking it gently behind my ear.

"You had me worried there for a moment. Your eyes blackened, and your body heat rose. It looked like you were in a trance. I was more afraid for you than me, even though it did cross my mind that I could be struck with your powers."

"Why didn't you push me off of you and protect yourself?" I ask. Why would anyone feel they need to put their safety at risk for someone like me?

Callian blinks back a few times as if it is odd to think this way. "It's a risk worth taking . . . because you owe me a new shirt," he teases, pointing down to the hole in his black tunic. I unexpectedly laugh, even though I notice he so fluidly danced around my question, but his relaxed expression is a good enough answer. I look at the small hole in his tunic from where I stabbed him. A piece of cloth dangles free. I poke a finger through the fabric, stroking along the faint pink scar left in its place. Dry, crusted blood surrounds the area. I quickly withdraw my hand, realizing I shouldn't be touching him. I clear my throat and quickly get off him, now sitting at his side.

"You owe me an explanation, remember?" I demand, hoping he doesn't notice my cheeks flush.

"What is there to explain? I was gifted by the gods from the stars, along with many others. Have you not seen anyone self-heal before?" His brow lifts with curiosity.

Truth be told, no. "There are rumors of self-healers, but my father doesn't allow anyone to use their gifts unless they want to lose their heads," I confess. Anger flashes across his face, and he looks shocked at the revelation. He opens his mouth to speak, but I cut him off to avoid any more mentions of my father or how secluded my life has been. "Did it hurt?"

My eyes drift back down to the healed area. I touch it once more, sensing his stare while my hand trails over the faint scar that I assume will soon fade, examining it slower this time, enthralled by this rarity.

"Yes," he says in a smooth, husky tone that makes me pause. I then realize my fingers have been lingering over the divots of his abs longer than they should. My cheeks flush again. I lift my eyes to his and withdraw my hand onto my lap.

"I take it you weren't a fan of the little gift I left you. That's too bad, because I enjoyed doing it." I smirk, trying to dismiss the desire still pooling in his eyes, ignoring the inexplicable guilt that still nags at me. "I've never seen someone with the ability to heal themselves before, I'll have to be more clever next time."

He laughs, looking at me through a hooded gaze. "I heal pretty quickly. A good power to have when fighting little flames like yourself," he teases, tugging on my strand of hair that fell loose again.

"You must think I'm a monster." My mind reels back to my vision.

"I like monsters." He smiles, catching me off guard again. My breath hitches at the sight of him holding my gaze beneath the morning light.

Huffing out a faint laugh, I rise to my feet and start gathering my things. He disappears into the trees to relieve himself, and while he's occupied, I do the same. I know we have a long way to go before reaching our destination.

I make sure the fire is completely out as Callian packs up the rest of our things. I walk up to the white horse and scratch him behind the ears while Callian gets him ready for the journey. When he's done, he hoists himself onto Cirrus' back.

There's a calmness in Cirrus' eyes. I never knew I could envy a horse until now. Callian reaches for my hand. This time, I hoist myself behind him.

"You're not going to be in front this time?" he asks, sounding disappointed under the guise of a flirtatious tone.

"No."

"Well, that's disappointing." Callian pouts, gently tugging on the reins. Cirrus pulls back and starts down the path.

"Why is that disappointing?" I know I am playing with fire by asking such a question, but a part of me feels adventurous.

A hum rumbles in his chest. "Your body heat has become a welcome part of our ride."

My heart flutters, but I say nothing more as we descend down the Sebina Mountains.

CHAPTER 10

W E HEAD NORTHEAST WITH the sun on our backs, high enough to see what our next few hours of travel will entail. Nothing but a vast, wide valley stretches ahead. I wonder about the people who dwell within the walls of Callisto and the events that will proceed after we enter.

"Cirrus knows his way from here. The rest of the journey will be an easy ride," Callian says.

The sound of Cirrus' hooves against the ground fills the silence. We don't speak for a while, but then the thought of my impending arrival in enemy territory starts to weigh on me.

"Can we take the longer road to the kingdom? I'd rather arrive at night than endure a grand entrance." I want to avoid being seen altogether, actually. Back home, I was a shadow, and I hope to remain that way in this new kingdom.

He sighs deeply. "We are already taking the long way. Lucky for you, we will be entering through the side entrance. You won't be seen much until you meet with the king," he confirms, focusing his eyes on the line of trees far east.

"Wonderful," I mock, rolling my eyes.

"He's a good man. You'll find out as soon as you meet him," he says. "I promise."

A promise. I scoff under my breath.

He laughs. "Are you always like this?"

"Like what?"

"Negative." His tone goes flat.

I cross my arms over my body. "I'm not negative. I'm just forward. Honest."

Cirrus neighs.

"Exactly my thoughts, Cirrus," Callian replies.

I scoff louder this time. "You can't seriously be talking to a horse."

"Why not?" he asks in that smooth, casual tone. He seems to find this conversation amusing.

"Because"—I pause—"he's just a horse!"

Callian shakes his head. "You're very strange."

"*I'm* strange? I'm not the one who takes women in the middle of the night while they sleep."

He goes still at the reminder. Whatever he was about to say dies on his tongue. As more time passes, my body starts aching from the ride. The tall grass starts to look like a nice fluffy bed. Over to the left is a wide river with a small line of bushes growing by the shore and a row of trees cresting the hill.

"How much further do we have to go?" I ask, pressing a hand to my lower back. I tilt my head back and forth, rolling it from side to side. A small moan escapes as I feel some of the soreness release. I want nothing more than to lean on Callian for relief, but I insist on keeping my distance, even if it's only by a few inches.

"You know, the offer to sit up front still stands, Princess."

The breeze wisps through his hair along the nape of his neck. My eyes trail over the shape of his broad shoulders, watching his arms flex handling the reins. That tethered pull blooms once more, an endless feeling I can't suppress.

"It isn't necessary," I say, though I'm picturing myself leaning my body against his back for relief.

A low chuckle rumbles in his chest.

We say nothing for a while longer, but I sense something stirring his thoughts. By now, he should be saying things that make me want to punch him in the face, but his silence is tense, only making the time drag on.

He finally speaks. "I have a question. I warn you, it might be an uncomfortable one."

"Okay . . ." Raising a brow, I try to ignore the feeling of my heart sinking into my chest, focusing instead on a bird perched on a log in the distance.

"We don't know the capacity of your powers right now. All we know is lore and prophecy. Of course, you know what comes with that: misinformation and uncertainty. We didn't know you existed until recently, but we won't know more until you meet with the Seer and we do some digging of our own." He takes a deep breath. My stomach tightens, knowing what he's getting at. "You explained your powers pushed through as if they were seeking me out . . . but why? In a moment where I—" He clears his throat. "In a moment where *we* were both . . . distracted."

Damn him for being so forward with this uncomfortable question. My mind reels to his moans as I moved my hips across his length. My face grows hot at the memory. I don't know what to say.

His question comes at the worst time—as Cirrus begins trotting down a steep hill. Gravity is a bitch, and it definitely isn't my friend right now. My chest goes flush against his back. Instinctively, my hands slide down past his waist and plant themselves on his thighs to stop my fall. Gods, they're so thick, and they're made of pure muscle.

Heat pools below my stomach. That's all it takes. One touch to flip my world upside down and forget how damned my future could be. These blooming feelings are disastrous. His body leans back a little, as if he is soaking up the feel of my chest pressed against him. Shame latches itself onto me like a plague. My breathing stills, my heart wants to flutter out of my chest.

"I didn't mean to do that."

I swallow hard with a shaky breath before taking my hands off Callian's thighs. I straighten myself back up. I have an inkling his question really isn't about me or Seers. It is about our morning, before the vision. He grips the reins tighter as tension hangs in the air. As soon as we're on flat ground, we go under a thin line of trees growing parallel to the path and the river shadowed by the treetops. At this very moment, I wish I could just disappear completely. I parry his question and add a few more inches of space between us, still not knowing what to say. He runs his hand through his hair.

"I guess what I'm asking is, was that *you* while you were on top of me, or something else."

Shame wins, claiming victory over me like an arrow striking my heart.

"It was a mistake." A mistake. The words come out so quickly, words we both know are untrue. My tone is cold and scathing.

"Is that so?" he drawls icily, straightening his shoulders.

"It was my powers pushing out, nothing more. I hope it won't happen again," I assert, masking my conviction. Yet, what I felt, I honestly don't know if it was me. I can't be sure.

Callian grows deathly quiet, putting thought into his next words. I slyly lean to the side, peering around to look at him. I guess he feels my eyes searing into the side of his face because he turns his head, and those piercing, green eyes stare back at me with a sliver of power peeking at the rims, reminding me of his wrath. Tension flutters in his jaw. I remember when he cornered me in the White Forest—backing me against the tree's bark while making dark promises to instill fear. I sneer back.

"Once someone shows you how to work with your powers, you'll have more control over them. Then you won't have to worry about making another *mistake* again," Callian responds coldly while looking straight ahead.

He nudges Cirrus to veer right and speed up. The abrupt pace has me grabbing onto Callian's sides as we ride hard toward the river. The sound of water flows rapidly downstream, beating against the rocks as we draw near.

"What are you doing?" I call out.

He rides without answering me, galloping along the shoreline until we find a spot where the water calms. Cirrus slows to a pacing trot.

"I need to stretch my legs, and Cirrus needs a drink," he says.

I glare at him as I take the initiative to dismount. Callian follows, making a loud thud as his boots hit the gravel. He searches around in the bags and pulls out my water skin, handing it to me with a deep scowl. I snatch it from his hand and turn away. He retorts something inaudible as smokey, green tendrils still brim his eyes, threatening to release. As angry as he makes me, seeing his hair whisk around his face makes me want to torment him, to push those boundaries out of spite.

He pulls his water skin from the bag with his back to me and walks over to the river's edge. The water gathers around his boots. He crouches down, unraveling the top to let the water flow in. My eyes skim over the terrain. Gravel crunches beneath my boots while I walk to the lapping water and put distance between us. The water is loud enough to distract me from the tension.

I just need to breathe, have a moment to myself, and possibly allow more time to pass to avoid the inevitable. We are only a short distance away from Callisto, and having no idea what awaits me or my future, my body needs a release. I stare at the water flowing downstream. I cannot escape the way the water has always called to me. The same way the moon does when it's at its fullest. I have to take what I have in front of me and try to make the most of it. I access the river, noticing the land dips off a few feet away. It's deep enough to conceal my body.

A smirk forms on my face. I glance at Callian. He has his back toward me while he tends to Cirrus, preoccupied with his precious pet. I pull the dagger from my boot so it won't flop out as I take it off. I remove my clothes with haste, tossing them to the side. My black hair dangles freely down my chest, concealing my breasts as I make my way into the water. My nerves get the best of me, and I get sloppy, swishing the last few steps until I take a quick dive.

The loud splash must have pulled Callian's attention toward me. When I come up for air, I see he has turned and is running like a fool up to the shoreline.

"What are you doing?" He seethes. "Are you insane? The waters are too cold for a swim!" he yells over the flowing sound.

I sink my head back under. His voice becomes muffled beneath the water. I raise my arm out, flipping him my middle finger, then swim a few strokes underwater, press my toes against the rocks, and swim back up to the top.

"I don't have time for this!" he says. Even from this distance, I can see the scowl on his face and his straight teeth glinting like a hungry wolf.

"I'm not ready to go to your kingdom yet, *captor*. I'm going for a swim," I call back, taunting him as I run my hands over my face and through my hair, dipping my body further into the water. I run my hands along my body, removing the dirt, dried blood, and grime from the nights of travel.

"Get out," he demands, but his words hold no power over me. I stare back at him, floating idly in the water. It's humorous to see his restraint as he tries not to let his eyes linger longer than necessary. "Now," he grits through his teeth, low and with great warning.

"No," I bite back.

His chest heaves. With each passing breath, his eyes grow darker. His fists clench until his knuckles turn white. My breathing stills. Fear wants to take over, but I refuse to be afraid. I refuse to be a victim of his wrath just because I'm not doing what he wants.

"If you don't get out right now, I'll—"

"You'll what?" I intercept, lowering my glare as my eyes narrow in on him. Beads of water drip down my nose and off my chin.

He pauses. Deep heavy breaths follow as he continues to stare below the water. "I'll come in there and get you myself." The warning in his tone fades as lust fills his voice. "Damn the consequences of what I might do."

"Seems to sum up who you are," I boldly say, ignoring the sudden shift in his tone, and the sudden pounding of my heart. "I dare you." My tone sings with a coated darkness mirroring his own.

A deep growl rumbles in his chest. His arm reaches behind his back and he pulls the tunic over his head in one swift motion, tossing it to the ground. My eyes lower to his abs. A warm sensation pools below my belly. I watch him remove his boots, one by one. My heart drops into my stomach as they hit the gravel. His glare never leaves mine. Those eyes are so beautiful and threatening; the way they brim with so much intent, it's intoxicating. I want nothing more than to push him, to play and see how far he will go. His black leather trousers fall to the ground. He's completely naked on the shore.

The challenge in my eyes fizzles, drifting downstream with the water as my treasonous eyes take in the full sight of him. My breathing stills, seeing the length between his thighs. Even though he isn't aroused, it's impressively large and thick. I swallow hard.

He stalks toward the edge of the water and my body tenses. The water ripples as he enters, rising higher until it stops under his ribs. He closes the space between us with his feet planted on the ground. My toes barely brush against the riverbed. The frigid water laps around our bodies.

"This is your last warning, Princess. Get out of the water." No threat in his words.

My raw hunger rises faster than the fluttering in my stomach.

"No . . . " I gently whisper, less bold, looking up at him through a hooded gaze.

With one swift move, he wraps his hands around my waist, lifting me from the water. I gasp at the shock of the sudden force as he thrusts my naked body against his—strong and primal.

I'm willing to give into his every whim. My legs wrap around his waist. My arms cling to his neck. Every part of me is completely open, exposed from my waist up. I close my eyes desperately, trying to find fault in how I feel, but that pull returns, drawing me to him in ways I can't seem to understand. Is this my darkness reaching out to him? The more I search, the more I realize it's just us. The reality of what I want is right in front of me.

"Tell me, Princess, what do you want?" he whispers in a smooth, sultry voice. A final plea for honesty and truth as his minty breath fans across my lips. I open my eyes to find his searching mine. His features are warm, and so much desire coils between us. In a world where everything is crashing down around me, all I can see is him.

"You . . . " I whisper, caressing the back of his neck. My heart pounds against my chest at my unveiled words. "What I want is you."

Without hesitation, he leans in, brushing his lips gently against mine before he claims them, kissing me slowly and tentatively. A low, throaty moan rumbles from his chest. His tongue licks in, soft and gentle. A tease before he pulls it out, leaving me breathless. I close my eyes, deepening the kiss, allowing myself to give in to his strong embrace, his warm touch. He breathes me in as if I am his remedy. I'm weightless. His kiss frees me from all the darkness surrounding my soul, chipping away at the hidden space where it hides. I'm coming alive again, taking what I want with his arms around my waist. The way he pulls my body to his feels as though he's pulling me to safety.

My hands comb through his long, dark hair, desperate to be closer. I open my mouth once more, and his tongue slides in; every stroke is full of talented, wicked sin. A soft moan escapes me. I want him to explore every part of my body with it. The barriers we put between ourselves have cracked, releasing all the hunger, need, and want that's been coiling between us for days. My heart beats faster as his lips move away to kiss the side of my jaw. My head tilts to the side, allowing his tongue to glide freely. His shadowed jawline rubs against my skin. It feels just like I imagined it would: perfect.

My eyes flutter to the back of my head. Callian's lips brush across the column of my neck before gently nibbling, drawing out another moan from me. He soothes the area with his tongue and more wet kisses. My nails dig into his back, pulling his body closer. A groan rumbles in his chest. Every time he makes that sound, the apex between my thighs aches. He brings his lips back to mine, crashing into me, so claiming and primal. Water swishes around my legs as I wrap them tighter around his hips. The tip of his cock is swollen with desire, gently brushing up against my slit and grazing my bundle of nerves.

He smiles against my mouth. "Fuck," he grunts. "You're such a greedy princess. Those sweet moans will be the very death of me."

He lowers my body so his length glides against my center once more, and my hand grips the back of his head. Another soft moan escapes me, pleading as more pressure builds between my thighs. I want more. I need more.

My hand runs down his chest. I pull away to glimpse the perfection before me. His abs are drenched from my wet hair. Beads of water trickle down between us. The sight makes my body hum.

"You're perfect," I whisper unexpectedly while my eyes rake down his body. He looks at me with a heated grin, showing a glimpse of those perfect, white teeth as he releases a deep chuckle.

"You're so devastatingly beautiful," he says, leaning in for another kiss, making it long and passionate and taking his fill. My hands trace over every hard line of his body, finding myself lost in him all over again. All while butterflies storm wildly inside me.

"We must get back on the road," he says in a heated breath.

That invisible tether wraps tighter around us, unwilling to let us part. I don't want to let go just yet. He turns around, still holding me, facing the shoreline. The sun beams across his face. He takes a few steps toward land, the water slowly beginning to recede. With every stride, he never takes his eyes off mine. He carries me back to shore in his arms.

When we reach dry land, I unwrap my legs from his waist. He slides me down his body, and I feel his entire length glide against my center before my feet touch the ground. I sneak a glance at his package, fully erect and glistening with desire. My chest heaves. I want him more than anything, but time is fleeting. He caresses the side of my face with the back of his hand, tucking away a loose, wet strand. Those broad shoulders are wide enough to eclipse the sun.

Callian curves a finger under my chin so our eyes meet. His dark hair dangles in wet locks around his face, eyes flaring with intent. I bring my hands to my bare chest.

Suddenly, insecurity, guilt, and shame rise and take complete control.

What did I just do? My mind begins reeling. That was more than just a kiss. It was an unrestrained frenzy of hands and tongues exploring one another. A bargain with the enemy is one thing, but now I'm kissing him?

He reaches for me. For a moment, I think he is going to lower my hands and say something that will make my cheeks flush, but he does the opposite. He brushes my face with the back of his hand once more. His eyes warm.

"If it matters what I say, just know you are perfect too." He leans down, kissing me. "I don't regret what just happened. I meant what I said. We will find your path together. *This* does not end when we pass through those gates." His hands fall away. As I watch him gather his things, one word stands out. One I've never had anyone use when it comes to me.

Together.

I fear two imperfect people have somehow found one another in the dark, and I can assume how this will end.

CHAPTER II

THE UNEVEN ROUGHNESS OF the terrain has my stomach wanting to expel its contents. Callian and Cirrus travel these uncharted lands like it's their first nature, unaffected by the constant roll of hills. This is what I assume a ship would feel like, based on the things I've overheard from sailors at our port. It's strange to think I grew up on the shores of Sao but have never set sail.

Every muscle in Callian's arm flexes while he measures the distance between the sun and the land. I draw in my lips, still picturing the kiss we shared at the river. His taste lingers like an echo from the stars. My mind drifts back to his touch and the burning desire in his eyes. It was an unexpected event. Foolish and reckless, yet I could have stayed in the water until our bodies pruned. Biting my lower lip, I focus on his hair sitting in the hood of his cloak. Handsome or not, I have to remember that beneath his emerald stare is a man who took me. He's still my enemy in some ways, and I have to remain leery, even though my body is telling me otherwise. I'm not sure what this will mean once we arrive in Callisto, but as I hold on to Callian's sides, I'm not bothered by the very little space between us. We crest the top of a hill, the spires of a massive castle coming into view.

"Callisto . . . " I whisper, taking in its beauty. The wind whips through my hair, obstructing my vision for a moment. I quickly brush the strands away from my face while Cirrus prances back and forth on the wide path with anticipation. I'm not sure if I share the same enthusiasm. My chest tightens, realizing how far I am from home.

Callisto is significantly larger than Sao. According to the dated map I found in my research on the White Forest, it is the biggest kingdom across Vendrelle. I swallow, knowing that means more people, more prying eyes, and more judgment. This kingdom is a fortress resting atop a large hill with mountains on each side. A large moat surrounds the palace. Callisto's walls appear to be well-fortified, stretching from the north and curving to the east. I've never seen a wall expand across an entire territory before. Also to the east is their port with ships anchored at the docks.

"This is definitely not the shithole I claimed you crawled out of," I admit, still struck by its beauty. Callian lets out a mirthful laugh before nudging Cirrus to ride forward. I grab on to his sides, feeling the hard plane of muscles beneath his tunic.

A gust of wind fans across my face, but there's no calm to the storm swirling inside. My nerves are caught in its whirlwind as we ride through the lush terrain. Guilt continues to play its role of tormentor. I'm a betrayer to the kingdom of Sao, and what would Alyce say if she knew I chose to go with him? My father always says everyone outside our walls is the enemy. I have gone to war with his words carved into my mind, crossing blades with anyone who challenged him. He turned me into someone I don't recognize anymore. It angers me that I've allowed myself to become an empty vessel, a weapon.

As Callian reaches down to gently squeeze my hand, his touch reaffirms his promise to find all the answers *together*. A promise he didn't have to make. How bad could the rest of Vendrelle truly be? I'm torn between two views of the world: the one I've been told to hate, and the one I'm seeing firsthand. Yet I can't help the raw truth of where my allegiance lies: with the enemy. But if my father is the one who betrayed me, then why do I still feel this way? I'm not ready to face the truth, nor am I prepared to find the answers I seek. A wave of panic hits me in the chest. I'm already considering jumping on one of those ships at the port as a stowaway.

We enter the thick forest surrounding the outer rim of the palace. Instead of riding through the main entrance, Callian keeps his word. We veer left, riding along walls with a bustle of life beyond them. People are laughing and talking, and ambient music is playing.

"The king's people live inside the walls with him?" I ask. The people of Sao live outside the outer bailey.

"Our king loves his people. In his oath, he swore to protect them and all the lands he rules over. The kings before him did as such too. If it weren't for the people of Callisto, none of us would thrive. We all work together. Everyone has a job to do."

My brows knit together. Their way of living is such a contrast to Sao.

Two guards spot us approaching in the distance. I slip my hand away from Callian. He takes notice. His mouth gapes as if he's about to respond, but he's interrupted by a guard with a thick, husky voice.

"Welcome back, Callian," the guard says in excitement, brushing away his thick, wavy, brown hair. He's tall with well-defined muscles, a few faint scars marring his warm, russet skin.

The other guard gives a curt nod. Taking a second glance, the two guards look almost identical, but this one is slightly younger and taller with deep-set, hazel eyes. His shoulder-length hair is tied back, though one wavy lock dangles free on one side.

"It's good to be back." Callian nods to the first guard. "You're only excited to see me because that means your shift is over."

The guard lets out a laugh that echoes through the woods and into the mouth of the well-hidden entrance beside him. "Well, you know what day it is. My wife is brewing up my favorite stew. I'm eager to get home." His brown eyes flare with delight while he rubs a hand over his belly as if he can already taste its savory flavor.

"You eat the whole gods-damn pot tonight, your brother won't be pleased with how much you complain during your shift tomorrow," Callian says, glancing at the second guard.

The tall, hazel-eyed man laughs. "For fuck's sake, listen to Callian. Don't eat the whole pot this time," he says. While they continue to converse, I can't help but snicker at their banter.

"Don't let their bickering fool you. These two men are some of our best sentries," Callian says, low enough for only me to hear.

The talkative guard quickly notices me and leans out to get a better look. "Who's this little lady with you?" he asks.

"Careful, Samuel," Callian drawls, reaching back until his hand is placed over mine. He slightly turns his head to meet my stare with a look so smoldering my breath hitches. "She's mine." He smirks, squeezing tighter.

I'm unsure if it's supposed to be a joke or if he's serious, but it makes my cheeks flush hotter than a flame. I retort by yanking my hand back.

"Excuse me, I am *not* yours. I don't know who the hell you think you are, but—"

Samuel lets out an uneasy chuckle. "If looks could kill . . . I've seen that same look from my wife."

"She's already killed me a thousand times and more with her steel-blue eyes." Callian slightly turns to look back at me. "Judging by the color of her cherry-red cheeks, I think she likes it."

I snarl in response.

Somehow, Samuel's mirthful laugh smoothes over the tension. "No need to get too upset, Miss. Callian is known for having a sense of humor. I'm sure he's just teasing you," he tries to assure me.

Callian slightly turns his body toward me. "Am I?" he whispers.

"Are you *what*?" I seethe, sharpening my tone while my heart flutters simultaneously.

"Just teasing . . . " He groans in the same tone from when we were in the river. My gods, is that all it takes for me to become undone? He chuckles, satisfied with the complexity of my expression as he flashes me a smirk. "Samuel, this is Viona," he continues, pulling his attention back to the guards. Samuel walks forward, extending his hand up to mine.

"It's a pleasure to meet you, Viona. My brother, Iván, is a little shy, but he's equally enchanted to make your acquaintance," he says, firmly gripping my hand in a handshake.

"Yours as well." I nod. I look at Iván to extend my greeting, but he's completely removed himself from the conversation, scratching the scruff of his jaw before brushing invisible dust off of an iron rod. He uses it to pull back all the vines and foliage dangling over the entrance.

Before we ride into the tunnel that will lead us into the village, I look back at Iván. "It was nice to meet you." My voice warms. A faint smile curves his lips as a sliver of pearly white teeth peek out.

"Likewise," he responds shyly.

The warm-lit lamps cast a soft, buttery glow along the cobblestone walls. I turn around to see that the brothers have covered up the entrance. At the end of the tunnel is a cast-iron gate with two more guards waiting on each side.

Callian breaks the silence. "I kind of like making you blush, Princess, but I apologize if I took it too far."

"Apology accepted, but remember, 'I kind of like' making people bleed. Next time you want to make me blush, I'll be matching the color with your insides."

His approving chuckle echoes throughout the tunnel. "Well then, the next time I make you blush, I promise it won't be with words, nor will there be an audience."

My stomach takes a dip as heat pools below my navel. Damn the stars, I might not survive him.

CHAPTER 12

IF I KEEP BLUSHING like this, I might ignite. I shove Callian's comment to the back of my mind.

"What else do you enjoy doing besides painting the walls with the blood of men?" he asks.

Before I can answer, we reach the end of the tunnel. The guards raise the gate, winching the heavy chains until a loud clang hammers against the ground as it closes behind us. The sound reverberates around me, reminding me that I have sealed my fate by deciding to come here. The hesitation trying to fester quickly vanishes when I see the town. They clearly live well, but that isn't the shocking part.

"People have powers here?" I ask, watching a woman nestle into a chair to read while a broom sweeps around her. Another down an alleyway is organizing their food without lifting a finger. I have so many questions.

They are allowed to use their powers freely with no punishment?

My father would have already slaughtered this woman and her entire family for it.

"Not everyone does. Some were gifted by the gods from the stars while others carry powers in their blood," he says. I study the woman exercising her innate control over the broom as her eyes slowly move down the page of her book. Watching me observe her, he comments, "There's no doubt she can do more, but not all want to move mountains, some are content moving small rocks, and they have to train to strengthen it. We leave it up to them to decide, and if they choose to further it, our resources are nearly endless." I look down at the palms of my hands, feeling a faint hum beneath my skin. I envy their control and their free will. "It angered me to find out it was forbidden in your kingdom," he says, sensing my shock, but before I can answer, children approach us.

Three small girls no older than ten years old run in our direction. The one with mahogany hair in tight curls runs alongside Cirrus as we ride down the street, her blue eyes beaming. The other two girls shyly keep their distance. All their cheeks are flushed from playing. The closest girl innocently stretches out her hand, holding a flower to me.

"This is for you." The little girl with tight curls reaches up. Callian gently tugs on the reins for Cirrus to stop momentarily. I lean down, smiling, and take the rose in my hand.

"Thank you." I roll the short stem between my fingers, viewing it on all sides, fascinated by the rarity of its colors. A rose akin to an illusion, reminding me of a soft sunset. "This is beautiful." Its satin petals brush the tip of my nose as I inhale its scent.

"It's for your hair," the girl calls out.

"Oh." I carefully place it on the left side of my ear, tucking it into my hair. Her eyes light up once more, watching me. Cirrus continues along the cobblestone streets, and the three girls still follow us. I glance back, a woman watches us while she continues to use her power to sweep the front of her doorway. She curtly nods in my direction.

"Do I get a rose, too?" Callian playfully asks.

All three girls laugh in response. "You're silly! Boys don't get roses!"

"On the contrary, but most men don't receive any flowers until they're dead," I tease.

They stop in their tracks, sucking in a sharp breath with their hands covering their mouths. Tension chokes the air until they all start giggling.

"She's funny!" one of them says.

I guess I have to work on my communication skills. Callian looks back with a raised brow. Already gnawing the bottom of my lip, I shrug my shoulders, but it takes everything in me not to laugh. He looks like he's doing the same before he turns back around.

"Come on, girls. It's time for dinner!" the woman calls.

"It was nice to meet you," the first girl says before the three of them rush back.

"I'm sorry!" I whisper. "I'm not very good with children, if you haven't noticed."

"Oh, I noticed," he drawls.

I pinch his sides, and a laugh ruptures out of his chest. He turns to stop me, and my heart flutters at the sight of his smile stretching from ear to ear in a flirtatious grin.

Suddenly, a dark figure appears directly in my line of sight, and a cold chill instantly washes over me. I turn to see a man clad in dark attire astride a large, black stallion, scowling in my direction. His horse is almost as large as Cirrus, ornate with armor matching his rider's. An array of guards are flanking his sides.

Callian sees the change in my face and, quite possibly, the glint of darkness in my eyes. The lightheartedness of our moment is gone as tension fills the air and he whips back around. Five men stand directly in our path. A scornful look splays across each of their faces. Judging by their hands firmly placed on the hilts of their swords, they must think I'm a threat, just waiting for me to do something disastrous. I should find that offensive—and maybe I do, just a little. My body thrums, striking an ember of my powers that seem to prickle beneath my skin. Their prying eyes watch my every move, and my own eyes rake over each one of them. Though I can't do shit with what's dormant inside of me, I know I could easily take them all with a weapon. I have no problem showing them why they should fear me.

Callian's back straightens and his shoulders widen. It's apparent the disdain is mutual.

"You're always one for theatrics, Ronan. What is the meaning of all this?"

Ronan rides forward. His long, black hair drapes down the front of his chest. His nostrils flare with arrogance, and his deep-brown eyes narrow in on me as he talks to Callian.

"The king has requested I meet you here in case you have any difficulties bringing in the captive."

Captive . . . My brow lifts. I smile maliciously as my senses continue thrumming with warning.

"She is no captive in the palace of Callisto," Callian states.

Cirrus paces us back and forth with his ears pulled back, head raised with bared teeth. Ronan rounds us. He's a fool for sizing Callian up.

"The king decides that, not you. Being as you're late, we assumed you had difficulties retrieving the *captive*."

His eyes rake up and down my body as disgust is woven into his words. My lips twitch up into a snarl. I'm close enough to see the sweat beading above his brow and his cheeks flushed from the heat.

"We had a few situations arise on our travels. Now step aside," Callian growls.

"Judging by the way you were so flirtatiously allowing the enemy to grope you just now, I can only wonder what *situations* you got yourself into," Ronan says in a scathing tone with a smirk that fuels my anger.

I lean to the side to get a better view of this asshole as he continues to circle us, and I see Callian's jaw tick, his hands gripping the reins so tightly, his knuckles turn white. It takes everything in me not to plunge a dagger into this man's chest, but I know there are bigger things at stake. I will not give into his mindless game.

"I'm sure the king will be very pleased to hear you were spending your time playing with"—Ronan pauses, distracted momentarily. He glares into my eyes, his words lost as if he can see something more—"the princess."

A sadistic look spreads across his face. Unease prickles my skin. Before Ronan can continue leading his horse around us, Callian leans over and grabs a fistful of his coat, yanking him inches from his face. Both horses purse up their lips. The tension spirals out of control as the two men flex their ranks.

"Don't tempt me to remind you who is in charge here." Callian grits through his teeth. "Stand down. Now," Callian orders the guards while keeping his glare fixed on Ronan. The guards break formation and move aside as their eyes bounce between the two.

Amidst the hostility, I carefully pull the dagger from my boot, hiding it under an article of clothing. My hand tightens around the grip. Sweat beads above my brow at the sudden flare of heat stroking my skin.

Some of the townspeople have gathered on the sides of the street, whispering to one another and pointing in our direction. My skin tingles as my power begs for some sort of release, an itch I don't know how to remedy. It's a battle, keeping myself at bay while everything is unfolding. I fear I will lose myself if I cannot figure out how to contain what's inside of me.

CHAPTER 13

T HUNDER CRACKLES IN THE air as a tremor rolls beneath us. A thick layer of ice forms around Callian's fist, locking his grip even more firmly around Ronan's tunic. They both share an aggravated look as they become linked together with frost.

"Are you playing ranks with your little dick again, Ronan?" A woman's voice echoes from a small alleyway to my left.

My head whips toward her to see a stark silhouette of a woman upon a horse against the setting sun. As she draws near, a faint hue of violet glints off her long, flowing, blond hair. It falls to her waist in thick waves, bouncing around her frame. She rides astride a large, white-marble horse. She seems to have an important role, maybe higher ranked, because her clothes are far more elegant than any royal woman I've ever seen at court. But she's riding in like a warrior, flashing a haughty look, not giving two fucks about the disagreement these two men are having. She hasn't made eye contact with me yet. Her violet eyes narrow in on Callian and Ronan. The men stiffen in her presence—not like they could move much anyway. She seems to be enjoying having them in her icy grip as a smirk forms on her face.

"When the king told me who he sent to welcome you back home, Callian, I reminded him that putting you two together is like throwing wild beasts into the same cage. So he immediately sent me here to ensure you two idiots play nice in front of our guest. Judging by how you two are embracing each other, I was right once again," she says.

Callian stops struggling, giving her a tight nod. "Point taken, Crystal. Let me go."

She rides closer, stopping ten feet away. "You say you understand, yet I always find you two in a scuffle. If only the both of you knew how to act civilly," she counters, lifting a brow.

Her features pull taut as her eyes continue to bounce between them. Seeing the power she holds over these men makes me breathless. She looks over to Ronan, waiting for him to speak. He says nothing, one final attempt at defiance. With a flick of her wrist, she manipulates the beads of sweat along the column of his neck to restrict his airway, forming a thick band of ice. Her hand splays in the air, controlling the tightness. His stubbornness quickly wanes beneath her magical grip. His face reddens. After a few more seconds, he quickly nods.

"You are to stand down now. Let Callian *and* his guest pass with ease," she asserts while ignoring the gurgling sounds erupting from Ronan. "The king's orders."

In the blink of an eye, the magic is gone, but Callian pushes Ronan back with one final jab. This whole thing could have been avoided if Ronan hadn't been such an asshole.

Callian turns his attention to me, gesturing to Crystal. "This is—"

"I don't need you speaking for me," she interrupts, waving his words away with a playful hand. Though she is clearly irritated, she still seems excited to see him. As she talks, Callian tries to get the warmth back into his ruddy hands by rubbing them together, and Ronan falls in line behind us. "I'm Crystalline Ryver Mira. I represent the king," she says. Light freckles splay across her face, and her eyes are big, vibrant, slightly lifted at the outer corners, and shining violet, like amethyst—a rarity in itself. Even with the sun behind us, her fair skin glows. She raises a brow, noticing my dagger which is now uncovered from its hiding place. "Everyone calls me Crystal," she says with a warmth that makes me thankful I'm on her good side. Observing how she treats people on her bad side was intimidating enough—I hate to admit it—even to me.

"I'm Viona Tarvas."

She nods, saying nothing about the dagger. It's a blessing from the stars to see a woman understand another wanting to protect herself. "I apologize we had to meet this way, but I'm glad you finally made it."

She winks. I nod, hoping my expression can somehow tell her thank you.

Now, glancing back at Ronan, I question how the other people of Callisto are going to treat me while I'm here. Seeing the array of expressions from the villagers' faces, it's likely there will be more just like him.

Crystal side glances at me with a smirk. "Ronan's job is to make sure all orders given by the king are fulfilled. As you can see, sometimes he likes to go rogue. Especially when Callian is away. Don't worry about him. He's an asshole, and everyone knows it," she says, trying to lighten the mood. A trait that reminds me of Callian, who seems to be able to effortlessly hold a conversation with anyone. "It's always the ones who bark the loudest who have the smallest of dicks. I would know, considering what my friend told me after a night with Ronan," she says, loud enough for Ronan to hear. I snicker, wondering who else heard her comment.

"Where I'm from, I was surrounded by them. What's one more?" I retort.

I hear Ronan click his tongue behind us while he makes small talk with some of the villagers as we ride in.

"I'm glad to be back." Callian turns to Crystal, changing the subject. "It's been a long journey. Food and rest are what we need right now."

We. My stomach dips, and my lips slightly part at the comment.

"Of course. I'm glad you're back too. It was starting to get boring around here."

I watch the two exchange an amused look, trying to see if there's something more between them, but I can't find anything. I feel stupid for even thinking this way—it doesn't matter—but it makes me question if this is the *she* he was referring to when discussing the maker of these clothes.

"The king will be delighted to meet you." Crystal glances over to me. The warmth in her tone remains. "After you have rested, of course."

"Yes, I suppose there's much to talk about," I reply with a tone of foreboding, staring straight ahead, swallowing any worry trying to spring to life again. "I have a lot of questions."

"Once we enter the palace, will you please show her to her room?" Callian asks Crystal. "Make sure she's given the room directly across from mine."

Before my heart has a chance to flutter again, he gently squeezes Cirrus' sides to ride faster. The unexpected thrust flings my body back, forcing me to grab on to Callian's waist.

"What the hell was that for?" I hiss.

He scoffs, "You'll find out soon enough." Irritation laces his words.

I turn my head, seeing Crystal's eyes wide with excitement and curiosity. Now I see why. I can see a thousand questions swirling in her mind. I swallow the lump in my throat, wishing she didn't have any. I surmise his little request was enough to convince her *we* have something. As if having a heated moment was even anything at all. My pulse quickens as my mind flashes back to the river.

Crystal rides faster to catch up. Thankfully, she doesn't make any comments about our arrangements. "You must be famished," she says, hiding her curiosity in the guise of friendly conversation. I can feel her stare searing into my side even more now. "Of course you are. I told him to bring more food, but he insisted the crumbs he packed would be good enough," she blurts before I can respond. I smile awkwardly.

"You know I'm not one for overpacking. I take what is needed and nothing more. Conversely, you would pack half the kitchen and the cook if you could," Callian's mocks.

A smirk plays across her face.

"Hey, I'm a girl who likes to eat, and I am not shy about it." Her chin lifts with pride. "I can eat more than all of you assholes combined. Don't make me shame you in front of your new ... friend," she drawls. Those violet eyes beam with way too much curiosity. I'm not used to this type of invasion of privacy.

"That's a competition I'd love to see." I add, trying to stay on subject. I don't know if hunger is starting to take over, but I would definitely be willing to see if I could eat more than her right now.

It's growing darker by the minute. Children who were happily playing in the alleyways between the streets have started to go back inside. I can smell hearty foods cooking over the hearths, making my stomach rumble. I hope I don't have to wait long for my own dinner.

I glance behind me, taking full notice of Ronan still wearing that prideful, glaring hatred for me; it's searing down my back. I wish I were riding in front of Callian so his large, masculine frame could eclipse me from the prying eyes of this asshole. It's evident Ronan's disdain will extend beyond today's events. I will have to keep my guard up.

An icy chill sweeps down my body as the hairs on the back of my neck rise. A heaviness blooms in my chest, causing my vision to blur. Lavender fills the air. I try focusing on my surroundings, but every time I blink, I'm slipping away.

I'm no longer astride Cirrus. Callian, Crystal, Ronan, and all the guards are gone. I'm standing in the middle of the White Forest in its harsh elements without the comfort of my cloak. My skin pebbles against the frigid air, causing my teeth to chatter. Between each frothy, misted breath, my eyes skim over the frozen terrain.

Adnama's voice echoes through the trees. The wind hits my chest like sheets of ice. Each breath of air burns my lungs, causing my breaths to become shallow and strained. My head whips around in all directions, trying to follow her sound, but she's everywhere all at once. My core is shaking, my eyes prickle at the stinging pain of these relentless winds. What lies dormant thrums beneath my palms. I tuck my hands under my arms, clinging to the remaining warmth of my skin.

"Viona . . . " Her icy breath runs down my spine, causing me to spin on my heels. Deep-brown eyes stare back at me. She's mere inches from my face, her hair, dark as night, falls down her small frame. Shadows begin cresting over the canopies of the trees. She grabs me by the arm, her grip full of warning as her eyes turn to pure onyx. Flashes of figures flicker in the back of my head, cycling so quickly, I can't seem to grab ahold of any.

Only one word starts to rise from the voices swarming around me. One word that unveils what I should do.

"Run."

CHAPTER 14

T HE WHITE FOREST DISAPPEARS, and a sudden rush of warmth thaws my skin. I exhale a breath of relief seeing my arms around Callian's waist and Crystal at our side. That feeling quickly wanes as I realize they remain in a steady conversation. Did I just have another vision? Blood pulses in my ears while I focus on the ground, watching all the horses' hooves slightly lift in place off the cobblestone streets. My heart thrashes against my chest as all the hairs on the back of my neck remain standing. Something ominous is in the air. My head whips around to see Ronan with the same calm demeanor as the guards. No one seems to notice. Realization hits. We're about to be attacked.

"We need to hurry." My eyes bounce back and forth between Callian and Crystal in urgency. Her eyes sweep over me, trying to discern my sudden haste, but it only takes Callian one second to recognize my tone.

He lets out a predatory growl and unsheathes his sword, creating a domino effect—metal slices in the air as, one by one, the guards follow his lead. Crystal tightens the reins, giving them a slight tug, signaling her horse to take a few steps back to create a barrier around me. A glowing sphere of ice forms in the palm of her hand.

Callian turns his head toward the guards. "Search the area!" His voice thunders through the streets and small alleyways and seems to rattle all the windows of the villagers' homes. Some of the people around us look up. His eyes narrow in on them. "Get inside. Lock all your doors and windows!" Fear spreads across their faces as they scurry inside, gathering children and loved ones.

"What's going on?" Ronan yells. A bright light takes shape, forming a sword in his hand. A blue shadow wisps around the blade in a controlled aura of light. His stark-black horse rears up. Ronan leans forward and pulls the reins down, whispering something only his horse can hear. The birds above us swarm the sky, flying out from the canopy of the treetops and fleeing from their hiding places.

"We have company," Callian warns. The air grows thick as the eerie calm before the storm settles around us. Nobody makes a sound. I steady my breathing while tightening my grip on my dagger.

"Can we make it to the entrance?" Crystal whispers.

"We can't risk showing them where it is," Callian replies.

I assume it's another well-hidden passageway to the palace.

"Right." Crystal nods.

He looks her in the eyes. "But they know she's here. Take her to the northeast entrance of the palace. NOW." The urgency of his tone sends my heart into a racing speed, but my eyes narrow in on him.

"What? No. I'm not going anywhere." Every breath I take becomes more shallow and comes quicker than the last as my emotions start to storm. "Why should I hide from the enemy when I'm the reason they're here?" I protest. I open my mouth to speak again, but he cuts me off.

"I didn't *ask* you, Princess. I'm *telling* you."

I blink back with knit brows. He used *that* tone with me. The same fucking one he used when we were in the White Forest.

"You are in no place to make any choices for me," I remind him, snarling, poking my finger into his back. I can feel Crystal wanting to chime in and defend him. "I'm not leaving." Finality fills my voice.

Callian turns to me, eyes flaring with anger, but there's a flash of . . . worry? An emotion I didn't expect to see from him.

"Yes, you are," he grits through his teeth, low enough for only me to hear. "We can't risk you losing control of your powers. You'll be a danger to yourself and those around you."

Feeling the knot in my chest return, I exhale sharply. He's right. Damn him for being fucking right.

Dark shadows breach the stone walls. Shrill screams tear through the streets and alleyways, sending a cold chill down my spine. More horrified cries echo somewhere in the distance. This isn't the only place the shadows have reached. The guards are already in pursuit. I think of those three little girls with their beautiful, bright faces and hope to the stars they're alright. My blood begins to boil, seeking revenge as dark shadows cascade down to the cobblestone streets, rushing in like thick waves billowing around the horses' hooves. The horses' eyes widen in fear, and some have their ears pinned back. The wispy shadows move around them like snakes. Cirrus lifts his legs, and Callian quickly presses a hand to Cirrus' neck, calming him beneath his touch. Darkness begins to shroud the sky above us. My mind is slipping, Crystal's voice muffled beneath a searing pain to my temples.

"Run." Adnama's words only exist in the depths of my mind. *"RUN."*

I'm falling far away into a hollow space as though I'm being held underwater. A woman's body appears in a flash, drifting in an ominous sea.

What is happening?

"You need to go," Callian says, but he's met with silence. His voice is nothing more than a faint sound in the wake of delirium. "Viona!" he yells. I follow the sound of his voice as time seems to slow. Suddenly, I feel the warmth of his touch as his arm reaches back, squeezing my thigh. All the senses come coursing through my veins at once. "Leave now." His voice is fierce, a finality masking a worry. "I trust her with your life, as should you."

I blink back a few times and nod. I know I could fight, but not like this. These people need *them* right now, not me. I'm an unpredictable obstacle that will only get in their way. I swallow my pride and snip any inkling of worry trying to rise about being separated from him. Crystal remains on guard, watching the shadows drift around us. Hesitation fills her eyes, and they bounce between Callian and me.

Time is fleeting. I move off Cirrus and onto Crystal's horse. The whole time, Callian's eyes remain on me. I adjust myself behind her and put my arms around her waist. I steal a glance at him, and the corner of his mouth ticks up into a smile. It's a small indication that it's going to be okay.

Although the shadows engulf us, my heart swells. It's a feeling I didn't know could exist until now, warring with the complexity of this newfound attachment toward him. He's beautiful even as the thick, inky swells of darkness surround us. He's close enough to lean over and cup his hand over my cheek, a sudden move I didn't think he would make in front of a crowd. I briefly close my eyes against the warmth as he runs the pad of his thumb along my lower lip.

"I will find you soon," he whispers, sweeping a warmth over me. His words wrap around my heart like twine. The invisible tether that pulled us together tightens in desperation as he lets me go. He gives Crystal a tight nod. As soon as he gives the signal, we take off.

A powerful force emits from Crystal's hand, sending a wave of ice to push against the tendrils of dark shadow and create an opening. We ride out of the dark as royal guards ride in. Their horses' hooves strike loudly against the cobblestone streets. Once we're out, we stand to the side as she holds the wall up long enough for the guards to get through. I look through the opening to see the enemy drop down onto the streets of Callisto with weapons secured in their grips. As I recognize who they are, anger courses through my veins.

Fucking Solas' men.

They move like a fading dream, drifting in and out of sight. Darkness shadows their every move as it whisks around them. Their sabres and swords are aimed and ready as their eyes glow an infinite blue. My gut twists in my stomach as guilt crawls up my spine.

"Gods-dammit," I curse. I should have killed them all when they were walking the halls of my home. Lives could be lost today, and I can't do a damn thing about it.

Solas' men move between worlds, but Callian slices through their flesh. One by one, the shadow pirates drop to the ground. His agility is like a somber dance, weaving through their shadows with an unwavering strength. His eyes find mine in a sea of chaos.

Callian turns away, driving his blood-slick sword up into the cavity of the enemy's chest as the man descends upon him. A solid, white light builds in the palm of Callian's hand, sending a powerful force blasting another in the torso. The enemy goes flying through the air; his body slams against the wall as fissures spread across his chest before he disappears into the shadows. More come into view, swarming around Callian, Ronan, and the rest of the guards fighting at full strength.

Crystal leans back toward me. "I have to close them in!" she calls out. "It's the only way to keep everyone else safe."

With her magic, the walls arc, trapping everyone inside an ice dome. Callian and the rest of them disappear from sight.

The streets are barren as we ride in. Word spreads fast here.

The sun is setting deeper over the horizon. Orange and purple hues will soon fade into twilight. Royal guards astride horses patrol the area. Up ahead, the palace of Callisto comes into view, sitting high atop a massive hill. The glorious and intricate structure displays many levels and layers within the palace walls. There's an enormous garden below, surrounding a large portion of it. I can only imagine how easily one could get lost roaming the grounds. The crescent moon is finally showing its shadow, peeking behind the palace. We make a sharp turn, veering right, and ride along the garden hedges. Soon, we round another corner. Two men clad in silver armor guard the large, wooden doors that hide under an overgrown entrance. One of the guards spots us. He quickly turns around to knock on the door. A third guard unlocks it from the inside.

"This is where we get off," Crystal says as her horse slows to a trot.

I nod in response as she hands the reins to one of the guards, whose green eyes flicker with curiosity through an armored helmet. We both dismount. Crystal remains on guard while putting her arm around my shoulders.

"This way." She gives me a gentle nudge. We enter a long, stone hallway with lanterns hanging on the walls. This one isn't so dingy. At the end stands another guard whose brows are knit.

"Lady Mira," he opens the door in haste and stands to the side.

"Thank you, Leon," she says, rushing by.

We enter another large hallway with tall ceilings. Marble pillars line the path to our left and stained glass windows to our right, with a few rooms at the end of the hall. We quickly walk across and head up a staircase. There's little time to take in my surroundings, but there's no denying how elaborate this palace is. Light blues, golds, and whites decorate the staircase. The banister is carved from fine marble and ornate with floral designs.

Crystal turns to me. "Callian, Ronan, and the guards will be able to handle it," she says. I nod, but the knot in my chest remains.

Every level we ascend has statues on each side of the windows—overly decorative for such a seemingly secluded part of the palace. I can only imagine what the rest of it will be like.

We make it to the third floor. Down the long corridor, I see four guards standing outside one door, which I assume is mine. I almost feel insulted at the sight. Are they posted there to make sure I can't leave?

"Lady Mira." They nod, wearing no expression on their face.

"I want you patrolling this entire level, we need a guard stationed at every corner," she says as we walk past them. One of them opens the door to my room, motioning for me to go in first.

"This is where you'll be staying." Crystal huffs as she closes the door behind us. I too, take a deep breath, trying to steady my breathing from not only the flight of stairs we just rushed up, but from the adrenaline that remains coursing through my veins from fleeing.

"Thank you," I exhale, noticing this room is far too prestigious for someone like me. I allow myself to take it all in as I remind myself what Crystal said—Callian will be okay.

There's a large, king-sized bed with two tables on each side. One corner of the room has a fireplace and two large shelves full of books, a settee, more small tables, and a lovely fur rug—and a bathing chamber off to the side. There's a dressing area with a privacy wall made of thin canvas and a cabinet behind it. My heart sinks, noticing the long, wide mirror beside it. I shudder, taking a step back. Crystal must see my reaction. She approaches me, placing a hand on my shoulder.

"Is everything alright?" she asks with a pinched expression, trying to piece together what stopped me in my tracks.

My cheeks flush. "I'm fine, but may I please have that mirror removed . . . immediately? I—I'm just not one to want to see myself in the mirror every day." I swallow the lump in my throat. Those amethyst eyes suddenly make me feel as though I'm under a looking glass. My chest tightens at the thought of her pressing into the matter, but she doesn't go any further.

"That's alright. You don't have to explain yourself to me." She walks out, calling for two guards to come in. "I need this mirror taken out of here, please," she orders. Her tone immediately shifts into that authoritative figure I met in the town.

Before I can see the reaction to the odd request, I turn away, drawing my attention toward the balconies, feeling ashamed for asking such a request right now. The truth is, what looks back is far more than just my reflection. Looking into mirrors has always felt like peering into a window to my soul with the constant reminder of what lies hidden beneath my skin—a place where the darkness festers. Right now, I feel it churning idly with every beat of my heart.

One of the men grunts beneath the weight of the mirror, pulling me from thought. They struggle while strategically trying to move it without dropping it into millions of pieces. I stare past the balcony, walking out into the setting sun, feeling the warmth against my skin. Nothing could have prepared me for a sight like this. It's not cold and angry like the shores of Sao. I was expecting to see the town below, hoping to catch a glimpse of Callian or any news on what's happening down there, but the town is off to the side, almost out of sight. Only the view of the docks and the town's edges can be seen. Every lantern looks like a star. A faint scent, mine, carries in the wind, reminding me of the many days of travel. My gods, I need a bath.

Crystal walks out to the balcony, taking a deep breath, and presses her palms against the balustrade. There's tension in her exhale, and she wears the same look of worry that I feel. Silence hangs in the air while we wait for the guards to leave.

"Thank you," I finally say when I hear the door close, turning to find her still looking over toward our view of the town.

She gives a tight nod, and her mouth curves into a smile.

"Follow me." Crystal leads me to the bathing chamber. "As you can see, everything you need is here. I hope you don't mind. I'm not very good at showing people around." She brushes a blonde strand of hair from her face, and I notice that faint hue of violet is gone. She walks over to the closet and opens it. "I'm a terrible host, actually." A ghost of a laugh. I'm not sure if she's laughing at being a host or the fact my closet is empty. "Sydney was supposed to have this filled to the brim, but being the perfectionist she is, it seems she'd rather custom-fit your wardrobe." Crystal turns around to look at me. "If you don't mind,

I'll be right outside waiting for an update. I'll send word to the king that you have arrived safely and are in your chambers."

"Thank you, Crystal."

She turns to leave but then quickly spins around on her heels. Her hair swirls around her frame. "Oh! The bath is filled with hot water. Feel free to make yourself comfortable. Fresh clothes and a nightgown are waiting for you there. No one else will be entering your chambers tonight. I'll make sure of it. When you are done, just let me know. I'll be right outside." She smiles and then rushes out before I can say anything.

Low whispers drift in from under the door. I can't tell what they're talking about. Only a few words here and there, but none make any sense. I can only discern the tones. My heart drops at the sound of Callian's name. *What are they saying about him?*

I suddenly withdraw, taking a step back. It's none of my business, really. He did his job, so there shouldn't be anything else to discuss unless it has to do with the reason I'm here.

I enter the bathing chambers and remove my clothes, tossing them to the side. My body slips into the tub. I already feel the heat loosening every tense muscle in my body as it envelops me. I submerge myself beneath the water, remaining here for as long as I can, drowning out the world for just a moment. Then, I slide myself up, resting against the tub, and watch my black strands of hair float above the water. A bar of soap sits on the edge of a small table nearby. As I begin to scrub my skin raw, the scent of vanilla fills the air. After, I lather my hair with a liquid soap and loosen all the knots. Though my body feels more relaxed, I know I shouldn't stay in the tub. It's a vulnerability I can't afford. When I'm done drying myself off, a fresh pair of black trousers and a matching long-sleeve tunic are waiting beside a sheer, white nightgown. I never thought I'd appreciate something as simplistic as clean clothes. Holding the tunic in front of my bare chest, I'm filled with gratitude for the choice of color. The trousers are snug on my hips, but I'm okay with it. While most women from Sao try to have the slimmest hips possible, I embrace mine. I'm not going to give up my pastries anytime soon. Alyce says a woman's power is in her hips. Not because of bearing children, it's the strength we hold when we fight.

Back in the day, I saw her toss men three times her size to the ground. My mind flashes to a memory of her using her hip to carry the enemies weight—a move she later taught me, and one that has never failed to knock a man on his ass. I smile with pride.

Crystal's already knocking on my door, pulling me from thought. I quickly slip on a fresh pair of socks and put my boots back on. When I leave the bathing chambers, she's already wheeling in a cart full of food, a bottle of wine, and a glass pitcher of water. The scent of salted meat fills my nose. There are buttery carrots and potatoes next to it, sending my stomach to rumble in anticipation.

"I'm not hungry, but thank you," I respond, even though I'm ready to go feral over the plate of food and devour it like a wild beast.

She scoffs. "You're funny." Her amethyst eyes sparkle with humor as a wavy lock dangles freely over her shoulder.

"Excuse me?"

She pushes the cart of food to an empty table. "You're funny." Her voice lifts as she repeats herself. My brows knit as I try to infer what she means. "Has anyone ever told you your eyes can tell more than what you say?" She assesses me while setting the table, placing two plates down.

I raise a brow and cross my arms. "I hear that quite often, actually," I say sharply, unamused with her accuracy.

She takes a seat and extends her hand out for me to sit. I exhale and pull the chair out.

When we are at eye level, she hums.

"Don't be so coy. It's just the two of us. I know you're famished, and so am I." Her tone softens. "Eat how you want. When it comes to hunger, there are no rules."

She winks at me, wearing a mischievous smile while serving enough for two men to eat. I can tell she's trying to create a calm atmosphere, despite what is going on. It is a kindness she doesn't have to extend for someone like me.

Picking up my knife and fork, I aim for the salted meat while Crystal picks hers up with her hands. I've never seen anyone eat that way before, especially someone of her status. A snicker slips free from under my breath.

She looks up from her plate with her mouth stuffed with meat. "What?"

My cheeks flush at the sudden attention. Her eyes are very intimidating. "I've just never seen anyone eat like that before, that's all. Or at least not women. Most of them back home wouldn't be caught dead eating like an animal."

Shit. Shut up, Viona. That came out rude.

She rasps out a laugh and continues to talk with her mouth full. "Well, you're very straightforward."

"I'm sorry, I don't get to talk to people all that much. I guess I'm out of practice with my social skills."

Crystal wipes her hands and pats my arm. "It's okay. Besides, it's really hard to offend me." Her eyes are warm, which settles the nerves in my stomach. A wavy strand of hair dangles in front of her face again. She uses the back of her hand to tuck it back. I place my utensils down, pick up a piece of meat with my hands, and sink my teeth in.

"This is so good," I hum.

"Callian should be cursed for the way he packs, barely enough to feed a squirrel," she says as she pours herself some water. Though I have many questions, I decide to enjoy this much-needed meal. Amidst all the chaos surrounding us, it's nice to smile. She has a way of making me feel comfortable already. I admire her carefree personality.

After I fill my belly to the brim, I finally begin to let her in on who those men were—our kingdom's enemies—retelling my encounters with them as far back as our history goes. Solas and his men are nothing but criminals with boundless chaos. I tell her about the time our kingdom fought against him in battle, how he conjured an army of those shadow pirates, and the destruction they brought to our doors. She sits back with her hands laced over her stomach, listening. Silence fills the air. I question if I am oversharing. Then again, what do I have to lose?

"We know who Solas is. He's plagued our seas for years. The fact that his men have stepped foot on land again tells me he wants to expand his horizon, and I'm willing to bet he plans on doing that with your capture to appease King Tarvas. I hope by Callian killing his men, it will send a clear message that this is the wrong territory to tread on."

She assures me all will be well again, that no other guards were called to the town's borders or the port, so I should get some rest. While she settles into a chaise with a book on her lap, I change into my nightgown and slip into the bed. My head rests upon the pillow with my eyes fixed on a candle burning at my bedside.

Little flame.

I watch the candle's wick flicker against the cool, night air. Every so often, Crystal turns a page. And soon, the two sounds become a night's song lulling me to sleep.

CHAPTER 15

My eyes flutter open to a dark room, and I forget where I am until the firm mattress reminds me that I'm far from home. The night air still carries the candle's faint, honeyed, musky scent. As I lie here reeling over the events from the past few days, a light breeze stifles the heat emanating from the untamed power just beneath my skin. My life has been flipped upside down. The only thing that has remained the same is the moon, and I'm not sure why that brings me comfort amidst the chaos.

My mind always seems to drift back to Callian, and somehow, every time he touches me, that power thrums in response, like a drop of water rippling the surface. He never came to check on me. My eyes move across the rest of the room to see if there's any evidence he was here, but I still can't make a single thing out. I'm not sure if I feel disappointed by his absence or angry. In truth, I shouldn't care, and things must be okay; otherwise, Crystal would still be here. She must have grown bored watching me sleep and left. I wonder if she's still nearby or if she returned to her chambers, wherever they are.

Tomorrow will be another long day. Getting sleep should be the only thing on my mind right now. Not Callian, Crystal, meeting the king, or anything else. I close my eyes, forcing myself to block everything out. It doesn't take long for me to drift back to sleep.

A SOUND JERKS ME WIDE AWAKE. The hinges creak as the door opens, sending my heart to pound against my chest. As it's shutting, my hand is already sliding under the pillow, feeling around until my fingers hit the pommel of my dagger. I'm still on my side, facing the balcony with my back toward the door. My hands become slick with sweat as the adrenaline starts to rise. I slowly slide the dagger down, inch by inch, until it's right in front of my chest. I steady my breathing, listening to the sound of their heavy footsteps as I count down the seconds before I can strike. They stop beside my bed on the opposite side. The weight of their body sinks into the mattress, lifting my side up. I swing my arm, hoping to hit flesh, but a giant hand catches my wrist midway, sending a sensational wave down my body.

"Changed your mind on how you feel about me already, Princess? You wound me." Callian seems to be musing on my reaction.

My breathing stills as heat flushes my cheeks. I can sense the smile in his voice as he hovers above me in the dark. With a gentle push, he guides my wrist back down onto the mattress, placing it against the sheets. The dagger falls from my hands, but I'm hit with instant regret as my anger spikes.

"I feel nothing for you," I hiss.

He has a lot of nerve, sneaking into my room unannounced like this.

A soft chuckle rumbles in his chest.

"Your tongue weaves such beautiful lies," he purrs, his minty breath fanning across my lips. My body responds, rebelling against my own words. This asshole is the perfect concoction to send my emotions to war, but he's so close, the velvety sound of his voice sends my heart fluttering. My thoughts wander to places they shouldn't. The bed creaks when he leans in closer. I can barely make out his smile, but his aroma drifts down. The smell of cedar and his musk envelop me. It's fresh and alluring, with heat radiating from his body, telling me he bathed before coming here. I'm relieved he's okay, but irritation still thrives in the back of my mind while I lie in this all-too-close position. Even in the faint moonlight, his eyes gleam. It's enchanting, and I'm finding myself caught in his trance. His hair dangles down his face with a few dark strands still wet and sticking to his jawline. My eyes trail down to the column of his neck. My gods, he's beautiful.

"Are you reminding yourself of how much you like me?" he teases in a deep, husky voice.

I swallow the lump in my throat, unable to think of anything to say. Damn the stars, I need to get away from him. "Quite the opposite. Now get off me," I reply as my chest heaves. "What are you doing in my room?"

Seconds pass. He looks at me for a few moments before letting me go.

"I'm here to do what everyone else does at this hour." He turns his back toward me and removes a boot.

"And what is that?"

"Unless you have another activity in mind, I was thinking I would sleep." I sense him musing over the thought as he slips the other boot off.

Sleep. I scoff.

My anger boils over. It takes just one word, a word I love so much, for him to ruin it for me. I exhale a sharp breath, tossing the blanket off my legs, and throwing it aside. I fumble in the dark. The cool, night air reaches my skin and sends a chill through my body that steals my warmth. I should just shove my dagger into his back and send him on his way. He has healing powers; he can bleed and heal in his own fucking room. I search the side table to light a candle. Its buttery glow ignites. The heat of the flame warms my skin for a moment. I set light to a few more. From the corner of my eye, I see him remove his tunic and toss it over one of the chairs. He barely misses. He really thinks he can just sleep wherever he wants.

Refusing to look at him, I round the bed, but his eyes remain fixed on me the entire time. It's not until I set the candle down and stand directly in front of him that I realize it was a huge mistake.

"You're not sleeping in my room," I repeat, but my eyes rake down his shirtless body and breeches that are way too thin for any modesty.

"After what happened today? Yes, I am." The corner of his mouth curves up into a grin as if my demands hold no conviction. My mouth opens, ready to spew a retort, but it shuts instantly.

My voice softens. "Was anyone hurt?" I ask, my stomach already tightening at the thought.

He gently shakes his head, and the tips of his hair sway back and forth against his shoulders. "No loss of life," he confirms.

"Thank the stars." I exhale, bringing a hand to my chest, but I notice his eyes catch on how I breathe, as if the sudden sound that escaped my lips reminded him of something else. He leans back, making himself comfortable and drinking up the view in front of him.

"Since all is well, you can come back to bed." He pats the place where I once was.

"You cannot be serious," I reply. I want to step back, but my body remains still.

Traitor.

"Oh . . . but I am *very serious,* Princess," he drawls with lust shamelessly filling his eyes, placing me into a looking glass. "Remember when I said you were mine?"

I swallow the lump in my throat. "No," I lie. The word unexpectedly slips out in a soft breath of air as my body thrums in response.

The words he spoke into the shell of my ear have lingered since he took me. "I also said I would come and find you. Here I am. Now, you're playing hard to get."

Silence hangs in the air.

"I'm supposed to keep you safe," he reminds me.

A duty, I remind myself, nothing more. I shouldn't care anyway. "Well, you've done your duty; you may leave now," I respond.

He sits back up, studying me with those very invasive eyes.

"I don't think I have." He grins. His velvety voice lifts in humor. My cheeks flush, remembering exactly where we left off.

"Oh, is that so?" My voice fluctuates in ways I thought it never could when angry. "Well, you have. Now get out," I demand, crossing my arms over my chest. I should have never let go of my dagger. The tip of its blade just barely peeks out from beneath my pillow over his shoulder, tempting me with its glint.

"How do you know this is even your room?" he teases. Humor flickers in his eyes, dancing with the flames. He remains sitting on the edge of the bed, unaffected by my hostility. "I doubt you've had time to wander about the palace and learn its layout. What if *you* are the one who's in the wrong chambers?" A mischievous grin tips the corner of his mouth, and those straight, white teeth shine. Every divot in his abs is illuminated in the candlelight while he leans back again, resting on his elbows against the bed. His hair is disheveled and still partially wet. If he weren't such an arrogant asshole, I might admire that he cleans up nicely. His face is freshly shaven. Everything about him is a sin, and he knows it.

My fists clench at my sides. "*You're* in the wrong room. Crystal told me this one was mine."

I stand my ground, but Callian's eyes wander down my waist, causing my heart to flutter. I become breathless under his stare as I realize the candle illuminates my shape, casting a soft glow against my skin. My chest slowly rises and falls, seeing desire churning in his eyes until they move up the rest of my body to meet mine. The tension in my hands release. I forgot how thin the fabric of my white nightgown is, but suddenly, I don't really care as he takes my hand and brings it to his lips. He kisses my knuckles. I never knew one simple kiss could remind me of the stars. My lips slightly part, and soon, my eyes close at the touch. He moves me toward him until I'm at the edge of the wooden frame, right between his thighs. My eyes drift open. When he leans forward, every passing moment intensifies the heat coiling between us.

"Even in the dark, you shine so bright, Princess," he says, unveiling me with his eyes as the flames from the candlelight dance in his irises. The pad of his thumb trails along my lower lip. My breathing deepens. He curves a finger under my chin. "Let us continue where we left off in the river."

I remind myself why I'm here and why I shouldn't do this, but my mind and body are on two different paths. Before I can try convincing myself not to, my hands are already moving up his body to his broad shoulders. I *want* to continue. I *want* to sleep in his arms and let my worries sail away like they did in the Sebina Mountains, but my mind flashes to the sudden burst of power that ended the larkin's life.

"I'm not very safe to be around. What if I have another episode? You could be in danger if I'm not able to control myself," I admit.

"Then I will be right here beside you," he says without hesitation—words that are so easily spoken for him, but for me, after I've spent so much time alone, this felt . . . nice. He places his other hand on the middle of my back. I softly exhale as my body hums beneath his touch. His desire, need, and want press into me. "Let me bear the weight of all your worries."

His hands move down past my hips and thighs. By the time they stop at the hem of my gown, I am welcoming this distraction. He starts to pull the fabric up. My hands lift in the air, giving him permission to remove it. His eyes never leave mine as he unveils my naked body before him and stands at his full height, tossing the gown to the floor. The cool, night air nips at my skin. I'm so exposed, but the back of his hand brushing along my cheek sends enough heat coursing through my body that I shudder. Threading his fingers through my hair, he cradles the back of my head with a heated gaze and pulls me in.

That unseen tether returns beneath his touch as our lips crash into each other. Each kiss is so untamed and claiming, washing away the fragments of darkness as all my worries fade into the back of my mind. There's nothing gentle in the way my hands run up his chest and around his neck. I'm starving to be closer. He pulls me flush against his body, moving his hands up my back. A deep moan rumbles in his chest as he soaks in the feel of my breasts against him. That sultry sound deepens the desire building between my thighs. With care, he tilts my neck to the side, kissing from my chin up my jawline, running his nose along the column of my neck as his long hair tickles my collarbone. My eyes close, moaning against the feel of him taking his time as his hands move with precision down to my breast. They're so sensitive to his touch.

"Callian," I purr, combing my fingers through his soft, silky hair as my nipple falls between his fingers. He exhales deeply, smiling against the crook of my neck as if I've left him breathless.

"Don't say my name like that, Princess . . . " he begs, resting his forehead against my shoulder. "It makes me so weak for you."

His breath heats my jaw. My body responds with a shudder, needing more. His lips find mine in a wild, tangled fury. I open my mouth to him, feeling the stroke of his tongue lash out with dominance and hunger. His moans reverberate around me, sending more waves of sensation between my thighs. The bulge in his pants pitches through the thin fabric of his breeches. He breaks away, panting, and kisses along my collarbone. I stand on my toes as he cups his mouth over my breast. His tongue laps around my nipple, sucking it into his mouth. The need building between my legs intensifies. I comb my hands through his hair as a loud moan escapes me. Every stroke of his tongue sends my core throbbing. My breathing becomes rapid, the yearning for him heating my skin as our hands start moving frantically over one another.

He lifts me off the ground and my legs wrap around his waist. He then turns, setting me back down on the bed as if I were the most precious and delicate thing to him.

"Are you doing okay, Princess?" He strokes my hair as he cages me between his arms.

"Yes," I pant out.

He wedges his large muscular body between my thighs. My breathing stills at the motion as heat spreads across my face.

"If you want me to stop, tell me, and I will."

"Don't stop." I pant, shocked to hear my own words, but they speak the truth.

"You sound so fucking beautiful when you purr for me," he whispers, caressing my cheek with his nose. His lips coast across mine before they claim me again, blindly pulling a pillow toward us and tucking it beneath my head. The weight of his body presses into me, and I welcome every bit of it. "You make me want to do such dirty things to you," he confesses, shifting further down the mattress.

He plants a soft, tender kiss above my hip and stares up at me, watching my reaction. My lips slightly part as his tongue glides across to the other side. He cups his lips over my hip slowly and tentatively, finishing with a kiss.

My head tilts back. "Please don't stop," I moan.

The corner of his mouth quirks up at my sudden urge, at my need for more. He lifts himself up, resting on his knees. The bulge in his breeches is at full staff, with light filtering between the thin fabric. My breathing hitches.

"Bend your knees for me, Princess." His thumbs caress my legs, sending pressure to build at my core. I follow his words while he slowly guides me wide open. He takes his time until I'm fully spread apart. My cheeks heat at the motion, baring myself entirely before him.

"Fuck . . ." he groans under a heavy, heated breath, gripping my legs firmly. His calloused fingers press into me while he looks starved. My heart flutters, watching him take in the full sight of my naked body. The corner of his mouth curves up. "You are perfect," he says leaning forward, running his hands up my thighs while he gently massages and works his way closer. "I want to know what your sin tastes like."

He leans down and lowers his head. When he presses his tongue against my bundle of nerves, my gods, I think my heart might burst. My hands grip the sheets as a wave of euphoria rolls through me. His tongue moves with precision as heat flares across my chest and face. A soft moan escapes me, washing every ounce of uncertainty away. Every stroke of his tongue sends me further into bliss, chasing the feeling of him—something I have been denying myself for far too long. His talented tongue strokes my clit with dominance as he glides it up and down the center of my folds. His moan reverberates around me as he teases my opening then clasps his mouth over the entire area, drawing out another whimper.

"Oh my gods," I plea, panting out every word in long, heated breaths.

"I told you, Princess, I am on my knees, ready to serve."

He slips his tongue inside me. My mouth gapes open as I grab onto the bed sheets, holding on as he spears me with his tongue. The sensation builds. Another loud cry breaks out. The throbbing between my legs intensifies, rising higher and higher. My hips begin to move in rhythm, wanting his tongue to go deeper, needing my fill. I become feral beneath him, chasing the feeling of pure ecstasy.

Suddenly, my skin starts to flare. Sweat breaks out across my brows and chest. I feel my powers flickering under my skin, coming alive in this heated moment, pulling me away from him. My eyes flick open in a panic, uncertain of how this will end. He looks up, reaches for my hand, laces his fingers with mine, and squeezes tight.

"Don't think," he assures me. "Feel. Give yourself this moment. Give yourself to me, Viona." He groans into my sex, wrapping his other hand around my thigh. A predatory sound escapes him. He pulls me onto his tongue as if challenging the darkness hiding behind my eyes. "Mine . . . " he growls.

I can't find the words to speak, so I nod.

His tongue is relentless against my clit. The ferocity in him unleashes as he claims me as his. I am chasing the desire again, chasing him in every unwavering stroke. My thighs tremble. I comb my fingers through his hair, letting his words echo in the back of my head.

Mine . . .

His . . .

Suddenly, a tidal wave crashes over me, and a sensational feeling of pure bliss courses through my body. My sex pulsates and dances around his tongue, spasming like hard, relentless waves over and over again. He moans into me, grabbing a firmer hold of my body as he takes in the feel of my orgasm wrapping around his tongue. Every bit of my pleasure is heard throughout the expansion of my chambers as I continue riding the pleasure. As my breathing slows, so do the movements of his tongue.

Callian gently pulls away as a look of satisfaction spreads across his face. He remains leaned back, resting on his knees, reveling in the sight of what he's given me. Those full lips are swollen and red, glistening with my desire. His chest heaves as he crawls over my body and hovers above me with his muscular arms caging me between them. Dark strands of hair fan around his face. He leans down, pressing his lips to mine. I can taste myself. I smile against the action. We move to the top of the bed, and he covers us with the blanket.

"I don't think that was part of your job description," I admit, catching my breath while settling into the bed.

"Perhaps not." He smirks, bringing me into his arms. I allow myself to nestle into his side as our legs tangle together. He lets out another deep, exasperated exhale. "You will be the very end of me, little flame," he whispers, sleep ready to claim him.

The way he strokes my hair relaxes me. I, too, grow tired. I am on top of the mountain, not ready to come back down, but there is a reality in his words that sets forth a foreboding thought in the back of my mind.

"I hope not," I whisper before drifting to sleep.

CHAPTER 16

A GENTLE KNOCK ON the door pulls me from sleep, and I look out toward the balconies. The sky is a deep shade of violet and pink. I've slept most of the day away. My body shifts to the other side to find an empty space. I place my hand where he was, feeling the fabric cold to the touch. He must have left hours ago. It was ridiculous to assume he'd be here.

The knock on my door returns, this time with more persistence. I blink away any more lingering thoughts about last night and quickly sit up in bed. The door creaks open before I can speak. A woman with dark-mahogany hair slips through, and I quickly pull the sheets up to cover myself. She strolls in, carrying a big, blue basket adorned with gems and other fancy embellishments with a stack of clothes draped over her other arm. Curiosity flares behind her rich-green eyes as she takes a quick assessment of the room. Her features remind me of a cat's; high cheekbones with big eyes upturned in the outer corners. Her skin is smooth and tight with a gentle stroke of rose brushing against her cheeks. The faint lines at the corners of her eyes reveal she is likely double my age, maybe in her mid-forties. My gods, she's breathtaking. Her confidence radiates throughout the room. She raises a brow at Callian's tunic thrown haphazardly across a chair, and her mouth curves up into a grin when her eyes land on mine.

"Good morning, Viona. It looks like Callian made himself comfortable last night," she says facetiously, using her magic to slam the door shut and lock it behind her.

My cheeks heat. I'm unsure if it's her comment or the sudden use of her magic that makes me feel powerless in her presence. Unease prickles my skin, but I keep my chin lifted. Her eyes rake over my partially naked body.

"He must have gotten lost and wandered his way into my room," I reply.

That was a stupid response! Shut the fuck up, Viona!

"Lost?" She lets out a mirthful laugh. "Honey, by the looks of your beauty, I can see why he might have found himself suddenly 'lost' in your room." Her eyes glint mischievously. I feel the sudden heat flushing my face again.

She unloads her things onto a table and walks over to me. Her dark-blue dress flows down to the floor, and her heels echo throughout the room.

"You don't need to worry about me." She smiles as she pats my thigh over the sheet, then strides back to the dressing area. "I'm nobody special," she calls out, waving her hand with an edge of sarcasm in her voice. "I've just come to size you for a wardrobe. It's always 'Sydney, do this,' 'Sydney, I need to be sized for that.'" She opens up her basket and starts sifting through its contents. "You've traveled quite a bit to get here. We all know Callian travels light, but I hope the clothes I packed gave you comfort on the road."

My eyes widen, realizing this was the woman he spoke so tenderly of back in the forest. Pride beams off of her when she notices my obvious admiration for her talents.

"Yes. The cloak did save me in the White Forest—quite a few times, actually. I had nothing on but a thin tunic and pants," I say, losing confidence in my words the longer I speak, remembering how I was taken. A little bit of embarrassment returns to my cheeks. Guilt strikes twice remembering I'm still sitting naked in the bed with his scent all over me. I feel like a traitor, but to whom? Myself?

"Where's the mirror?" She rests an elbow over a crossed arm.

"I . . . requested for it to be removed."

She looks at me again as if expecting me to continue with the reasons why. I run my hand through my hair. "I'm just not one for seeing my reflection," I awkwardly state as my fingers get caught in a knot.

"That's alright, my dear. We can work around it." Her voice warms.

I slip my nightgown on and walk over to Sydney. She starts going through the fabrics and holding them against my body. Inaudible words murmur under her breath while she works her way through each color. She curves her finger under my chin to meet her stare. The sudden close contact has me tense as she looks into my eyes, holding another piece of fabric against my chest. Her eyes bounce between my face and the soft cloth.

She hums under her breath. "Your eyes are a very rare shade of blue. Interesting."

I blink a few times. My throat is suddenly dry.

"Is that a problem?"

"No." She smiles. "Actually, none of this is a problem." She lowers the fabric to really look at me. As if her eyes weren't intimidating enough. "What you two do is none of my business." She winks.

I'd like to fade away into thin air right about now, as I'm reminded of how his tongue ascended me to the stars.

"It was a mistake. He shouldn't have been in my room," I blurt out.

"A mistake? You sure didn't sound like you were regretting it last night."

My head whips around toward the door to see Crystal standing there with a grin stretching across her face.

"How did you get in here?" My eyes narrow in on her beneath knit brows.

She dangles a set of keys on the tip of her finger. "While you were sulking in self-doubt and wishing your orgasm away from last night, I unlocked the door and let myself in." My mouth gapes open, blindsided by the boldness that flows so freely from her mouth. "And we are going to talk about that later. I want all the details." She gives me a wink, beaming with excitement while bringing over a food cart.

"We will certainly *not* be talking about it." I cross my arms tightly over my chest.

"Oh, shut up, Crystal. Why must you be so nosy?" Sydney sneers. "You don't see me prying about what *you* were doing last week when I found you in the pantry with that cook."

"What?" Crystal casually shrugs. "He was teaching me how to churn butter." She picks a piece of food off my plate and sticks it into her mouth.

I snicker under my breath.

Sydney scoffs, "Please, Crystal, you're a woman of war. The day you want to learn the crafts of the kitchen will be the day I question your sanity. That's just as ridiculous as Viona saying Callian simply *lost* his way into her room last night."

My smile quickly wanes, and my jaw drops open. Are they seriously forgetting I'm standing right here?

"Did you say lost? Okay, Viona wins the award for the most ridiculous excuse of the week." Crystal laughs. I look over to see her picking up my apple.

"Do you mind!" I finally blurt. My retort stops her from taking a big bite. "Have you both forgotten I'm right here?"

I didn't realize I was signing my privacy away the moment I agreed to come here. I'm not sure if I'm more angry at the fact that Crystal keeps picking at my food, or how they keep casually discussing my business in front of me. Probably both, because it's been years since I've had this much socializing. This is all too much, and I'm suddenly reminded of the benefits of solitude.

"You're right, Viona. We apologize. Now, hold still." Sydney points my shoulders toward her. "You need to stop moving or one side of your tunic will be longer than the other."

Crystal plops onto one of the oversized chairs by the fireplace and picks up the same book she was reading the night before.

Sydney keeps the smirk on her face while she measures my waist and continues speaking to herself. "Between Callian and Crystal, I'm surprised I haven't started graying yet."

I give a tight smile, feeling a little envious at the relationship between Sydney and Crystal. It reminds me of what Alyce and I could have been if my father didn't keep her from me so often. I swallow the lump in my throat.

Sydney finishes my measurements and gathers her things. A pile of clothes remains behind.

"After you've eaten dinner, Crystal will help you get ready and escort you to the Great Hall where you will meet King Valor." My heart sinks, realizing meeting him is inevitable. I can't risk hiding in this room and having people see it as a sign of weakness.

"Thank you," I reply.

"Speak nothing of it." A warm smile spreads across her face. She takes her leave, carrying her things with her. Crystal's bright-violet eyes peek mischievously out from her book when the door closes behind Sydney. She snaps it shut, and her brow lifts as she stands and walks over to the table. I scoff, seeing those eyes already prying. She was probably pretending to read, waiting for us to be alone this entire time.

I walk over to see what's on my plate. A thick piece of meat with potatoes, and bread with butter dripping off the sides. My stomach rumbles at the sight. She pulls out a chair to sit, and I'm already forking a potato in my mouth, trying to ignore her intrusiveness.

"For such a dangerous woman, you are also very timid, closed off, and easily tempered. You will be a danger to yourself and those around you if you cannot learn to control your emotions." Crystal says, crossing her arms over the table. My brow lifts. Now, *this* might get interesting.

"Really?" I drawl, spearing another potato into my mouth, this time with aggression, my eyes remaining on my plate.

"No offense at all; I'm just trying to understand you better for when I train you. You see . . . " With a small gesture of her fingers, she pulls the water from her cup, and a spherical form floats idly in her palm. "I can create and manipulate water and ice. If your powers get out of control, I can cool you down." A crackling sound hits the air. Tiny snowflakes spread around the sphere, closing off its translucency. She gives a gentle push and it floats back over her cup before disintegrating into tiny shards of ice and falling back in. "May I?" She holds out her hand, asking permission to touch me.

"You may not." I bring my hands to the edge of the table.

She chuckles. "You'll be fine, trust me."

Trust. I don't even know what that means anymore, but I humor her, offering her my hand. She gently wraps her hand around my wrist. Immediately, her powers push through in a soft, faint aura of purple light thrumming against my skin. My eyes flick to hers, feeling a rush of cool, winter air flutter through me. For some reason, I feel more at ease, but there's . . . more. I sense goodness in her heart. Something inside me blooms: behind a hidden veil is a layer that maybe she doesn't know I can see. A vision slowly begins to reveal itself—a fragment of a memory of a man and woman, heavily guarded by a misted haze. Their features start pushing forth. Crystal quickly releases me, her back hitting the chair. There's a glint in her eyes, but it disappears before I can gather what she is thinking. She slowly places her hands back onto the table and laces her fingers together.

"Callian asked me to take up residence next to your chambers. The king agreed it would be best if I remain close in case you need me. He requested this last night, and I was happy to oblige." She smiles, but I can see something looming behind her eyes from what just happened.

"Thank you." My voice softens. Picking the fork back up, I take another bite of my food, finishing the rest of our meal in silence.

"I'm not wearing this." I hold the dress up to my chest, trying not to hurl at the sight of lilac fabric embellished with too much floral. There's so much frilliness, it makes me sick.

"Why not? It's what a princess would wear," Crystal mocks. She casually leans against the wall and takes a bite of my apple.

I roll my eyes. "I am far from being a princess."

"Are you not the heir to your father's throne?"

She's a little too inquisitive, but why should that still shock me? It's a difficult question with an answer as sharp as a double-edged sword. Technically, I am, but because my father saw me as useless, it wasn't a role given to me. I shudder at the thought of him.

"A title I was not groomed for. I am one of the highest-ranked knights in the kingdom of Sao. I'd throw myself off a cliff or drown myself in my own blood before I ever take that throne." I say, placing the dress back down on the table. I suddenly find myself caught in the intensity of her stare while she studies me. Was I oversharing again?

"Who do you consider your enemies?" she asks, tipping her chin, putting much emphasis on the last word. My eyes remain fixed on hers in a hooded glare. There's a darkness wanting to push forth, wanting to protect myself in such a foreign place.

"Anyone who sees me as their enemy. I now hold no alliance to anyone but myself," I counter, realizing it is a vow I just promised, and that the guilt I've had about betraying my father's kingdom has started to wane.

Crystal nods, as if she understands that I'm someone who is only seeking survival. The tension in the air quickly dissipates. She raises the apple as a form of salute.

"Seems like you and I are going to get along just fine." She takes one last bite before setting the apple back down on the table and starts sifting through the clothes with me. "I'm not one for dresses either, but I like an elegant yet dramatic touch to my attire. Something that has a little flair. Once Sydney gets to know someone, she really has a way of weaving their personality into their wardrobe. It's one of her many powers."

After a couple of minutes, she pulls out a pair of gray trousers and holds it up to my hips. "How about these? They complement your bright-blue eyes." She tosses them back into the pile before I can answer.

"Where are the clothes I wore yesterday?" I ask, picking up a brush.

"They are being cleaned and pressed for you."

I let out a sigh and start brushing my hair. The knots are unmanageable. My fingers become entangled in this matted mess as I try to free each one.

Crystal pulls a chair and swings it behind me. "Come, sit. Let me help you."

I freeze, not expecting the gesture, and slowly sit back in the chair. She takes the brush from my hand and begins working on the knots.

"If you brush your hair from the top, you're going to damage it. You must start at the bottom by brushing the tips."

She holds my hair just above the base, combing through the knots. Little by little, working her way up. Her touch is gentle and calming. Memories of my mother flash into my mind. Every morning, she would come into my room and brush my hair. Even though we had hand-maidens to do those tasks, it was one she enjoyed doing herself. I place the palm of my hand over my chest and run my fingers down the empty space where my necklace used to be. The only thing I had left of her, and it is far from reach. The dagger Alyce gave me is also lost, probably dropped somewhere amidst my abduction.

"Who taught you how to brush your hair?" I ask.

She briefly pauses. A heavy silence hangs in the air before she continues brushing. I can sense her locking herself into memories. A ball forms in my throat as I already know her answer.

"I'm sorry, I shouldn't—"

Her voice softens. "It's alright. It was my mother." She says, brushing the side of my head.

Sadness swells in my chest. It's a topic I will push no further on. I rub my hands together, fidgeting with my nails.

A gentle knock breaks the silence. Sydney is back, carrying an article of clothing draped over her arms.

"Did you like my little surprise?" Sydney smirks.

"If you mean the purple dress, no," I reply, keeping my focus out toward the balcony. Sydney places my clothing onto the table, and a small vial lies atop. Leaning forward, I take the vial in my hand, thumbing it around in my palm as the liquid swishes around. "What's this?" I ask.

The sudden burst of Crystal's laugh sends my hair flying to the front. Sydney glares at her, and she quickly goes silent.

"That, my dear, is a tonic to prevent pregnancy. I brought it up from my apothecary."

My cheeks instantly flush, causing me to set it back onto the table like I touched something hot. She picks it up and places the vial back into my hand. "Drink it," she demands.

I lean back into my chair. "How do I know you aren't trying to poison me?" I sneer, realizing how stupid that was as soon as it left my lips.

Somehow, I can sense Crystal enjoying every moment of this. Sydney challenges my glare, and it only takes one second for me to comply. I open the vial and drink it. The pungent smell assaults my nose and burns down my throat.

"We can't waste any more time." Sydney rushes me from my seat and strips me down so quickly, I have no time to react. She pulls a deep-maroon, sleeveless tunic over my head and down my body. The material stretches with ease, hugging my shape. A low v-neck dips down, ending at my sternum and allowing the cool air to hit my chest. I'm a little too exposed, realizing this is a similar style to the one I wore before, except the bottom slightly fans out behind me, and the front cut off just below my navel. She senses my unease. "There's no need to feel embarrassed. There's nothing you have that I haven't seen before."

She hands me a pair of black trousers, and I quickly slip them on. I'm relieved to see the trousers hide my midriff. She fastens a thick belt around my waist with a dark-silver emblem clasp. I hold out my arms while she slips on a small coat ending at my ribcage. My fingers trail along the crushed, maroon, velvet sleeves. Crystal hands me a pair of socks and black boots. When I'm done, they step back to look at the masterpiece I'm wearing.

"My gods, you are stunning." A smug look stretches across Sydney's face. Her small, pursed lips curve into a smile. "A stoic warrior stands before me." It's easy to see why Sydney is so prized within these walls. She looks me over from head to toe and walks around me, proud of her creations, but something more seems to stir in her mind. She places a hand on my shoulder. My body hums under her touch, feeling the magic beneath her fingertips like a soft, thrumming vibration. Something tells me she's much older than she appears to be. Her features pull taut as she continues to stare at me, as if she, too, sees something I can't.

Sydney's brows pinch together with a reluctant look in her eyes. "The woman who holds his heart, holds his soul. And if that's you, Viona, then may the gods help us all."

CHAPTER 17

FOUR GUARDS ARE STANDING in the corridor when we leave my room. I'm shocked to see this many, wondering if it will be a recurring event. One briefly skims his pale eyes over my attire, his gaze lingering long enough for me to notice a faint scar above his brow.

"If you want to keep your head intact, I suggest you divert your eyes," Crystal reminds them.

"Apologies," he says with flushed cheeks.

"As you were, Rossburn." Crystal nods.

She escorts me to the Great Hall while the four extra guards flank behind us by a few feet. As we walk in silence, every step is weighted with uncertainty, having had very little time to sort through my thoughts. She must sense my unease.

"If it helps, the king will not be discussing any details tonight. There will be too many prying ears and eyes at court."

She notices my sigh of relief.

"It seems like the king spared no expense in the décor," I surmise, trying to change the subject as I observe the white marble floors stretching throughout the halls. A faint breeze drifts in from each of the balconies tucked between tall, ivory pillars. The sun is nearly setting, casting deep-violet and orange hues across the sky. Lanterns burn in the distance, giving the town a faint glow. I didn't realize how high up we are. We enter another large corridor with an array of warrior statues carved from marble lining the walls. They look so real, as if they were frozen in time.

"Are these people from Callisto's history?" I ask, staring at one of the statues of a woman garbed in a dress. Crystal slightly shifts her eyes to me in confusion.

"Some of these statues are the gods of the stars. The ones who created these lands thousands of years ago. You'll find that we have many different versions of them throughout the palace."

As I pass by each one, I look at them in awe.

After descending a few flights of stairs, we round the corner to the Great Hall. I swallow hard, feeling the sudden rush of nerves clenching around my heart when I hear the bustle of life on the other side of the gilded doors. I glance back at the guards still following our every move.

"Are they necessary? I thought I was a guest, not a prisoner," I say, trying not to draw attention to my rising panic.

Crystal glances at me. "Though it is unnecessary, it was Callian's orders to double up security due to the events that unfolded yesterday," she replies.

"How unnerving. Who does he think he is?" I mutter under my breath.

A look of shock spreads across her face. Before she can speak, one of the guards steps forward.

"Lady Mira." He bows.

My heart won't stop pounding against my chest, but I straighten my back and wipe my clammy hands down the front of my clothes. The doors swing open. I hold my breath as the loud creak of the metal hinges grates my ears. The conversations come to an abrupt halt as silence washes over the crowd. Men and women born of nobility fill the room. All eyes are on me. I'm not shocked that the darkness tying me to my name has followed me to this kingdom. Some of their expressions are a great reminder of that. I can't escape it, no matter what kingdom I travel to. Whether I like it or not, I was born into royalty. My chin lifts, letting them sense whatever they feel from me. I will not falter.

"Shall we?" Crystal turns to me with pride gleaming off of her as she revels in my transformation the moment those thick, heavy doors swung open.

In a sea of courtiers, I quickly find Callian standing on the dais beside the king with his sword sheathed at his side. The most beautiful man I've ever seen is in a black coat, a tunic, and thick-fitted trousers—every muscle in his body bulges. Every head turns to follow me as I walk down the light-blue carpet. The moment my eyes lock with Callian's, everyone else in the room fades beyond sight. He looks at me with such a deeply sated expression that his smile alone has him undressing me before the entire court. My breath hitches as he stands shamelessly beside his king. I redirect my attention before my cheeks can turn bright red.

King Valor sits on a throne made of gold, wearing rings on every finger. His salt-and-pepper hair is combed back, and he looks to be in his mid-fifties. His crown is made of gold with a sapphire adorning the center. It's hard to see his size from a sitting position, but his arms are muscular, reminding me of one of the statues in the hallways. The last bit of light from the setting sun shining through the stained-glass windows highlights his chiseled jawline.

I sense magic thrumming within him, though the ability to heal might not be one of them judging by the faint scars that mar his hands, quite possibly from war. War my kingdom did not participate in due to the haze around the White Forest. The possibility of unknown history stretching beyond my knowledge, limiting my already-narrow view of the world, causes me to feel naïve, but I'll tuck that away to dwell on later.

Crystal announces my name with a loud voice full of authority and pride. "Your Grace, King Valor, I present to you Viona Tarvas, daughter of King Mal Tarvas, and member of the Royal Guard serving the kingdom of Sao."

She steps out of the formation to join the other guards on the side. I bow respectfully before the king. Though hearing my father's name was jarring, I'm touched by the care she used to present who I was. Not a princess nor an heir, but a title I will always be proud of: a warrior.

"You may proceed forward." The king's voice echoes throughout the room, holding much power and wisdom. I'm now merely fifteen feet away from his throne. Moments seem to stretch on for an eternity under his bold, green stare—I'm not sure whose is more penetrating, his or Callian's. "We finally meet. If I am correct, you are the kingdom of Sao's princess and the heir to its throne. Why do you not wish to be announced as such? One should be proud to honor their kingdom holding such a title." The crowd hums with low chatter.

"Your Grace, it is a title I do not wish to hold, nor is it how I wish to be addressed. I will be so grateful if you refer to me as Viona." I bow again respectfully.

A few gasps are heard from the crowd. Whispers spread. Improper etiquette or not, I refuse to be called by a title I wasn't given. He studies me for a few moments with a raised, salt-and-pepper brow. He turns his head toward Callian with an approving nod.

"My my, sounds quite like someone else I know." He smiles casually, amused, even though a slight edge remains in his voice. "Come closer, my dear."

I step forward, reaching the edge of the dais and glancing at Callian, catching his prying eyes raking over my body. A wave of awareness rushes over me. King Valor's eyes warm the moment I look at him.

"It is a pleasure to meet you, Viona. Traveling across Vendrelle is no easy feat, but I am glad you finally arrived. You're welcome to roam freely throughout the palace, the town, and the docks within our fortified walls, but you are forbidden to leave until further notice. Due to the attacks last night, it is for your safety."

Forbidden.

The word strikes a chord in me, but I suck it up and politely bow as graciously as I can.

"As you wish." The words feel like ash on my tongue.

"My most trusted guard will be responsible for your protection. I'm sure introductions aren't necessary." His gestures over to Callian.

My stomach takes a dip, and my eyes slightly widen, seeing him take the first step off the dais, then another. I swallow the lump in my throat, straightening my back as if him closing the distance does nothing to me. My chin lifts, trying not to let my eyes give away anything that he and I have done, but Callian does the unexpected. He gets on one knee—a motion that steals my breath as he stares with a hooded gaze. That look alone might give away our physical attraction to one another. I swallow hard.

"It would be my honor to be by your side." He places a hand over his heart. "I vow to protect you, serve you, and keep you safe until my last breath."

Callian's words are so powerful, so promising, that my body responds with an awareness of his truth. He gently kisses my hand, sending a wave of heat fluttering against my skin. As he rises to his feet, that penetrating stare never leaves mine. He stands beside me, now facing the king. I can feel the heat radiating off his body. Gods, this can't be good. I think I nearly fainted.

"Why should she be allowed to roam freely throughout the castle when most of us consider her an enemy?"

My mood wholly dissipates to the sound of that familiar voice grating across my skin. My head whips up in his direction. Of course I find Ronan—a face I had not seen when entering the hall—standing within the first few steps off the throne. He must have slipped through the crowd, snaking his way to the front. The same guards as yesterday stand to his right like some sick posse. I'd like to carve that smug look off his face. Side glancing Callian, I see the vein on the column of his neck pulsating with rage.

"She is an enemy hiding in our fortress!" someone musters the courage to shout. The crowd breaks out in chatter.

"Will we be safe, my king?" Another voice echoes through the Great Hall.

Ronan's words spread like poison throughout the room, and these people are taking the bait.

"Don't be foolish. She is our savior," a woman scoffs from the front row, wearing a fitted, blue dress. Her sapphire eyes beam with joy.

Others chime in to agree with her. It's only a handful of mindless comments until the room quickly becomes divided and starts to spiral out of control as arguments catch flame. My eyes narrow in on Ronan. Satisfaction stretches across his face. It's evident he's baiting me for a reaction to make me look like the enemy. I will give him *nothing*. I remain calm and unaffected while his venomous words start an uprising within the room.

Moments stretch on. It takes everything in me to rein back the anger I'd love to unfurl, all while Callian is quickly losing it. His eyes grate over the crowd with a vengeance, memorizing every face that blurts insults.

"She's a liability and a risk to our people!" yells a man holding a glass of wine, dabbing the sweat off his face with a handkerchief.

King Valor abruptly stands with such force, his throne grates against the marble floors. The physical power is felt within the room as he towers over us all. Those eyes that were seemingly kind moments ago are now flaring with anger. The hard lines of his body prove the decades of wars fought and the training he still does today.

"*Leave*!" His voice thunders across the Great Hall, leaving a wave of silence in his wake as the clamor of division comes to a brief halt. A newfound respect for him blooms to life. This is something my own king would never have done for me. One word is all it takes to clear an entire room. The crowd slowly disperses out the doors, but Ronan remains. King Valor cuts him a look of warning. "Take your leave at once," he orders. "There is no room for mindless theatrics here."

Ronan smiles and steps down. He stops in front of me. Darkness tips the edges of his brown eyes as they slowly dip toward my chest. With a sharp inhale, he breathes in my scent as if he detects something potent.

"You smell as sweet as the promise of death. Tell me, *Princess*, does he like the way you taste?"

A predatory growl erupts from Callian's chest. The sound sends a chill down my spine.

In one swift motion, Callian stands wedged between us, wrapping an arm around my waist, placing me directly behind him. His other hand shoots out, gripping Ronan's throat.

"If you were smart, you'd keep your eyes off her and your mouth shut. Our shared blood will not restrain me from ripping your spine from your body, *cousin*." He seethes.

Cousin? I blink at the word.

Before I can process that they're related, King Valor takes a step forward. "That is enough!" The ground rumbles beneath us, causing me to stumble.

Callian releases Ronan.

Ronan staggers back, gasping for air but then smirks. When he catches his breath, he grins and straightens his coat. "Apologies"—he stifles a look, giving a mocking bow. His eyes glare up at Callian—"my prince . . . "

CHAPTER 18

Prince? My eyes narrow in on Callian as I take a few steps back. I have the impulse to punch him right in the face, but my nerves are so rattled, I can't think straight.

"Oh, my," Ronan drones. "He hasn't told you? Seems like you two have lots to discuss tonight after he's done burying his face between your legs." His smile widens, taking one last look at me.

Callian's fist goes flying into the air, hitting Ronan in the jaw. Ronan's body takes flight, skidding across the marble floor. King Valor runs a hand over his face in frustration. Ronan sits up, wiping the blood trickling down his mouth with the back of his hand and looks at Callian with a grin. Blood glints off his teeth. The sick fuck looks to be brimming with satisfaction. I expect the both of them to battle it out, but Ronan's eyes bounce between Callian and me before he gets up and leaves.

The betrayal lingers in his absence, stealing all the air in my lungs. Callian steps forward. I hold my hands out, taking a step back.

"Don't," I bite out.

Crystal clears her throat. "I'll be waiting outside," she says. My eyes flick to hers; I forgot she was even here.

Anger and embarrassment sting my eyes. The king now knows what's been going on. A fucking prince, what was I thinking?

King Valor glares at Callian. "Looks like you have much explaining to do," he says, jaw fluttering with irritation. Probably for not telling me who he was. Serves him fucking right.

"There's no need to explain anything. I'm done here. If you'll excuse me, King Valor," I reply, trying to keep my composure and hide the humiliation coursing through my body. He gives me a tight nod.

Without making eye contact with Callian again, I storm out. I refuse to be in the same room with someone who made me feel like an idiot.

I ignore Crystal waiting outside and rush up the stairs. Callian swings the doors open with such force that they hit the interior walls.

Crystal's voice echoes through the stairway while watching him chase after me. "I'll take the long route back to my room after I talk to the king!"

I pick up my pace, trying to navigate through a palace I have yet to explore. Callian calls out. The sound of his voice sends my heart plummeting to the pit of my stomach. My pace quickens. My emotions gnaw at my gut. I make a slight turn and run down a long hall I've never seen before. Fuck, I'm already getting lost. My eyes burn with frustration. Tears threaten to break free.

How could I have fallen for this? I keep asking myself over and over. The back of my throat tightens.

"A fucking prince of all people," I murmur under my breath, feeling a tear finally escape.

I've been such a fool, naïve for having feelings for someone who was not only the enemy, but a prince. Was this part of his plan? To seduce me into coming here so they could use me for their gain? I try to calm my breathing, but my body thrums with a power I still don't know shit about. My vision blurs, trying to decipher where to go as I look down the corridor. My thoughts no longer make sense.

At the end of the hall are two large, wooden doors forming an arch with no guards at the entrance. Desperate to disappear from sight, I run the rest of the way. I open one door just enough to slip through, and I enter a dark room dimly lit by the moonlight. Its glow filters in through each massive window. This isn't just any room; it is a treasure trove. Thousands of books line the walls from top to bottom. Small reading nooks span out down each row. There are desks placed throughout the vast room with more books and papers on top of them. The expanse of this library seems infinite.

Voices reach the doorway, snagging my attention. With caution, I take a few steps back. My breathing stills, expecting to hear Callian's voice among them, but it's two women walking down the hall. I exhale deeply, but behind me, a familiar voice sends chills down my body.

"You can hide in the dark all you want, little flame, but I will always find you." Callian's darkened gaze narrows in on me as he leans against a bookshelf with crossed arms. I lunge forward, shoving him in the chest. Of course, he barely moves a muscle.

"Damn you for startling me!" I hiss, running a hand through my hair. "How were you able to find me so quickly?"

"This castle has many secrets. Would you like to explore how many more we can find in the dark?" His calm demeanor is smooth, his sultry voice replaces the primal rage I witnessed in the Great Hall. I scoff, crossing my arms over my chest, and flick my eyes to the trim of the library windows, wishing I were alone. Callian pushes off the wall and uncrosses his arms, making his way over to one of the tables. We stand in the dark with only the moonlight shining in, holding back all the words we have to say. He strikes a piece of flint with steel, and embers spark to life, highlighting his face for just a moment before dimming to a small flame. The intensity in his eyes makes my chest tighten. "We need to talk about this," Callian says, bringing another candle to flame before sitting in a chair. He leans back with his hands laced together and elbows resting on the desk. Candlelight dances in his eyes.

"I have nothing to say to you," I lie.

"You have plenty to say. Did you forget how expressive those bright-blue eyes are?" he says with a glint of humor.

I press my palms onto the ledge of the table and lean in. "Why didn't you tell me you were a prince?" I seethe into a harsh whisper. I'm close enough to smell his scent. Damn this prick. He leans closer as the humor drains from his face.

"For the same reason you despise being called a princess. It is not a title I recognize myself as, nor is it of any interest to me to run an entire *fucking* kingdom." His jaw feathers, biting out the last few words with an icy edge. We are now mere inches apart. His eyes drift down to my lips. "We are more alike than you think, little flame."

"How so?" I demand. "I don't go stealing sleeping *princesses* from their beds at night." For a moment, humor flickers in his eyes as he weaves together that fantasy.

"You and I prefer to serve justice in bloodshed, not by sitting on a throne." His mouth curves up into a grin. As much as I don't want to admit it, he's right. He leans back into the chair, satisfied when he sees my expression change.

My back straightens.

"What if this was some plot to seduce me into doing what you want? What if your plans are similar to my fathers? To hurt me and take my powers?" I'm foolish to allow the words to slip from my mouth so mindlessly, but it's too late. Hurt flashes in his eyes, something I didn't expect to see. They cut into him like shards of glass, but that look doesn't stay long enough for him to think I noticed. The mask of his cockiness remains even though I challenged his morals and honor.

"I might be a man with dirty thoughts, but being a sly, dubious one has never been my angle." His jaw ticks with tension. My emotions remain warring inside me as silence hangs in the air. He leans forward over the desk and wraps his hands around mine. The sudden touch electrifies my senses, and my body responds. My lips slightly part, watching his thumb graze over my wrist.

"I'm sorry," he says as he gently kisses the top of my hand, and it remains there while he speaks. "As I told you in the forest, you have no reason to trust me, but I'd like to show you I'm worthy of it if you'd give me the chance. I don't want you to fear or hate me or ever have to worry that I'll hurt you. I would never do such things."

"I don't understand why," I whisper in a shaky breath. "Why do you care so much about me? You don't even know—"

"I know enough to see you deserve much more than what you've been given. You deserve to have the right people around you. Though I can't guarantee everyone will accept your presence, let that be my problem, not yours."

My breathing hitches. Living in my body weighs heavily on me some days, spending more than half my life without understanding or really knowing who I am or what I will become. The weight of my powers are on *my* shoulders. I've endured many moments alone with no one to confide in.

Callian must sense the war inside my head as I fight back the tears. The chair pushes out from behind him. It only takes him a few strides to move around the desk before closing the space between us. The heat radiating off his body envelops me. He reaches for me, reassuring me I don't have to stand in the dark alone. His hand gently presses against the small of my back. The way he pulls me against his body is so secure and comforting. As his arms tighten around mine, I realize something.

"You heard those people in that room," I remind him. "You saw the chaos my presence brings."

"I don't care," he breathes, brushing my cheek with the back of his hand while his eyes search deep within my soul. I lean in, resting my head against his chest, letting the rhythm of his heart ground me.

"If one day you decide to rule, standing by me right now will taint your name." I pause, sucking in a sharp breath. "I am the enemy to most here, as well as a curse. What chance will you have by knowing me?"

"Again . . . I don't fucking care," he whispers, light and airy.

He should. There's more at risk than him being an heir. I close my eyes shut to the painful emotion swelling in my chest and listen to the steady beat of his heart against the shell of my ear. I hear mine beating in a rhythmic motion with his. When I search deeper, the darkness sleeping inside me beats slower than ours in a low, deep hum, like the one that beats beneath the waves in my visions, reminding me the inevitable is catching up quicker than I can grasp.

He rests his chin on the top of my head as his chest gently rises and falls. We stand silently in the dark, embracing each other in a place I know all too well. The tips of his dark-brown hair brush the side of my face. My hands wrapped around him somewhere amidst my anger and resistance, and I didn't notice how tight I was holding onto him until he held me tighter, in the safety of his arms, stroking my hair.

"No matter how far I run, what I have inside me will always follow," I confess, lifting my head to meet his gaze. Callian's eyes illuminate in the soft, faint glow of the candlelight.

"Then give me all your darkness," he whispers, full of desire.

He curves a finger under my chin and dips his head. Slowly and tentatively, his mouth presses against mine as if he's searing my lips to memory. His words echo in my mind as if they were a gift from the stars. I give into him, giving him all the weight my soul carries while his kiss frees me. I push off my toes and pull him closer. My hands move up the side of his neck. Tears finally break free, falling between us. When he feels the dampness on his cheek, he cups the back of my head, deepening the kiss. The way he moans into my mouth pulls at my heart in ways I thought I'd never get to feel—wanting to take the pain as his own. He briefly breaks away to lick the trail of tears off my cheek. My heart swells. He holds me against his body and stands in the dark, ripping through the poisoned vines that bind my heart. My body hums in response with a feeling I cannot describe other than pure ecstasy.

"My stars," I whisper, sliding my fingers beneath his tunic to explore the hard lines of his chest. Callian leans his body up against the desk while I begin moving on him in a heated frenzy, seeking more friction. The bulge in his pants presses against my body. It throbs against his trousers. I palm his length in my hand for the first time and whimper into his mouth, feeling how big he is. A throaty groan escapes those perfect, full lips as I move my hand up and down. When I start to reach into his pants, he smiles into my mouth at the unexpected touch, stopping me.

"As much as I want you to touch me in every single way . . . " he groans, kissing the side of my jaw, "and believe me, I fucking want it . . . I am here to serve you, Princess, not the other way around."

His hands caress my face as he devours my mouth once more. I open to him, letting his tongue lash against mine. His rough hands glide down my frame, cupping my breasts. They move down to my waist, gently tugging on the fabric of my belt. He teases me with his fingers as they slide between the material to caress the skin just below my navel.

"May I?" His eyes flare with desire. I nod, watching him tenderly unfasten my belt. The strap slips from around my waist, dropping onto the desk. The thick, silver emblem makes a loud thud against the wood, sending an echo throughout the expanse of the library. "Will you let me fulfill my duties?" he pleads with hands running up my waist. His fingertips press with need against my stomach, sending heat pooling between my thighs.

"Yes . . . " I pant.

He slips his hands inside my trousers, rubbing the small bundle of nerves. My mouth opens at his touch, and he catches my moans with his perfect lips. My body lurches forward, gripping his arms. Soft moans begin to push out as I steady myself against him. His scent of cedar and musk is rubbing all over me while his fingers continuously work between my thighs with precision. My hips thrust against his hand, chasing the way he keeps teasing me along my entrance.

"You're so wet for me, Princess." His eyes darken when he slips his hand free from beneath the fabric and holds it up to the faint candlelight. His fingers glisten. His eyes lock on mine while he brings them to his mouth. Shock rolls down my body as he tastes me. I bite my lower lip, moaning at the sight.

He groans, "You taste so sweet, like strawberries."

Something predatory comes alive as he lifts me off the ground. My legs around his waist. I use this time to remove my coat, leaving it where it falls while he carries me to a chaise against the window and gently sets me down.

"You know"—he leans down and gently sucks my lower lip into his mouth—"I found it captivating the way you strode into the Great Hall. Power dripped off your perfect body." He groans into the crook of my neck, sending another wave of heat through me. "It made me think of the not-so-graceful things I'd like to do to you in front of a room full of courtiers."

"You are treasonous," I softly purr. He has my body humming in more ways than one.

"That may be true. You have set my heart on fire. Your whole body is treasonous. Right now, I want to see you glow in the moonlight while I make you come."

I bite my lip again, soaking in his words like a remedy, moaning to how his velvety voice sounds when he speaks to me this way. His fingers work magic as he unfastens my trousers and slips them off my body. I'm left with nothing but my tunic as it fans out from above my navel and around my naked frame. His hands work my thighs, massaging them with his rough hands while his thumbs glide closer to my center. The heat between us deepens. He pulls me to the edge of the chaise, and this time, I don't wait for him to spread me open. My knees glide to the sides.

"Show me how you like to serve," I whisper. The corner of my mouth quirks up, realizing my words have become bolder under his touch. His grip tightens around my thighs as he stares down at me. I pant out a soft breath.

"You're a goddess, woven by the silver threads of the moon."

My breathing hitches. Callian drops to his knees and removes his shirt, baring his chest as the night sky shines in, casting moonlit shadows along the dips of his body. He wraps his arms around my thighs, locking me in place while his muscles bulge with every movement. My gods, his skin is so smooth. Passion floods his eyes, one final look before dipping his head between my legs. The way he presses his tongue against my sex makes me ascend to the stars. He takes his time, watching me as every stroke of his tongue fills my body with pleasure. I arch my back, rolling into his rhythm.

"Little flame, you are perfect." His voice reverberates over my bundle of nerves. Lost in the talents of his tongue, I don't notice he unhooked one of his arms from my thighs until he slides a finger inside me. My mouth gapes open with a loud moan.

I suck in a sharp breath and cover my mouth. "What if someone hears us?"

"I don't care," he exhales. His heated breath fans against my thighs as his tongue continues to work my sex. "Let them know you are mine." He continues to work my center, sliding his tongue between my slit. My eyes roll into the back of my head, and I collapse back onto the chaise. "Let them hear how their *prince* pleasures their so-called *enemy*."

There's a darkness in his tone my body begins to chase. My core tightens around his finger. Another loud moan escapes me, this time uncaring who hears us.

"Fuck," he growls, panting against my thigh. "Do that again for me, Princess. My tongue wants to feel the tightness of your grip." Every word he breathes is full of wicked sin. His finger slides out as he replaces it with his tongue. The way he spears me deepens my urge. My entrance tightens around him as my body starts to chase the feeling of ecstasy. My heart thunders against my chest. I desperately run my fingers through his hair, pulling him closer between my thighs as my body searches for that release. His tongue is punishing, thrusting deeper inside of me, drawing out another cry. He moans in response and looks at me through a hooded stare as he continues to devour me. I become undone, my entrance tightening at the sight. Then, I explode, riding my release against his mouth while his tongue continues to spear me. The more I moan, the louder his guttural sounds rumble in his chest, shattering me whole. I ride the waves until they become a steady, rhythmic calm. He pulls away, breathing ragged as his lips glisten with my release. He lies down beside me while we both catch our breath. I turn to him and nestle myself against his body. We lie in the moonlight, caressing one another, enjoying each other's company for the rest of the night.

CHAPTER 19

*M*Y GAZE TRAILS DOWN *to Callian beneath me, his eyes an ominous gray, and his dark hair lying flat against a plum-colored pillow. My name rolls off his lips in pure ecstasy, slipping into an endless echo around us. We're in a room cloaked in shadow on a purple bed with tiny specks of light glowing between us. They cast shadows that flutter against the hard lines of his body. He cups the heavy swell of my breast in his hand while the other is warm at my hip. I inhale the scent of sex and magic as our bodies ride deeper into one another. He watches me with a lifeless gaze, gliding me along his length. My head rolls back, and my nipples pebble from the pressure building between the apex of my thighs. The emptiness emitting off of him remains, all while my body surges with my growing sense of power. It's searching for him through a thick haze. I'm desperate for those emerald eyes to find me. I revel in the way he's succumbed. The more I see, the more I need. The darkness is slipping through the cracks to reach him, whispers beneath the surface. There's a clamor in the rhythm of his pulse, sending a tingling awareness down my body.*

My eyes drift up toward the mirror above the bed, ornate with obsidian stone. My pupils are dilated to the brim. This hollow space is waning, showing me in all its truth that these are not speckles of light floating between us. They're embers raining down. I ride him, unaffected by the heat as they sink into my skin. Callian's body reacts the same way; the embers disappear into his flesh like kisses from my soul.

"Callian," I whisper his name. His eyes transform into the warm, bright-green I know. He cups the side of my face, thrusting his hips to drive his length deeper inside me.

We are transforming together in a seamless, weightless space, but then darkness beats below the surface of his bed with a pulse growing louder, stronger. A dagger appears in my hand, cold to the touch. My arms rise into the air until they're above my head, clenching the hilt between my palms while I continue riding him. His gaze won't leave mine. He sees me, really looks into my eyes with an acceptance I can't seem to understand.

"No," I plead in the back of my mind, but I strike down, piercing the blade into his flesh. I feel every tear, every shred of his muscle the deeper I go. I'm screaming, but I can't speak. Screaming for it to stop, but onyx tendrils fill his eyes.

He grabs my hand, forcing the blade further into his chest. Blood pools in the center, trickling down in thick, pulsating ripples synchronized with his heartbeat.

The room fills with his blood, Callian's blood, and I can't make it stop.

I GASP, SHOOTING UP IN BED with my hand on my chest, desperate for air. My throat and chest are burning as if I've swallowed hot liquid. My eyes go wide, searching around the room, and I don't even know what I'm looking for.

The door swings open and hits the wall, pulling my attention to the loud sound. Sydney's stark silhouette blurs against the morning light as she enters my chambers with something in her hands.

"You two have no shame, do you?" she scolds, dropping it onto the table and making me wince in pain as the sound reverberates around me. She moves about the room like a shadow. My mind is whirling. I run my hands through my dampened hair and look down to see my nightgown slick with sweat against my body.

It was just a dream. Everything is okay.

Or was it a vision? Or a warning?

"Do you hear me?" Sydney's voice breaks through my thoughts. "You forgot half of your clothes in the library last night," she says, pointing over to the items which I now notice are my belt and coat.

"I'm sorry." My cheeks are flushed, but it's not from embarrassment. I hover my hand above my forehead, squinting my eyes to adjust to the morning light, and wipe the sheen of sweat off my brow.

She looks me over. "My gods, child, you look feverish," she says, pressing the palm of her hand to my forehead. Her brows knit with concern. "And you're scorching hot." Her eyes skim down my body, seeing the disheveled state I'm in. She reaches for the pitcher that's on the bedside table and pours me a cup of water. "Here, drink this."

I sit up in bed. My hand shakes uncontrollably as I bring the cup to my lips, swallowing every drop as if I'm parched. I hand it back to her. "More," I rasp as her eyes widen.

"Where's Callian?" I ask, feeling the stickiness in the back of my throat.

Sydney refills my cup. "He's just outside the door. Do you want me to grab him?"

My heart drops to the pit of my stomach.

"No!" I lurch forward, grabbing her wrist with a crazed grip. Water shakes out from the cup in a big wave, spilling onto the table and partially wetting the cuffs of her long-sleeve dress. She shoots me a look of warning with an irritated brow lifted. I gasp. My mouth gapes, realizing what I've done, and I instantly let go.

"I'm so sorry, Sydney. I didn't mean to." My hand withdraws back to my lap while shame creeps up. "I had a nightmare. I don't want him to worry or see me like this." She eyes me once more, assessing my current state.

"He does seem to overreact to the slightest of things, especially when it comes to you," she says with warmth. She walks over to the armoire and begins looking through my clothes. "I heard about the tussle Callian had with Ronan last night in front of King Valor." Silence lingers in the air as she waits for me to fill in the gaps. Even though my body feels like it's burning hot, the sound of Ronan's name grates against my skin, sending a chill down my spine.

I take another gulp of water. My words become stiff. "That man has nothing but hate for me."

"Don't let that entitled, big-headed prick get to you, Viona. His words might be laced with poison, but from what I see, they're driven by jealousy." She hangs articles of clothing into my cabinet.

"Why would he be jealous?" I ask, tilting my head to the side.

She turns around and sighs, clearly irritated, as if I should already know why. Now I'm letting the silence linger in the air, wanting *her* to fill in the gaps. She stops what she's doing and walks over to the side of the bed. She sits down, placing her hands in her lap, and leans in. Even when she is tense and her features tight, she has such poise in all she does. Her hair is pulled back into a loose bun today, two strands of hair hanging in waves on each side of her face. The collar of her cyan button-up dress is at the perfect length to still showcase the beauty of her neck.

"Callian has it all," she continues in a low tone so that her voice doesn't bounce off the walls. "He's the heir to the throne, the prince of Callisto, Commander of the Royal Guard, and his father's pride and joy. People seem to gravitate toward his kindness and his unyielding determination to have our people live in peace. Ronan is quite the opposite. He is an opportunist who is using his father's death as leverage to sneak his way to the top. So far, he has succeeded. Standing on the other side of the king. Being that Ronan and Callian's fathers were brothers, Ronan feels he should be the king's successor since Callian refuses to take the throne. Now that Callian has his eye on you, the—pardon me—princess of Sao, and he's made it *very* apparent that he does . . . " She pauses, her lashes fluttering as she grins teasingly. "It's plain and simple. Your presence is a threat to Ronan because you have the potential to one day bear an heir with a more legitimate claim to the throne."

I start placing all the little pieces together. "I suppose that does make sense . . . " My words fade as I go deeper in thought, pushing away the idea of bearing an heir.

"You're young, but when you become a woman of my age, reading between the lines becomes first nature. You start to know things about people long before even they do." She winks.

Wise words. I'll have to sear this to memory, but my dream keeps pressing to the front of my mind. Something foreboding hangs in the air.

"Don't let your dreams follow you in your waking state." Her voice interrupts my thoughts as she can clearly read my expression. "You should worry more about being late to your training. Crystal is waiting for you in the west wing of the gardens." She pats my leg and proceeds toward the bathing chambers. Even though I barely know her, she somehow made me feel . . . better. There's a familiarity with her, as if I've always known her.

"You're right, and stop reading me!" I tease, smiling.

"I'm going to draw you a quick bath, but don't linger." Her voice bounces off the marble walls.

My eyes glance around the room, making sure there are no other mirrors I have missed. I push myself off the bed and head toward the bathing chambers. I dip a hand into the water and notice that Sydney set my bath to a cool temperature.

"You'll get used to it eventually," Sydney calls out from the dressing area.

"Get used to what?"

She leans back so that her head peeks through the doorway. "Your body is trying to acclimate to the changes as your powers push forth. Everyone's experience can be a little different, but fevers are the most common side effect."

"Oh?" I say faintly with my pulse returning like a hammer against my ribs.

I quickly blink back the thoughts, pin my hair up, and slide into the tub. Already, my body has cooled down. I quickly rub my skin raw, pushing my dream to the back of my mind, then hop out and dry off. I pluck the pin from my head as my dark hair cascades around my naked frame. Crystal isn't here to do my hair. I'm not certain why I was expecting her to come in with Sydney, but talking to her would keep my mind occupied.

A sudden, cool breeze drifts in. My hair gently brushes across my bare chest, causing my skin to pebble. In my search for a shirt, my vision draws toward a box with a black bow wrapped around it. An orange rose placed atop. The same kind of rose that little girl gave me when I first arrived in Callisto.

"*Princess,*" the note reads.

The corner of my mouth slightly turns up, seeing the handwriting of the only person who *might* be allowed to call me that. I still haven't fully decided. I drag the box in front of me and remove the top, sucking in a sharp breath when I see what lies upon a blue, satin cushion.

"My mother's dagger," I whisper, picking up the blade as it hums beneath my touch. What I thought was lost now sits in my hand, and I'm clenching it tight within my grip, stifling a sob.

"Callian can be quite the charmer if you give him the chance to be," Sydney says from the entryway of the bathing chambers.

"How did he—"

Sydney raises her hands and shakes her head. "That is something you have to ask him."

I quickly put on my clothes, slipping my legs into a pair of black trousers with a matching sleeveless tunic—both form-fitting against my body. I flex and move around, testing their durability and finding them to be perfect for training. I fasten the custom-made sheath Sydney created and strap my mother's dagger to my thigh. Before opening the door, I hear Callian engaging with the guards. I take a deep breath before stepping into the corridor.

"Good morning, Princess." He smiles at the sight of me. He's clad in black with his hair pulled into a small tie. A few strands hang loose down his face. His long-sleeve tunic is unlaced at the chest, exposing just the top of his pecs. His sword is strapped to his back in its sheath. Today, between the dream and his gift, I force myself to withdraw a little.

"Good morning." I faintly smile, creating an awkward silence stretching between the guards as we all stand here.

Callian's beaming expression doesn't change. He motions down the hall. "Shall we?"

I nod, quickly peeling my eyes away from him. Silence drifts between us. He takes notice of the dagger strapped to my thigh. I can already sense many questions brewing, but he keeps them to himself as we continue down each corridor.

"Thank you for returning my dagger to me," I finally say with my eyes still fixed down the hall. "I thought it was lost forever."

Today, the palace is bustling with life. Each person we pass gives him a nod. It feels strange to expose the dagger, remembering Alyce told me to keep it hidden. I remind myself I'm not there, I'm here. Far, far away.

"You're welcome. I found it in the White Forest. I figured, if you ever stopped trying to use it against me, I would return it."

"And what if I still wanted to?" I smirk, but a pang of dread hits my chest from the memory of last night's dream. I push it back down, keeping the steady pace of our conversation. He grins, those perfect, white teeth shining. When he stares at me, my heart drops a little.

"I would have kept it as a reminder of our little rendezvous in the forest."

I laugh loud enough that my voice echoes down the hall, catching two males' attention. They sneer at me, recognizing who I am, reminding me of what my presence has brought. I dip my chin and glare back at them.

"You look like an angry wolf ready to pounce on its prey."

"It's hard to be kind to people when they look at me with such disdain," I scoff.

"So you give them more reasons to do so by giving them death stares?"

His humor tingles along the side of my face, but something in my returning expression grabs his attention. He catches my hand, stopping me in place. I feel his next question pressing on, so I sigh, looking away as he closes the distance between us.

"You had another vision last night, didn't you?" he asks in a low whisper as his eyes scan down the hall. My head whips in his direction. Both his hands gently press into my shoulders, waiting for me to answer. I gnaw at my lip with knit brows, afraid if I stare too long, it might pull me right back into the nightmare. His hands run down the side of my arms. The warmth emitting from his body seeps into me.

"Come." He takes hold of my hand and leads me out toward a balcony.

We step out into the sun. My eyes fix on the ocean and the port in the distance. He stands beside me. The fresh air lifts the heaviness in my chest. The ocean is so close yet so far from reach. I glance at Callian, seeing a longing in his eyes for what lies beyond the ports toward the shimmering sea. The wind picks up, blowing a few strands of hair across my face. I tuck the strands back behind my ear.

"Have you ever been out to sea?" I ask.

"Countless times." His mouth quirks up into a half-smile as peace washes over him. He closes his eyes in a soft flutter and inhales the faint smell of the salty sea air. A feeling of contentment seems to bloom in his chest which I can only surmise comes from warm memories. If I could only feel that for just a moment, just one second. "Sometimes it feels like I have spent half my life at sea," he continues. "There has always been something calling me to the ocean. Like a siren, sending her song through every wave and every drift in the wind. When I set sail, as our ships went against the current, when the wind blew through my hair, I always felt it was the most freeing thing I could feel . . . until I met you."

He turns to look at me and threads his fingers with mine. My heart skips a beat. His eyes shine as if my presence alone grounds him, as he has done for me countless times on this unexpected journey.

"Have you ever sought adventure beyond the ocean, Princess?"

I smile shyly, looking back out to the sea, going back to a time when things felt more at peace. "I used to spend all day telling my mother where we would go and all the things we would see, the ships we would ravage, all of the gold we would steal from them as I picked up seashells and built sandcastles."

He lightly chuckles. That rumble in his chest reminds me of how safe I feel in his presence. "You were even a little flame back then, I see." The pad of his thumb caresses my hand.

I tuck a loose strand behind my ear. "This dagger means more to me than you know. It once belonged to my mother. I haven't had it in my possession for long though. It was given to me a day before my birthday." I pause. "Which . . . was the night I was taken." I clear my throat, feeling the reality setting into him as guilt follows.

I begin to tell him a bit more about my mother. A small chapter in my life where things were simple. When I had it all and my life felt complete. I don't need his sympathy or apologies for what he did. I'm here, making the best of things. He watches me as I talk through it, looking beyond the words flowing from my lips when I speak. The whole time, he never takes his eyes off me, caressing me through the memories with the stroke of his thumb. For the first time, speaking of her doesn't pull me back into the dark.

"I've never been permitted to set foot onto a boat, much less to roam the seas. I still walk down to the beach, dip my toes in the sand, and watch the waves until the sun sets. That's as close as I've ever been to living a life at sea." I shrug, unlacing our hands, and lean my elbows against the stone banister, looking back out to the ocean. He does the same, resting beside me. His body heat radiates through the fabric of his shirt as his arm brushes up against mine. "I guess since my mother died, I have been asleep for far too long and missed plenty of opportunities," I admit.

That invisible, tethered pull wraps around us. He slightly turns his head and smiles. "I would like to show you someday—what lies beyond these mountains and the seas—if that's an adventure you'd like to go on with me."

My chest tightens with his words.

"When the world doesn't seem as though it's on my shoulders, it would be a dream I wouldn't mind trying," I reply, side glancing at him with a mischievous glint. "As long as you're aware you're traveling with a future pirate who wants to raid a few ships for fun." I nudge him with my shoulder.

He laughs. "If raiding ships means I get to see more of that breathtaking smile of yours, then I'd love to watch you revel in your darkest desires, my Princess."

"That's a dark statement coming from a prince," I tease, and for a moment, it does sound like a fun adventure.

"You'd be surprised how deep I'd dive for you." A flirtatious grin tips the corners of his mouth. I blink back as something else strikes my heart, but it quickly disappears before I can understand what it was. I laugh, pushing him away.

"You are shameless, Callian." There's so much more behind his laugh as he looks at me through a hooded gaze. We both fully stand as I realize I still have to train with Crystal. "Thank you." I clasp my hands behind my back, making my way into the corridor.

He joins me at my side. "For what? Saying I would raid ships with you?" he teases, but he knows exactly what I meant. "You don't ever have to thank me, Princess."

CHAPTER 20

WE REACH THE GARDENS and find other people training in the vast, open space. Some spar with swords while others wield their magic. I'm still shocked to see the freedom this entire kingdom has when it comes to using their abilities. It is a comfort to see their king doesn't suppress them. Crystal is talking to a tall guard with broad shoulders, his back turned to us. I see he's holding something up to the sun and hear him saying something about how to use a certain herb and the effects it has when dried and crushed up into a tea. He seems quite fascinated with it, going into great detail. He made such an impression at our first meeting that I recognized that odd behavior immediately.

"Good morning," I say loud enough for them to hear.

Crystal peeks over his shoulder. "Where have you been all morning?" She steps to the side and walks over to us as her eyes bounce back and forth between Callian and me. She stops in place. "Actually, never mind, don't answer that." Her hands raise in protest. I glance up at Callian, lightly chuckling.

"Good morning to the both of you." Iván smiles, dipping his head, and gives a slight bow to Callian.

"Iván was just explaining to me a new tea I should try. He says it should knock me right out." Crystal pats him on the back hard enough that he stumbles forward a bit. For a man as tall as he is, I hold in the laugh that wants to escape.

Iván rubs the back of his neck sheepishly, smiling. "Well, it's not something I discovered personally. It's been around for quite some time, but it's a herb I've been cultivating here in one of the gardens.

It's thriving in our soil, so we don't need to have it imported anymore. We can start using it as a sleeping aid."

"That sounds like something I'd love to try myself," I say, eager for any remedy to help me sleep. "Would you like to try some with me, Callian?"

He almost falls into a laugh but catches himself when my sharp elbow jabs into his abdomen. He rests an elbow on his arm, scratching his chin. That shy smile breaks free. One I rarely see other than when I surprise him. Like when I grabbed his length while we were in the library last night. He's beautiful when he does that. The sun filtering through his dark hair, showing hints of auburn hidden within. He can feel my glare seeping into the side of his face and glances at me with heated eyes. It is evident between us, even though we are in the middle of a conversation, our minds are doing other things.

"I mean, I'm not one for tea, but—"

"Perfect!" I cut him off, looking over at Iván. "Would you mind making extra for us?"

Something in Iván's eyes shifts, the shyness melting away. "Really? Yes, of course! I would love to make you some. I'm already making a batch after my shift today. My brother, Samuel, snores like an ox, so his wife asked me to make extra to help her sleep. I'll bring it up to your room when I drop some off for Crystal."

"That sounds wonderful, I can't wait. Thank you, Iván," I say.

Crystal puts both her hands over Iván's shoulders and nudges him forward. Callian and I step to the side, letting them pass. "Okay, guys, now it's time for you two to leave. Viona and I have to get to work."

We watch Crystal hang onto Iván as they continue their flirtatious play. Her hair glints in the sunlight casting off that beautiful, lilac hue. Her eyes beam as she talks to him. She's a woman of power, but it's nice to see the softer side of her come out. It makes me wonder if they have something going on, too.

I shyly glance at Callian, smiling, realizing I haven't smiled like this in a very long time. A soft gust of wind drifts between us, swaying that rebellious strand of hair along his cheek. I reach out, tucking it behind his ear, noticing how his breaths become deeper. I catch him staring at me with a hooded gaze.

Somehow, our bodies always seem to naturally gravitate back together. With one quick swoop, he picks me up, pulling me flush against his body, and swings me in his arms. A laugh erupts from my chest as we spin in place, and my heart flutters at the swift movement. He gently sets me down, nestling his face in the crook of my neck, and lowers his voice into a seductive tone.

"I'll see you in a few hours, love."

CHAPTER 21

LOVE. MY BREATH HITCHES.

Low, seductive, the way it rolls off his lips. Something blossoms in my chest at the sound of his voice saying that word. I'm already counting down the minutes until I see Callian again. This all feels so exciting and new.

My lips curve into a smile watching him leave. I overhear him discussing where he will have Iván posted. As their voices fade out, Crystal turns around and walks over to me. Her demeanor shifts into training mode. Gravel crunches beneath her boots. Her hands clasp behind her back as she studies me, assessing my character. I challenge her stare, following her every move. There's not much of a size difference; she and I have similar statures, toned arms, and firm bodies. Except my thighs are a little thicker thanks to my love of bread and pastries. Also the fact that she's wearing her seemingly traditional, light-colored clothing in contrast to my dark attire.

Suddenly, she pulls a dagger from a sheath hidden in her waist. It cuts through the air, whizzing by me. I duck into a roll and spring back onto my feet.

Tricky bitch, she's testing my agility.

I hear the dagger land somewhere in a bush behind me. My eyes peer at her midriff. Three more remain hidden on her waist, all discreetly lined up on each side. She spins in the air, this time landing a blow with her fist connecting to my jaw. I stumble back, snarling. The taste of metal fills my mouth as heat flares beneath my skin. I grunt, moving into a stance with my left foot in front and my fists held up. My eyes narrow, and I send her a smile as blood trickles down my bottom lip.

"There you are." Her violet eyes flare. "Now it's time to play."

She pulls another dagger from her sheath and lunges forward, swinging down the blade. I grab her by the wrist with one hand as a faint glow ignites in my palm, passing heat through her. My body is reacting to the force she's using against me as the tip of her blade inches its way closer to my body. A wave of awareness rolls through me with the sudden growing ability. She smirks. Her body emits a cold chill to counteract the heat, gaining the upper hand with more force. Before I can use my other hand to grab her, she breaks free by twisting her body around and blindsides me with a jab to my stomach. I stumble back with a grunt, trying not to lean forward into another strike. Crystal turns around to face me again and sends another dagger slicing through the air, only this time it's aimed for my chest. My senses peak and my body drops down to the ground. I watch a strand of my hair float down and land beside me.

My gaze flicks to hers. That one *barely* missed.

Two daggers left.

I still haven't unsheathed mine. We continue to flow in this chaotic dance. From the corner of my eye, I notice people have started gathering to watch us from a safe distance.

She twists her torso, pivoting on her front foot, and attempts a horizontal elbow strike. I block her move by closing the distance between us with a head-butt. She stumbles back, shaking her head as blood trickles down the side of her face. She laughs, wiping it off. The tips of her fingers are coated red.

"Now we match." I grin, running my tongue along the top row of my teeth, tasting the blood.

Crystal mirrors my expression. She pummels forward, every hit as powerful as the next with unwavering strength. I block every single one. She throws another dagger, and I quickly move to the side.

One left.

My powers are thrumming beneath my skin, but for the first time, I feel a little bit of control, like a faint beam of light coursing through my veins.

"You're doing well, *princess*. Let's turn it up a notch." Her violet eyes flare as she hisses out the title she knows I despise so much.

The temperature in my body rises, and two spheres of ice form in the palm of her hands. Without warning, she releases them in my direction. I turn to dodge one, and it flies by me, shattering against a statue, but the other strikes the back of my knee, causing me to stumble onto the ground. The palms of my hands scrape against the gravel.

"Fuck," I wince in pain, feeling the burn sear into me.

As she approaches, she sends another blast of ice, relentlessly striking me all over my body. It isn't strong enough to break the skin, but it's painful enough for me to know it will leave a bruise. Every time I try hauling myself up, my arms buckle. The frigid temperature is slowing me down. Crystal is undoubtedly powerful, but as the darkness makes its way out, so am I.

Something snaps inside me. My body hums as my powers push forth. Darkness weaves in and out as it fights the power running through my veins with unmatched speed.

My heart slams relentlessly against my chest as I slip out of control. The next moments feel like a blur. It's one thing for her to use her powers around other people, but it could be deadly for me to use mine. I roll out of the way with an unexpected, fluid grace, quickly jumping to my feet. The struggle between the ebb and flow of my powers unleashes. A blast of flames shoots out from my palm, ripping through the air. She moves out of the way as everything in its path is set aflame. My knees buckle at the sudden release. I drop to the ground, breathless, the palms of my hands are scorching hot.

Immediately, Crystal's attention is snagged from me and directed toward the garden. She uses magic to stop the fire from spreading. My upper lip twitches into a snarl. I dart forward, come up from behind her, and unsheathe the last dagger from her waist.

"Looks like you ran out of daggers," I pant out, satisfied, holding the blade to her neck.

Sweat forms on the top of her brows.

"Looks like I did," she says, smiling.

I step out from behind her, placing the blade in her hand. Suddenly, the sound of clapping erupts around us. My head whips around, and I see a large crowd that seems to have tripled in size during our training. Are they clapping for me? I swallow the lump in my throat, unsure what to do with my body. My back straightens; I hold my head up high.

"What do I do?" I whisper, unaccustomed to the attention.

"I guess you know how to put on a good show." She shrugs, giving me a wink. She waves to the crowd, wearing a smile from ear to ear. "Either way, soak it up. It's making you look good, even to your enemies."

Her eyes motion over to a familiar face. The gentleman from last night who spoke of his disdain for me is now clapping. As best as he can, anyway—tapping the tips of his fingers against his wrist while his other hand holds a glass of wine. A tiny laugh bubbles out of me. It's a little too early for drinks, but it appears he doesn't think so. The crowd starts to disperse. Crystal locks her arm around mine as if we are friends. The sudden gesture shocks me at first, but I say nothing while we walk back to the garden's center.

She steps in front of me, getting into a fighting stance again. A grin spreads across her face. "Let's go for a few more rounds, but this time, no magic. I don't want to be the reason you accidentally set the entire garden on fire."

I scoff, mirroring her stance as we get back into position. "Isn't that why you're here?" A smirk dances across my face. Her eyes narrow in on me as she begins to close the distance between us.

"I'm here to train you and to teach you control, not to use the palace gardens as a playground," she says in a humorless tone—all business.

Well, damn. I blink back and nod, still grinning. "You're the boss."

Over the next few hours, we continue to train under the hot sun. We use a plethora of weapons from daggers to swords. She teaches me how to have better control when the enemy is trying to get inside my head. Something I know I'll have to work on to keep my shit together. By the time we're finished, we are drenched in sweat.

"Can't you just use your powers to cool us off?" It sounds like I'm begging, feeling the sun's heat scorching into my skin.

She tilts her head back and laughs. "I *could,* but wouldn't that be wasteful?"

From the corner of my eye, I see two men setting up a table with food. Finally, my saving grace.

Crystal takes one good look at me. "You got lucky. It's time to eat."

I wipe the sheen of sweat off my cheek. She pats my back as we approach a table full of food. Thankfully, it's set up under a thick tarp.

"Thank you gentlemen, we are quite famished," she says to the men.

One lifts his head. His bright, golden eyes warm when he sees her. "Lady Mira, I know how much you love your bacon, so I made sure there was extra for you and your lovely guest."

Crystal sighs in wonder at the array of foods and says, "This is quite a sight, thank you again."

"Yes, thank you," I reply, wearing the same wide-eyed expression.

"You're welcome. Enjoy, ladies." He dips his head before they take their leave.

My stomach rumbles at the sight of all the delicacies spread out. I fill my plate with bacon, eggs, two muffins, and a fresh bowl of fruit. Crystal stacks on just as much food as I have.

"You did well today, but that doesn't surprise me. I knew you were skilled the moment I laid eyes on you. To find out you are also at the top of your ranks in Sao is impressive. Doesn't surprise me you gave Callian such a hard time on your way here." She spears a piece of egg onto the fork and plays with it, dabbing the corner into a greasy spot on a slice of bacon.

I scoff under my breath at the memories and toss a piece of strawberry in my mouth. I can't help the pride beaming off me at her praise.

"Callian filled me in before he entered your room the night you arrived," she says with a mischievous grin on her face. Her mind appears to be whirling with questions as I meet her stare and clear my throat. I don't think she realizes how penetrating her eyes are.

"It's been *interesting*, to say the least," I admit as I begin breaking my bacon into smaller pieces with my fork. "Some days, I feel like I haven't had time to process anything. It's been . . . *different* having him around, even though he sometimes infuriates me."

She reaches across the table and squeezes my wrist. "You have to give yourself more credit, Viona. I don't know your whole story, but you have adapted well to your surroundings."

She smiles.

The sincerity in such a small gesture warms my heart. "So far, whenever someone has shown their animosity toward you, you have not yielded. You seem to be indomitable. It's quite inspiring. Callian is just the icing on the cake. Enjoy it." She winks before packing more eggs onto her fork and then shoving them into her mouth.

I faintly smile at the thought that she could be right. I am still here. Even though I was taken, it was *my choice* to come willingly. I've taken chances not many would take.

"I can see why Callian is infatuated with you. I haven't seen him this happy in quite some time." Crystal's expression changes slightly, and I'd have missed it if I hadn't glanced at her in that split second.

My mind goes to thoughts of him having other women before me. He is handsome, after all. Seemingly overly experienced in the way he touches me. Should I be jealous? The expression she quickly masked stopped my thoughts from going any further. Maybe he experienced loss, but haven't we all?

I give a tight smile. "Your encouragement is appreciated. If I can learn more from the Seer and harness my powers, then I'm sure I can be as great as you someday." I hold my cup out, keeping the conversation light and airy.

"I have no doubt you will." She clinks her cup with mine.

We continue to eat in comfortable silence. Crystal needs no powers. Clearly, she isn't just a woman with a sharp tongue and bold personality. She's a warrior like me, but with far more control than I feel I will ever grasp. My admiration for her continues to grow.

She bites into her apple, ignoring the trickle of blood on the side of her lip. I wince in pain, trying to take a big bite of my muffin. We're a mess, falling into a steady flow of conversation as we fill our bellies to the brim. She briefly talks about how she has been spending more time with Iván. They both have a thing for herbs and their healing abilities, something they have been bonding over as of late. She mentions how they go beyond the fortified walls together in search of new herbs. He brings his bow and arrow into the fields and does archery, and she is learning how to curate archery into her magic. As curious as I am, I keep all the prying questions to myself and let the smile on her face fill in the gaps, which is good enough for me.

Crystal looks over my shoulder. "Oh, good! The healer is here."

"Healer? Is that all I am to you?" Sydney pulls up a chair beside me. Its cast-iron feet scrape against the gravel. Sydney's scent fills the air, a sweet aroma of bergamot.

Healer? My eyes perk up when she looks at me.

"How many healers are in the palace of Callisto?" They're rare back home . . . unless my father kept them hidden, too.

"Apparently, not enough since I'm here right now." She sighs full of mirth, facing the chair in my direction. I snicker under my breath as she turns my head from side to side to assess the damage. "You both look rather disastrous."

I glance over to Crystal, who's now raising a brow and trying not to scoff as she drinks her coffee.

"Face me, Viona. This will only take a moment." Sydney presses the tips of her fingers against my lip. At first, I wince in pain, but then I feel a soft surge of energy vibrating beneath her touch. It slowly weaves in and out of the wound, healing it. Within seconds, the pain is gone. I rub my fingers over the area, feeling the dry blood flake between my fingertips.

"Incredible," I whisper. My mind reels back to Callian healing himself after I stabbed him in the White Forest. I didn't see how he did it, but I wonder if he used the same methods.

"She is, isn't she?" Crystal beams with pride, and Sydney slides her chair over to her. Crystal sets her coffee down and turns in her seat to face Sydney but keeps talking to me. "I've assessed your abilities through your fighting skills. It seems you have control of your powers only when you don't feel threatened, which is a double-edged sword because you're always on the defensive. Easily unhinged." I cross my arms over my chest with a brow arched in protest, but she continues. "Luckily, I could easily read when you were losing control." She keeps her eyes looking straight ahead. Within seconds, the side of her face is healed.

Sydney pulls a piece of cloth out of a small pocket of her dress and pours water onto it. She rings it out, wiping the blood off Crystal's face. I study the woman who was just throwing daggers and spheres of ice at me, only now, she reminds me of a young girl being tended to by a motherly figure. With Sydney's looks, she could easily pass for a young mother, being blessed with aging like the gods. It tugs on my heart, and my chest tightens. The haunting melancholy of my past sneaks up on me. The only sound I can hear is my mother's faint voice in the back of my mind. I feel the tears swelling, so I look away and take a big gulp of water.

"Good afternoon, ladies." A tall male in his mid-thirties approaches us. The pale-blue suit he wears matches his eyes. I'd consider him handsome if it weren't for the grin planted on his face.

We give him a tight nod. Sydney, of course, gives him dagger eyes, saying nothing while she continues her work. Her glare puts him on guard, but he quickly recovers.

"I'd like to formally introduce myself to our new guest here." His eyes sweep over me as he takes a few steps closer. His hand extends to mine, lifting it from the table.

"I'm Vincent de Vaunt." He places a kiss on the top of my hand. "It's a pleasure to meet a woman with . . . such an extraordinary amount of talent." My skin crawls at the way his eyes rake me over. I try to imagine what they would look like on a stick.

I slide a glance over to Crystal. She lifts her brows, the only response she gives.

I guess I'm on my own. Behind her poised facade, she's too busy trying to hold in a laugh that I know very damn well wants to escape.

So much for my savior.

An uncomfortable grin spreads across his face after I catch him glimpsing at my chest while my head was turned. I'd love to jab a fork into his eye socket. Tension hangs in the air as I glare at him. Suddenly, boots are crunching against the gravel—wide, long steps coming toward us. My stomach takes a dip.

Callian abruptly pulls a chair out from the table. He doesn't look away from Vincent as he sits beside me. He casually leans back, staring Vincent down with a glare that clearly makes him uneasy. A look like that would incinerate him where he stands if Callian could wield fire.

Suddenly, my chair grates against the ground. The metal sound is jarring, but the sudden yank makes the apex between my thighs heat as

Callian pulls me next to him. The tension is palpable. Vincent's smile wanes.

Callian puts one arm around me and picks up a strawberry with the other. The way his luscious lips wrap around the fruit is purely wicked. He takes a bite, and the end pops back out of his mouth with a sinful, wet sound.

"Mmm, so sweet." He groans out each word. The predatory sound rumbles in his chest, staking claim as his arm tightens around my shoulders. It is apparent he is becoming territorial. I grin, my eyes narrowing in on Vincent, watching him swallow the lump in his throat.

"My prince . . . " Vincent bows. He's being eaten alive under the prince's scrutiny.

Crystal is now living and breathing in this moment, happily watching it all unfold before her. Sydney rolls her eyes, unamused at the situation unfolding. Callian lifts his chin, holding a darkening gaze, watching this poor man weaken in his presence.

"Vincent," he icily responds.

"If you'll excuse me. Good day." Vincent retreats, leaving in a haste like a dog with a tail between its legs.

"That was unexpected." I sigh, tucking a loose strand of hair behind my ear. Callian's arm remains around my shoulders. Butterflies flutter in my stomach.

"That was sickening," Sydney counters. "I don't ever want to eat another strawberry again."

Crystal bursts into laughter, but Callian stares at me long and hard as the world around us fades. There's something feral behind those flaring eyes. He gently brushes his knuckles against my cheek, cupping my face.

"You should wash that man's lips off your hand before I go insane."

"I agree," Sydney chimes in. I catch her gaze. "He may be handsome, but he's a sleazy bastard. You can't fault the man, though. I mean, look at you."

I scoff, "I'm no one." I try brushing her words off by straightening my shoulders. I'm not used to getting so many compliments or so much attention.

"You think he's handsome? I'm wounded," Callian cuts in, teasing Sydney. He stands up and pushes his chair back in. I take that as a sign that it's our time to go, so I do the same. He gently places his hands over Sydney's shoulders and gives her a kiss on the cheek. She's stubborn, but she gives in. I can see the love in her eyes like a mother for a son.

"I'll catch up with you guys tonight after Iván brings me the tea," Crystal reminds me as we take our leave.

I take a deep breath, mentally preparing myself to meet the Seer. I'd at least like to make myself look presentable before hearing the truth of my fate.

CHAPTER 22

THERE'S A COMFORTABLE SILENCE between us as we walk back to my room. A sudden breeze whisks around my face, all the while feeling Callian's stare as a reminder of his feelings for me. The sound of our boots echoes off the walls. His strides are so long, it takes me almost two steps to match his.

In the silence, my mind drifts back to my session with Crystal. I've always felt my abilities would be a curse, but now, I revel in the small amount of control I had over it, which is an inkling of victory.

"I saw how you handled yourself today while training with Crystal." He beams, as if reading my thoughts.

"So you were spying on me, huh?" I glance up, smirking.

He laughs with a broad smile, one he rarely displays around others, and it plucks against the tethered pull we seem to have. Those white teeth sparkle in the brief sunlight. I playfully nudge his arm with my shoulder.

"To watch a beautiful woman bloom, bend her body in ways that would make the heavens shake. How can one not watch with awe? You're very skilled."

I chew on my lower lip, holding back a smile that wants to stretch from ear to ear.

"Tell me something I don't already know, *prince*." There is a teasing edge in my voice, and my chin lifts as we continue down the long hall.

"Something you don't already know? Hmm . . . " He playfully brings his hand up to rub his chin. A few loose strands of hair bounce around his face with every step as he stares straight ahead. Suddenly, he stops walking and gently grabs me by both my wrists. He pulls me into a small, dark hallway with no lanterns to light the way to the other side. He presses me up against the wall. The sudden force leaves me breathless. His rough hands move up my body, and a deep moan rumbles in his chest. "I didn't like how that prick was staring at you."

He takes the hand Vincent kissed, pinning it above my head. My heart instantly dives into the pit of my stomach, seeing that primal rage come to life. I look at him through a hooded gaze as his other hand glides down to my hip. I suck in a sharp breath as my body responds to how he caresses me with his thumb. It gently slips between the fabric of my trousers.

"I—I already knew that," I manage to stammer.

"Do you wish to know more?" he purrs, breathing into the shell of my ear as if he can't contain his need to touch me. Every single word is laced with something sinister.

"Yes," I plead, and it's almost shameful to hear how easily I melt beneath his touch.

"I wanted to cut his fucking lips off his face for kissing your hand," he says into the side of my neck. "And when I saw him leering at your chest, I wanted to rip his eyes out, too. He's lucky I let him walk away, but I can't promise what I'll do the next time something like that happens."

My breathing stills. Callian's words are the sexiest and most danger-ous combination.

"That's funny," I pant out, "because I thought the same thing."

He grins with satisfaction.

"Why didn't you?" I whisper, almost in a challenge.

I see his mind whirling, and I know I am playing a dangerous game. He smiles, and something dark glints behind those eyes. I bring my leg up, wrapping it around him, chasing it, feeding off the source that would make him lose his mind for anyone who lays eyes on me. I like it. He runs his hand along the length of my thigh and, in a fluid motion, lifts me off the ground with one arm. My legs straddle his body while he stills my hand and pins me against the wall.

"That's not something a *prince* would do." He groans, a faint mock-ery in his title. It seems as though both of us hate using the term. If my hands were free, I would cup the side of his face and soothe him, but all I have are my lips.

"You can be whatever you want with me, Callian," I whisper.

He exhales in response.

We hear a clamor of armor and heavy footsteps walking down the hall. We share a look, and our breathing stills as the sounds draw near. His smile eases my nerves. I bite the inside of my cheek, trying to halt the laugh that wanted to escape. One voice grows louder, and in that moment, all the playfulness in Callian's face drains. His features pull taut, and he shakes his head, telling me not to make a sound.

King Valor walks past us with guards flanking his side.

"Yes, Your Majesty, I'll be sure to let him know as soon as I find him."

"Good. In the meantime, I will await word from the Seer as soon as he's done meeting with Viona Tarvas." King Valor's voice makes me shudder, but at least he has enough respect to refer to me correctly even in my absence. Their footsteps fade off down the hall.

That's right, the Seer. Shit. As soon as their footsteps fade completely, I unhook my legs and slide down Callian's body.

"Fuck," he grunts, leaning into the crook of my neck. He lets go of my wrists and takes a step back. "You will be the end of me, Princess." I can feel his smile against my flesh as he reaches inside the front of his trousers, adjusting what I assume is his length. He peeks out from the darkened hallway, making sure no one else is coming. He nods his head and extends his hand for me to follow.

We resume our silent walk to my chambers, deep in thought. As I look down the corridor, my eyes are fixed on the statues of gods, etched into every part of this palace. There's so much pressure and responsibility within these walls. I understand why Callian doesn't want the title of a prince, but he is destined to rule, regardless of what he wants. I've seen the glint in his eyes. It is a look that tells me he will eventually do what his father asks of him. Not because of the honor but because of the love they share, the respect, the lineage.

I realize I have finally forgiven Callian for not telling me who he was. I share the struggle in my home kingdom, but at least he is seen. His father speaks to him, sees him, considers his opinions, even searches for him, which is something my father has never done until now. Callian waits outside as I hurry into my chambers, quickly running a wet cloth over my face and arms. This time, I pin my hair back, or at least attempt to with the few pins left for me in my room. I rush back out, and we make our way to the Seer.

I notice we begin taking the path that leads to the library. As we approach those thick, heavy doors, we turn right down another long hallway. At the end is a beautiful, cast-iron staircase spiraling up a small tower. I place my hand on the railing. A vibration hums beneath my skin, startling me. The same tangible energy fills the air.

"Do you hear that?" I ask, glancing at Callian. He hovers his hand over the pommel of his sword. I place my hand over his. "No, it's different," I assure him. "There's a faint hum in the air."

Relief sweeps over him, and he looks up, putting it all together. "You must be feeling the Seer." His eyes study me.

After way too many stairs, we finally come to a stop. As we stand outside the door, I can smell fragrances and oils drifting out from under the doorframe.

"Come in," a male's voice beckons. He has an accent I can't place. Then again, how could I know anything when I've spent my entire life in the same kingdom?

Callian opens the door for me, and I walk under his arm into a small space with countless shelves filled with old books and relics. There are a few tables with papers scattered about and scrolls tucked away in every corner. More shelves line the walls, reaching the ceiling with various jars of dried flowers and other things that seem rather questionable. I don't let my eyes linger for long out of fear of insulting him.

"Please, take a seat, Viona." The man sits on a cushion next to a large slab of stone and motions to the other across from him.

Callian tries to find a space among the clutter to lean against the wall. I look back over to the man. His eyes are glowing like amber. Long, blond hair drapes over his chest in wavy locks with strands that seem to be touched by white moonlight. He looks to be in his early thirties, but his soul feels much older. His pale-blue robe hangs open, putting his lean muscles on full display. His nails are long, pointed at the tips, somehow beaming like the moon's luminescence. His left hand is adorned with rings. Blue markings cover his smooth, brown skin, starting at his hands and continuing up his arms in swirls, reminding me of wind from a painting. I notice they extend up the sides of his neck to his chiseled jawline.

A lump forms in the back of my throat, unable to find the words to speak as I stare at this man whose beauty not only allures me, but whose power emitting off of him frightens me—ancient in the way his body hums with ethereal magic. The sensation overwhelms me, like a pressure building in my chest, yet I can't seem to look away. I've never felt this from anyone before. I'm staring at a man who holds so much wisdom. He stares back from across the slab of stone, wearing a grin as those eyes narrow in on me with curiosity. I wonder how much he can see by just my presence alone. I clear my throat before taking a seat on the cushion.

"I am Gareon Samial," he says with a smooth voice, then curtly nods. "You, my dear, shouldn't fear me. There are far greater things at play."

How can he—

"I don't have to read your mind. I could feel your fear and hesitation when you placed your hand upon the railing of my stairs. It only grew as you drew nearer. It is a weakness that will get you killed by any other person who possesses as much power as we do."

"We?" I ask. "What do you mean?"

"I can confirm my suspicions with a drop of your blood," he says coyly, holding out his hand.

His moonlight fingernails look sharp enough to penetrate flesh. Even though I don't want to, I lean across the stone slab and extend mine. He wraps his large hand gently around my wrist. His skin feels soft and cold to the touch. My eyes widen, feeling a chill sweep up my arm and down my body, taken aback by how close he is to me. As I admire his beauty, a half-smile curves his lips as if my thoughts are playing across his mind.

Shit, Viona. Stop thinking.

He brings his other hand up and hovers it above mine. A soft, white light begins to glow between his pointer finger and thumb. A needle weaves to life before my eyes. When it's fully formed, it shifts position. With a gentle push from his fingers, it drifts closer. The motion startles me at first, seeing its sharp, pointed tip glinting by an unknown light source only a few centimeters from the end of my finger.

"This will only sting for a moment," he assures me.

I glance at Callian who is watching us with curious eyes. He gives me a tight smile and dips his chin. I look back at the Seer. As soon as I nod, the needle pierces into my skin. Fire and ice shoot up to my arm, but the feeling quickly passes. Blood drips down onto the stone slab between us. He pulls out a small jar of soil from his pocket and begins to shake it out little by little, letting the dirt and blood mix together. On contact, the two begin to emit a red glow.

"Why soil?" I ask.

He looks at me intently as if I interrupted his train of thought. "This isn't just any soil, Viona. This is from the grounds of which you were born." He pulls out another vial and uses his thumb to flick the cork off. "*This* is from the waters that surround your 'prison.'" He lets it drip out until magic expels in a plume of glimmering light, all the while keeping his eyes fixed on me. My brows knit together at his choice of words. "That's what you call your home, is it not? A prison?"

"I suppose," I reply, not trying to pick a fight with this man.

"I just need you to blow gently onto the three elements as the final ingredient for wind," he commands.

I swallow, pursing my lips together, and blow softly. Suddenly, the ground shakes, and the wind speeds around us, spinning in one direction. My hair whips around my face. Callian disappears from sight as a blue-and-white sphere forms around us. My eyes dart over to Gareon whose amber eyes have turned ice blue, and all the swirls on his body begin to glow.

I'm not afraid. Somehow, a calmness washes over me as our bodies enter a space hidden between a veil. I'm weightless with a being who holds so much power. I feel it coursing through my body as we begin to levitate.

"This is where you learn the truth. This is where your journey begins." His lips remain sealed, his voice merely an echo surrounding me. He's everywhere all at once. *"You must listen, Viona. We only have a few moments."*

The wind picks up speed, spinning around us. He extends his hands, willing my body to drift toward his. The elements he used get sucked into the sphere and become one with the controlled chaos. Lightning crackles in the air, distorting the space, chipping away into something else.

"What's happening?" I speak, but no sound comes out. My hands clasp over my mouth as panic rises to the surface.

"The fact that you can communicate with me like this tells me a great deal about you," he infers in a tone so soothing, it settles my nerves.

The moment he takes hold of my hand, the wind stops. We become the eye of a storm, landing in a place I've seen before. My eyes widen, realizing he is walking with me through one of my visions.

Ash and bones cover the ground.

"The world is burning," he says, but we cannot feel the heat. My feet barely make a sound as I try to step out. He pulls me back, shooting me a look of warning. The side of my body goes flush against his. *"Careful. If you wander too far, you will be lost, and I cannot protect you once you leave my grip."*

I nod. *"I've seen this before."* My eyes scan the land. The smell of death is potent in the air. All the trees have been set ablaze with flames rising high. When they fall, a plume of embers scorch the sky. *"Is this the end?"* I ask.

"This is only the beginning, but you are looking with the wrong set of eyes." His words keep weaving into a riddle.

"What do you mean?" This seems to be the catastrophic effect of my powers. How could it be anything else?

"Look closer." He points to a figure shadowed by flames. I can't make out the silhouette. *"You've dreamt it. You've heard it calling out to you. You've tasted darkness with every vision. I'm sure you want to know why."*

I don't have to answer. Gareon can see the desperation in my eyes. Suddenly, the wind shifts, and the figure starts to take shape. It's me, but there's someone else standing directly behind me, almost like they're *hiding*. A steam-filled fissure splits the ground as if the world has been split in two. Flames rise between the crack and scorch the sky. The ground is shaking. There's so much ash and ember raining down, all I can see are two shadows in a plume of smoke. There's so much haze, I lose sight.

"It is not only your *powers calling out to you, Viona. Your powers are shared with someone else."*

"Someone else? Who?" That's impossible.

The veil starts to falter. Gareon grits his teeth as he struggles to maintain our safety within the sphere. Between the fraying lines of this inferno, an ocean appears, trying to take over. Back and forth it flashes between an unwanted war and a raging sea; two visions are trying to collide.

"Get behind me and hold on!" he calls out, shoving me with one swift motion behind him.

The wind pushes us back a foot. My arms wrap around his waist as tightly as they can. Blue-and-white light emits from the palm of his hands as he tries to seal the cracks. The blunt force pushes us back another foot. The sphere turns into a gravitational pull. We are about to be swept up. With all my strength, I plant my feet on the ground and push against his body, trying to stop us from moving. But I'm losing my grip. Suddenly, I hear a low, heavy drum, beating slowly and arduously. I'm drowning in its melody. I look under his arm to see a faint crimson glow beating my heart's rhythm. The same vision I saw in the forest with Callian. It sings to me as it floats idly beneath the waves. My eyes flutter to the back of my head. My grip loosens from his waist. I'm slipping.

"Viona!" Gareon's voice is a faint sound as my body calls for serenity. He shouts my name repeatedly.

It isn't until I hear Callian's voice thundering from beyond that my trance is broken. I suck in a sharp breath, regaining consciousness. Gareon gains control and closes us off. We are back in the safety of the sphere. He quickly turns around, brows furrowed as he looks me over.

"Are you alright?"

"Yes, I think so," I say, rubbing my temples. *"What the fuck was that?"* He looks down at me, still not convinced by the way his icy-blue eyes remain flaring while he looks me over again. *"I said I'm fine."*

When he finally believes me, his eyes return to deep, dark honey. I'm led back to the cushion, still within the swirling sphere, and he retakes his seat across the slab of stone.

"Your blood runs deeper than I thought. We saw something not of this world cloaked behind your powers, yet it was somehow a part of you." His eyes narrow in on me. *"It grows stronger by the day, just like the fondness you share with your newfound lover."*

Callian. I look over at him, pacing back and forth outside the sphere. As soon as he sees I'm okay, he leans against the wall, but the look on his face tells me he won't be until I'm in his arms.

"He's not my lover, trust me."

Gareon scoffs loudly with a smile so wide, it exposes his pointed canines I didn't notice he had.

"Funny, I'd say otherwise with the energy emitting off the both of you. He is your destiny, just as much as you could be his demise."

"Demise?" My stomach takes a dip.

"What do you mean by that?" I demand, sucking in a sharp breath as if I need air, feeling the nerves gnaw at my insides. A foreboding look stretches across his face. The images of Callian from my vision start to flash before my eyes.

"Stop. Don't say anything else. I don't want to hear it." I stand, trying to find a way out. *"Get me out of this . . . this fucking space!"* I yell in my head.

Gareon approaches me, but I use all my force to push him back. It does nothing to his tall form. He grabs hold of both my wrists. His nostrils flare as I struggle in his grip. Those deep-honey eyes look at me in warning not to test him. Callian pushes back off the wall and approaches the sphere, but he can only watch. Anger storms in his eyes. He looks menacing, like he will rip Gareon to shreds once this sphere falls.

"I am not the enemy, Viona. You chose to come here for the truth, and here it is. Sometimes, truth feels like a slap in the face or a dagger to the heart. This is life, and it isn't always pretty. You, of all people, should know that. If you care for him, you need to gain control of yourself. Find the source of your powers within you, and take control. There are people here who will help you, not destroy you."

His words burn into me like acid rain. My fists clench together. I'm filled with rage as the reality becomes palpable.

He continues, *"Look at the way he hovers, the way he looks at me maliciously, all because I gave you the slightest discomfort."*

Callian stalks in place with a deadly look piercing into Gareon, who seems unfazed by the threat as his mouth curves into a grin.

"There is a gravitational pull bringing you two together. Callian is territorial, protective, and just seeing another man's hands on you in any way drives him insane. Watch." Gareon still has me in a gentle grip. He caresses my wrists with the pad of his thumbs in a soft motion while looking over to Callian. Callian walks up to the sphere, the wind starting to blow his hair back as he's inches away from trying to enter. *"If he tries to enter, he will be blown back against the wall so hard, his skull would crack open. His healing powers would do nothing for a split-open head. He knows this, and yet he stands along the edge for you."*

Gareon's words bring so much truth. Callian's eyes darken as he glares at this ethereal being. Gareon is playing a dangerous game with a man who would do anything for me.

"Your prince is so easily unhinged. He is your light as easily as you are his dark."

It pains me to see Callian so crazed. I unclench my fists. Gareon releases me.

"Now I'm going to break the sphere. It would be best to tell your . . . prince to restrain himself so we can resume."

With a wave of his hands, the sphere disappears. Callian's anger fizzles. He rushes to my side, pulling me in against his body, and cradles my head against his chest.

"Are you alright?" His voice softens as he cups my face, but he releases me and strides over to Gareon before I can answer. Tension chokes the air as the two stand face to face. "What the fuck did you do to her Gareon!" He seethes, commanding an answer as he meets Gareon at eye level. Callian's chest rises and falls rapidly as his rage tips over the surface. His power fills the air.

"Step aside, Callian. We have no quarrel," Gareon responds, relaxed and unaffected.

"Like fuck we don't. What did you say to her?" Callian says, baring his teeth.

"As you know, what a Seer shares with another is sacred," Gareon replies, his lips curve into a grin. They share a look I can't discern. "If she wishes to share it with you, she will. If she doesn't, then that's her decision." Callian pauses, letting the words set in. "Let me remind you, *soldier*, I do not serve your king nor do I belong to this kingdom. Any foreseeing I do is for the good of *everyone*. Not just royalty."

I nudge myself between the two angry, towering men, pushing them apart at arm's length. "Alright, stop it! Callian, I'm fine. Please let us finish."

With a heavy breath, Callian sighs, giving a tight nod before stepping away. Gareon and I sit back down. A small ball of light forms in the palm of his hands.

"This one represents one part of your powers. It is tamed, controlled, and strategically powerful." He holds out his other as a dark shadow forms. "This represents the darkness within you. See how much larger it is when compared to the other?" My eyes bounce back and forth, noting the stark contrast. "Look deeper into the shadow, Viona. Do you see anything?" I tilt my head to the side and squint my eyes, zeroing in on the dark orb as it swirls unyieldingly. Flames dance within each orb, but it is harder to see it inside the one cloaked in dark shadow.

"I see fire, but it almost looks . . . confined." My brows knit, studying its movements. The flames shift side to side, then up and down. There are moments when the flames swell so high, begging for a release. Gareon watches me as I soak in the knowledge.

"Exactly. We need to find out why. I feel some of what we just witnessed has to do with your lineage." I can sense the hesitation before he even speaks. He's being meticulous with his words. "It seems one of your parents could be immortal."

My gut squeezes tight at the mention of my parents. My eyes sting as tears threaten to break free. "My mother is dea—" I struggle to force out the words. The memories of my mother are kept hidden in a thick cloud of haze. Any mention of her is a rift in the tide. I swallow the lump in my throat. "If your words are true, it must be my father. I am nothing like him. And I am mortal, last I checked," I state, crossing my arms over my chest.

Gareon's stare sears into the side of my face. "Don't be so quick to assume. I believe it would be beneficial for you to access the prophecy and see what you can find on your lineage. Sometimes, immortality can skip generations, depending on which genes are stronger. In the meantime, I'll be returning home to do some research within my own personal collection. What I possess would never be found in the archives of any royal family. It would be best if you remained here. Continue to train and educate yourself on the scrolls in the palace." His eyes bounce to Callian. "I assume you will ensure she has everything she needs." Gareon lifts a darkened brow at him. "I'll return in a few weeks. I have faith you'll be much stronger by then. The more control you have, the better the chance you won't lose yourself to your powers. What we have here has been written in prophecy. We need to have all of our cards lined up and figure out how deep your bloodline runs to understand what this truly means for us."

Within the blink of an eye, the orbs disappear in shards of mangled light. All that's left are little speckles soaking into the ground.

Gareon leans back, reaching for his tea. His pointed nails chime against the cup as he loops his fingers through the handle. He eyes me from the brim, his full lips pressed against it as he takes a long sip. While the two of us remain silently staring at one another, my reality sinks in, and it's beginning to drown me.

"Thank you for your time, Gareon, and for your protection." I nod, rising to take my leave. His eyes warm as he mirrors my move. He strides over to us, using his powers to open the door. Callian walks out first.

"*Viona.*" Gareon's voice echoes around me. I turn to look at him, shocked he can still communicate with me telepathically outside the sphere. "*Do not let comfort blind you. Do not let safety soften you. Keep your guard up, and stay by his side regardless. I'll keep our connection open. If you ever need me, say my name. I will hear you.*"

I smile the best I can.

CHAPTER 23

I T'S BEEN A FEW days since my reading with Gareon, and I've finally mustered up the courage to do the research. The thick, wooden doors to the library swing open with force, stirring its occupants, and about a dozen eyes look up at me. Some have stopped pulling books midway off a shelf. My mind flashes to the last time I was here. It was in the middle of the night. Only the two of us, half-naked and basking in the moonlight. As memorable as it was for me, it would be just another untold story for these books to hold. Callian's footsteps pull me from thought when he catches up. I remain unscathed by the dirty looks some were giving me.

A woman stands in the center of the room with short, black hair fanning around her shoulders. Her head whips in my direction. She wears dark-brown trousers and a light-beige tunic under matching stays that flawlessly outlines her curvy hips. The look on her face is almost as devastating as her beauty as she continues to glare at me with irritation. Her book snaps shut. The small pouch tied at her hip bounces with every step as she strides toward me. I am about to move forward, but she stands in my way with a hand on her hip, the book in the other.

"Excuse me," she says, glaring at me with eyes dark as night. "You can't just walk in here like this, disturbing other people. We have rules set in place while in the library. If you can't respect them, then you must leave."

The tension fills the room. I realize she is the librarian, and by the looks of it, she'd go to great lengths to ensure peace within these walls, despite who stands behind me. I've not spent much time in libraries, but I know it's her duty to protect the contents of this room. I also realize I've been foolish. I have to remember I am a guest. People are watching.

I clear my throat and take a step back. "My apologies."

"Good." Her voice lifts. She brings the book back up to her chest. "Now, how may I help you?"

Callian steps forward, his body slightly pressed against my back, making my heart flutter. He speaks in a low tone. "I apologize for the disruption, Seveena, but we're here to access the archives." Her eyes widen as she takes another long look at me.

"The library is closed for the day. I need everyone to leave!" Her voice echoes throughout the vast space.

Low chatter fills the room. Chairs scrape across the floor, and people start gathering their belongings. We stand silently for the next few minutes. Once the last person leaves, Seveena clears her throat.

"My prince, I do not mean to be so forward, but it is forbidden for anyone *not* from the royal family to enter the Alora Archives." Hesitation fills her voice.

Forbidden? My brow lifts. Now, I'm curious.

"I can assure you, if the king disagrees, he can take it up with me. You will not be at fault," he confirms.

Seveena pulls a tight smile and lifts her chin. "Alright, follow me," her words snip. The small pouch tied to her hip swings around as she walks ahead. Our boots fill the silence while we follow through the ample space.

I see the chaise by the windows from the corner of my eye. Callian's hand presses against my lower back, and he leans down to the shell of my ear. "I loved the way your body glowed in the moonlight," he whispers, his velvety tone sending a wave of energy down my body. I nudge him hard enough for him to grunt. I glance at Seveena, hoping to the stars she didn't hear him.

We approach two large doors in the shape of an arch. Seveena uses her powers to swing them open with just as much sass as she does to close them. We walk through another section of the library. This room has a loft with small nooks, and straight ahead are more desks and working areas. We reach the end of the room, stopping in front of a wall of books that expands the entire length from floor to ceiling.

Two ladders with wheels rest on the wall on each side. Seveena sets her book down on a nearby table. My brows knit as she stands facing this wall. Her hands move in a circular motion, and the air buzzes with an energy that makes the hair on the back of my neck rise. She begins weaving magic in the palm of her hands. A steel-blue light forms.

My eyes widen, watching the light seep into the wall of books. Two metal doors replace its shape with Callisto's royal crest adorning the center.

Seveena steps aside, smiling, even though the kindness doesn't reach her eyes when they rake over me.

"How long do you need?" she asks, walking back over to the table to retrieve her book.

"Give us a few hours, Seveena." With a wave of Callian's hand, the doors part open. He looks at me, gesturing to go first.

I step through the metal doors into a space carved into the side of a mountain. There are a few large bookshelves on each side of the room. Two chairs are pushed under a small desk. Tall windows curve with the shape of the mountain. I gravitate toward the windows, and my heart drops watching the waves crash against the cliff edge down below. My vision slightly blurs while I hear him thanking her in the background. I rub my temples, trying to smooth out the tension behind my eyes. I don't see the shores of Callisto or its welcoming docks. Instead, a vast ocean stretches for miles.

"It's beautiful, isn't it?" he asks, placing a hand on my shoulder.

I turn around, noticing our entrance has disappeared. Nothing but jagged, rough stone left in its place. *Have we been locked inside this fucking tomb made of rock?*

"No, it's wickedly devastating," I scoff, pivoting from his reach. Confusion contorts his face. "Where are we, Callian? Tell me we aren't hidden on the side of the mountain in the middle of fucking nowhere." My unease quickly latches on, growing roots. My arms fold across my chest as my hip shifts to one side. "We aren't in the palace anymore, are we?" My eyes skim over all the scrolls, books, and other parchment papers lying around, taking in the confinement of this space.

"No, we aren't." He sighs, leaning against the table with his hands resting on its ledge.

Great.

"Every kingdom has a secret place where they keep their scrolls, books . . . items not always meant for public viewing. Our power connects us to this place, and the magic keeps it concealed. Only the kings, their royal families, and trusted royal court members know where they are," he confirms.

The wheels in my head start turning. My father must have a place like this. I am of his blood, yet he never shared its location.

"Right." I walk away, only half listening as he continues. My fingertips press into the divots, cracks, and any little crevices I can slip them into, hoping to find a hidden lever, anything to make the doors reappear. His voice fades into the back of my mind as I concentrate.

"I think someone has a bit of claustrophobia," he teases.

I press my ear against the wall, hoping to hear life beyond it. Maybe even a simple sound of a crisp page turning as Seveena reads her book. Anything. But I hear nothing. Only the growing sound of the waves as they crash up against the side of the cliffs from below. I sigh, pushing myself off the rock, and dart my eyes over to Callian. He saunters over to me, trying to pull me away from the wall, but I wave him off. He laughs once more with amusement beaming off his face. I grab him by the tunic.

"Tell me you can open the door," I hiss, eyes flaring with anger. "I couldn't give two fucks about the contents in this room. I will light it on fire and burn everything inside of it." My words are empty. He knows it. I need this place and the secrets it holds. Besides, I have no clue how to summon my power.

His eyes grow dark.

"You're very tempting, little flame, but we don't have time for this. After we are done here, we have the rest of the night to play," he says in a sultry growl. Though his patience is fading, and his eyes give warning not to challenge him.

"Don't tempt me with a good time, *prince.*" I seethe.

For the next hour, we don't speak. The rustling of papers fills the silence. I was supposed to hate him. This man took me from my home against my will, but the desire for him runs hotter than the flames flickering beneath my skin. Now, he stands barely ten feet apart from me, taking my burdens as his own. The intensity in his eyes burns through the pages as he flips through each one—eager to help me find clarity. I watch him over the brim of my coffee cup. The light shining into the windows is growing dim.

Seveena is kind enough to bring us coffee and a few sugared pastries without being requested. It's past evening, so we're surprised to see her still outside the doors. Callian reminds her she doesn't need to wait around for us, but she asserts she will finish her work at the front desk and then head off.

Most of these books seem useless to my situation. Maybe I'm looking in the wrong place. I move to the next shelf. Finally, one sticks out. *Whisper of Immoral Sins*. It is bound in white vellum with a decorative, red application to the spine. I flip through the book. A heavy smell of lavender blows off the pages. This might come in handy, so I walk over to the table and place it on Callian's stack. He picks it up and reads the title aloud.

"Sounds dark," he replies. A smile finally tips his mouth as he looks up. They're the first words he's said in over an hour. Something in his tone tells me he is ready to end the silence, and so am I.

"I always like to start where I feel most comfortable." I smirk, splaying my hand over the book's front while my mind drifts to a million other things. Facetiousness has always been a good façade.

Something catches my eye, and I look past him at a pile of scrolls nestled between the wall, varying in size. I pick up the scrolls and spread them one by one across the desk. A low hum is now tangible beneath my touch. Some of the dates on these scrolls are illegible. Many lifetimes ago, someone inked these pages and brought them to life. Echoes of their existence are left between the pages. The scrolls are in such great condition I'm almost afraid to touch them. My fingers trail over the edges until one hums against my fingertip. Red ink splays across the parchment scroll.

"'A ruler born in blood,'" I read aloud, pulling Callian's attention.

"I know that phrase," he says. The words tighten around my pounding heart. The heat of his arm brushes up against mine as he leans against the table. "What does it say?" he asks, looking over my shoulder. His hair tickles the top of my head as he stands behind me.

"A ruler born in blood,
from a king who sees no son.
The gift that shall be brought,
can be taken when the moon turns red.

The rightful heir to the throne,
is the one whose powers grow.
Not too early, not too late,
the timing marks their fate.

Gathered through death,
the shadow holds the crown.

Fires rage, a guided mage,
two decades from the start.

Souls of a triangle unite, and a leader emerges from the ash.
A blindfold under a veil worn, love that cuts like knives.
Only this survives the blood moon night."

"The prophecy," he murmurs. Another wave of phantom chills course through my body like an icy grip wrapping around my thundering heart. He runs both hands down my arms to comfort me. Our eyes scan the symbols sketched onto the ancient scroll in inks of red and black. It's a triangle drawn inside a circle with more text written over them. Callian begins reading aloud.

"'Love is bound in darkness,
igniting the unforeseen.
Found through stars,
rebirth between the trees,
guards its keep.
The world will bleed in two if the distant world is breached.'"

My eyes skim over the text, repeating the words, each drifting to a place in the back of my mind where the darkness sits in a corner and waits. I exhale another sharp breath, trying to swallow the lump in my throat as my emotions build. My body is fighting against the thoughts stirring within me and the longevity of the day. My mind begins reeling, wrapping itself around the words of this prophecy.

"I've spent so much time in the dark, so much time in my head and barely being spoken to. The more I'm here, the more I realize how confined my life was. I never searched for more. It angers me that I just accepted it. I never asked questions. I just lived in a haze because I was filled with . . . " I bite the inside of my cheek to parry around my own emotions. "I was filled with grief," I rasp. "I hated that place. It was cold and empty. Yet, I couldn't bring myself to leave because it was a constant reminder of her. It was as if I had bound myself in chains and thrown away the key. There was a necklace she gave me the year she died. It was her last gift to me, and now it's so far from reach."

He lifts my hand to his lips, placing a gentle kiss atop it. A faint smile appears on my somber face. His gaze meets mine, eyes glossy as he listens to me pour my heart out. I take a deep breath, combing my fingers through my hair. He gently pulls me to his side and wraps me in his arms. The slight motion tightens my chest. I listen to the steady beat of his heart in an embrace that seems to last forever.

"I think you should rest," he suggests. "We found the prophecy." His breath fans the top of my head.

"That sounds like a good idea," my words barely whisper as I sift through my thoughts.

Being hidden from the world on the side of this cliff doesn't seem so bad now, and soon, the sound of the crashing waves brings nothing but serenity. My situation has no quick resolve, but at least we can revel in the notion that we aren't leaving empty-handed. We found something, and I have the rest of the night for the words of the prophecy to settle in.

CHAPTER 24

*V*OICES ARE BEING WOVEN *into the dark as the scent of sage and sea fill the air. I faintly hear the low murmurs of a girl speaking with a male. A constant, soft chatter that becomes a vibration. My eyes drift open to a void, a dark space, as their voices continue to rumble beneath the pillow against my ear. All the little hairs on the back of my neck rise, realizing who the voices belong to. I sit up in bed and step onto a cold, stone floor, seeing myself as a little girl standing in my room back home. My father rushes in with tears brimming in his eyes. Moonlight beams in from the balcony, illuminating our silhouettes.*

I am tethered to a moment in time, hidden by the haze of a dream. I take another step closer. A faint aroma of honey fills the air. My mother's favorite type of candle. There's a pressure building in my chest, knowing what is about to happen.

He drops to his knees to meet ten-year-old me at eye level. I stand in my nightgown, rubbing my eyes with the back of my hands.

"Daddy, why are you sad?"

He hesitates, brushing the hair from my face and tucking it behind my ears. "Something happened to Mama tonight," his voice rasps.

"What do you mean?"

He searches my eyes as they begin to fog. Finally, a tear breaks free. "She—" He chokes on a sob, trying to catch his breath. Pain fills his voice as he struggles to speak. He blinks, and another tear streams down his face as I watch his mind reeling to the horrific event. "There was so much blo—" He stops himself and looks down at the floor to quickly recover. "Mama is nowhere to be found." His voice strains, but his demeanor falters.

Not fully understanding, I take him by the hand. "It's okay, Daddy. She must be hiding somewhere. Maybe she is waiting for us to find her?"

"She's gone . . . " He lets go of me and runs his shaky hands through his dark hair. "She is resting with the stars now."

I watch reality sink in as he starts to repeat it.

My ears ring, seeing the moment my heart was ripped out of my chest.

"No, she's hiding. I know it!" I see myself, those little, bright-blue eyes swelling with denial, taking him by the hand to lead him toward the exit of the room. He yanks his hand back so abruptly, I see myself flinch.

"She's dead, Viona!" he yells, anger flaring in his voice. I bring my hands up to my chest, frightened as he starts screaming it over and over again. "She's dead! My love, my Yelena!"

A name we have left sealed in our past and locked away. My little hands cover my ears as he screams her name at the top of his lungs. Madness claims him just as quickly as it claims me.

This was the moment he barricaded himself from the world, even from me. I watch from the shadows as he wails. This was when both of our souls died. Watching the little girl harden as tears fall off those little round cheeks. Alyce rushes in, pulling little me into herself to shield me from the sounds of his madness.

A darkness forms behind his eyes. One I couldn't place back then, but standing here now, it's clear something is different. He brings himself to his feet with a crazed look that sends chills down my spine. He rips Alyce away from me, grabbing her by the wrist. My small hands slip through the fabric of her gown. I begin screaming frantically for her touch.

"Get out," he screams in her face. "Do not comfort her. Leave her be." He yanks her out of my room and locks me in. I throw myself against the door, banging on the hard, wooden surface until my hands are sore. Did he think I was to blame?

I run toward myself to comfort who I used to be, to the little girl who was left in the dark to grieve on her own. When I reach to touch her, my hands go right through the silhouette. My ten-year-old self disappears into the cold, night air.

I'm left on my hands and knees, alone in the moonlight as old wounds are reopened and ripped apart. All I can do is sob. Not only for the little girl in me, but for a life I felt was stolen from us. I beat my fists against the ground until the pain forces me to scream. What happened to him?

What happened to us? All the stars in the sky seemed to fall the night my mother died. Of all things, why would he blame me?

I'm losing myself in a memory that I have spent my entire life trying not to relive. Here it is, like a slap in the face, reminding me of who I've become. Grief pays its visit, scraping its claws against my chest. My jaw clenches as the unbearable pain in my heart becomes too much to bear.

"Viona . . . "

A voice calls from beyond the halls. The door drifts open. The honey aroma grows stronger. I use the sleeve of my nightgown to wipe the remaining tears from my face. The voice calls me once more, pulling me to my feet. I slowly step out into the hallway. Cold, frigid air hits my chest. Snow fills every nook and cranny of the hallway. The bones of my home are still the same, accompanied by the emptiness of silence. A thin layer of ice covers each door, highlighting my path. It leads me to the very end of the hall where an apparition of a staircase appears. I follow the voice as it leads me down a dark flight of stairs. This was never a part of my home before. The cold resides, heat rises, and the air grows dank and musty. Old lanterns hang on the walls every ten feet or so.

When I reach the bottom, a small corridor with a big metal door is waiting for me. I slowly make my way toward it. With every step I take, the door creaks open wider. My heart hammers against my chest as the smell of rotten flesh grows pungent. Even in a dream, I begin to retch. I pray to the gods I won't expel the contents in my stomach. The darkness of the room reverberates around me. The voice turns to faint whispers drifting in shadow, wrapping around me. My eyes flutter to the back of my head. The heaviness of the room is like a thousand stones crushing my chest, yet I take another step. Warmth envelopes me. The sudden contact pulls me into a light.

"Wake up." A male's voice echoes throughout the space, over and over until the sound of who it is grows clear.

"Viona." Callian's scent fills the air. My eyes slowly drift open to the sound of his voice. He says my name a few more times before I look at him hazily, adjusting to the morning light. Tears prickle my eyes as a wave of grief strikes, remembering where I am. Another day, another reminder she is gone. I cover my face, distraught as I dissolve into sobs.

He quickly crawls into the bed and lies beside me, placing an arm over my body and pulling me against his.

"Shhhh. I have you, Viona. I have you."

I turn around, nestling my face into his chest to hide while I cry for what has been lost. I miss the smell of my mother's hair and the sound of her voice. The small rasp in her tone every morning while the both of us adjusted to the day. She always slept in my bed because I was afraid of the dark. I've remained there all this time without her. Anguish swells inside me, igniting my rage. My body feels hot to the touch. Another reminder of the curse inside my body and the precarious state of my control. I could suddenly burst at any second, and yet Callian doesn't seem to care. He isn't pushing me away, he holds me closer, shielding me from the world so I may mourn. Pressing a kiss to the top of my head, he cradles me against his chest.

I cry.

I cry until there is nothing left, until my throat runs dry, until the sound of his voice comforting me becomes a faint sound in the back of my mind as I drift back to sleep.

The sun is beaming against my back. Our legs are entangled. The moment I sit up, his body shifts with mine, but I cannot for the life of me meet his stare. I must have expelled a lot of energy while in my dream. My throat ran dry thinking of my father. I can't help but feel like something was about to loom from it.

"I'm sorry," I murmur, turning my head toward the balconies.

"Hey," he whispers, curving his finger under my chin as he gently turns my head to meet his gaze. "You don't ever need to apologize for how you feel." Those bright-emerald eyes warm. My eyes lower to his chin, catching the prisms of light along his shadowed jawline. His voice is deep and comforting. I reach for him, cupping the side of his face as I run the pad of my thumb along his chin. The light in my dark. He's been so kind and patient through this, a kindness I feel I don't deserve. With a soft exhale, my hand lowers.

"What time is it?" I faintly say, shifting my body to stand, noticing the placement of the sun as it's past noon. I stumble, grabbing onto the corner of the bed frame to catch my fall. He immediately jumps up and rushes to my side. I grab a handful of his dark tunic, feeling as though I could fall again. He helps me sit back down onto the bed.

"It's past noon," he confirms. "But nothing else matters right now outside this room."

Shit, but I'm already late.

The weight of the bed shifts as he sits beside me.

"I'm supposed to meet Crystal for training." Though my will is stronger than my fight, I can't ignore the faint ringing in my ears.

"Well, lucky for you, Crystal canceled training for the day. She had something personal to attend to."

"She canceled?" My voice is hoarse. I hope everything is okay. Even though my body feels like I've been hit by a larkin, my concerns are all for her.

He holds a hand up in reassurance. "Don't worry, she's fine. I'm sure she will tell you all about it when you see her next." He gets up and heads into the bathing chambers.

"What are you doing?" I ask. I can hear water splashing around and Callian moving things about.

"I'm taking care of you!" he calls out playfully.

"Why?" I'm nearly in disbelief over the way he's been tending to me. His head peeks out from the doorway with his hair suspended to the side, exposing the column of his beautiful neck. That smoldering look he's giving me stills my breath.

"Do I need to have a reason?" he purrs.

"I suppose it's because it is your duty." I swallow hard, peeking up at him as the heat continues to burn through me. I look away, focusing on every curve and divot of the smooth, marble walls as tears threaten to release.

His bare feet pad against the floor. Every step he takes toward me tightens my chest. I look further away, trying not to meet his gaze because I know I'm a wreck. He kneels in front of me, running his hands along the tops of my legs. Rubbing them in such a soothing motion, sensing the pain behind my words.

"I'm taking care of you because what I feel for you burns deeper than any duty placed upon me," he says.

Another tear slips free, but I wipe it away with force, feeling so undeserving.

"You don't even know me," I retort. I know I sound foolish, but the words have already left my lips.

"I feel like I always have," he confesses.

I finally look at him, and he holds my gaze, long and hard, searching my eyes. That unseen tether tightens around my chest. He brushes a lock of hair away from my face, not caring that I'm hot and sweaty. My eyes soften at the motion.

"I know you're stubborn. You'd rather let your body heat up and burn than ask for help." That might be true, but I faintly scoff, the corner of my mouth quirking up. "So please, let me have the honor of taking care of you," he says, cupping my cheek. I bite my lower lip and give a silent nod.

He helps me to the bathing chambers and sits me down on a chaise while he dips his hand into the water. As it swishes between his fingers, I feel the water calling me.

"It's cool," he warns. "But your skin is as hot as fire, I don't think it'll be a problem." He strides back over to me. "Can you stand?" That velvety voice is like a calm to my storm.

I nod. He helps me to my feet once more and walks me over to the bath. There is a tenderness in the way he undresses me as he slides the gown over my body. The breeze drifting through the doorway causes my skin to pebble. My hair is slick with sweat against my neck, and I know I don't smell very pleasant. I'm in my rawest form with my emotions open and bared. The light beaming in from the balconies reflects off the walls, making the room brighter and every part of my body visible.

I step into the tub and slide my body in, welcoming every inch of cool water to soothe the heat. My head rests against the rim of the tub.

"Here." He puts something soft behind me to cushion the back of my head.

"Thank you."

We don't speak. Instead, the sounds of the water fill the space. He kneels beside the tub, dragging a sponge gently across my forehead and down my arms. There's a comfort accompanying the silence in the way he tends to me. I don't remember the last time anyone has taken care of me in this way. Alyce wasn't allowed to be by my side the way she had been for my mother. She was the only kindness I knew in my world back home, and even then, she was withdrawn in fear that my father would take his anger out on me. Despite all the darkness I seem to find myself surrounded by, Callian does not fear it. He is either a fool, or I've finally been granted some godsdamned luck. Maybe a little of both.

"When Crystal informed me she was canceling your training today, I didn't want to wake you. I decided to work from my room and took my documents there while you slept in. Shortly after, I heard you crying out in your sleep."

He runs the sponge along the side of my neck, down to my chest, repeating the motion on the other side. I turn my head to the side and look at him with gratitude. We're quiet for a little while longer. He leaves and brings me some of Iván's tea I left by the bed to help me relax.

"What do you want to do today?" he asks. I pause mid drink, realizing I can't remember the last time someone asked me that.

"Can we go to the library?" I reply softly, biting the bottom of my lip. "That is, if you aren't needed anywhere else."

Humor flashes behind his eyes, probably because we were just there yesterday.

"Anything you want. The moment your schedule was cleared, so was mine." A smile curves his perfect, full lips as he tucks a strand of hair behind my ear again. He rustles behind me, looking for something. I hear the sound of a cork popping then falling to the ground.

"Lean back," he says in that deep voice I'm growing to adore. I shift my body to see what he's doing, but he scolds me. "No peeking, Princess."

"Fine," I hum, leaning back.

Vanilla fills the air the moment his hands start to comb through my hair. He begins to wash it, massaging my skull with slow, strong strokes. The sensation is relaxing. The tension in my shoulders releases slowly. He carefully uses his fingers to comb through the strands, gently undoing the knots. He uses a wooden bowl to scoop clean water from a bucket and runs it over my hair. I tilt my head back, letting the coolness of the water soak into me. My hair billows around my naked frame.

"Can you sit up for me?" he asks, lathering a bar of soap in his hands. It smells of fresh vanilla, cinnamon, and roses. I sit forward, bringing my knees to my chest, resting my head on them while he massages my back. I hum in response. I can tell he's being respectful in the way he touches me, working around the parts that drive him mad. He washes my body, gliding the soap along my back and arms.

"So you're only a gentleman when bathing a woman?" I tease, staring at him from where my head rests, hoping the somber nature of the room will shift.

He smirks, massaging my body and soothing out the tension in every muscle. Bubbles begin to fizzle into the water.

"Are you able to stand?" He calmly smiles. I nod, grabbing ahold of his arm while he helps me to my feet. His eyes rake over my body.

"May I wash your delicates?"

A laugh bubbles out of me.

"Delicates?" I smirk, raising a brow.

He laughs, looking down at the floor as his hair slightly conceals a shy smile and rosy cheeks I don't see often. It's heartwarming, the way he looks at me with his head slightly cocked to the side and a dark lock of hair brushing across his face.

"Trust me, Princess, I have chained up all the dirty words for now. I will only be thinking chivalrous thoughts about you with the most respectful hands."

"Really?" My voice dips low as I steady myself against him. He takes a small step forward, leaving very little space between us.

"Really," he whispers with no hint of lust or wandering eyes, just warmth and understanding. My grip tightens around his arms as his gaze burns through me. "I will always honor you," he vows, lathering the soap in the sponge. He waits for my approval, and I nod. He glides it over the apex of my thighs a few times in the most respectful way. Through the next several moments, my heart becomes a steady calm as his love and tenderness chase away the remnants of my dream. As I caress the nape of his neck, smiling, something blooms inside me.

I am content because of him.

It was a feeling that rarely happens.

He draws the sponge away.

"Thank you." My words leave in a soft whisper.

He curves a finger under my chin and looks at me as if he felt it too.

After he finishes bathing me, I see that a fresh set of clothes were set out on the marble counter. I quickly put them on and head over to the dressing area of my room, drying my hair as much as I can.

"Would you like me to braid your hair?"

"Where did you learn how to do that?" Taken back by his question, my brows knit with curiosity. A soft chuckle rumbles in his chest. He takes me by the hand and leads me to the empty chair looking out toward the balconies. He stands behind me, parting my damp hair in three sections.

"Every time Crystal won a bet, she would make me brush and braid her hair. After losing so many times, I eventually became really good at it."

"Hmm," I respond. The bond they share is evident. "Is that what it feels like to have a sister?"

He sighs, tying a small, black ribbon at the base of my braid. "Yes. I can't speak for others, but there has always been a battle of dominance between us. Behind it is loyalty. As annoying as she can be at times, she is my sister. Though we share no blood, that has never really mattered to any of us. Except for Ronan." His voice dips lower with such disdain for his cousin. I feel the same way. "There has always been this disconnect with him. It's as if he's the result of a bad deal made under a moon."

Suddenly something strikes me. "The moon," I murmur under my breath.

"Exactly."

"No, that's not what I meant." I brush him off and begin pacing back and forth. "What does it mean to make a bad deal under the moon?" I study him intensely.

"It's an old saying, 'Never make any decisions under a full moon.'"

"Odd saying, but you have me thinking. There was a mention of the moon in the prophecy. Something about a blood moon night," I ponder. He raises a darkened brow and leans against the table. The weight of his body pushes it back by a few inches. We ignore the sound.

"I'm listening."

"My mother used to tell me that even the darkest of stories seek the light. They want to be told. There has to be more to this prophecy, perhaps a story. I need to find out more about my birth. Maybe the knowledge isn't all stored in the alcove after all. Maybe some answers are lying in plain sight."

He falls deep into thought, staring at the ground. There's a silence in the air as both our minds begin brainstorming. He pushes off the desk, taking a few steps toward me.

"You know, I think you're onto something."

CHAPTER 25

"HERE GOES NOTHING," I mutter under my breath as Callian opens the door for me. A few familiar faces look up from their books. I quietly exhale, feeling embarrassed that I made myself look like an ass the last time I was here. I raise my chin and walk over to Seveena, who began eyeing me from her desk the moment I entered. She leans forward, lacing her fingers together as she factitiously smiles. I restrain myself, returning the best smile I can, but I think all I do is bare my teeth because her lips twist up into a snarl.

"That's frightening," she scoffs.

My smile fades, turning into a grin as I cross my arms over my chest and shift my hip to one side. "Well, that's me trying," I admit.

"It's a start," she says in a friendlier tone. "How can I help you today?"

I uncross my arms, taking a step closer. "We need to access any records you have of the past moon phases."

Her eyes skim over my braided hair as it drapes over my shoulder. "Of course."

She stands, making sure her chair doesn't drag across the marble floors. Her eyes bore into mine as if she's showing me how to be quiet in a library, putting emphasis on closing the book slowly and gently. I roll my eyes waiting for her to be done with her silent lesson.

I can feel stares upon me as we make our way toward the left side of the library. We enter a side room where bookshelves line all four walls. The desks in the middle have plants dividing the spaces between them.

"It's been a while since I've been in this room. How far are you looking to go back?" She turns to me.

"The last twenty years," I reply.

The connection Seveena has within the space is palpable because she immediately knows where to look. "Let me know if you two need anything else." She hands the book over to me.

Callian nods.

As I flip through the pages, I'm reminded of my connection to the moon. The most consistent thing in my life is something so far from reach, and yet it has always kept me tethered to a hidden part of myself through the ocean. A part of me I'm still trying to understand. Back in Sao, I always ended my days looking at its luminescence, watching the moon move through the darkness of an onyx sky painted with stars. Each night I was cloaked by darkness, it was the sliver of light that always guided me back, through the ocean and to the shores.

"Here it is," I say, pointing to the year I was born written in black ink. I trail my finger to the date. My eyes widen seeing red ink coloring a full moon.

"I was born on a lunar eclipse," I whisper.

The world will see you. They will know you. My mother's words echo in the back of my mind. A reminder that always drips down my spine like an open wound marked by fate.

"The blood moon," Callian whispers. He looks at me, eyes narrowing in thought. "'A ruler born in blood, from a king who sees no son.'"

His words send a chill down my arms. I swallow. "Maybe there is a possibility something dark wove itself along with my powers when I was born, but what?" I'm hanging onto a glimmer of hope, but I cannot deny the words of the prophecy. I look to Callian, trying to understand it all. "I've been told different things about myself. I could be the end and the beginning, but all I've seen is the division my presence brings. Especially since coming here."

He puts his hand on my shoulder, giving a comforting squeeze. "If the prophecy is right, you were meant to bring the lands together, not to rip them apart. It says 'a leader emerges from the ash.'" He shakes his head, refusing to let me accept the doubt that's trying to take root. "You were brought here to hone your powers, strengthen your skills. So far, I've been impressed with your resilience and your innate ability to resolve. Don't let anyone cloud your thinking, not even the words of the prophecy. Focus on you. Remember what I said, I will handle everything else."

A darkness glints in his eyes as his words sound more like a promise wielded into steel, as if he would handle anyone who got in my way. As comforting as that may be, it still wouldn't change much. Adnama warned I could lose myself to my powers. My visions are always so destructive and chaotic, visions that only lead me into self doubt. It feels more like they're a curse for the darkness that follows me. I am constantly searching for a connection to fully understand myself. The weight of this knowledge comes in waves, and right now, it sits heavily on my chest.

"You're right." I try tucking all those worries away as I close the book and place it back onto the shelf. "We will wait for the library to close, then visit the royal Alora Archives. In the meantime, I'll see what is here and do as much reading as I can. You can stay if you want, but you're not obligated to."

"A choice between hanging out with foul, wretched guards or being in the presence of an invigorating woman? I think I'll choose the latter." He winks. Once again, that perfect smile appears as a light in my dark, pulling me to safety before I drown.

My head tilts back in a laugh. "You are shameless."

After hours of reading and an abundance of caffeine, I start feeling the effects behind my eyes. We're sitting in the Alora Archives in a hidden alcove. I got ahead of myself, taking on so much in such a short amount of time. The words of the prophecy are now becoming a blur. I try regaining my focus. Though I have it memorized by now, it doesn't change the motives of my father. King Valor can see me in the light all he wants, but as I stare into the black and red swells of ink that mark my fate, all I see is darkness.

Callian notices me lost in thought. I hear him walk over to a book-shelf. He places a book on the desk and drags his chair closer to mine. I blink a few times, adjusting my eyes as my brows knit together.

"What are you doing?"

He uses his power to yank the paper from my hand. A small, con-trolled force of wind places it on a shelf far from reach. He must sense my emotions. He turns to see me glaring at him and closes the space between us. His skin smells like cedar mixed with a fresh, citrus scent. I'm overcome by the intensity his touch brings me every time. Though it's so raw and new, there's no denying it's there.

He gazes down at me with hooded eyes.

"This room holds many pieces of Callisto's history. This is our past, present, and future." He laces our fingers together. "You are a part of *my* story, Viona. I want every moment with you written in our history. I don't know what the future holds, but I know I don't want to forget any of it," he says with a shaky breath as his thumb trails over the top of my hand. "I want every part of you etched in my time."

My breathing stills. He unlaces our hands and reaches for a feathered quill, dipping it into the inkwell. He begins to write. My head cocks to the side as I study him, watching in awe at the way he motions the quill with fluid grace, honing his skill with every stroke. This moment, the way he holds me close to his body with one hand while he writes with the other, ascends my feelings for him beyond the stars.

When he's done, he slides the book over to me.

Its white leather cover feels coarse against my skin.

I read aloud. *"We were here, and this was us. Hidden between the earth and the sun. - Callian Valor."*

There's a sudden shift in the air as I speak the last word, igniting a soft glow to cast from the pages of the book. His letters begin to shim-mer in small speckles of soft, white light reminding me of fireflies as they charge the air and dance around us. I watch them, all-consuming as they illuminate the space. They're almost as beautiful as catching a glimpse of him smiling when he looks at me.

"What is this?" I gasp in wonder. My eyes widen as my head tips back, marveling at an unseen magic.

"This is the book of us, Princess." He tucks a loose strand behind my ear as my heart beats rapidly against my chest.

We're enveloped in a swirl of light, each small ember casting a fiery glow to our skin.

"When I say I want every moment with you written in time, I mean it." He looks at me intensely with a thirst in his eyes only I can quench. I've kept myself to the shadows for so long. I can't understand why anyone would want to remember someone like me. His face becomes a blur as tears swell in my eyes.

"I don't understand," I whisper.

"This book will automatically transcribe every moment of our time together. It's something my ancestors had the ability to do. It was a gift I never saw reason to use, until I met you. Only you and I will be able to open it, and only you and I could create it. As the years pass, we can go back and remember all we lived through."

"But how?" I shake my head in amazement.

He hands me the quill, my lips quirk up.

"Write something," he tells me with a hooded gaze.

A small laugh escapes me as I shyly take the quill from his hand. "I don't know what to write."

He breathes into the shell of my ear. "Writing is a form of expression, feelings that are pulled from the deepest parts of our soul. It is freeing as much as it is frightening. They are words that live forever." I close my eyes and lean into him, listening to the soft, sultry tone of his voice.

I begin to write. Words start weaving themselves together. My heart is beating so hard against my chest, I fear my hands will shake.

"'Promise you will always find me. – Viona Tarvas'"

The words leave my lips as I write, confessing a bold truth. When I stroke the last letter of my name, a beam of shimmering gold light disperses into the air, sealing the book we have just begun together.

He exhales, smiling as if I've left him breathless while he slides a hand into my hair. I watch his hardened shell crack, eyes glistening as the pad of his thumb trails across my lower lip.

"All of time and space couldn't keep us apart." His deep, sultry voice becomes strained. Embers of light drift in the shadows of his irises as he confesses a bold truth. "My heart will always call to yours, and yours to mine. I would rip the stars from the sky to find you."

I close my eyes to his words fanning across my lips, encasing me with his promise. He presses a kiss onto my forehead and pulls me into his embrace. In this moment, all the darkness in the world couldn't pull us apart. I wrap my arms around him so tightly, I forget to breathe. The gold, shimmering light starts to fade and I swear I can feel them seeping into our skin. He has my powers humming in more ways than one. I also feel our attraction weaving through a light that hasn't waned since he took me. He curves his finger under my chin.

"My heart is yours, Princess."

Those perfect lips brush against mine, I'm savoring how they feel. He opens his mouth, tenderly unleashing a soft, gentle kiss with a stroke of his tongue. I deepen the kiss, letting him in. He groans into my mouth, and my need for him breaks free. I reposition myself, straddling him in the chair. Another moan rumbles in his chest as his hands move with fluid grace up my back.

The sun is setting, its soft, orange glow fading behind the sea. We stay in this position for a little while longer. Until the skies turn into twilight. Exploring one another between small talk and light kisses.

When it's time to go, he places the book back on the top shelf. Its spine bears the inscription, "Callian Valor and Viona Tarvas." Our story, as long or short as it may end up being, will be etched in time. A small piece of his history as well as mine.

CHAPTER 26

"**T**HAT'S NOT TRUE." My head tips back into a laugh. Callian hovers over a table of breads and pastries while I sit by the fireplace on a thick, fur rug.

"Oh, but it is." He smiles while he cuts into the pie's crust. His sleeves are rolled up, exposing his forearms. As he cuts perfect triangles out of the pie, his muscles flex. "As true as it could be for any child." A loose strand of hair dangles free from his face as he leans down to hand me my slice. He licks the filling off his thumb.

"You really believe you saw a mermaid?" My voice lifts in curiosity, setting my slice to the side. I take a sip of my tea.

Over the last week, Iván has been dropping off chamomile tea on his way to Crystal's room. I've grown accustomed to the way he knocks on my door. Three quick knocks. He keeps the conversations short, eager to get to her. As much as I would like to get to know the man who's head over heels about my newfound friend, I'm happy they find comfort in one another.

Crystal has been dedicating her early mornings to training me. Every day, she starts by doing a series of movements to loosen me up, followed by a few lessons on strength and skill. She is helping me hone my powers by working on my mental strength as well. I fail every time, setting things aflame against my will. Sometimes, I think her random obstacles are just another way to torment me.

Around midday, I usually spend time in the library studying, sitting on the same chaise by the window. It has become my favorite place to be since that one night with Callian. Seveena occasionally checks in on me.

I read things from the history of elemental magic and power. This has been a lot to take in. Once gifted by the gods, people's abilities can grow through practice. People here are simply given the choice, and if they choose to, it is then woven into their lives. They aren't suppressed or hunted down for wanting to further their abilities. It seems like Sao is the only kingdom with a ruler who despises it. I've also learned some carry power without being gifted—through the bloodline of their flesh and bones.

I have also been studying each type of ability. Crystal said I must learn it all. Knowing our enemy is knowing how to succeed. Which tends to lead me back to the larkins.

Every time I walk to the library, I think of Gareon. Each time I look down the hall, staring at the cast-iron staircase that leads to the Seer's study, I wonder what he has found so far. I've debated calling out to him telepathically a few times, but no news is good news. I'd like to keep it this way for as long as possible.

After a few hours in the library every day, Callian has been joining me so we can study more in the Alora Archives. Other than meetings with the king, we've been spending the rest of our time here in my room. Callian is all I think about at the end of the day. So I suppose I can understand how Iván feels about Crystal.

Callian's voice pulls me from thought. He continues to tell me about a story from when he was a boy. He was off on an adventure with his father, and when their ship docked on land, he wandered off alone. Hours passed, and he realized he was lost.

"That's when I saw the mermaid. I swear it, cross my heart." He makes the motion over his chest. The muscles in his forearms flex. "I don't know what would have become of me if the mermaid didn't lead me back to my father. Not only was I granted one of my powers that day, but she saved me from a lion."

"A lion?" I scoff. I've never seen one before. Only illustrations in a book from a long time ago. "Do lions live here too?" I feel silly asking, but what do I know about this land? He chuckles, sitting across from me by the fireplace, hovering his fork over the pie.

"No, they don't. They live on one of the islands far northeast of our port. By the time I knew I was being stalked, he was already flying through the air. A sudden force came through my palm, and I willed the power to hold him in midair. I didn't have it in me to kill him, knowing I had the upper hand. I held him back long enough for me to escape. My father said the mermaid was one of the gods from the stars, and she had blessed me."

My eyes widen with fascination. "I read about being blessed, but I never knew the ones from the stars could *walk* the same grounds we do."

"Oh, they certainly can, just as easily as the gods from the Shadow Realm. All of the gods can decide to grant or tempt you. I assume the god I encountered knew my heart before granting me this gift," he confirms. I feel so out of touch with this world, but I remind myself it isn't my fault my father kept this knowledge from me.

A comfortable silence hangs in the air as we continue to eat our pie by the fire.

"Well, for what it's worth, I'm glad you saved the lion," I reply with a smile before forking a piece of apple into my mouth. The flavors explode—cooked apple, cinnamon, and nutmeg swirl around my tongue. "I've never tasted anything so sweet," I moan.

"I have," he groans while spearing a piece of his pie, then smiles at me before he takes a bite. Apparently, all he has to do is groan two simple words, and I become liquid in his hands. Every time he speaks, I fall apart. I look down at my plate and play around with a piece of the pie's crust, hoping the fiery glow from the fireplace conceals my flushed cheeks.

"A taste one could get used to, I suppose." I smirk. "Your cook here is amazing, by the way."

"I hope you never mean in the same way Crystal does, or else I would be terribly jealous," he teases.

I take this as an opportunity to pry just a little.

"So, what about Iván then? Are they also a thing?" I take another sip of my tea, hoping it will warm my insides. The fireplace can't expel the chill that's taken over my body tonight.

An unexpected laugh erupts from his chest. "Iván is her friend. He always has been, and he always will be if he doesn't grow a pair and woo her. She's as fierce in battle as she is in love, but I know her heart. She lives for romance. Which, I assume, is why she probably has a thing for the cook."

"Oh, I see." I wonder how Iván feels about that. They seem very happy when they're together.

"Don't worry. There are no secrets between them. Iván is well aware of her late-night pantry raids. They may flirt endlessly with each other, but at the end of the day, she wants to be pursued."

Callian devours the rest of the pie, sets the plate onto a small table, and leans his body against the settee.

The wheels in my head start turning. "Maybe you can show him how to pursue? Seems like he could use some encouragement."

He wipes the corner of his mouth with the tip of his thumb. Even the way he does that makes my body yearn.

"Would that make you happy?" he asks, knowing I have a soft spot for Iván.

"Yes, it would." My eyes harden. I normally never pry into anyone's business, but it wouldn't hurt to give him some advice.

"Alright, I'll do it because it will make you happy."

"Thank you." I yawn. Every muscle in my body aches.

"I think it's time we head to bed." His voice matches the weariness of mine from our long day.

To bed. Such simple words that are so weighted. He hasn't been sleeping in my room every night. Over the past week, he has been leaving it up to me to decide where he sleeps. Things have been moving so quickly since I arrived in Callisto. He has been here for me during my struggles, but ever since my vision, sleep has been an obstacle. He hasn't pressed for a reason when I've said no. I still haven't mentioned the vision I had of us with the whole dagger thing. It's not an easy conversation to have. Each time I think I have the courage to tell him, I freeze. How does one tell someone they had a vision of them being burned alive under a trance? *Oh, and by the way, I was riding your cock while doing so.* Something we haven't even done yet. The tonic Sydney made me drink should be working by now in the event we do. She left a handful in my room, telling me to drink one every month. As much as I'm reminded of how much I want it every time Callian touches me, I also don't mind the wait. I'm enjoying my time with him, every minute, as short-lived as it will be if the prophecy is true.

"Love that cuts like knives," those words that seem more like a curse emerge from the darkest part of my mind. I swallow the lump forming in my throat.

I hate keeping this from him, but what am I supposed to do?

Lost in thought, I exhale from exhaustion and frustration.

His eyes soften. The crackling sound of the fireplace fills the silence. He leans forward, gently kissing me on the cheek. I close my eyes, leaning into the warmth of his hand as it cups my face.

"Goodnight, Princess. I'll see you in the morning. If you need anything, I'm right across the hall."

I want nothing more than to be wrapped in his arms, but fear wins tonight. I'm afraid it always will.

"Thank you." A ghost of a smile appears, wondering if my constant indecision will start a rift in the tide, but it hasn't yet.

"Goodnight," I whisper.

The sound of his footsteps leaving reminds me that darkness will always win, no matter how happy I try to be. I can smile all I want, I can train until my body breaks and wield my sword until it shatters. But there's no denying what is rising inside me.

My eyes drift to the empty space where he sat, the fur matted down by his weight. His sword glints in the flames of the fireplace. He must have accidentally left it behind. I lean forward, wrapping my hand around the hilt, and drag it across the rug toward me. My hands trail along the metal sheath, admiring the designs as they spiral and weave into one another. With force, I pull his sword free. The sound of metal slices in the air, reminding me of when I first took it from him. I stand, feeling the weight of his weapon as I remember the way I carried it through the White Forest. Cumbersome and unpleasant then, but now it's weightless. I raise it to my side. Every sweeping motion is done with fluid grace as the sword and I dance.

Callian has a love for things that are dangerous, including the one who holds this sword. I move with the blade, feeling it hum beneath my touch, sharp and deadly, cutting through the air with precision. With all its sharp curves and edges, I manage to grasp what is expected when carrying this. It speaks to me in a low, vibrational hum, a language lost in time, but there is so much more that holds me.

So much duty comes with the weight of this sword. He is a prince, afterall. He will rule Callisto one day. The back of my throat burns. I swing around in a spinning motion, taking another jab into the empty space. I hold my stance, my eyes landing at the door.

This can never be mine. It is clear what I have to do. I could never claim this weapon or the man who wields it. I can smile and laugh in his presence, but when alone, the gravity is shifting beneath my feet, and all I can see is that dagger plunged into his heart. I cannot keep living in this fantasy of *us* when it can be taken at any moment.

It only takes two knocks for Callian to answer. As the door swings open, a rush of energy swarms through me. My chest tightens, seeing the way he greets me with an assuming smile.

"Miss me already?" He grins, leaning his elbow against the frame of the door. His shirt has already been discarded. Every divot of his hardened chest glows in the dim light of the corridor.

"You forgot your sword." I extend out his weapon, but he doesn't take it. Instead, he wraps his hand around my wrist and leans down.

"What's wrong, Viona?" The urgency in his tone sends my heart sinking to the pit of my stomach, and my throat tightens hearing him say my name. A word he rarely uses unless it's important. He looks out into the corridor, staring at the night guards. "Come in so we can have privacy." Callian steps aside, motioning for me to go in. I swallow the lump in my throat and enter.

Upon my entrance something hums in the air, a feeling so profound, a chill sweeps over my body. I'm standing inside his room for the first time. Horror spreads across my face.

My vision . . .

Tears swell in my eyes as I take in the exact scenery from the vision that has been tormenting me. A large, purple bedspread with tufted upholstery, ornate with leaf crowning. My eyes rake up to the large, black-framed mirror, bold as death, right above his bed.

"I can't do this anymore," I rasp. The air suddenly feels thick as I hold in a strangled sob. He rushes to my side, gently placing both his hands on my arms.

"Do what anymore?" His brows are tightly knit as he desperately searches for reason.

I look away, unable to watch as I break his heart. "I'm a fucking fool for ever thinking this could ever work."

"You don't mean that," he almost growls out the words.

"I do," I snap, whipping my head in his direction, returning his gaze with a stone-cold look. "Get your hands off me." I seethe.

He releases me as confusion pinches his brows. Everything is unraveling so fast. My heart wants nothing more than his embrace, but my mind forces me to take a step back.

"If you'll excuse me, Prince Valor, I need to get back to my room. I have an early day tomorrow." I turn to leave, but he grabs me by the arm.

"You don't mean that," he repeats.

"Yes, I do."

His chest heaves with anger as he runs a hand through his hair. "I know why you're doing this," he says. I pull myself from his grip. Silence hangs in the air as I walk toward the door. Every second that goes by, I hear his breathing grow more rapid. "You're afraid, and all you can think to do is run."

My eyes flutter shut, stalling my grip on the handle as the truth of his words sear into me. "You're a fucking asshole," I retort with my back still toward him.

"Why, Viona?" He makes his way toward the door. "Is it because you know I'm right?"

I turn the knob, but as the door opens, he slams it shut. I turn around, glaring up at him with hatred in my eyes. "I will rip your fucking soul apart," I snarl through my teeth as I take one step toward him.

All the air is sucked out of the room. His jaw flexes while his eyes brim with emotion. He opens the door to let me out.

"You already have."

CHAPTER 27

T HE FAINT SOUNDS OF the night still cling to the air of the early
dawn. The candle by my bed is nearly burnt out. I lie on my back,
staring up at the ceiling, arguing with myself for everything, anything
my mind can grab onto. I've been reciting what I will say once I make it
to the Great Hall. With barely any sleep, my thoughts and words have
slowly started to collide, and now they are one big, catastrophic blur. I
can't wait any longer.

I push to my feet and get myself ready. My cabinet is full of clothes;
Sydney must have added more to my wardrobe. I sift through a stack
to my left and pause when I find a very flimsy nightgown with the
thinnest straps I've ever seen. I hold it up to my body, its delicate
fabric fanning over the front side of my frame. The black material is
so see-through that I might as well be nude. I scoff faintly.

She's a sly old gal, but I no longer need this. I fold it up and place it
back into the pile, pulling out my cloak next. It's the same one I wore
through the White Forest.

"Hello, old friend." My fingers trail over the embellished vines and
roses. I swing it over my shoulders, fastening it around my neck.

I slowly open my door, praying to the stars that it won't make a
sound. As I peek into the hall, two guards are fast asleep. One is leaning
up against the wall while standing. I cock my head to the side, trying
to grasp how one could stand in such a compromising position. The
other sits against the wall with his head tilted back. His mouth hangs
open, letting out faint snores. I wrinkle my nose, and my upper lip
twitches in disgust. I slide out of my room.

Before taking another step, a dull light catches my eye. Candlelight
flickers beneath Callian's doorframe, causing my heart to sink, won-

dering if he's still up. Before the sadness can swell, I leave, tiptoeing down the hall and keeping to the shadows of early dawn. When I reach the very end, I slide against the wall and descend the stairs in haste. I make it through the first two corridors, but as I turn the corner leading to the Great Hall, I run into a tall, ample form.

My body flies back, sliding against the cool, marble floor, knocking the wind out of my chest.

"Viona, are you alright?" King Valor asks, extending his hand, but every muscle in my body freezes. He pays no attention to his drink, which is now partially spilled over the tops of his hands and onto the floor. He's shirtless. Salt-and-pepper hair lightly covers his chest. A thin string clings onto his beige trousers as they hang around his hips, and he's barefoot. For someone his age, he's in fantastic shape. His body is chiseled. Light scars mar his skin on the side of his ribs. They almost look like claw marks.

I quickly look away, already mentally throwing myself off a cliff for seeing the king so exposed. I think I want to throw up from my nerves.

"I apologize," I say, extending my hand while refusing eye contact. His big, calloused grip wraps around mine. With one effortless tug, he pulls me to my feet.

"Seems like you and I like to roam the halls when we cannot sleep. Let's go for a walk, shall we?" He motions in the opposite direction of the Great Hall. With a curt nod, I fall into step with him. Before we leave, I notice the two guards on each side of the doors to the Great Hall have remained silent, staring straight ahead into pure nothingness. There's no doubt in my mind they saw everything that happened. I can't help but feel embarrassment brush my cheeks again. The puddle of water is left spilled all over the ground.

King Valor must sense my unease. "Don't worry. I wasn't going to drink it all anyway. It's what Sydney suggests I start my day with." He then looks from side to side as if we're sharing secrets. He whispers, "Between you and me, a slip of the ole whiskey in my coffee does my body better than the water." A smile curves the corner of his lips as he winks at me. His white, warming smile reminds me of Callian's, except the king has dimples. His relaxed demeanor smoothes out my nerves, pushing me to finally smile. I lock both hands behind my back, and we continue down the hall.

"These are the times I enjoy the palace the most," he continues. "When the bustling of life and duties are at rest, when silence fills the air, and the only sound I can hear is my bare feet against the floors. This is when I think best."

He leads the way as we step out onto a veranda and walk beneath it. What is left of the moonlight peeks between each pillar, making an arch shadow against the smooth stone floors. The cool, early morning air drifts in, accompanied by a faint smell of the ocean with a hint of jasmine. There's a calmness in the air. I can easily see why he embraces this hour.

"Where do you like to go to escape?" he asks.

I softly chuckle, staring at the ground as the shadows from the trees dance across my boots, remembering the path to my place of solace. "As a child, I would run along the stone wall that led me down to the ocean, jumping every few feet to slap my hand on the railing. Each time I'd jump, I would get a peek at the water. If I could have flown down, I would have. There is a perron leading from the castle to the beach with sand sprinkling the steps like powdered sugar. It was always that first leap out onto the warm sand that made me feel the most content." I take a deep breath, missing the one place I truly feel at peace. "The shores of my home hold many memories, good and bad, but when listening to the sound of waves washing up on shore, all my worries seem to disappear."

I feel his gaze as I speak, as if he's finding comfort in my words. "Seems like the waters are calling you, dear. One cannot deny that," he says, but something foreboding lingers in the back of my mind.

"Yes, I guess it does seem that way, doesn't it?" I reply. His observation does hold truth. Water always seems to find me, no matter what corner of the world I'm in. "I haven't seen the beaches of Callisto up close yet, but they're breathtakingly beautiful from my balcony. The waters here are so blue and vibrant. Such a stark contrast to the dark and ominous shores back home."

We step out into a garden. Hues of orange and pink have begun to brush the skies.

"Nothing compares to the shores of Callisto. The first time I took Callian to the beach, he waddled his way into the waters. As soon as he could walk, it was where he wanted to go. He spent so much time in the ocean, his mother used to say, 'One day, that boy will grow fins and swim away.'" His cheeks flush a rosy color while he laughs. "We have one of the most beautiful beaches I've ever seen," he boasts, puffing out his chest. My eyes glance over to the faint scars below his ribcage. I want to ask how he got them, but I don't want to pry. "Callian will have to take you there sometime soon."

The heaviness in my chest returns. I have to take this opportunity to speak to him.

He leads me over to a stone bench overlooking the garden. "Let us sit," he says.

I nod, taking a seat as close to the edge as possible. Mourning doves begin their cries somewhere not too far. He sits beside me, but we don't speak for a few moments. He closes his eyes, soaking in the sounds around him. Unfortunately, it's now or never.

"Speaking of Callian . . . " I pause, taking a labored breath. "I was wondering if you could assign someone else to accompany me during my stay here at the palace." Hesitation fills my voice as I fidget with my nails, feeling my heart pounding against my chest.

"Oh?" He side glances me, bringing his hand to his thigh with a raised brow so similar to Callian's. "Has something happened?" he asks.

Though it seems like my heart can't pound any harder, it does. "Things are . . . complicated. I want to focus more on my studies and training without distractions." I hesitate some more and parry around the reason. How can I tell him about my vision when it involved piercing his son's heart? Not only his son, but the prince of Callisto, the heir to his throne.

He says nothing for a moment, scratching the salt-and-pepper stubble growing on his face. "Well, love is complicated."

"*I'm not in love with him!*" I blurt louder than I intended. I stop, taking in a deep breath. "I apologize. I'm not in love with him. He's great and amazing, but I would like to focus all my attention on what's important."

I wait for a heated response, wait for him to take offense, but he does the quite opposite. He smiles as if he understands all I am going through.

But then he asks, "What's more important than discovering who you choose to love?" he says in a soft breath of air, staring off into the sky. It's evident his heart is drifting far from here.

Then he turns to me, bright-green eyes searching beyond what the human eye can see. He continues talking. "You know . . . sometimes, my nightmares become too much to bear. Even though the dreams are gone when I awaken, they never truly fade. When I'd return to bed, my wife would tease me and say they were an excuse to get away from her snoring. Sometimes, I'd let her think so. Anything so she wouldn't worry, but my stars, that woman could see right through me." He pauses, smiling under a short breath as memories take hold. "Let me tell you, I may be old, but I'm not a fool." He stares into his empty cup before placing it down beside him. "I am certainly not blind. I've known how much my son cares for you since the moment you entered that Great Hall. I have never seen him light up like that before. The way you looked at him was a match, undeniable. It reminded me of when I first met my wife."

The sun filtering between the clouds casts a soft glow on the garden's hedges.

"I'll appoint someone else to be your guard if that is what you wish. I hope you won't end up like me. Walking the palace halls like a ghost among half-spilled water because you refused to let anyone in." He pats me on the shoulder before rising.

We both chuckle, but the sadness is tangible in the air. The king misses his wife. My heart breaks for both him and his son. Callian barely speaks about his mother. I've never pressed the matter, trying to respect his space. We are all hurting for someone we lost, they just seem to manage it better than I ever will. My eyes drift to King Valor. He's such a fierce-looking man, but today, he showed me a softer side.

"Well, it's about time this old man gets ready for the day. Would you join me for coffee?"

His offer brightens my spirits a little. "Yes, I'd be honored," I reply.

"Wonderful." He beams. We stand, and he looks over my shoulder. One motion from him and a guard is at our side. "Please take Miss Viona Tarvas to the Great Hall."

"Yes, Your Majesty." He bows.

The king takes one last look at me and smiles. "I will join you shortly."

The king casually walks away with his hands clasped behind his back, taking in the last few moments of his quiet morning before his day begins. I barely know this man, but I enjoyed the comfort of his presence. Him allowing me to be here is already a risk, one he was willing to take for the greater good. He treats me with kindness. He doesn't see me as a curse or an asset. Even after losing the love of his life, he is still strong.

How can one hold grief so close and not let it burn?

I let the conversation with the king linger as I leave the gardens. Soon, the sweet aroma of breakfast wafts from beyond the doors of the Great Hall, pulling me from thought. The scent fills my nose, making my stomach growl. Even with the doors closed, I can hear the laughter and loud chatter filling the room. I swallow hard, realizing that I'm having coffee with the king . . . and breakfast with an entire room full of people. I've been taking all my meals in my room since I arrived. Before I muster up the courage to step through, the guards swing the doors open for me.

"My lady," one says.

"Thank you," I reply. He awkwardly smiles, watching me enter.

Almost two dozen people sit at one of the most extensive rectangular tables I've ever seen. Some conversations drop into a low chatter while others never take notice of my entrance. I walk into a room full of unfamiliar faces, skimming over the crowd until a friendly face emerges at the end of the table. Those bright-violet eyes can light up any room.

"Viona! Over here!" Crystal yells over the crowd, waving her hand in excitement.

A wave of relief washes over me seeing her bright, wide smile. I make my way over to her. Quite a few sets of eyes watch me from the brims of their cups. Either they're questioning why I am wearing a cloak to breakfast on a hot summer day, or they are still bothered by my presence. I couldn't care less. I'm not here for them.

Big floral arrangements decorate the space in a wide assortment of blue and white flowers complementing the tapestries and Callisto's crest which hangs on the back wall. Endless plates of food line the table.

I quickly notice the king's sizable, empty chair at the very end. Two empty seats are across from Crystal; I assume one to be mine.

Before I reach my seat, one of the royal guards steps out from the side. "I present to you, the king." His voice echoes throughout the hall.

Everyone stands to their feet. I freeze watching the king stride out. He looks dapper in his white tunic and tight-fitted, blue coat, gold embellishments lining the front. The intricate design is clearly the work of Sydney. His white trousers display his muscular legs. Rather fancy for this time of day. His thick, heavy boots echo throughout the room as he makes his way over to his chair. When he sees me, he nudges his head to the side, telling me to join him. I move with haste to stand by my seat.

"Let us enjoy this good food as we eat in peace and harmony." He raises his cup into the air. Before he can continue speaking, a loud explosion tears apart the entrance of the Great Hall. Thick shards of wood that used to be doors explode on impact, slamming into the side of the walls. A chill sweeps down my body.

Everyone turns their head to the figure appearing in the center of the doorway. The moment it happened, the king abruptly stood with his sword drawn, creating a ricochet effect as every guard, including Crystal, did the same.

Callian . . .

My heart drops to the ground. He's barefoot and shirtless, wearing nothing but loose-fitted, black trousers that hang desperately by a thin string around his hips. Each breath he exhales sounds like a growl. Every muscle in his body bulges with heated rage. The veins along his forearms are prominent, and his eyes glow a fiery green. The entire court is struck with shock, and some probably fear for their life seeing their prince ready to rip anyone apart if they stand in his way.

"Viona's gone!" he roars, a sound so feral, it rips from his chest. A dozen knights flank his sides, standing behind him in full gear, ready to fight . . .

My mouth gapes open. *All this for me?*

Callian scans the crowd. Fear and murderous rage are a dangerous storm to trek. For a moment, the regret about ending things with him last night sinks in. The knot in my chest tightens. I'm motionless, watching his feral rage, feeling my heart moments from combusting just like the doors. I've never seen him this way before.

The crowd is still silent with everyone's body frozen in place, but their heads turn toward me.

I step out from the crowd.

"Callian, I'm right here," I reply, my words angry and clipped.

As soon as he hears my voice, his eyes soften. He moves forward with such haste, my stomach takes a dip. The back of my throat burns. I motion to step forward, wanting to run to him, but I stop. I just can't. Clenching my fists at my sides, I step back.

He rushes to my side, wrapping his arms around me, cradling my head against his bare chest as if our conversation never happened. I inhale his scent of cedar. For a moment, it feels like it's just the two of us, once more swept up by this storm. He holds me so close, I can feel his heart beating wildly against his chest, like a throbbing ache only my presence can soothe. Every beat cuts into me like a knife.

The king breaks the silence. "Alright, everyone. Now that this has been taken care of, let us eat."

Low chatter replaces the tension in the air. Plates and utensils chime as people fill their plates with food. I could sense the anger in the king's voice, but not at me, thankfully.

"Are you hurt?" Callian whispers in a heated, minty breath while I'm still wrapped in his arms. The warmth fans the top of my head. I pull away, pushing both hands against the hard lines of his chest.

"No, I'm fine. Can we sit down?" I lie. I want nothing more than to run my hands through his hair and say I'm sorry before kissing his beautiful, full lips. Instead, my words are colder than I wish them to be. He goes to speak, but I cut him off before any words can form. "Stop. I don't want to hear it," I press. He searches my eyes, but I look away to sit down before he can see through my façade. I start pouring myself water as my brows lift, carrying the weight of tears in the brim of my eyes. I stop myself from blinking so that the air can steal them away. "Crystal, can you pass me the fruit?" I extend my hand out, feeling his glare searing into my side.

"Fine," he exhales, gritting through his teeth. He pulls out the chair and takes a seat beside me. In the corner of my eye, I see his father fuming as if this conversation is not over between them.

"She was taking an early morning stroll throughout the palace and so happened to grace me with her company while I went for my walk." The king serves himself a few pieces of sausage and begins to cut the links with his fork and knife. "It was quite lovely, wasn't it, Viona?" A smile stretches across his face.

"Yes, it was. I've never seen that part of the palace before. The gardens were exquisite," I reply.

King Valor's voice calms my nerves. My tears have already dried when I make eye contact with him to extend a smile. I place a few pieces of strawberry onto my plate.

"Yeah, that's nice, so what's with the cloak?" Crystal blurts, taking a bite of her bacon. I glare, watching those amethyst eyes yearn for any drip of information. I shoot her a look of warning.

Callian side glances at me. He sits with his plate empty and anger palpable.

"Yeah, I'd love to know too," he retorts.

I notice the flutter in his jaw from my peripheral vision. The last time he saw me in this cloak, I was running from him.

"What a woman does with her mornings is never a man's concern, Son," King Valor chimes in.

I nod in agreement in his direction. "Thank you." I look over to Crystal. "You two are nosy this morning, but it's a long story. I'll tell you about it later," I reply.

She hands me the plate of bacon while her eyes bounce between Callian and me. She smirks, eyeing me with a look that says, *"You'd better."*

I roll my eyes, trying to signal her not to pry any further at the table. I only serve myself two slices of bacon. Honestly, I'm not hungry at all. This morning's events have left my appetite nonexistent.

"Oh my, my. Trouble in paradise, I see."

My head whips in the direction of the voice that gives me goosebumps. Ronan glares with those prying, brown eyes as he pats each side of his mouth with a napkin, pinky up. I did not notice him before, as he sits five people down. He runs a hand along the front of his long, dark hair. The proper prick smiles in a guise we all know is full of disdain. I glance at him for one second before forking a piece of strawberry, refusing to give him the satisfaction of a response. He places his handkerchief back down next to his plate and cuts his sausage into tiny pieces. I sense Callian's tension rising, but at least it isn't entirely directed at me now.

"We all know your words are equivalent to your dick size Ronan: both insubstantial." Crystal jabs her fork into a piece of potato and pops it into her mouth. I snort along with several other members of the court. If I weren't looking, I would have missed the smile on King Valor's face. It quickly wanes before anyone else takes notice. Though Callian's humor has drained from his face, he faintly scoffs under his breath as he stares straight ahead into nothing. His bright smile briefly glints in the morning light. He and his father have so many similar traits. It's a shame I'll never learn of any more similarities between myself and my own father.

Ronan's features tighten as he clears his throat. "Of course, Crystalline. You, of all people, would know the size of every man's parts in the palace." He smiles, proud of himself for his weak little retort. Crystal tilts her head back and laughs.

The king sighs, pulling a flask of whiskey out of his coat pocket. A wink flashes my way as he pours a little into his cup. I chuckle while trying to keep my composure. He quietly gestures, asking if I'd like some. I shake my head as I bring the cup of coffee to my lips.

"This is exactly why a man needs a drink to start his day." He takes a long pull off his concoction. "Now that the three of you are here, I would like to inform you that some changes have been made to this arrangement." Callian and Crystal exchange a look of confusion before looking at their king. My heart plummets to the ground and crushes into millions of pieces knowing Callian will be upset by this news, but I refuse to let him see.

The king lowers his voice so that only a few of us can hear. He looks Crystal in the eyes as he leans an arm on the table. "Crystal, my dear, I have appointed you as Viona's new royal guard. You will accompany her anywhere she needs to go."

"Yes, Your Majesty. I will guard her with my life." She gives a curt nod. All the humor drains from her face as the seriousness comes to light. She shares a look with Callian. That sibling connection is coming forth.

"What?" Callian grits his teeth. His fists tighten, and his knuckles turn white. A few people look up. He angles his body in his chair so his back faces the rest of the table and glares at his father. I can only imagine the look of betrayal etched in his eyes. It almost sounds like he's challenging his father's words. Tension chokes the air, and I suddenly wish I weren't sitting between them.

"You heard what I said, Son. Do not question my authority," King Valor warns.

Callian's disappointment is burning into my soul. Fuck, I didn't want any of this to happen. If only he knew it was to protect him from *me*. I turn to look at him, my throat suddenly dry, but I lift my chin and mask any emotion trying to break free.

"Is this your request? This what you really want, Princess?" he whispers softly, a final plea just low enough for the two of us to hear. His features tighten.

I inhale a deep breath, biting down on my jaw before I speak. "Yes, it is for the best. I'm sorry, Callian."

He briefly closes his eyes and exhales a long breath. I watch the pulse in the column of his neck. When he opens his eyes, I'm met with a stare so penetrating, it tightens the knot in my chest, and then something changes. Before I realize what I'm doing, I reach for him, inches from pressing my hand against his thigh as if to soothe him, but his words cut off my movement.

"Fine," he icily responds in a tone that sends my hand back to my side as if his words have snapped at me like a tight band.

I do the only thing I know how to do. My upper lip twitches into a snarl, and in a low tone, I say, "Fine. So be it."

BETWEEN THE FLAMES

PART II

CHAPTER 28

OVER THE NEXT WEEK, I stick to my routine, training with Crystal and spending time in the library. The only difference has been that I now take more of my meals in the Great Hall with the others. Callian has only joined us on a few occasions. I assume he wants to give me my space.

"I think today is the day you learn self-control," Crystal calls out.

"Now why would I want that? I quite like my chaos," I tease, looking back at her, feeling my hair whip around my face.

We ride into an empty field northwest of the palace, far away from any distractions. I can feel Cirrus' excitement in the way he gallops. Every curve of the land allows more freedom the further we go. I gently pull Cirrus' reins, and he slows down, trotting up the rest of the hill. We come to a halt when we crest the top. I dismount, surveying the land with my hand raised above my brow to shield my eyes from the sun. Even from this distance, the palace is glorious.

"You have too much rage, Viona. The only time your power comes out is when it is unwilled. Today, you will summon it yourself," she calls out.

There is a bit of truth to her words. All this pent-up rage has to go somewhere, but as I take in the view, I wish I could shut the world off just for today and let myself be, but it's a peace I feel won't ever come. My eyes trail up the tall mountain cutting through the sky with all its sharp edges. The higher my eyes go, the more it appears the weather would be too relentless and unforgiving for anyone who dares to travel up. Snow powders the top, casting an ominous haze. Such contrast to the sun forming a halo above the sky. Bone-white sand dusts the bottom of the mountain, leading into the ocean. Wildflowers grow between large rocks and around the evergreen trees.

This is the closest I've ever been to Halos Mountain. My heart flutters with excitement. Callisto's stone walls are the only thing separating me from ditching today's lessons to explore. One section of the wall seems like it's seen better days. Vines and shrubs vein up the side, weaving through small cracks and crevices. It's clear nature has been reclaiming it for many lifetimes. My eyes follow the rest as it stretches miles away until it disappears deep beneath the waves.

I turn to find Crystal still astride her white mare, watching me with a smile. The sun hits her light-blonde hair, casting that radiant violet hue to match those eyes. I turn back around. A sudden gust of wind brushes against me, and my hair whips around my face. There it is, the faint smell of the beach filling all my senses—saltwater, blossom, and driftwood. I close my eyes, hoping to get just one more fleeting smell. I hear her dismount behind me. Her boots make a soft thud against the ground.

"It's nice and quiet, isn't it?" she says, tightening the belt around her cream-colored trousers. She always seems to match. The sleeveless tunic complements her beige corset. Her dark leather arm guards with silver-plated studs match her boots. She managed to braid her hair sometime between breakfast and before we left the stables. There are two on each side, curving with the shape of her head in a tight uniform. Maybe, one day, I'll care a little more about my appearance. I turn to her, still shielding my eyes from the sun.

"Yes, it's a good distraction. Thank you." I offer a smile that doesn't quite reach my eyes.

I realize how much I leaned on Callian for comfort. There was more than coiling heat between us. We enjoyed each other's company. Every time my mind would wander, he had a way of making me laugh, grounding me back to reality. I hate to admit it, but I wish he were beside me.

She reaches out and squeezes my arm. Her eyes search mine. She must sense the tension hiding behind them. "Come on," she says.

We lead the horses under a large tree to shade them from the heat. There is a comfort in the way the tall blades of grass rub against one another in the wind with fluid grace. I tie Cirrus to the tree, and he nudges me in a way that tells me he wants more. I stumble backward a little and chuckle.

"That's right. You like getting scratches." I smile, gently running my hands along his head and over the backs of his ears. Then I scratch his chest. He seems to like the extra attention. I turn to leave, but he nudges me once more.

"Hey!" I snort. "What's gotten into you?" Grinning, I then remember the weird little thing he and Callian do. Cirrus lowers his head slightly toward me. He wants me to rest my forehead against his. "You're shameless," I tease, placing both my hands on his face and pressing my forehead to his. My eyes close. We stay in this position for a few moments. "You, sir, are just as stubborn as your father."

He snorts, puffing out a breath as heat blows from his nostrils.

"I think all of you are," Crystal says. She searches around our satchels and pulls out our water skins. "Let's go."

I give Cirrus one more rub before falling into step with Crystal. My mind reels back to when we were at the stables. I was ready to take any horse they gave me. I was confused when the stable lad led me to Cirrus' stall. He said, "The prince wanted to ensure you took him out today. Something about how he trusts him." I was just as shocked when he handed me Callian's sword. I had my mothers dagger at my hip, but I haven't been given an official sword yet.

There is another tree not too far from the horses. We walk over to it and take shelter in its shade.

"Sit," she says, motioning to the space in front of her. I plant myself in the same position as Crystal: cross-legged but with my back to the palace.

"Close your eyes, and listen to your surroundings," she says. "Do you hear it?"

I straighten my shoulders, close my eyes, and lift my chin. A few moments of silence go by. There's nothing.

"I'm not sure what I'm listening for," I admit.

"That's because you're not focusing. Now pay attention," she scolds. "Tell me what you hear."

I take a deep breath, focusing on my surroundings. The wind is rustling through the grass, and I hear the sounds of idle horses, but nothing significant seems to gravitate toward me.

"Allow your body and mind to not just hear it, but feel it," Crystal says. I begin pulling the sounds around me.

"I hear the grass bending to the whims of the wind. There's a faint sound below the surface. Small mammals are running about. I hear the horses' hooves making soft thuds against the ground."

"How does that make you feel?" she asks.

"I feel connected, at peace."

"Perfect, keep going. Let your mind search further," she encourages. I allow myself to do so—remembering the smell of the ocean and the shores of Callisto. My mind travels through the landscape until I can see cresting waves. I pull the sound from its path. Suddenly, I hear it.

"I'm by the beach. The waves are crashing down against the sand."

"Wait, what?" she blurts. "Never mind, ignore me. Keep going."

"The waves wash ashore, lapping in a slow, rhythmic calm." I pause as something familiar pushes forth. "A beating heart."

My brows pinch together at its distinct rhythm. I sense Crystal watching me with leery eyes as my mind pushes deeper, further. I'm caught in the current, and it's pulling me in. I see my body waist-high with my silhouette stark against the horizon. My hands rest at my sides, feeling the cool ocean lap against the palms of my hands. Only this time, I'm not scared. There's a serenity blooming as I succumb to the sea. Then, somehow, my soul moves backward, up the shore and through the fields, until a wave of energy jolts back through me.

My eyes flutter open seeing Crystal's mouth hanging wide. Our emotions equally match. This is something I've never felt before, and she just witnessed the black tendrils of smoke filling my eyes. The darkness recedes instantly.

"Where did you go?" she whispers, seeming unsure of what to do next. She looks more fascinated than anything. I explain to her what happened. The more I talk, the more she understands. "Viona, do you know what you just did?" She leans forward, squeezing my legs in excitement.

My brows furrow as her claws dig into my thighs. "First, you're grabbing me too tight." I gently brush her hands off. "Second, no, I don't know, so do you mind filling me in?"

"You just soul-traveled!"

"I did what?" I pause. My lips slightly part. *Did I hear her correctly?*

"It's when your soul is able to go somewhere without you physically being there. This is incredible and extremely rare. The most astonishing thing about this is you did it so effortlessly. Do you realize how extraordinary you are?" She beams.

I scoff under my breath. "I don't think I could ever see myself that way."

She can't stop the smile beaming across her face. "I mean, it's slightly scary. The way your eyes did the whole all-black thing, but *this* is a rarity."

I lift a brow and cross my arms over my chest. "Duly noted."

"I'm sorry, that was insensitive of me. Has Callian seen any of this?" Her voice softens.

The mention of his name makes my heart sink. "Yes, unfortunately he's seen more than anyone ever has." I look away, tightening the grip on my arms while focusing on Cirrus and how happy he looks grazing on the grass. His life is so simple, and now I feel like an idiot for envying the life of a horse.

I try to see the point of this useless exercise, but one thing is clear. I look up at her. "There was a slight difference this time. I wasn't pissed off or scared. That could be why I had more control. I was able to pull myself back. Other times, Callian has been there to do it." He didn't have to be, yet he made it seem like such an easy choice.

She softly nods her head, soaking in the information. "We will work on that so you'll be able to pull yourself back each time. For now, let's continue."

"Okay," I reply. My arms uncross, and I let my shoulders fall to the sides. I relax my body and exhale. She scoots back a little, creating more distance between us.

"Hold your hands out like this." She extends hers out, both palms facing each other, and shapes them as if she's holding a large circle. Suddenly, the ground trembles. I look down, watching tiny beads of water rise from the compacted dirt. There is a profound beauty in the way she borrows from her elements so effortlessly. The droplets swirl together, forming a sphere of water. I mimic her form. She sends me a quick nod. "Good. Search for that fire inside you. Try doing it in the same manner as our first exercise."

I close my eyes. My brows knit while I begin searching for those strands of light inside me. The more I search, the more those little shadows appear, weaving through like tendrils. The moment I hesitate, they pull back.

"It's there, but I can't seem to grab onto it." I steady my hands. All the muscles in my body seem to seize, and my jaw ticks. I can feel a sheen of sweat above my brows. "I can't." I exhale sharply as I abruptly lower my hands back down to my thighs. I can taste defeat on my tongue.

She gently wraps her hands around my wrists and brings them back up. "Clip those words from your vocabulary." She leans in, keeping that strong eye contact. "I won't accept that. Tell yourself, Viona. Yes. You. Can."

I nod, licking my lower lip. I form my hands into a circle, palms facing together, and close my eyes. This time, when I feel the tendrils of light, shadows appear again. I'm pushing further, searching for that build-up. I begin to crave the feeling of it snaking through my veins, but my hands shake. I'm holding myself back, but why? Why am I so fucking hesitant all the time? I'm sure Crystal sees my struggle as I grit through my teeth. Tears of frustration fill my eyes while anger simmers beneath the surface.

"You can either let your powers make you their bitch, or you can bring the darkness to its knees and own it. Choose a side, Viona, because the weak and the evil do not play nice together. Right now, you are the lesser."

In this moment, I realize all the hurt, anger, and rage created that spark of power inside me. Every time grief kicks down the door, I'm there submitting myself to it, on my knees. My hands tremble as I will the power coursing through my veins to come forth. A faint, white light appears in the palms of my hands. I see the light beaming in through my eyelids.

"That's it, keep pulling from that source," Crystal encourages.

I reach beyond the darkness for those tiny tendrils. All those moments where I stood frozen in time, watching my mother from the balcony. That feeling I would get when she smiled. The beautiful memories of her fight against all the memories of rage each time my father cast me aside. I want balance. I want the peace I know I deserve, needing both the dark and the light to coexist so I can have control. I can contain this chaos within me without letting it set me and everything else ablaze. This time, I wait. I become the predator waiting for darkness to come. Before it begins to intertwine itself around my light, I grab onto it and begin weaving it myself. All of a sudden, a sharp roar of fire hits the air. Heat warms the space.

My eyes fling open. Orange-yellow flames flicker and dance between my palms. My jaw drops. I look over to Crystal, watching the angles of her face illuminated by the source of light as a cluster of clouds pass above us.

My eyes water at the miraculous sight of fire churning.

"I did it," I faintly whisper under my breath, not sure if this is real. "I finally did it!" Confidence blooms inside me. Tears of joy run down my face, and I feel the heavy, thick wall of pressure and worry chip away. My eyes lock with Crystal's. "After all this time of uncertainty, all the doubt, and feeling so lost within myself . . . I fucking did it."

"Not only did you do it, Viona, but it's also contained. Think about how you did this." She watches in awe at the sphere swirling between my hands.

"Darkness ignites the flame, and love controls the chaos," I whisper, watching the flames swirl idly in unison. The more I hold it in my hands, the calmer it becomes.

"When love weaves into the threads of your magic, you can achieve many things. This is just the beginning of all you are meant to be. Don't draw back with doubt. Allow yourself to marvel at your power," Crystal says, beaming with pride.

I release my hands. As soon as the flames disintegrate into the air, Crystal leans forward, hugging me so tight we fall over onto the grass. Shrill laughter fills the air as the both of us roll onto our backs. Cirrus makes a sound. Our eyes dart over to our horses. He rears up and snorts.

"Sorry, Cirrus!" I yell.

My stomach hurts from laughing so much. I roll on the ground and look over at Crystal.

"Your hair." I snort.

Laughter-induced tears well up in her eyes as her fingers feel all the foliage embedded into her braids. "Who cares? It's bound to get messed up anyway. If not by rolling around in the grass, then when I'm on my back for the hot cook."

I wipe the tears from the corners of my eyes and try to catch my breath.

"Do you even know his name?" I ask.

She takes one good look at me. We pause, letting that question hang in the air, then cackle again. Amidst our laughter and picking grass out from her hair, I realize it's nice having this feminine energy around. Even though I miss Callian, being here with Crystal is what I needed. I allow myself to feel all the complexities of this moment without falling apart.

As our giggles subside, we decide to lie under the shade of the tree and fall into a comfortable silence. I catch glimpses of clouds moving swiftly across the sky through its swaying branches. The wind is picking up, drifting toward the harbor.

Is this what it feels like to have a friend? You do things together, laugh, bicker, and just settle into this quiet place of comfort? Surely, she must feel the same. Otherwise, we would have started our journey back to the palace.

"If you could travel anywhere, where would you go?" Crystal asks, turning her body toward mine. She leans her head against her palm, and her braids rest against the ground. I smile. A pleasant sensation infuses my body.

"I'd love to lie on a warm beach somewhere with my ship anchored in the distance. In a wild world, I would be a pirate. All my stolen treasures would be on board. I would end each day watching dusk turn to twilight and have good ale in my cup to warm my bones from the night's chill."

"Hmm," she says. A faint smile splays across her lips while she gets lost in deep thought. "I think you'd make the perfect pirate. You certainly are mean enough to be one."

My head tips back as I chuckle. "Sure you don't want to join me? You have a tongue sharp enough to cut out any man's heart."

She chuckles, throwing a piece of grass at me that only goes half the distance.

"You could enchant them with your beauty while I steal the goods. It's a win-win," I admit.

"I'd be up for a few nefarious adventures." A villainous look forms on her face before she breaks into another big smile. I turn my body toward her, mimicking her position, and she continues, "Do you see anyone on your ship with you? Perhaps a handsome, green-eyed prince who is absolutely weak in the knees for you?" She raises a brow.

I sink down a little. "It's complicated." I sigh. My eyes lower to the ground where my dark hair is sprawled across the grass, searching for any pieces of foliage I can pick out, but to my surprise, there isn't much. "He's upset because I asked for distance. Whatever 'it' was between us, it's over. I just don't think the timing is right, knowing what lies ahead of me. I have to focus on why I'm really here." I know I am trying to convince myself more than convince her.

"What relationship isn't complicated? That's how you grow to-gether. Does he make you happy? Does he treat you right?" she says, catching my gaze. "Callian is like a brother to me. I've known him most of my life, and one thing I know for sure is that he doesn't hand his heart out to just anyone. He has so graciously given it to you. I want the both of you to be happy."

Words spoken like a true sister.

I look away. Each word slams into me like thick, heavy bricks. Yes, he does make me happy. I would scream it at the top of my lungs if I could. He's everything.

"Those are questions you should ask yourself," she continues. "It's not always perfect. At times, it can be a daunting task, but that's what makes a couple evolve. If you two found happiness in each other, why stop?" Her features tighten, tension filling her voice. She takes a deep breath as if she can finally breathe after releasing the weight of all her built-up thoughts.

I'm clenching my teeth so hard, my jaw hurts. *Well, here goes nothing.*

"I had a vision that I killed him," I rasp. I quickly sit up, bringing my knees to my chest and wrapping my arms around my legs as a surge of images flashes through my mind. "In my vision, he was in a trance. He was under me, but he really wasn't there. He didn't even react as the blade pierced into his heart. When I looked at the mirror above the bed, it was me holding the dagger, yet it wasn't. I don't know how to describe it, but my darkness had taken him. So, yes, I ended it with Callian, but not because I stopped caring for him. I did it because I'm afraid the vision will come true." My voice cracks as tears swell in my eyes.

"Hey, it's okay." Crystal soothingly comes to my side and wraps an arm around me.

I look at her with a glassy stare. "It won't be," I mumble. "When I went into his room, the night I cut him off, everything I saw in my vision was confirmed. The same room, the same bedsheets, the same mirror, the energy in the room charged with tainted darkness. I panicked. I said some regretful words and ran." I pause, hearing his words echo in my mind. "It's what I do best, run."

She holds me tighter, rocking me back and forth while making a soft hush. My chest tightens at the amount of comfort she is enveloping me in. Her hand brushes away a strand of hair that's clinging to the side of my face from my tears.

"I wish you would have come and talked to me about this. You know I'm here for you, right?"

I rub the back of my knuckles under my eyes. "I suppose."

"I'm serious," she asserts. "I'm not just your *current royal guard.*" She rolls her eyes as her mouth quirks up into a grin. "I want you to know I'm also your friend."

My eyes swell once more. I pull her in for a hug, this time, wrapping both arms tightly around her small frame.

"You have no idea how much that means to me, Crystal. Thank you," I whisper.

She cups the back of my head. "You can always ugly cry with me. Any time you need to." I can feel her smile stretching across her face. We both chuckle.

The air suddenly shifts. My smile wanes, and my eyes narrow in on the tall, stone walls just beyond as a small fissure appears. Every single crack already embedded in the relic of a wall expands. The ground shakes, setting off a ricochet effect. The structure is crumbling. Crystal and I jump to our feet. Before I can process what is happening, the wall explodes. What used to be sections of Callisto's fortified walls are now pieces of large, sharp, jagged rocks, and they are flying our way.

CHAPTER 29

"**L**ook out!" Crystal shoves me out of the way.

Large pieces of rubble fly through the air. My body slides against the grass as my head thrashes back. Crystal conjures a tall sheet of ice from the ground, shielding her from the impact.

The pieces barely miss.

The blunt force of the rocks crack her barrier. There's a ringing in my ears. I stagger to my feet as my eyes dart over to the hole created by the explosion. Six snarling larkins push their way through, picking up enormous pieces of rubble and tossing them out of their way like tiny pebbles. A being who I can only assume is their commander sits astride a dark mare between the broken wall. This beast is slender with yellow eyes that contrast the wisps of smoke swirling around his charred skin. His eyes skim over the landscape until they land on me. My lips curl into a snarl.

With a deep, guttural voice, the commander raises his spear and points it in my direction. "Retrieve the princess!" His eyes bore into mine, smiling with a mouth full of decayed teeth.

My adrenaline spikes. Of all the things that could come for me, why them? I have no weapons, only my dagger sheathed at my thigh and a power I can barely summon. My mind flashes back to the moment the larkin's hands wrapped tightly around my throat. I was close to death, tasting the last bit of life on my tongue. I was barely able to fight off *one* outside the White Forest. How the fuck am I supposed to fight off six?

The ringing in my ears subsides. Able or not, the larkins are all headed my way. I don't have time to think about how. We only have seconds to act, and I need my weapon.

"Cover me!" I shout to Crystal as I dash over to the horses. I can hear shards of ice hitting the air, metal clanging together, and the beasts' grotesque sounds. I quickly turn around. Crystal is managing to hold them off, but she's being surrounded.

I pick up speed, running faster than I ever thought I could toward Cirrus, all those early morning jogs paying off. As I approach, he rears back, letting me know I'm being followed.

I untie the reins from the tree. "I'll keep them away from you, Cirrus, but don't run too far." I slap him on his hip. He takes off, and Crystal's horse follows. I unsheathe Callian's sword.

I whirl around to see a larkin standing twenty feet away. The skin around his knuckles crack as he clenches a sharp dagger in each hand. He's much bigger than the one I killed outside the White Forest, well over six feet tall. A growl ripples from his chest. I want to hurl from the smell already assaulting my nose but don't have time to linger on the thought as the larkin launches a dagger my way. I drop to the ground, feeling the air whip above my head as the blade zooms past. My awareness rises, sending a wave of heat unfurling beneath my skin. I rise to my feet, tightening my grip on the sword.

"I'm going to enjoy playing with your insides, pretty girl," he growls.

He glares at me through the brim of hot air fogging from his mouth, then advances, unsheathing a short blade. While larkins possess impeccable strength, they're heavy-footed and slow fighters. I dodge his attack, ducking low. My sword slices clean through his flesh. Another gargling scream rips from his throat, putting his sharp fangs on display.

The smell of blood taints the air. He stumbles back but quickly regains his footing. He swings the blade in the air, and our swords collide with a clashing force. His form towers over mine as I hold my stance. Chaos storms wildly behind the larkin's fierce, yellow eyes, and the stench coming from his mouth enshrouds me in waves of heat. He pushes me back, eyes narrowing as a growl rumbles in his chest. My boots skid against the ground, inch by inch. I hold the position with all my strength until I can regain my footing. With a hard thrust, I push forward. Our swords slip free of each other. He growls another heated breath and strikes out. I parry his next move, falling behind and striking his other leg. He drops to his knees. One swift motion is all it takes for his head to be cut clean from his shoulders. Blood sprays the side of my face. The air is misted in red as his head goes rolling. His carcass falls, hitting the ground with a heavy thud.

The blood of my enemy coats my teeth, and I feel a small tendril of darkness weaving through my veins. It's his death, something in his blood that binds me in a strange, guided light, giving me the ability to sense the rest of the surrounding creatures without looking. Their hearts beat hard and heavy, like slow war drums. I snarl, turning to meet another larkin's stare. I swing my sword, landing an uppercut straight into his abdomen, feeling the tip of the blade slicing through every organ and corded muscle that kept this fucking retched beast alive. His eyes widen, and his body writhes until he expels his last breath. With one hard thrust, I draw my blade back.

My eyes search the terrain for Crystal.

With fluid grace, she fires a shot of ice toward a beast holding a longsword. The force pushes him back a few feet. His eyes dart down, watching the ice liquefy and soak into the ground.

"Your powers are weak." He laughs maliciously, swinging his weapon at his side. A grin spreads across Crystal's face as the ground rumbles beneath his feet. The sudden shift throws him off balance. He looks at her with saliva dripping off his teeth. "YOU BIT—"

With one quick motion of her hand, palm facing the sky, a large blade of ice shoots up from the ground. It slides through his flesh, cracking every bone in its path, impaling the larkin right through his center. A growl gurgles in his throat as the icy tip protrudes from his mouth.

Two more larkins are closing in, but she uses her powers to push them further back, blasting them with waves of ice. She saunters over to the impaled creature, steel eyes scaling up and down his almost-lifeless form, watching his body convulse. Blood pours out of the sides of his mouth, cascading down his neck and arms. Every orifice in his face bleeds. He can no longer move his head as the massive piece of ice holds him in place. One of his eyes manages to find Crystal. In his last moments of life, she whispers something in his ear. He takes one final exhale before perishing. His face points toward the sky, but there is no forgiveness where he's going.

I feel another set of eyes searing into my back and turn to see yet another larkin snarling, observing what a mess we're making of his friends. He moves forward and strikes. I counter each attack until one lands, cutting my arm. I hiss, feeling his blade's sharp edge cut into my skin. It is just enough to send my powers coursing through my veins. He jumps into the air and lands behind me.

One enormous hand wraps around the back of my neck and picks me up. My body is suspended in the air with my back to him as Callian's sword clashes to the ground. He swings me around, showing his leader he has me. The larkin's ear-shattering growl reverberates around me. Blood pulses in my ears as memories of the larkin outside the White Forest flash before my eyes again. But this time, I won't let fear seize me. I blink back the memories before they can take control. My eyes glance over at Crystal.

Before I can even register how she's faring, I feel my stomach take a dip, as though I'm flying through the air. He slams me into the ground. All the wind knocks out of me as I land on my side, gasping for air. I feel as though every bone in my body has broken, but the pain subsides when I move onto my back.

My eyes flutter open to the sound of him approaching. His dark-yellow eyes go wide as he stops in his tracks. My own eyes sting before I feel a warm sensation fill the space instead. When I start to feel the shadows pulsing with the beat of my heart, I know my eyes are shifting to onyx. His steps falter. He looks over to his leader, then back at me.

"Don't just stand there! Get her, you fool!" his commander orders, still astride his horse by the rubble.

I use the few seconds I have to jump to my feet and extend the palm of my hand out in front of me. A surge of energy races through my body. It shoots up my arms so quickly, it almost throws me back. Flames ignite beneath my skin. Everything slows to a halt, and it seems as though time has stopped. I let out a soft breath. In that exhale, fire scorches through the air, sending a devastating blow to the larkin's face. A scream rips from my throat, taking with it all the anger these beasts have inspired. My powers are unforgiving.

His hands fly to his face as an ear-splitting growl rips from his chest, and an even fouler stench assaults the air. He jumps out of my fiery path, landing directly behind me again.

Predictable.

But this time, he's blinded. He lowers his hands from his face, and I see that his dark-yellow eyes have liquified, dripping from his eye sockets. His screams are agonizing.

My power recedes, and my chest is left heaving in its wake. "That's the last time you put your fucking hands on me, you revolting piece of shit!" I drop to the ground to retrieve Callian's sword and send him an uppercut blow, piercing my blade through his heart. His throaty growl soon goes flat. Blood oozes out as the weight of his body slides toward the hilt of my sword. I push him off with all my strength, and his body slumps onto the ground.

The clamor of metal pulls me from my kill. My head whips around, finding Crystal in an up-close battle with a larkin who holds a mace and chain. Crystal moves with pliant grace every time he takes a swing. The way she fights is like a memorized dance, with a ferocity for malice. Her magic comes out like blades of ice tearing into his flesh. He's losing momentum. His weapon falls, and he drops to his knees. A pool of blood saturates the ground as he bleeds out.

I run up behind her. "You're wicked." My lips curve into a grin, watching the larkin grunt.

"You can give your compliments to the chef. He showed me where the main arteries are when prepping meat."

"Hm, interesting." I reply while observing the larkin's chest rise and fall.

Her smile wavers as she kneels beside the larkin. He struggles to speak, choking on his words, but they hold no importance to us.

Crystal is winded from the fight, but I finally hear what she whispers to her enemies as they take their last breath.

"The stars will not claim you, you will not join your brothers. Your soul exists no more." Her words are a finality to their death. All the air in his lungs expel, and suddenly, the mood shifts.

She looks up at me with knit brows. Her eyes flutter as she struggles to keep the tears from falling. Her features tighten, and something flashes behind those amethyst eyes.

"They have taken so much. They do not deserve grace. None of them do." She straightens her posture as she struggles to find the right words. Her kills need no justification. I would kill them all if it meant she would have more peace. I faintly exhale, knowing the power memories can hold. We can suppress the bad ones all we want, but when they decide to crawl their way out of the shadows, they can sometimes feel like death brushing its reminder of where we once were.

I place a hand on her shoulder, giving it a slight squeeze. With my other, I reach out so she can take hold. I pull her up. Our hands remain clasped together, and our arms lock across our chests.

"We got this, Crystal."

She nods against my forehead.

We turn to find the commander pacing back and forth on his horse. His growl becomes louder. His teeth snap as bloodlust fills his eyes. He tightens his grip on the reins and charges for us.

"Do you want to fly?" Crystal blurts out.

"What?" My head whips back in her direction.

Is she delusional?

I quickly sheathe my sword. Determination fills her eyes.

"I'll take that as a yes," she says, grabbing the front of my clothes.

"Are you insane?" I yell. Every muscle in my body grows tense.

"Next lesson: How to create a distraction," she says.

Before I can blink, she tosses me into the air. I go flying toward the charging larkin. I tighten my grip on the hilt of my sword as my other hand flares out. I'm falling, but somehow, I regain my position and land on my feet. Wide-eyed, as shock sends a chill down my body, I look back at her in astonishment and see she's running our way. The larkin snaps his face toward me just as icy blades protrude from his chest. His eyes go wide. Blood spills out of his mouth, and he slumps over, falling off his horse.

Crystal rushes toward me and the larkin.

"When you said I'd learn to create a distraction, I didn't think I would *become* one!" I pant, placing both hands on my knees, trying to catch my breath.

She shrugs. "It worked, right?"

I scoff.

The larkin coughs out blood, bringing our attention back to him, and his lips turn into a grueling snarl as he watches us. Crystal leans down to the creature. Suddenly, her body jerks back and her breath shudders as she tries to suck in air. I see her hand clench at her side.

The larkin laughs with an icy edge that chills me to my core. "You will not curse me as I take my last breath." He seethes.

Crystal's body falls back. My eyes focus on the red gushing out from between her fingers as a blade sticks out from her side. Her eyes widen as she hits the ground.

"No," I whisper. Time seems to stop, the wind in my sail frozen as my chest tightens. Tears swell in my eyes, watching all the color in her face drain. All the light and beauty she emits begins to drift.

"No!" I scream. My chest heaves. Both my hands grip the hilt of my sword. I raise my blade into the air and pierce the larkin right through his chest, finishing what she started. I twist my sword, screaming at the top of my lungs with all the rage consuming me. His bones crack, reverberating around my blade. I drop to my knees and drag her into my arms as my hand compresses around her wound. The warrior who can take out beasts twice as large as herself now lies in my arms with such fragility, it frightens me.

"Crystal, wake up." I gently pat the side of her face. "Please." My vision fogs. "No, no, no, please don't take her from me," I beg the gods, the stars, or anyone who will listen. My hands shake. I've seen so many wounded, but this is different. I care about her, and I am not ready to let her go. My mind flashes to everyone she loves. "I have to get you back to the palace," I whisper.

Finally, she opens her eyes. I choke out a smile.

"There you are." My lips quiver.

"There's a vial in my pouch. Give it to me," she pants out, struggling with every word. Each breath she takes is torment for her. I search for the little, brown pouch secured at her hip and feel around for the vial.

I pull it out, using my thumb to flick the cork off. I bring the vial to her lips. She opens just enough for me to pour some in carefully. Adrenaline runs like fire through my veins. My hands shake and some of the liquid drips off the sides of her mouth. Whatever this is supposed to do, I hope it's enough until we can get help.

The ground rumbles again. My breathing stills as I look over to Callisto's shattered wall where the leader once stood. Whispers are all around me. My powers stretch beyond the wall, sensing what draws near. I must be soul-traveling, because I can see horses riding forward. Their hooves strike hard against the ground like rolling thunder as they descend the hill toward the broken wall.

Larkins.

More of them.

"They're coming," I faintly whisper. My expression grows grim. My pulse is sent to a racing speed. She tries to stand, but a flash of pain causes her to stumble. We fall back to the ground. She cries out in pain.

A small army of larkins sit astride their stark-as-night horses between the rubble with fire-tipped arrows pointing in our direction. The voices in my head grow so loud, they're deafening. My breathing becomes rapid and heavy. I extend my hand, willing fire to push through, but nothing comes out.

"Fuck!" I yell. My hands begin to shake as nerves seize me. The archers bend their bows and release their fiery arrows into the sky. I try again, screaming at the top of my lungs, a mournful last attempt to expel the rawness cutting deep into my heart. I brace for the impact of what will likely deliver us back to the stars.

CHAPTER 30

I NSTEAD OF ARROWS, BOLTS of lightning strike the ground around us. I lunge forward, hovering my body over Crystal's and inhaling what I think will be my last breath, but I live long enough to feel the ground rumbling beneath us.

How am I still breathing?

Blue-and-white light illuminates her face. I look up through the soft, swirling fissures of light to see the silhouette of a man moving with precision through the enemy. Bolts of lightning emit from the palm of his hand, splitting open the cavity of a larkin as this man filets him with one strike. Blood mists the air, but it doesn't reach us. We're enveloped in a glowing light. It hums, protecting us from the remaining fleet of beasts.

Crystal moans.

"Don't worry, I've have you," I reassure her.

"Since when do I worry?" She faintly smiles with her hand still pressed against her side. Her witty sense of humor lightens the tension.

I choke out a laugh. "Apparently, never,"

I brush the wet strands of hair from her face. Her eyes widen at the hovering display of lights, and the shield around us disappears.

"Gareon?" My mouth gapes. He looks nothing like the calm man I met before. Chaos storms in his blue, moonlit eyes. With every breath he takes, the markings on his arms flare brightly along his rich-brown skin, pulsing between blue and ivory, sprawling up his neck and jawline. Every single muscle on his body is on full display. He's in nothing but dark-blue trousers and brown, knee-high leather boots.

My eyes skim over the terrain. He killed every single larkin without drawing a sword—a strength and power I envy. He drops to his knees beside us, his eyes narrowing in on Crystal. They return to that glowing honey color as his features unexpectedly soften.

"How did you get here so quickly?" I ask, still shocked by his sudden presence.

"I'll explain later. We need to get Crystal to the palace."

I nod, turning my head to call for Cirrus. His hooves gallop across the field toward us within a few moments. Crystal's white mare flanks his side. I look down to see the dagger embedded deeply into her hip; the hilt sticking out between her fingers. I'm afraid she'll bleed out if we don't hurry.

"Give her to me, Viona," Gareon says, reassuring me as he takes her in his arms.

"Viona gave me a healing potion. It should be enough . . . for now." She pants. "But the pain." She pauses, staring up at him. "Take me to Sydney."

He nods.

I quickly mount Cirrus and look over to see Gareon cradling Crystal and resting her head into the crook of his neck astride her horse. Every wince she makes sends chills down my spine. With the bit of strength she has, she holds on.

We take off. As we ride, gut-wrenching guilt squeezes the air in my lungs.

Gareon presses his hand against hers as she compresses her wound. Blood slowly seeps through his fingers. A bright, glowing light emits from his hand. He glances over to me.

"This will seize the waves of pain while we ride. It's the best I can do until we get her to Sydney," he calls out.

I nod, my hands tighten around the reins, and I look straight ahead.

We ride as fast as we can to the northwest entrance of the palace. There's already a fleet of guards riding toward the site of the explosion.

As soon as I'm within calling distance, I yell, "Get Sydney now!" to the two guards who remain by the entrance. All the emotion held in my throat releases. I look over to Crystal. Her eyes are closed, and blood spills over the side of her hip. That fucking vial didn't do anything.

As soon as they see Crystal in his arms, one of them yells and rides with haste toward the palace. The other rushes toward me.

"What happened?" The guard's eyes widen seeing the amount of blood all over us.

"Larkins broke through on the northwest side of the walls. We need Sydney," Gareon replies.

"She will be heading toward the infirmary. Follow me." The guard clicks his tongue. He turns his horse around and squeezes its sides, leading the way.

We arrive in less than a minute and see a large number of guards already here along with townspeople lining our path with grief-stricken expressions, showing their support. I overhear some asking if there is anything they can do to help Crystal. Just like the day I first arrived, word spread fast.

The guards lower her body off the horse, and I quickly dismount and follow them.

A strong force of energy swings the doors open. Sydney stands in the doorway with an apron over her dress. Worry pinches her brows.

"I've prepped the table. Bring Crystal into the infirmary quickly," she orders, stepping to the side to let them pass. She looks me over, searching for any wounds, and skims over the cut on my arm. She cuts me a look, one I cannot discern. I'll have to sort through those emotions later because shame is creeping up my spine. I can't help but feel that I failed Crystal.

"We were attacked," I blurt, not really thinking of the words coming out of my mouth.

"No shit. Tell me something useful," she bites back. "Who attacked you?"

"Larkins," I confirm, keeping my features tight. Her eyes go wide as though she's been thrown back into a memory that was sealed away.

"No . . . " she whispers, eyes darting toward the guards as they carry Crystal in. All the color in Sydney's face drains. She whispers under her breath, "Please don't let it be what I think it is."

As soon as Gareon makes sure Crystal is in the infirmary, he disappears. A few moments later, Callian bursts through the door. His arms stretch wide across the doorframe as he murmurs a word under his breath. His eyes darken as they search my body for injury.

"I'm fine," I say the moment he finds the cut on my bicep. Then his attention shifts toward Crystal lying across the table. All the color in his face drains. The emerald tendrils of shadow that were brimming his eyes recede.

Sydney says nothing. The look on her face is enough. She's straight to the point, pulling all her focus in on Crystal. "I need to see what kind of dagger the larkin used. Hand me the scissors," she orders her assistant who already has it in his hands. The young male has not said a word since we arrived, but he works fast. His short, dark hair is tied back. What they're wearing makes me a little uneasy, as if they're already prepping for surgery.

Guilt flashes behind Callian's eyes, and he shakes his head in disbelief. I grab ahold of his arm.

"Hey, it's not your fault," I remind him. He meets me with a glassy stare. Though he says nothing, it seems my voice stopped his mind from slipping.

We watch Sydney cut away the fabric around Crystal's side as she peels off the soaked material. There's so much blood, we can't see much else. Sydney's assistant brings over a stack of clean cloths and warm water. They begin gently wiping away the blood.

"Her bleeding has slowed," the male observes.

"After she was struck, she told me to give her a vial from her pouch," I say, struggling for words. Everything is happening so quickly.

Sydney nods, analyzing the wound. She exhales, pressing a hand on her chest. "Thank the stars this is just a regular blade." She and Callian share a look that I can't read, then she looks at me. "Some of them wield weapons not of this world. If one of those happens to penetrate the skin, a venomous poison spreads throughout the body. If not treated immediately, it can result in death."

My brows knit as I take in this information.

"The fucking assholes," I murmur, lowering my eyes to Crystal. There is a sense of serenity watching her sleep, seeing her thick, blonde lashes resting over her cheeks.

"That vial you gave her slows down the process. Poison or not, between that and Gareon arriving just in time, it gives me a head start on her healing."

Callian remains silent with his eyes fixed on Crystal. His jaw ticks with tension, and the column of his neck pulsates. I can sense a storm brewing inside him.

"Is she going to be okay?" I ask Sydney. I already know she is, but I'm seeking affirmation for Callian's peace of mind.

"Yes. She'll make a rather quick and full recovery." She looks over to Callian.

I exhale sharply. "What can I do to help?"

"Hold her hand and keep her still. I need to remove the blade and stop the bleeding."

I nod.

Callian takes a few steps back and runs his hands through his hair, inhaling deep breaths repeatedly. He knows what's about to come.

"Callian, I need you to rein your shit in and help me." Her words are stern. I can't even begin to fathom how she is doing this, knowing who lies on the table.

"I know." He exhales in a growl and goes to stand beside Sydney on the other side of the table. Our eyes lock before we firmly place our hands on Crystal's body.

Sydney barely touches the blade. Crystal's eyes fly open, and an excruciating scream rips from her throat. Her pain is felt throughout the room. Beyond the doors, a clamor of distress begins from those who stand beyond it. I clench my teeth at her ear-shattering scream.

Sydney takes a deep breath, trying to block out her cries, but I can tell she is shaken. We all are. Callian and I continue to hold Crystal down while Sydney wraps her hand around the protruding weapon. Sydney's eyes narrow in on me. She silently mouths a countdown so I know when she's about to pull the dagger from Crystal's side. At the last moment, I hold Crystal tighter. Callian grits his teeth. We brace for what's coming. With one swift motion, Sydney pulls the dagger free. Her assistant immediately puts pressure on the wound.

Another cry rips from Crystal's throat, echoing throughout the halls. This time, her eyes stay open. She makes eye contact with me and grabs my arm, digging her nails into my skin. I hold back the grimace of pain.

"It's okay, Crystal. You can do this," I remind her. I glance at Callian, hoping my words also reach him. The pain she's inflicting on me is nothing compared to what's coursing through her body. I'm sure the entire palace can hear it. She could rip my arms apart if she needed to, as long as I can see her smile again. She looks up to the ceiling as tears flood down the sides of her face, trying her best to bite down on the shock of pain. Every moment feels like an eternity as Sydney and her assistant work.

I hear Iván arguing with the guards posted outside the infirmary doors to let him in. Hearing the distress in his voice makes my heart sink, but he can't see her, not like this.

Suddenly, Crystal goes quiet, and her grip loosens on my arms. My blood runs cold, thinking the worst has happened. My head snaps back in her direction to see a bright, white light emitting from Sydney's palm as she works her healing magic over the wound. The dagger now lies in a pool of blood in a large bowl off to the side.

Crystal's breathing is stable.

"I've lulled her into a deep sleep to work on her wound," she says, concentrating on her magic. I nod, noting that she has the same magic as Callian. She must sense my apprehension, because she says, "I had to . . . for her sake."

"It's alright. I understand it is needed sometimes," I whisper, glancing at Callian.

My hand strokes Crystal's beautiful, long, blonde hair. A blade of grass sticks out between one of her braids. I pluck it out as another tear slips free. She looks so peaceful; it almost looks like she isn't even breathing, but the subtle rise and fall of her chest gives me comfort.

"Thank you, Sydney." Callian's voice is hoarse. He presses a kiss to her temple before joining me at my side.

"You can bring Iván in now," Sydney says. There's a calmness in her voice as she continues to work her magic.

I open the doors to find Iván a mess. He rushes toward me. "Is she okay? What happened to her?" Tears brim his eyes.

"She's going to be okay. A larkin stabbed her, but Sydney is in the process of mending her wound."

"Thank the fucking gods." He exhales. He pulls me into his chest and hugs me so tight, I can't breathe. On contact, I see something flashing before my eyes. It is him in the middle of a field, surrounded by haze, but his back is turned. My eyes widen at the sudden image.

He leaves to go to Crystal before he can see the look on my face. I'm reminded this sometimes happens the first time I touch someone. It's like peering inside a veiled dream, only I can't interpret what it means. I rub my temples before following him in.

When he approaches the table, he laces his hand in hers. Though she's asleep, he talks to her.

"My sleeping beauty," he whispers, caressing her face.

I go up to Callian, placing a hand on his chest. He looks down at me, calmer but still at a loss for words.

"Let's give them some privacy," I whisper.

A tear finally breaks free, running down his cheek when he nods. I brush it away with the back of my hand. He wraps his arms around me. I inhale his rich scent. It is the first time in what feels like an eternity since I've touched him. We embrace and hold one another through something forever etched in our time together, and I can't help but wonder how our book will record this moment.

CALLIAN AND I MAKE OUR way back to our chambers, but before we ascend the flight of stairs, I pause. "Gareon saved us today. We wouldn't be here if it weren't for him."

Callian's features pull tight at the knowledge of far more happening. He nods, already knowing what I want to do next.

We head toward the library and then veer right, down the hall. I pause at the bottom of the cast-iron stairs.

"Stay here. I'll only be a moment." He takes a step back and watches me ascend.

Before I can knock, the door swings open. Gareon sits shirtless behind a dark, wooden desk with an inked quill in his hand. I notice his hand is bandaged, but I say nothing. When he sees me in the doorway, he gives a curt nod.

"Well, hello, Viona." He stares at me with narrowing eyes and a look that I can only assume means he was expecting me. He turns to reach for his robe. His blond, moonlight hair drapes down his bare back. The markings on his body are only on his arms and neck, so beautiful on his rich-brown skin. There's so much mystery to this man. Every muscle in his back flexes as he drapes the robe over his body. When he turns to me with a fiery amusement, I quickly look away and clear my throat.

Humored, he says, "Your presence here has caused quite the stir. I apologize for all you have had to endure."

I want to tell him it's alright, but honestly, it isn't. I stay silent. He sits back behind the desk and extends his hand out, waiting for me to sit. I swallow hard. "I can't stay. I just wanted to thank you for saving us."

His elbows rest on the desk, and his fingers lace together. "No thanks needed. You two made quite the mess before I arrived."

The side of my mouth quirks up into a half-smirk. "Glad you noticed."

I step forward, noticing he has a stack of new scrolls and books stacked in one corner.

"How did you arrive so quickly?" I ask, trying to read what he has, but it is impossible when it is upside down.

"Teleportation, my dear, but I already know your next question. It is unsafe to teleport the wounded, otherwise, I would have done so for Crystal."

"Oh," I reply, crossing my arms over my chest and shifting my weight to the side. "Are you always so invasive with people's thoughts?"

"Yes." He smirks, lifting his chin. I blink a few times. His honesty shocks me. I guess that's part of his allure. He lowers his hands and leans back into his chair. His amber eyes glint with humor as he studies me. The silence hangs between us before he speaks again. "You are quite the mystical one yourself. I heard you while I was sifting through my scrolls. The attack summoned me to come back sooner than I'd expected." I open my mouth to speak, but he holds a finger up. "There are still a few things I need to research. When I'm ready to speak with you, I will let you know."

That's it? My mouth clenches shut. The finality in his tone warns me not to press further. He gracefully nods his head, and I take that as my cue to leave.

"You know where to find me," I say before leaving. I descend the stairs, the door closing behind me.

Callian and I part ways and head into our rooms. Before we left Crystal with Iván in the infirmary, he assured us he would remain by her side for the duration of the night, allowing Sydney and us to rest.

I enter the bathing chamber, peel away my blood-soaked clothes, and toss them into a pile, hoping never to see them again. I slip into the bath, soaking until all the tension in my muscles loosens. While I scrub my skin raw, I remember the many times I've soaked in a bath full of the blood of my enemy, but never of a friend. This is different. I realize that love comes at a cost. It's a vulnerability. Crystal came so close to death, I don't know what I would have done if I—

"Fuck." A sob finally breaks free. In frustration, I throw the sponge into the water, cursing. I finally allow myself to cry. I don't have to hold back. I can just release all the tension in my throat for good. I run my hands through my hair, my eyes fixing on the tiny ripples of the water. I have to stop thinking about the what-ifs. My mind cannot go there right now. Yet, the more I stay in this blood-tinged tub, the more my mind drowns in it. I quickly finish bathing, making sure no remnants of battle remain. There is a fresh set of clothes on the counter, so I slip on a pair of black trousers and a long, gray tunic over my body and continue to dry my hair. I crawl into my bed, rest my head on the soft, down pillows filled with goose feathers, and pull the blankets over my face, letting sleep claim me.

CRYSTAL'S LOOK OF HORROR as the larkin struck her flashes through my mind and pulls me from sleep. I shoot up in bed, haunted by the memory of her blood spilling over between my fingers. My heart thrashes against my chest and the pulse in my ears thickens. There's a gentle knock at my door. Barely a sound, but enough to pull me from the thought.

She's fine. She's safe now. I repeat the mantra in my head, expelling any fear that wants to take root. I throw my blankets to the side and stagger my way toward the door.

"Who is it?" I call out, leaning up against the wall and waiting for a reply before opening the door.

"It's me."

My eyes widen, feeling my heart skip a beat.

I can't think of a good response quickly enough. "I don't know who 'me' is. Come back later."

My cheeks flush. That sounded really stupid. I walk away, reminding myself this isn't the time to be vulnerable. I quickly rip apart all the butterflies trying to flutter around in my stomach.

"Viona . . . " Callian sighs in a deep, frustrated breath.

I pause, hating how my name leaves his lips and how it affects me. I turn around and step near the door.

"What do you want?"

"Let me in, please." He keeps his voice low because the guards are constantly patrolling the halls, especially after the attack. There's a longing in Callian's voice.

"What for?" I sigh.

He hesitates. *Why do I feel like I'm going to regret this?*

I open the door to find Callian leaning against the entrance with a raised arm. His hair is disheveled, chest bare. There's a perfect amount of hair below his navel. I can't help but follow the trail that leads to his

. . .

My gods.

I mentally curse the string that is barely holding his black trousers up.

My eyes trail back up his form until I'm met with a smoldering look.

"It's not very polite to stare, Princess."

I scoff. "I wasn't staring, you fool. I'm . . . still waking up."

He grunts in response. "Whatever you have to tell yourself." A hum trickles out from his chest. I can feel my cheeks flushing at that sound, that grunt. I inhale a sharp breath and step to the side. I've concluded I will definitely regret this.

"Come in." I swallow hard, trying not to let my eyes wander up and down his body while his back is turned. His dark hair barely touches the tips of his shoulders. He has the body of a god, and it makes every part of me want to gravitate toward him. My eyes are nothing but betrayers.

I hear the heavy patter of his bare feet as he moves with haste toward the balcony. I close the door behind us and lock it. He then proceeds to check my bathing chambers. When he walks out, he looks relieved, but a somberness still hangs in his eyes. He runs a hand through his long hair and takes a deep breath.

"It's hard to sleep knowing you're out of my sight," he admits. His voice quiets as that cocky demeanor wanes. The side of his jaw flutters.

There's a stillness in the air as my heart squeezes. "Well, that's something you will have to get used to," I reply.

"Can I sleep in here?" he asks. I'm shocked at his question. Some time ago, he walked into my room, acting like he owned it. Now he's asking?

I cross my arms and look away, refusing to allow my body to feel what it wants to. Moments stretch on as I think of all the ways this could end, but when I see the look on his face, it reminds me of all the times I needed someone. All the times I was left alone to deal with all my emotions in solitude. My entire fucking life. He doesn't deserve to feel that way when I stand ten feet away. Sometimes, monsters can bloom amidst pain and grief, and though everyone seems to have a darker side they keep hidden, I won't allow him to become everything

I am. I look over to the fireplace at the settees. They aren't big enough for him to rest comfortably.

I sigh, uncrossing my arms. A little piece of my calloused self chips away. I walk over to the side of my bed and pull the sheets back, sitting down and patting the space beside me.

"Come on."

I expect a mischievous grin to spread across his face, but his expression doesn't change. He wears the same look of worry he had in the infirmary, all tensed up like a massive muscle ready to explode. I hated to admit that part of me misses his annoyingly carefree side. It has become a comfort in my chaos. With a few strides, he's on the other side of the bed. We both climb in, and I cover us. Though worry knits his brow and those green eyes stare at me through a haze, a ghost of a smile appears. No words need to be spoken, I know he is thanking me. I reach out, tucking a loose strand behind his ear. He closes his eyes to the touch as my fingers trail along his shadowed jawline. As I turn my back to him and focus on the long, sheer curtains swaying in the wind, I can still feel his eyes on me.

Crystal is safe. She's safe, and I'm only going to sleep, I tell myself.

He exhales and turns. The relief is palpable as we immediately feel comfort in one another's company. For a moment, it feels normal again. We rest back to back without saying another word.

CHAPTER 31

As I stand outside of the infirmary, I prepare myself to see Crystal still lying in bed, but her laughter fills the room. I push through the doors.

"You're awake!" A wave of relief washes through me. Crystal looks up from where she's sitting, and that big, wide smile beams across her face. I cup my hand over my mouth and stifle a sob. Tears sting my eyes. At this moment, I don't care if she sees them. I rush across the room and wrap my arms around her. "I'm so glad you're okay," I whisper into her ear.

Thank the gods. Thank you, thank you . . .

She stands without wincing and lifts her tunic. A faint-pink scar remains on her flesh. "See? Good as new."

I run my hand over the scar and faintly smile. "Yeah, I guess you are." My mind flashes to the memory of her wound oozing with blood. She seems to notice. Her soft grip pulls me out of my thoughts as she takes a hold of my hand.

"I'm more than okay," she assures me. "We were just about to leave when we got done eating. Care to join us?"

My eyes bounce between her and Iván. I look at him to see if it's okay, I don't want to intrude. He pulls out a chair.

"Please sit with us." He smiles at me and nods. His bronze-colored hair is pulled back into a bun. I serve myself an elderberry muffin and tea, then drift back into a clouded space as I stare at the center of the table. Though she seems to be fully recovered, I don't think I mentally am.

I don't have much to say while I sit back and observe Crystal and Iván fall into a comfortable conversation. He reaches across the table and laces his fingers with hers. His warm, russet skin glows in the candlelight. Crystal smiles from ear to ear at the contact.

"You're coming, right?" Crystal says, but I assume she's talking to Iván. She nudges me as I'm bringing my tea to my lips. A little spills over my hand.

"Hey," I blurt and chuckle.

"You're coming to the tavern tonight, aren't you? Please say yes." Her bright-amethyst eyes widen in excitement. Iván shares the same expression.

My brows lift. "The tavern? Why would I want to go there? If you haven't noticed, I'm a bit of a recluse." I eye them from the brim of my teacup before taking a sip.

"Oh, come on. It'll be dimly lit. A recluse like you definitely needs a change of scenery every once in a while. You can't spend all your time training and *being so serious*." Her voice goes a few octaves lower as her features tighten. She mocks me, bringing her cup of tea to her face and drinking it with a sullen look.

Iván laughs. I grin as my fingers play with the handle, tapping my fingernail against the side of the cup. Crystal does the same. I scoff, but then tip my head back as I break into laughter.

When my eyes meet hers, I say, "Fine, challenge accepted. I'll go."

"Good."

"Why does my life have to be such a fucking mess?" I squint with one eye, looking into the empty bottle before waving to the bartender for another drink. "Maybe I should just jump onto a small boat and row my ass out to sea and sit there until my body ignites into flames."

All you do is run. I scoff as Callian's words echo in the back of my mind. I can't help but loathe the truth of them.

"Please don't do that," Crystal says. "Callian would drown swimming across the entire ocean to find you."

The bartender comes over, taking a cloth to a cup's rim and eyeing me up and down. "I know that look," the woman says as she studies me.

"What look?" My chin rests on my knuckles as I slide the empty bottle to her. She catches it and places it somewhere under the bar.

"The look that says you need some dick," Crystal chimes in, smirking, before she downs the rest of her whiskey.

"Crystal!" I yell, my cheeks turning several shades of red. I quickly whip around to see if anyone heard her, but luckily, I don't think anyone did. Her head tips back into Iván's chest as she laughs. The kind of laugh that I can tell leaves him breathless.

There's such a vast height difference between the two. He begins to lean down but then stops. She presses onto the tips of her toes and pulls him down to her with force so they can exchange an upside-down kiss. He shyly smiles against her mouth while one of her hands runs up the side of his neck and the other holds her now-empty glass. My brow lifts. Is this their first kiss? Watching them makes my heart tighten, but I am happy to see them this way.

His wavy, brown hair is brushed back, though a few strands have fallen loose, barely touching his brow. He's wearing a clean, beige, short-sleeve tunic with a deep v-cut in the front, exposing his muscular chest. Dark-brown trousers, black boots, and a big dagger sheathed at his hip. He cleans up nicely. It makes me wonder if he has anything planned for Crystal after this. Maybe a stroll in the gardens or by the shore.

She slams her empty glass down in front of the bartender when they break apart. "Another, please, my lovely Elora."

As if she needs anymore. She's about seven shots of whiskey in, while Iván has only had two. For Crystal being such a petite woman, she can hold her liquor. The bartender laughs. I notice the creases around her eyes under the dim lighting of the tavern.

"I don't know where you're putting all that whiskey, sweet dear, but as long as you keep filling my tip jar, I'll keep serving you." Elora shakes her breasts. They both fall into a laugh.

Crystal leans over the counter and playfully pinches Elora's cheeks. She drops a coin between Elora's cleavage with the other. "You know I love you. You always bend the rules for me."

"It's only because purple is my favorite color, and you so happen to be the only one in the kingdom born with eyes and hair like that." Sadness glints in Crystal's eyes. I would have missed it if I weren't looking, but she smiles back and quickly downs her whiskey, wanting more.

"She is the rarest of gems." Iván leans down against the bar beside Crystal. His hazel eyes search her face as if he's studying every one of her features. She leans into him.

Elora's eyes warm as she watches them. "I don't know what Callisto would have done if we'd lost our light."

The knot in my chest returns as my mind flashes back to the event. I swallow the lump in my throat and focus on Elora. Her black hair shines next to the candelabra, highlighting hints of hidden red. Though she looks to be in her mid-forties, her essence reminds me of Alyce. Beautiful, bold, and fierce, with a look that could put any of these men in their place.

"What about you?" Elora looks over at me. "You could have any of these fine men and women in here. Do any catch your eye?" When she laughs, the swells of her breasts peeking out from her stays bounce. My eyes focus on them, and suddenly, they multiply into two sets. I feel dizzy. I press my fingers into the sides of my temples, blinking, waiting for my eyes to focus.

"Ugh. No, thanks." I scoff with an eye roll. Finally, her breasts shift back into one pair. "I'd like to forget the past few days, so please make that two." I look at her hazily, give her coin for my drink—Crystal was kind enough to give me a pouchful before we left—and place her tip into another pile.

That pretty much sums it all up. I want to wake up in my bed tomorrow and sleep the rest of the day away.

"None of these men are good enough for her, Elora. She's the prince's lover." Crystal drawls the last two words an octave higher while lazily hunching over in her chair.

"We are not lovers." I reply. "Why does everyone keep saying that as if it is a fact?" I blurt out, throwing my hands into the air in protest. I realize I was much louder than I intended to be.

"It *is* a fact, Viona. Your actions prove just that." Iván holds out his glass. I scoff and look away, focusing on the two women dancing as they embrace one another. Everyone seems to be in love tonight.

"I'll drink to that!" Crystal and Iván chime their drinks together. Crystal slams hers down, and Iván follows suit.

"Hmmm, that burns sooo good." She wets her lips and arches into him. He melts right into her, wrapping his arms around her body. I smile for the first time tonight, seeing how much they enjoy each other's company. At least two of us are happy, and I might as well embrace it. I raise my drink and extend my pinky into the air with a wide grin spreading across my face.

"To the facts!" I drink until it is empty, feeling the liquid roll down with ease. "Fact: you two will be fucking before the night ends," I blurt, smirking at Crystal and Iván. The three of us break out into a laugh, and Elora chuckles under her breath as she turns away, shaking her head.

The clamor of nightlife swells in the tavern. Two people take the stage beneath a dim firelight and begin playing. It's catchy, quick, and upbeat, as it draws the crowd to gather. Everyone stomps their feet along with the rhythm. Iván pulls Crystal away from the bar and into the crowd. She grabs ahold of my hand and yanks me to her side.

"You need to stop thinking about Callian and have some fun," Crystal yells over the music. She pardons us as Iván pulls us through the crowd and to the center of dancing people. My heart begins to race as their bodies move around me.

"Come on! Dance with us!" Iván says, smiling. He takes ahold of my other hand and tries to spin me. Crystal's giggle surrounds me as I make the most awkward spin I've probably ever done.

"I can't dance," I admit, but Crystal responds by pointing to her ear, pretending she can't hear me. I smirk, crossing my arms.

A woman comes up from behind me and spins me around. She's beautiful. Her long, dark hair flows in braids around her curvy shape.

Her green attire complements her umber skin and amber eyes. She waves her finger at me and uncrosses my arms.

"You need to move your hips like this." She begins to move with such confidence, it makes my cheeks flush.

"I do not do any hip moving, miss," I reply. She chuckles, waving away my words, and places her hands on my hips, causing me to break into laughter.

"Sway them back and forth. As one hip goes up, press up a little on your feet. Feel the rhythm of the song and let it move through you."

The corner of my lip curves into a smile and I nod. My arms lift into the air as I begin to sway my hips, gently pushing off with every step.

"That's it! You got it!" she says. Her eyes flare with vibrance and life. "Now, let your arms sway with the music." The woman begins to show me. I hesitate at first, but then a burst of courage springs to life as the warmth of the liquor settles in. My arms lift into the air again. My hips sway. Soon, I'm smiling, closing my eyes, and moving to the rhythm of the music. It's flowing through my body. Every beat reverberates around me, and I start dancing with her. We blend into the moving crowd. A mixture of sweat and perfume fills the air. I never thought I could feel so free in the middle of a crowd. I let it carry me away. She gently grabs ahold of my hand and spins me, then hands me off to two male lovers who are dancing together. They welcome me with open arms as we move to the music.

I look over to find Crystal looking at me with a smile so wide as she dances her way over to my side. I bring her into my arms and say, "Thank you for this."

"Always!" she yells above the crowd. She takes both my hands, and I have more confidence in my moves this time. I close my eyes and let the rest of the song take me.

When I open my eyes, I look to see the woman staring at me with pride. I glance among the other patrons of the tavern and realize that there is no right or wrong way to dance here. It's about the feeling. The way it moves you. Dancing might be one of the ways to access the splendors of happiness. When the song stops, we all come to a breathless halt. The crowd erupts into cheers, telling the fiddlers to keep playing. I give the woman a nod of gratitude, and I hope she feels it through her soul. She disappears back into the crowd, then Crystal, Iván, and I breathlessly make our way back to our seats.

"I don't think I've ever done that before," I admit, waving my hand in front of my face to cool down. My heart still races with adrenaline from the high of dancing, and I suddenly have a newfound admiration for anyone who can do this all night.

"We can come here whenever you'd like, Vi," Iván says. I hum in response at the new nickname he's made for me. In the dim candlelight of the tavern, Crystal's eyes light up. It's the first time anyone has ever called me that. I smile, looking at my friends who have done more for me than they will ever know.

Suddenly my drinks hit me hard, accompanied by something...dark? My head hurts. I don't know which is worse: how sick I will be tomorrow, or not knowing where this foreign feeling is coming from. It's definitely not mine. My senses go on full alert, and I can suddenly hear every little thing around me.

A man's shadow eclipses me. A thick, coarse voice groans, so aroused that it sends a chill down my spine. My grip tightens around the empty bottle, feeling his eyes skim over the shape of my body like I'm one of his new favorite desserts. I'm already relishing what it would look like if I broke this bottle over his face. The heavier he breathes, the more I hear particles of dried mucus dangling in his nostrils. Bile wants to work its way up my throat.

"You have five seconds to step the fuck back," I warn, staring straight ahead, not even bothering to turn around to look at him. I can tell by how his stench envelops me he isn't a pretty sight. From the corner of my eye, I see Iván step forward, ready to defend me, but Crystal puts her hand on his arm and quickly shakes her head as if she's telling him, *"She can do this."*

Good, she knows I can handle this bastard on my own.

Out of nowhere, my chair spins around while I'm still in it, scraping across the wooden floor. It makes such a loud sound that the music stops and everyone in the tavern looks our way. The drunk bastard has spun my chair to face him. It's enough to elicit a charge in the air. A foreign energy, not my own, courses through my body. As I look into this useless bastard's eyes, I know it's not coming from him.

And he's trying to intimidate me?

Laughable. Fuck him.

My lips curve into a snarl.

"Your pretty little mouth is going to get you into a lot of trouble." A malicious grin spreads across his face. As he hovers over me, his sweaty scent assaults my nose. He plants his hands on the counter behind me, encasing me with his arms.

"Last time a man spoke to me like that, he lost his head." I lift my chin, glaring at him in warning.

From the corner of my eye, I see people move back. There's hunger in his eyes as he licks his lips. The slight glint of darkness is enough to tell me he has done far more than *look* at unwilling women. He is a predator looking for his next prey. This intense feeling leaves a taste in my mouth that I have to get rid of.

"You think just because you're friends with that little blonde whore who's fucked her way into the palace that I'll go easy on you?" He grits through his teeth. "Maybe the both of you can show me how you did it."

I knee him in the groin. He yells, grabbing onto his crotch and dropping to one knee. With one quick motion, I break the bottle over his nose. Shards of green glass decorate his face and glitter the air before they fall to the floor. He stumbles back. The skin on the bridge of his nose rips open on impact. The crowd winces at the sound.

"You bitch!" he rasps, wailing in pain. "What did you do to my face? You fucking bitch, I'll kill you!" He holds his hands out in front of his face. They shake with rage while blood drips onto the floor.

"I just wanted to make your face match the ugliness of your tainted soul." I kick the chair back and stalk over to him. I grab a fist full of his hair, forcing him to look up so everyone can see who this piece of shit is. "This is the last time you speak to a woman with such disrespect. If I find out you can't contain the shit that spills from your rotten mouth, I'll cut off your tongue and watch as you swallow it," I promise. Anger pulses through my veins. He's lucky I don't slit his throat right here.

I throw his greasy head out of my grip. Four more men, who seem to have an equal amount of disdain for me, step out from the crowd. Iván and Crystal join my side, but when one of them sees the size of

Iván and notices Crystal standing beside him, he goes pale and runs out of the tavern. Okay, make that three men. One takes another step toward us, standing between his bleeding friend and me, wearing a dirty, long-sleeve tunic and baggy trousers. He unsheathes a dagger, but it shakes in his hand.

Adrenaline is a bitch if you can't control it, and he's the perfect example of why. He looks menacing and out of control. He seems more likely to attack, being how unstable he is compared to his friends.

"What did you do to my brother, you fucking whore?" he yells.

So that's why. I can sense all the nerves in his body being rattled, hearing the gurgling sounds coming from his brother. My eyes briefly bounce back and forth between them, realizing they are twins. I almost laugh, but my eyes narrow in on him. I would have missed that tiny detail if I didn't just bash his brother's face in.

"Well, now your mother can tell you two apart." I unsheathe my dagger and raise it to my side, smirking at how my words seem to push him over the edge.

Someone off to the side yells, "*Fight!*"

The musicians begin to play their instruments. The fast melody charges the room as the tempo rushes through the crowd and they begin to stomp their feet, watching as onlookers. Well, this is rather odd. I've never seen a group so excited for something like this.

He lunges forward with a scornful yell I can hear over the music.

He aims for my throat but misses. I grab him by the arm and thrust my knee into his stomach. A guttural sound erupts from his throat as all the air knocks out of his lungs. I twist his arm behind his body and hear every muscle in his upper arm and shoulder rip apart, reminding me of the crackle of a fire. There's a loud pop. He falls to his knees, dropping the dagger the moment his shoulder dislocates. I kick his weapon away from him, and from the corner of my eye, I see Elora take it. I grab an empty bottle and break it over his face too.

His brother comes up from behind me and lifts me off the ground. I can smell his sweaty, musky scent mixed with the scent of metal still pouring from his nose. I thrash around in his grip, trying to break free, but my arms are held at my sides. My hair obstructs my vision momentarily, but I see Crystal several feet away in a knife fight with his friend. He's already bleeding, and she looks like she's relishing in it. Iván has the other with his hands pinned behind his back.

Suddenly, a sharp, loud thud fills the air. Someone struck his head.

"Ooo," the crowd reacts—some wince at what they just witnessed.

He suddenly releases me, and I stagger forward as my attacker's body stumbles back. He falls to the ground, knocked out cold. I spin on my heels to see the woman I was dancing with holding a metal pitcher in her hand. I smile ear to ear and give her a quick nod as a thank you.

My eyes quickly skate over the room. I expect death stares directed at me, but they are . . . cheering? My lips twitch into a smile. I can't believe what I'm seeing. The music stops, and we're surrounded. People are cheering for us and the woman who helped. I work my way through the crowd toward Crystal and Iván. Between the handshakes and pats on the back, my chest still swells, still feeling the effects of adrenaline.

My friends meet me with broad smiles. "Well, that was unexpected. Are you alright?" I ask Crystal, inspecting the bloodstain on her arm, but upon further inspection, thankfully, I find it's not hers.

"Couldn't be better."

Iván comes up to her side. His eyes skim over my body to see if I'm injured.

"I'm fine," I assure him. We go back to our seats. I pick my chair up from the floor and dust it off.

"I thought you wanted their mother to be able to tell them apart?" she observes, seeing that the twins now have matching wounds.

I assess them. "Eh, changed my mind."

I break into a smile. Seconds go on before the three of us laugh. Crystal sees a few guards walk in and motions for them to arrest the brutes.

I turn to Elora. "May I have some water, please?" The tavern is hot, and the air suddenly feels muggy, or is it my power thrumming? I'm glad I didn't think about using them tonight, I might have unintentionally scorched this place to the ground.

The tavern falls back into the bustling of drunken life. Elora falls into a conversation with Crystal, and their voices become distant sounds in the back of my mind. She hands me a cup of water, and I drink the whole damn thing in one gulp before slamming the cup back down.

"More, please." She pours another cup and leaves the pitcher with me. I'm about halfway through downing it when something catches my eye. That charged energy returns.

A hooded man sits in the corner of the bar, cloaked in the shadows cast by the candle on his table. I recognize the hilt of the sword sticking out of his sheath. My eyes trail up, taking in that familiar, shadowed jawline.

Before my brain can protest, I'm already marching right up to him and yanking the hooded cloak back. A pair of bright-emerald eyes find mine. He looks a mess, tired, but his stare remains penetrating, and I know he saw everything that just went down.

"What are you doing here, Callian?" I hiss. There's a storm of fury blaring behind my eyes.

"I'm enjoying the scenery," he motions to the pile of men beaten to the ground who are now surrounded by guards. "You put on quite the show tonight."

My stomach takes a dip. I hold back the smile by clenching my teeth and lifting my chin, returning his look with a stone-cold glare. Although it would be nice if he joined us, if he sat beside *me* at the bar, but for the sake of the vision that keeps plaguing my mind and for his safety, he needs to remain at arm's length.

"Well, you need to go because I'm trying to enjoy myself tonight, and I don't need another pair of eyes studying me, or rather"—I look him up and down with disdain written all over my face—"another man breathing down my neck." My nostrils flare.

For a moment he looks hurt, as if I've clumped him together with the pile of shit men who are now slipping on their own blood and staggering away in cuffs. His brows knit and his hand tightens around his mug, but he quickly squashes that look and mirrors my glare. He leans forward with eyes lingering on my lips before he looks up at me.

"This was my bar before your pretty little feet ever stepped into it," he retorts, smiling wickedly. A few loose strands of hair fall forward. There it is, that damn smile and annoyingly smoldering look. He casually leans back, takes a sip of his ale, and sets it back down.

"Well, it's my bar now, so get out." I demand. I turn to leave, but he grabs my wrist. Both our bodies react to the sudden contact. He's hanging on to every second, watching my glare bounce between his hand and eyes that look so starved. "Let me go, or you'll be on the floor painted in red like the rest of them."

"Why must you do this, Viona?"

My name. He never says my name unless it is important. The way I feel as it rolls off his lips is a reality I don't want to feel right now.

"Do what?" I whisper, trying to ignore how beautiful he looks even in this dim lighting.

"Why do you keep running from me?" His words, though soft and gentle, blast me in the chest. I hate the way he can read me like a book.

"I—" I have no answers to give. At least, none that I can tell him.

"You don't need to answer me. You need to ask *yourself* why. I only came here to think, it's what I do when I've had a long day. I saw you sitting at the bar, so I stayed back to give you space. When I watched you dance"—he pauses as if searing it to his memory—"the freedom you felt. It left me breathless. *You* leave me breathless every time I see that smile. What I wouldn't give to have you feel that way all the time."

"Where were you when that man was breathing down my neck?" I question, smothering the moment because it's too painful to hear him speak like this. I try to pass the blame onto him. I yank my wrist free and bring it back to my side. There is hurt and frustration in his eyes at my sudden withdrawal.

"You didn't need saving today. I knew you could handle it. I've also known Crystal most all my life. If I would have even attempted to set foot in her path, she would have my balls hanging on a pike. And I'm sure you'd do the same." A smirk tips the corners of his mouth. His beautiful, straight teeth are slightly exposed. My heart skips another beat.

My chest rises and falls with the coiling heat and tension hanging in the air. He licks his lower lip, looking at me with such longing, but he gets up, stepping into my personal space and placing his hands over my arms. His scent of cedar and mint finally envelops me. I breathe it in, briefly closing my eyes, wanting nothing more than to fall into his embrace and feel the warmth of his body pressed against mine. I miss him. I want him, but my back stiffens.

His lips press thin, sensing my icy stubbornness. It squeezes my lungs tight, just as much as I'm sure it gnaws at his heart.

If he only knew the real reason why.

"If I'm being honest with you, you can handle more than you give yourself credit for, Princess. I hope you start to love yourself one day so you can truly see how magnificent you are." The back of my throat burns, and tears fog my vision as I stare off, looking into the lantern's buttery light casting over the bar. "Even if it takes you an eternity, I pray to the gods above I will be here to see it. You deserve to feel free in all that life has to offer you. Even if I'm just another mortal in your story . . . fading off into your memory, I'd just like to see you truly happy."

He leans closer, his minty breath fanning against my cheek.

Just kiss me, I silently beg.

My heart sends out a plea. He pauses for a moment, but then his hand caresses the side of my face with a warmth that settles into his eyes.

Kiss me and tell me everything will be alright.

He leans down, pressing his forehead against mine. His breath ghosts across my lips. I inhale a shaky breath as I close my eyes at his touch, but then I feel his forehead move away. When I open them again, it's just me standing in the corner of the tavern, staring down at his empty cup.

CHAPTER 32

T HE TRUTH HURTS, SHARPER than the edge of any knife. I unsheathe a small dagger hidden in my corset and toss it at the bullseye.

"Fuck…" I exhale sharply. I hate missing. Another one flies through the air. This time, past the target, landing somewhere in the bushes. In a fuming rage, I throw the other two.

Miss and fucking miss.

I growl. Crystal and I begin walking toward the bullseye to retrieve my daggers.

"You're not very focused today," she observes, crossing her arms as she studies me with a side glance.

"You're right, I'm not."

The gravel crunches beneath our boots. Every step carries the weight of Callian's words from last night, haunting me to the point where I barely slept. We retrieve my daggers and I slip them back into their hiding places within the corset over my tight-fitted tunic, then perch myself up onto the wall. I rummage through my bag, searching for the leather water flask. When I find it, I take a long drink. My migraine is punishing, and my ears are still ringing from the loud music. Last night's liquor is still swimming through my system.

I look over to see Crystal's knuckles bruised from the night before.

"I'm sorry about last night. I shouldn't have lost my temper, but I didn't like how that bastard disrespected you," I say, smoothing my hand over hers, trying not to touch the area.

"It was one of the best nights I've had in a while, Vi," she laughs.

"You are quite the badass," I reply. It's clear we both share that fight in us, only, hers is so controlled. She tossed those men aside like they were nothing.

"Sydney usually gives me a tonic to rid the hangover, but she's not pleased we went out last night so she's making us suffer with these brutal migraines."

"And bruises," I finish her sentence. "Sydney reminds me of someone I used to know. Her name is Alyce." Before I can let tears slip free, I quickly take a long pull from my water skin to shield my quivering lips. I drink nice and slow while focusing on the clear, azure skies, and yet a single tear still manages to slip down my face.

"I'm sorry for your loss," Crystal's voice warms. She places a hand on my shoulder.

While resting my arm on my thigh, I clear my throat. "She's not dead, she's . . . " I pause as the words become harder to say. "She's somewhere back at home, still under the rule of my father."

"Oh, well I'm sure she's doing quite alright. If she's anything like Sydney, then you can take comfort in knowing she's a survivor." Somehow, those words comfort me.

I gently nod. "Yeah, I guess so."

She reaches for my water flask. Her head tilts back, and I watch her take down the rest. The column of her neck thrums as her throat bobs up and down with the water. She's beautiful, every part of her, even as she sits beside me with sweat beading down her face.

A thought crosses my mind. There has always been a little space in my heart that felt empty; I have holes in my heart filled with shadows, longing for a lot of things I know nothing about. But, Crystal has started to fill those holes. If this is how it feels to have a sister, then I will cherish what we share for as long as I live.

Something catches my eye: a marking made of ink behind her ear. One I never noticed before.

"What's that behind your ear?" I ask. I can't stop myself from reaching out to touch it, running a finger over the inked skin, tracing the heart-shaped lines and what seems to be flames. It feels similar to a scar, with the skin slightly raised.

She laughs. "*That* is what I call foolish love."

"Foolish love?" My black brow lifts, the side of my mouth pulling up into a grin. She stares off into the gardens and sighs, reliving moments around the heart seared into her flesh. Though it could be a painful memory, I want to hear it. I want to know more about her.

"Love is foolish when you're so blinded by it you can't see the person for who they are, or the harm they've done, until it's too late." The beam of light fades from her face. Her brows furrow as she's caught in memory. Even now, in her waning light, she seems to carry her grief so well.

"There was a time when I left Callisto," she starts. "I went back to my hometown in Diamonvel, located in the southeast mountains. It's a town outside the kingdom of Sebina. At the time, when I was searching for myself, I found *him*. This man was poetic, beautiful, and had all the charm any woman could ask for. He was the light in every room he walked into. I met him at a time when I often questioned my existence. When I felt I had no one. In his company, I found solace in the light he created around my heart, but all he did was shield me, not help me heal. Over the few years of knowing him, he broke barriers I kept so thick around myself. While in this process, he also broke me. One day, he snapped. He told me he had a near-death experience during one of his hunting trips. The fear of losing me consumed him, and in return, he smothered me. It was as though someone had stolen him away from me, taken him in the middle of the night and given me someone I didn't recognize anymore. I tried to understand, to have patience. That maybe, just maybe, this would fade in time. While I stood by his side, he started questioning my every move. I felt like I couldn't breathe. I couldn't go anywhere. I was no different than a caged bird. He even went as far as convincing me not to use my powers because I could hurt myself. One night, I couldn't take it any longer. When I told him I was going back to Callisto and he wasn't coming with me, he wouldn't let me go. As I tried to leave, he went too far. That was the first and last time he put his hands on me, because that's when I left. I left everything behind except the clothes on my back. I arrived at the doors of Callisto with nothing but a broken soul, and King Valor welcomed me back with open arms." She takes a deep breath and tilts her head to the side, showing me the inked area.

"He convinced me to get this as a reminder that his love burned for me."

"Do you regret it?" I ask. The wind picks up. She gathers her hair to one side and drapes it over her front.

"Never." She turns to me and smiles, lifting her head with pride. "It's all a part of my journey. I used to spend a lot of nights being cross with myself for never speaking up. A lot of time was spent thinking about what I could have said to him. I won't waste my time anymore. I had to fight to become who I am today. It's still a battle, but it gets easier to fight as time goes on." She gently pushes her pointer finger into my shoulder. "*You* have to keep fighting for yourself, Viona. It's like going to war. You wake up each day, never knowing what will come at you. You have to take it head on. Do not settle, and don't let anyone get in your way. We are capable of achieving all our dreams. You just have to grab life by the reins and ride the fuck out of it."

I chuckle under my breath. "You make it sound so easy."

That stern look forms on her face, one that reminds me of Sydney when she knows I'm hesitant. "That's because it is. Change how you see things."

That's the hardest part. There are so many times where I don't want to look, afraid of what will stare back at me. My jaw flutters with tension, focusing on the tiger swallowtail fluttering from flower to flower.

Crystal glances at me with her warm smile. The morning sun glints off her hair, bringing out that violet color in every strand. "This journey has led me back here for a second time. Back to Callian and his family. It is clear this is where I belong. Now I sit beside a beautiful soul who could quite possibly end the world with the flick of her wrists, and she has her eyes on my brother, the prince of Callisto from the East-lands. I am grateful you have found your way here too." Her eyes flare with pride, but every time she talks about Callian, there's always a mischievous grin on her face.

I nudge her with my shoulder and smile. "Seems like you have quite the task on your hands with training me."

"I've always liked women with a mean streak," she teases. "If I were to die by your fiery hand, then I would gladly die beside a friend." She wraps her arm around my shoulders and pulls me in.

"Is it crazy that you saying that brings me more comfort than you can know?" I ask, as my smile is beaming.

"We are devastatingly toxic." We both erupt in laughter.

"You're lucky to have found all this. I can see why it's worth fighting for."

"Callian is the brother I never had. I grew up coming to Callisto with my parents. They sold imported goods to the royal family, and our mothers had grown a friendship from the very start. Callian and I would play together every time we came for a visit. Sometimes, my parents and I would stay the whole summer. This was our getaway from the life we lived back home. One day, while we were traveling back, we were raided by a bunch of larkins. They killed my parents right in front of me. I don't know how I managed to escape, but I did. I found my way back to Callisto, and they took me in. I was only fifteen. I'm twenty-seven now. Some days, memories of my parents seem like a lifetime ago. Sometimes, I can still hear my mother's last breath. I've grown to accept it will always haunt me."

Tears sting my eyes. It makes sense why she hates the larkins as much as I do. They *have* taken so much from her. I realize maybe that was the vision I saw when she first touched my wrist. I can see now why she holds it so close to her heart.

"Those fucking demon spawns," I mutter under my breath. "How are you able to be so strong when you have suffered so much?"

"I have to live the life I know my parents would have wanted me to live. I refuse to relive that moment and have it become a stone on my chest. I let it be the fire in my fight, the reason I pick myself back up every time I fall. I miss them, but I'm not ready to go beyond the veil. I will not leave this place without putting up a fight."

"That freedom seems so far from reach." I sigh.

"You have us. Whether you like it or not, you have Callian."

"He infuriates me more than anything."

"Why? Because he cares for you? I don't see that as a heinous crime. Like it or not, you two are more similar than you care to admit. I just hope you don't wait to realize it until it's too late."

I TAKE THE LONG WAY BACK to my chambers, trying to get lost, because exploring is far better than being locked inside my head. As I walk down a corridor I haven't ventured into before, I hear King Valor's voice echoing from down the hall. I slow my pace until I reach the doors of the room he's in.

Shit, they're slightly open.

I pause, holding in my breath as if he could somehow hear me exhale. I'm about five leaps from freedom when I hear Callian in the room with him.

"Are you sure you're thinking with a clear head, Son? You don't seem like yourself lately," his father says. I hear papers shuffling around. Heat flashes up my face as a cold chill sweeps down my spine.

"I'm thinking just fine, Father. You don't need to worry." There's a long silence that seems to stretch on for eternity.

"Do you know what is at stake if you continue to have feelings for Viona? Do you know what can happen? It is a rarity within itself."

What rarity is he talking about? My eyes widen.

There's a longing in Callian's next exhale.

What is King Valor talking about?

"There's more to it than I can say." Callian breaks the silence. "Being the king has always been your dream, but it has never been mine."

"Well then, what is your dream, Son? What more do you want if being on the throne isn't it?"

Suddenly, having a pulse is really inconvenient. It's thrumming so hard in my ears, I can barely make out what they are saying. I take a slight step closer to the doors.

"I was never meant to rule this kingdom. We of all people know how short our lives can be. Though you might feel you have lost yours, do not attempt to take away mine. I love you, never question that, but what I seek exceeds the duties of the crown."

"Are you sure about how you feel? Are you willing to accept what might happen?" King Valor says.

That is as much as I can take. I'm afraid to hear what Callian really wants. Holding my breath, I slip down the hall until I find a flight of stairs to take me as far away from them as possible.

CHAPTER 33

I T'S BEEN WELL OVER a month since I arrived in Callisto, and several days have passed since the tavern fight. I'm back to my routine of training in the mornings with Crystal, and I'm growing stronger by the day, slowly harnessing the darkness surrounding my powers. There is something ancient about it. I guess that's why I've been anxious, worried about what Gareon will find. He still hasn't come to speak to me, and I'm beginning to grow frustrated by it. I keep expecting him to appear at my door or find me in the gardens or library. I thought about reaching out to him with this telepathic power he says we share just to piss him off, but that would be childish.

Before I enter the library, I look down the hall toward his quarters—light filters in through the window, highlighting the cast-iron staircase leading to his door. I look behind me, then down the other side of the hall. I'm tempted to go up there and barge in, but that courage is quickly squashed when I see two guards take up their post for the night.

Dammit, perhaps another time.

I walk into the library. It doesn't take me long to accumulate a stack in my arms. My eyes skim over the rows of books with spines of various colors, but my mind keeps drifting back to overhearing Callian speaking with his father.

I feel rather foolish walking into the section of books written about love and relationships, but I gravitate toward a few that spark my interest. *Chosen by the Stars.* I look side to side to double check no one notices me pulling this book off the shelf before placing it in my arms. I quickly leave and wander down a few more rows until another catches my eye. *The History of Callisto Rulers,* bound in dyed, royal-blue leather and gold gilt pages, matching the royal colors.

I turn to retreat back to my table, but a white spine sticks out from a row of brown leather books. Its vellum cover has letters gilt in gold and looks much older than the ones it surrounds.

I read the title aloud, *"The Lore of the Larkins and Other Malicious Creatures."* My eyes widen.

I can't help the sheen of sweat forming above my brow. I should spin on my heels and leave this section, yet curiosity tells me to take the book. The tug of war begins. I'm suddenly feeling uncomfortable within this quiet space.

You're being ridiculous, Viona. Take the fucking book.

Fear will always remain if I don't walk through the fire. I need to face this, all of it, so I won't feel like I'm drowning every time I'm lost in a memory. Without any more hesitation, I take it. I return to my table, collapsing around the heavy stack. The books land with a loud thud against the weathered desk. I exhale, searching to see where the larkin book landed.

"Shhhh!!"

My eyes dart over to Seveena who still has a finger over her lips.

"Are you serious? Nobody's even in here?" I state. My voice echoes throughout the library. Her black hair sways back and forth as she shakes her head.

Apparently, talking in a normal tone is forbidden, even if this place *is* empty. Duly noted. I take my seat and emphasize my etiquette while keeping my eyes locked on hers. The way I slowly sit looks more like a bow. Seveena responds by rolling her eyes before going back to her work. I study her for a moment. She looks like she could be my sister, only her hair is short, while mine billows down to my waist.

I tuck a loose strand behind my ear and pick up the book about the larkins.

While flipping through the pages, I stumble upon a drawing—no, a diagram—of a naked man with his arms and legs spread apart. He is drawn in various angles from the front, back, and sides. Below is a larkin, illustrated in the same position. Were they human before? I flip back to the beginning of the chapter.

When Men Become the Predator

Men will go through great lengths for desire, greed, and power.
A dark lord may grant this but cannot reverse it.
Their souls are sacrificed. It is then that the transformation takes place.
Once a man is born a larkin from the depths of darkness,
They will rise and do the bidding of the dark lord who created them.
Loyalty remains for their maker, but when called,
they only serve one ruler,
The one who wears the crown of the Underworld.

I stare blankly at the pages. They were once human, all of them. It proves what people will go through to get what they desire, just like some of the Blood Moon Knights back at home who serve my father. I'm reminded of the void in some of their eyes. They are no different, except for the physical change the larkins go through.

A chill sweeps down my body. All the men who have turned wanted things that would not make life whole. They are the evildoers of a darker force. I know my father hired the larkins, but what if there's more to it? What if he is a "dark lord," and what does that even mean for me? He has oppressed his entire kingdom, and I'm only now seeing it with the right set of eyes. My mind begins to run through all the possibilities.

Who is the ruler of the Underworld if it isn't him? I must speak with Gareon.

I REMAIN AT THE BOTTOM of the staircase, looking at Gareon's door. Faint light still glows from beneath the frame. I take a deep breath and ascend the stairs. The sun is setting behind the ocean. I pause momentarily, staring out the window, watching that last glimmer of light flicker above the water and dancing between the clouds, illuminating the storm that will soon come.

"The calm before the storm." Gareon's voice echoes throughout the stairwell. My head whips in his direction. He stands at the top, draped in a blue, crushed velvet robe with his hands clasped behind his back. His hair is tied back, but a few loose locks dangle free in a moonlit wave. He sees the startled look on my face. "Didn't mean to pull you from thought."

I straighten my tunic, unsure what to do with myself as his amber eyes peer down at me.

"It's quite alright," I lie even though I know my tone doesn't match the stern look I'm giving him.

He smirks, nudging his head to the side for me to follow. "Come, I have warm tea waiting."

When I enter his study, he's already mid-drink with his pinky extended out. I sit on the cushion across from him. An awkward silence hangs in the air while I wait for him to finish his long drink.

"What do you know of the dark lords?" I ask, getting straight to the point. My heart is hammering against my chest. He casually sets his tea down. Steam curls above his cup. My question didn't take him by surprise, as if he was waiting for me to ask.

"As you know, we have gods from the stars—to make it short, 'the gods above.' Then we have the gods from the underworld, the Shadow Realm."

"'The gods from below,'" I add.

He nods. "Many dark lords have existed throughout history. Whispers in the wind told me of one who roams our lands, but his power kept him concealed. Unfortunately, I could never detect it either. Limitations of being a demi-god," he smirks. "Dark lords are what we call fallen gods—banished by the gods above for going against their code." Something flashes in his eyes, but it's gone before I can interpret it. He sees my mind whirling with questions. "Yes, the gods can be quite wicked when bored. As you know, the gods above grant powers to good-doers while the gods below tempt the weak. It's what they call 'balance,' and though I don't agree with how they run things, who am

I to say? I can go on and tell you all their names, but I know that's not why you're here. Perhaps we will save that lesson for another day."

There's something ethereal to his words as his eyes narrow in on me. While he continues to speak, my body thrums in response as if my powers are affirming something, but what?

My lips slightly part, hesitating to speak because it still stings to admit it. I slowly exhale, releasing the tension that wants to build in my throat.

Just say it, Viona.

"I have a feeling my father is more than what he appears to be. He hired the larkins to find me. He is the reason they keep coming. He is the reason Solas' men breached the village. Something tells me he is a dark lord. The more I reflect, the more I see it." I take another deep breath, hoping it will loosen the knot in my chest. "It says in *The Lore of Larkins*, they're loyal to their maker, but when called, they'll serve the one who wears the crown of the underworld."

Gareon smiles as if satisfied with my findings. He gets up and walks over to the desk. "I want to show you something."

A book bound in vellum lies flat upon it. I slightly cock my head to read the title, finishing in a whisper, "'. . . *Immoral Sins.*" My eyes instantly flick to his. "This was in the Alora Archives, but"—I pause, picking up the book and feeling its weight in my hands—"this is a lot thicker than the one in Callisto's archives."

Gareon smirks. We are so close, his scent fills the air—lovely mahogany tea and sage. I notice there are no fine lines on his face even though he feels so ancient. He lifts his head slightly and smiles.

"This is the original. The copies other kingdoms have are much smaller, only containing *half* of what is inside this." He reaches for the book and opens it. "As it should be. Most cannot handle all of the truths." He flips through the pages. "This story is about an ancient god, a ruler from the Shadow Realm. Long ago, both the gods above and the gods below developed a treaty to keep to their own sides, only engaging in the balance of good and evil. This ancient ruler had fallen in love with a woman he had tempted. He would come to her in the guise of a man, walking the grounds as if he were allowed. The gods above found out, killed his lover, stripped him of his powers, and left him wandering among the living. With his last trickle of power, he forged his soul with hers, binding them together to be reincarnated until they recognize each other again."

The knot in my chest tightens as a chill rushes down my spine.

"'*Love bound in darkness,*'" I whisper. "It's in the prophecy. But wait, why would the gods care about another falling for a mortal? It seems rather selfish if you ask me," I admit.

"It's more work for them to do. Who wants to babysit a bunch of angsty, teenage demi-gods? In their world, they see it as forbidden love."

Demi-gods? I swallow.

"I suppose you have a point, but I still don't see why it's any of their business who anyone loves."

He casually shrugs.

I begin flipping through the pages of this story, thinking about how my parents met. Suddenly, a symbol sticks out, making me pause. A red triangle drawn inside a black circle. I look closer, seeing the ink splay across the page behind the letters of the story.

"This symbol is the same one that was sketched onto the scroll of the prophecy in the Alora Archives," I observe, feeling Gareon studying me.

"It is an ancient symbol of balance," he says. I look at him, finding myself beneath his stare. His amber eyes churn like distant galaxies; far too intimidating for me to look at for too long.

"How do you know all of this?" I ask, dropping my gaze to the book.

"I've been alive a long time, Viona. The whispers in the wind have searched for him, waiting for his rebirth, waiting for his ear to catch the secret that will allow him to regain his powers," Gareon says. "No one knew when this dark lord would emerge again or when the one who was prophesied would appear. Until, one day, the whispers stopped, and that is when I saw you."

Another chill sweeps down my body. "The sacrifice," I whisper. "*A gift that shall be brought. Taken when the moon turns red,*'" I say aloud.

"It seems you have memorized the prophecy quite well." He smiles with pride.

"I really didn't have a choice." I huff out a dry laugh as my eyes drift over the symbol. There's a stillness in the room as a heaviness tries to settle in my bones. "He won't stop until he has me, and he'll keep going until he has all of Vendrelle," I remind myself, snipping away the feelings that stem from the knowledge. "When is the next blood moon?" My head turns toward Gareon.

"In three weeks." His words send my stomach rolling. "He has three weeks to take you."

"Unless I get to him first." I smirk. "But we're going to need a really good plan."

He raises an approving brow. "May I share the discovery about your father with King Valor? This information will strengthen his plans."

"Of course, but why couldn't you have told me sooner?" I lightly shake my head, as the inner struggle of my emotions war together. I inhale a deep breath and steady my breathing—something I've learned to do in my training with Crystal. It relieves the tension in my chest, slightly.

Silence clings to the air.

"You must understand, there are some things I cannot interfere with. I cannot misuse what I see or change things." He stares at me intensely. "I can guide. Nothing more. Since returning, I have been waiting for you to come to me. Here you are, at the right time, as I expected."

I force my shoulders to relax and give a tight nod. "It must be hard to carry so many burdens on your shoulders. How do you deal with the knowledge of seeing people's fate?" I ask, my tone slightly softening.

He turns, elegant and graceful as he moves toward the window and clasps his hands. Moonlight filters between the strands of his hair, creating tiny prisms of light. His soft-brown skin glows. I join him at his side, noticing his window peers directly into the garden Crystal and I have been training in almost daily.

"It becomes numbing, I suppose. As you just learned, there *are* ways around the balance of longevity and love, but they are ones I choose not to interfere with," he replies, resigned to his choices. His voice drifts off, lost in thought. What he possesses is what others would give their souls for, yet, he deals with it humbly. "You and I are the same, Viona." He says with a sigh that carries much weight.

"What do you mean by that?" My brow lifts.

"We are the outcome of forbidden love."

CHAPTER 34

A STORM IS ROLLING across the kingdom of Callisto. Sheets of rain pelt against the stained-glass windows as I ascend the stairs leading to my chambers. It's late, I'm famished, and all I want to do is eat and go to bed. Sleep feels so far from reach because my mind won't stop reeling. Part of me has gained clarity, knowing now what I must do, but Gareon's parting words remain looming. He and I are the same. Does this mean my lifespan might be longer than most? If so, that can only mean one thing. I *could* be a demi-god. Thunder rumbles in the distance, pulling me from thought. I blink back a few times, pinning these thoughts for later when I'm not so mentally drained. I shift my book bag to my other shoulder to even out my strain. A flash of lightning cuts through the sky, and I jump at the sight of a stark silhouette glaring down at me from the top of the stairs.

"I apologize, Miss Viona. Are you alright?" the guard says.

"Yes. I'm fine, Rossburn." My tone is sharp like a blade. Instinctively, my arms cross over my chest, feeling uneasy beneath his stare, but my stone cold expression remains.

When I enter my chambers, the candles are lit. My brow lifts, noticing food on the table with a golden candelabra in the middle. I place my books down as the aroma of fresh bread and chicken increases my appetite. I didn't request my dinner to be served here, but that doesn't stop me from reaching out to break off a piece of bread or taking a big bite into a drumstick. There's a note leaning against a bottle of wine. I fumble the message open with my thumb, and take another bite of chicken.

"I promised to always find you. I saw you in the library and thought I would send for your dinner so you could eat while reading. Remember, I am never too far from reach. – Callian"

"Hm," I grunt. If I weren't stuffing my face, I'd be smiling ear to ear. I wipe my hands over my clothes and pull out the books. On top of the stack is *Chosen by the Stars.* I suppose I'll start with this. I quickly fork a piece of carrot into my mouth, flipping through the pages. I skim through a story that talks about the gods from the stars making embers of light that would fall onto the chosen ones below. I flip through a few more pages and spear another carrot into my mouth as I continue to try to read, but I realize I'm too distracted.

Within a few moments, I'm outside Callian's door, full of hesitation as my hand remains idly in the air. I glance over my shoulder, looking at one of the guards who quickly turns away and is suddenly amused by something on the wall. I shoot him a look of warning then turn back and knock. Callian swings the door open with that charming smirk, almost as if he were expecting me.

"Took you long enough, Princess." His hair is tousled to the side, and the tips are wet. Tiny droplets of water are cascading down his bare chest. My eyes shamelessly follow the trail of dark hair disappearing beneath his towel. I clear my throat.

"Do you ever wear clothes in here?" I scoff, arching a brow. "Actually, never mind. I want to inform you of what Gareon told me. If you're not busy, will you come to my room? *Clothed.*" I sneer at him, taking another glance at his chiseled body before my eyes meet his. I'm trying to avoid watching the water struggle to make it past his abs.

Callian's eyes peer into mine, searching behind my glare. Whatever he finds makes the corner of his mouth tip up into a grin.

My gods.

"You're so persistent about clothes, aren't you, little flame?"

I huff, stepping closer so the guards can't hear us. One step, and I instantly regret it because his aroma hits the air. That radiant heat emits off his body, reminding me of how it feels against mine, the deep groans he makes when he is between my legs. It all becomes too much. My cheeks heat at the memories.

"When you look like *that*, yes," I bite back. Before he can respond, I retreat back to my room, feeling his stare the entire time.

I quickly close the door.

Shit, this is going to be a mistake. I take a deep breath, trying to steady my pounding heart.

I hear him chuckle before closing his door.

I go back to the table and resume eating. Food is my favorite distraction. Focusing on the savory flavors is the perfect way to dull the moment. I continue to read my book about how the gods from the stars can gift powers to mortals, reminding me of how Callian got his. "Blessed" is what he called it. There were also other chapters about bonds, some being fated and what can happen if one power is too strong.

There's a light knock on my door, and Callian strides in, clad in a black, long-sleeve tunic that hangs loosely over his body. The top laces are untied, exposing the muscles in his chest. His breeches are tight-fitted, as if the material is thin enough to rip the moment he sits down. There's a plate of food in his hand. I quickly shove the books back into the bag.

"I was just about to eat too," he says, sitting across from me. We quietly eat between the candlelight—the sound of rain patters lightly against the balconies. The thunder is drifting further away. "What did you find out?" he asks while pouring himself a full glass of wine. I continue to fill the silence by stuffing my face. Between my nerves and being famished, it's the only thing I can do while I sort through my emotions.

"If you don't mind, I'd like to finish my food first."

"Anything you want, Princess," he replies. The words flow off his lips, causing my core to tighten. I look up from the edge of my chicken and pause, cheeks already flushed as heat courses through my body. He catches my stare, pausing to rest his elbows on the table.

"What?" I snap, slowing the pace of my chewing. I glare at him with flaming blue eyes.

"I could watch you all day." He hums, wiping the corners of his mouth as he wears a smirk.

"Well, it's not polite to stare," I remind him through a mouth full of chicken.

"And I'm not very polite," he says, eyes narrowing in on me. I swallow my food and reach for the wine. Thank the gods for wine.

"Well, then you need to learn some manners." I keep my eyes trained on the lush red liquid pouring into my cup.

"Teach me," he challenges, leaning back into the chair with his legs slightly spread apart. I suck in a sharp breath of air as my mind goes to activities that will be far more fun than just *teaching*. What I wouldn't give to straddle him in the chair right now. I place my hands on my lap. The silence stretches across the table, but his eyes flare with desire every second that goes by.

"Have someone else teach you. I'm sure there are plenty of suitresses," I retort, slicing my butter knife through the soft skin of my potatoes.

"True, I can have anyone I want. I can knock on any woman's door and they will take me, no questions asked." He runs his finger along the rim of his cup, watching my every move to notice his words hit me like ice, so hard that I think my knife stumbles. My teeth clench together. "But, they do not have my heart." He purrs in a way that feels like a release. My back straightens. I lower my eyes to my plate and stab a piece of potato with my utensil, doing my best to block out my feelings.

"You know"—I place the piece into my mouth—"you're making this *very* difficult."

"Why?" he says, causing my breathing to hitch. He stands from his seat and picks up his chair, placing it beside mine, but he leaves his plate stranded where it is. I look away, still refusing to make eye contact, refusing to feel what I most desperately want from him. I take a sip of my wine—anything so I won't kiss him.

When he sits down, his lovely scent envelops me. It's everything that makes me weak because it belongs to him.

Callian angles his body toward me, elbow resting on the table. Suddenly, I find myself caught beneath his stare. He uses his hand to brush the hair away from my face, and I lean into his touch. Those thick, savory lips peek out from his shadowed jawline. When I meet his gaze, it all ends. He has a way of setting the thorns I keep around my heart aflame. Every time they grow back, he effortlessly sets them on fire again.

"You're making this difficult because . . ." My voice trembles. I look down, staring at my hands, feeling stupid for how I feel. The world is likely falling apart around us. So much guilt springs to life when it comes to this. If I am like Gareon, where my lifespan is longer, then all Callian and I share is useless—another reason why I feel so torn between his world and mine.

"Tell me," he pleads in a deep, soft exhale, curving his finger under my chin and gently nudging me to meet his gaze.

"I—" Words evade my every attempt to speak them as I look into his emerald eyes. His lips part slightly, hanging onto my every word as if his life depends on it. "You make this difficult because . . . while my world falls apart, I cannot bring myself to . . ." I pause again.

Fuck, I'm no longer making any sense.

The frustration stings my eyes. "I've missed you," I finally admit. "But I've kept you at arm's length because of a vision I had of killing you. When I walked into your room that night, that's when little pieces of it came flooding back. I was frightened, so I did the only thing I knew how to do. I ran because I'd rather suffer in silence. I'd rather miss you than lose you, because I don't know how to suffer any other way."

Suddenly, the air is too thick, I can't breathe. Heat simmers under my skin. I'm about to unravel before him. My chair grates across the marble floors as I abruptly stand. I rush out onto the balcony, immersing myself in the rain.

Dark, ominous clouds flash as lightning strikes in the distance. Another balcony, another ocean view. I want to think of another me out there who doesn't always have to feel like she's being torn in half. I suck in a sharp breath, and my hands grip tightly onto the stone railing.

I close my eyes, letting the rain pelt against my face like shards of ice. Just as I feel myself slipping into the depths of my mind, two strong hands slip between my arms and wrap around my waist. Callian blocks out some of the rain as he surrounds me in a warm embrace. I exhale a shaky breath, feeling so undeserving of his touch, but I can no longer fight against what my soul has been longing for. He leans down, resting his chin on the top of my head, the tips of his hair tickling the sides of my face.

"You think I don't know what it's like to be in the dark?" He begins to sway our bodies back and forth. "It's a place I know all too well, Princess. If this is where your darkness hides, then let me stand here with you," he whispers into the shell of my ear.

My body responds with a tingling wave across my skin. Lightning silently flashes above the clouds; another faint roll of thunder rumbles in the distance.

"Callian, I—" I softly beg, placing my hands over his.

"There is nothing to be afraid of, there is nothing to fear. Do not let your visions hold truth over your own heart," he reassures me. There is no music, only the patter of the rain against the palace walls. His hands are doing more than touching me in the dark. He reaches through the veil of shadows. We slip away into the dark, into the shallow parts of our minds.

"I cannot stop thinking about seeing you that night in the tavern. The way you danced in the dim light, the smile I've longed to see stretching across your face. The way you closed your eyes and moved your body to the music. The people loved you. What I wouldn't have given to slip through the crowd and dance with you then." His voice is low and sultry. I can feel the smile on his face. "I'm here now, though," he says. "It's just you and me."

My eyes flutter open. "You? Dance? I don't believe it." I softly chuckle, feeling my heart settle into a steady beat.

Humor rumbles in Callian's chest. His laugh is so deep, the sound vibrates against my back. I stare off into the distance, looking out to the faintly lit ports and the little peek of Callisto's village, all cloaked by night. Moonlight filters in through the rain-filled clouds as our bodies continue to sway back and forth. I close my eyes, envisioning how he'd look dancing. I can only picture every step being full of passion and wicked sin.

"Maybe one day, I'll show you," he says.

"Show me now," I softly demand.

That little sip of wine gives me the courage I need to get through the next moment. My body does the rest. I turn toward him, our eyes lock, and suddenly, our breathing becomes more in sync. I look at him through thick lashes, rain catching on their tips. The palm of his hand slides up my waist, sending heat dipping below my navel. Confusion spreads across my face as he brings his other hand to mine and extends it.

"Will you dance with me on this somber night?" His breath fans across my lips as he stares in a hooded gaze. I'm immersed in his eyes as they shine against the faint moonlight.

There have been many times when I stood alone in the rain, looking out into the dark with only the sounds of the waves to comfort me. Many nights like this one, but with one significant difference—the way Callian holds me against his body becomes a sanctuary. I take his hand, letting all those lonely moments slip away into the ocean's depths.

Callian's palm presses against the small of my back. With one swift motion, he pulls me close. I yelp, and he grins in response. We're close enough that I'm sure he can feel my heart thundering against his. He moves us in a dance I have only seen from afar, and one so long ago that it almost feels like a dream. His lips slightly part as his eyes linger on my lips with need. He turns us around so his back is to the ocean. In another swift motion, he dips my body back. Rain pelts against my chest, drawing his eyes to the outline of the two hardened peaks. Desire burns in his eyes. His chest heaves at the sight, enough for me to notice how he slightly draws in his lower lip. When he pulls me back up, I'm flush against his body.

I rest my hand on his chest. Darkness blooms, but it isn't mine. It's his, thrumming against the palm of my hand in rhythm with his heart. My breathing stills. This feeling is new yet familiar. It's unexpected, but I'm not afraid. He's opening a part of himself I had not felt before. It's rage, chaos, sadness, and so much pain. All-consuming. He's the kind of darkness I could dance with forever.

"Kiss me," he whispers. Lightning cuts through the sky, highlighting his chiseled jawline. "Kiss me before I rip these clothes off your body."

Suddenly, I'm no longer counting down the seconds until thunder strikes. "What if I want you to do that?" I reply, holding his stare.

My boldness catches him off guard. His chest begins to rise and fall as if he can't stand not kissing me any longer. I press up on my toes, treading my fingers through his hair. Before I can reach him, before I can claim him, Callian's lips crash onto mine, moaning into my mouth in a deep release, and there's nothing soft about it.

Two enigmatic forces are trying to weave their way together. His hands run through my hair, fisting the back of my head. I gladly deepen the kiss and open my mouth to his. He rolls his tongue inside, devouring me, pulling me closer as if it still isn't enough. It's been far too long since I've tasted him. Far too long since I've felt his touch, something I thought about night after night. Heat pools between my thighs as I feel his length throb against my body. Our clothes are soaking wet, clinging to our skin and weighted by the rain. His shadowed jawline rubs against me. I am feral with desire.

"Take me inside," I demand.

He doesn't hesitate. One swift motion, and I'm in his arms with my legs wrapped around his waist. In our blind kissing frenzy, he hits the corner of a table, knocking over a vase. I jump, turning my head at the sound, but he catches my chin with one hand and gently nudges me to face him.

"Eyes on me, Princess. I don't want to miss any more moments with you."

"But the vas—"

"Fuck that vase, just tell me your favorite color and I'll buy you a thousand more."

I chuckle, but it comes out as a soft moan. The sound makes his cock throb against his breeches, and it almost makes me whimper.

There is a fragility in how he holds me, like I am something precious to him. He sets me down by the fireplace, my feet hitting the soft rug and the heat warming my back. Our eyes lock as we remove our clothes. There's nothing smooth about it, the way we struggle against the wet fabric, led by desperation. My breathing stills, watching his breeches drop to the floor. My eyes fill with desire seeing the veins along his cock that's so prominently hard for me. Flames cast shadows on every muscle of his body. His beautiful, rich-tan skin is glowing.

I can't seem to get my clothes off fast enough. I've only managed to remove my trousers when he says, "Let me help you," in a tone so smooth and sultry that it makes my breasts tingle with sensation. I lift my arms, keeping my eyes on him, wanting to savor how he looks at me as the wet fabric is pulled from my body. There's a rumble in his chest and fire in his eyes.

"You are so fucking beautiful," he groans in a heated breath as he takes in the full sight of my naked body glistening with rainwater.

He steps forward, taking my breast in his hand. His thumb rolls across my nipple, causing that ache to return in the apex of my thighs. I moan in response, they're so sensitive beneath his touch. He trails his hand down to my waist, just under my navel, dragging the tips of his calloused fingers across my flesh as he walks around me.

"Every part of you is perfect," he says.

My eyes follow him, trailing down to his ass. My gods, *he's* perfect. He lies in front of the fireplace, resting on one elbow with a knee bent. His length is beading at the tip. A longing pulse throbs between my thighs, warm and desperate with need. My heart races at the sight of him, those rippling abs illuminated in the glow of the fire.

"Please come here," he says. I comply, sitting beside him in a flutter. The fire is warm against my skin, but it doesn't stop my nipples from pebbling. I try to let the sounds of the crackling wood calm my nerves, but the more I stare at him, the more my insides begin to sizzle with need. "You look cold, Princess. Let me warm you," he purrs. My body shudders as he reaches for my hand and brings it to his lips. I moan, feeling the soft kisses he places on each finger. He pauses midway with sated eyes locking on mine. Then, he sucks one into his mouth, showing me the talents of his tongue. I pant out a heated breath, and his cock throbs in response, sending heat through me. My core tightens at his slow, languid licks. He begins kissing my wrists, moving down my arm, each kiss pulling me closer and closer until my chest is against his.

I straddle Callian's body, and his silky, hard length presses against my sex. I suck in a sharp breath at the feel of him beneath me. The lust has chased away my nerves. There's no stopping me from moving my hips across his length. I moan loud. My nipples pinch with arousal, matching the heat flushing on my face.

His head drops back. "Fuck," he grunts. "You're so fucking wet for me, it's maddening."

We continue to play the teasing game of grinding. I lean into the pleasure and chase the need with a pulsating drum beating against my sex. Water drips from my hair onto his chest. I glide to the very end, feeling his slicked pleasure rubbing against my opening.

"That's it, Princess, use me as you will. Remember, I am all yours, every part of me."

His moans are so deep, they steal my breath every time. I thought he would be leading, but he handed me the reins—allowing me to go at my pace.

My mouth opens in a cry of pleasure as his hands grip my ass. He helps guide me along his length at my pace, but his urge is too strong. The sudden movement lunges me forward as his head leans up. He catches a nipple in his mouth, licking and biting me in ways that further the pleasure in my clit. The connection between the two parts is a feeling I never knew was possible. I begin taking what I want, moving with precision up and down his entire length as his tongue continues to swirl around my nipple. He moans in response, a deep rumbling sound that vibrates against my body. Combing my hands through his hair, I'm craving the need, wanting more.

"I like it when you're greedy," he groans against my chest as his words continue to pierce my soul. There's something sinful about hearing the prince of Callisto telling me I can use him however I wish. I can feel his cock slick with my pleasure as I glide my way to the top of it. His tip teases at my entrance every single time. He angles it ever so slightly, barely pushing against my slit.

I whisper into the shell of his ear, "You are sly, Prince, and such a deadly tease." He cups the side of my face and pulls me to his lips. Our tongues lash in the most wicked ways before he presses his lips to mine.

"Forgive me. I am only a man, weakening beneath a feral flame." He smiles against my mouth. I don't know how I will survive this, nor do I care.

Callian slides his hands down my body, gripping my ass firmly, spreading me open to the cool, night air as it hits both my entrances from behind. I'm spread so wide, my slit parts. I arch into the feeling, grinding harder along his cock. Wet sounds smack the air, and I'm desperately reaching the tip of the wave.

"Tell me where you want to come," he growls.

That sultry voice sends my heart thrumming. Though every part of me says *"Just slide down his cock,"* I can't resist the urge to sit on his face.

"On your face," I admit, panting through every breath. "I want to come on that beautiful face." Heat spreads across my chest as a sheen of sweat forms above my brow.

He responds with a dark grin as his eyes flood with deviance and in one swift motion, Callian thrusts me above him. He shifts down, aligning my entrance perfectly with his lust-filled lips and locks his arms around my thighs. Every inch of his tongue slides inside my entrance. My gods, it's so long. My head rolls back as his arms tighten. His moans reverberate around my clit. I'm chasing the feeling as I grind harder against him. His tongue feels so good inside me, I'm about to lose my mind. Every time he makes that deep, guttural sound, my stomach dips.

Callian begins stroking his cock. It is all for me, every stroke of his hand, every thrust of his tongue. The heat intensifies, and I'm tipping over the edge. My pace rushes forward, grinding harder and faster against his mouth. A loud cry escapes me as I begin riding the wave of ecstasy. My orgasm dances and pulsates around his tongue, throbbing. The muscles in his arms tighten, and a deep moan rumbles in his chest as he comes too. We ride the wave together over and over again. I feel as though my soul has left my body; it now floats with the stars. My thighs shake as I pull away. His lips remain swollen with my pleasure. His head falls back against the soft fur rug, and he smiles, staring up at the ceiling, catching his breath.

"You are perfect. You will be the end of me, little flame."

My eyes widen, seeing the trail of his release going up to his abdomen and chest. Suddenly, that courage I felt while riding his face wanes, and I become a tight knot of nerves.

"Let me get you something," I whisper, rushing toward the bathing chambers. When I return, I hand him a cloth. He wipes himself clean and tosses it onto the pile of wet clothes.

I lie beside him, resting my head on his chest with our legs tangled together.

"I'm going to burn those clothes," I hum, nestling myself closer to the curve of his body. His hands caress my side.

"What if I like that shirt?" he says. I can feel the smile forming. I close my eyes, listening to his heartbeat as I trail my finger along the divots of his abs until I'm stroking the hair that leads downward.

"Do you think that would stop me?" I tease.

He laughs. "No, but if that would make you smile, then burn whatever you'd like." He shifts his body toward mine, encasing me in his arms. I'm so small in comparison to him. My feet barely reach his calves as our legs tangle together again. He runs the back of his hand along my face.

Though we are sealed away from the world, the reason I came knocking at his door pushes toward the front of my mind, sending a wave of nerves down my body. I don't want to talk about it yet.

"Tell me about your time at sea." I yawn, trying my best to stay awake. His brow lifts, studying me for a moment as humor flickers in his eyes.

"Such an interesting request for a bedtime story," he hums, kissing my forehead. I'm surprised he still has his wits, considering how tired he looks.

My lashes flutter. "Tell me," I reply, teasingly pushing a finger into his hardened pec to wake him up.

He looks at me, closing his eyes as sleep starts to claim him. "Is that why you came knocking at my door? For me to tell you about my time at sea? You wound me. I thought you came to thank me for the note and dinner." His eyelids grow heavy. The tips of his fingers begin to slip away from my face as sleep claims him.

"No, it can wait." Something foreboding hangs on my emotions, but I can only blame myself for putting pleasure before anything else. I quickly squash it before guilt tries to ruin this moment.

His breathing deepens, and I watch the rise and fall of his chest while laying in his arms. I cup his face, running my thumb along his shadowed jawline, and I take a deep breath, inhaling his scent, brushing back his hair, exposing the column of his neck. I tenderly kiss his throbbing pulse, tasting his salty sweat on my lips. Everything about him is perfect. I kiss him again. He hums again, but this time, he's asleep. Those beautiful lips curve into a smile. I close my eyes and drift away, listening to the beat of his heart.

CHAPTER 35

"PRINCE VALOR!" A FIST hammers against the thick, wooden doors.

My eyes fling open. The abrupt sound sends my pulse racing, and I can feel my heart slamming against my chest.

"Wake up. There's someone here." I shake Callian. He is lying on his stomach with his arm wrapped around the pillow. Some time in the middle of the night, he picked me up and carried me over to the bed.

A green eye hazily peeks up from the cushion of the pillow. Dark hair covers his entire face. I shake him once more, but he replies with a deep groan. His shoulders are like mountains, curving with the land. It distracts me for a brief moment. When the pounding returns, his eyes shoot open, and something dark flashes in them.

"Prince Valor! Are you in there?" The man continues to pound at the door. There's panic in his voice. Callian jumps out of bed, taking a sheet with him to cover his front. He unlocks the door and opens it just a crack.

"This better be important," he growls.

"They found something at the site of the attack. You need to see it."

I begin searching for my clothes and boots. My eyes skim the room for my dagger while the two men speak inaudibly to one another. At the end of the secretive conversation, Callian nods. "I'll be right there."

The blade of my dagger slices in the air as I sheathe it to my side. He turns to look at me. I can already see that whatever this is, it is big.

"You're not going. You're staying right here."

I slip on my first boot. "You speak as if you hold power over me."

Callian growls. Heavy, bare footsteps saunter over to me as I continue getting ready. "I need you to stay here," he says. I ignore him, slipping on my other boot. "Are you listening to me?" Anger flares in his voice. "You are staying here. That's final."

"Final?" My head tips back in a loud laugh. That word stroked my skin like the blade of a knife. "You're funny," I counter. His face contorts into confusion as I walk past him. "So your men can half-ass stand guard? Because if you haven't noticed, they're doing a shit job." I raise my voice. I know the guards can hear me, but I cannot care less.

His fists tighten. I see the struggle in his eyes as he bites back his next words. The veins in his forearms throb. He knows I'm right, but he turns to leave anyway. I run up behind him and grab him by the arm. He barely moves back, but it's enough to get his attention.

"*Don't* you dare turn your back on me when I'm speaking to you, Callian. Prince or not, I won't allow you to treat me this way." My breath becomes shallow. Am I taking this too far? I begin questioning my own words, but my past suddenly creeps up on me thinking about being locked in my room. My mind switches back to survival.

His jaw ticks and his nostrils flare as he exhales through his nose with a steel expression. "You have to remember, little flame, just because I am the son of a kind king doesn't mean I'm innately good. You have no idea what lengths I will go to in order to keep you safe." His words encase me in a chain made of shadows. He wears the smirk of someone I am about to return to hating.

My eyes narrow on him as he takes a step closer, but I don't falter. I stand my ground. He closes the remaining distance between us, which isn't much. His bare chest presses against my body, and I'm glaring into those emerald eyes. The tension tightens the air. What is flashing in our minds is evident, and we are flaming with ego.

"You don't get to order me around, *prince*. Let us not forget that I, too, am royalty, and my entire kingdom *isn't* kind. Coaxing out my darkness will be your biggest regret." His features tighten, the tension in his brows loosen, and after a few seconds, he nods.

"Do not doubt what I can handle. This is my mess that followed me here, so I'm going with you," I state.

"You are more than capable of handling anything, I never once doubted you. I'm just afraid of losing you. But you are right, that is my burden to carry, not yours," he admits, rubbing my arms and pressing his thumbs in a circular motion. He pulls me flush against his body, wraps his arms around me, and says, "I'm sorry."

SEVENTEEN.

Seventeen bodies are in a pile.

Men and women. My eyes frantically search the mound of carcasses, praying to the stars there are no children among the dead. Callian joins me at my side.

"There were no children involved." I nod in relief, staring at a young man with his mouth agape, horror spread across his face. The ground beneath us is painted red. Tears sting my eyes. I look away, seeing Crystal approach astride her white mare beside King Valor. Ten guards flank their sides. Sydney is among them, already wanting to dismount and ready to assist, but there is no one left for her to heal.

Iván's brother, Samuel, drags the back of his hand across his forehead, wiping off the sheen of sweat from the thick and muggy air. He takes a deep breath before he and Iván lift a woman's body from the pile. Her head is bashed in. Her bones crunch like broken glass as they place her in the wagon. I shudder at the sound. Each body lies side by side, draped in cotton sheets. Samuel whistles, letting the guard know this wagon is now full, and the guard voices a command at the horse that aids him forward. Samuel wipes sweat from his brow again and jerks his head, trying to fling the hair away from his eyes.

"A moment in private, my prince," Samuel says.

Callian looks down at me and sighs. "Excuse me."

The smell of death singes the air while the guards sort through the rest of the bodies. Deep animosity brims their eyes with angered glares all directed at me.

As more time passes in the palace of Callisto, division is growing. Not against each other, but against me. I knew this was coming. Like the anticipation before drawing a blade from your wound. You know you will be able to feel every tear of your flesh hitting each nerve. Nothing gets missed.

One of the men hasn't taken his eyes off me since we arrived. Callian notices the glares and the hatred, the animosity for me as he walks toward Samuel. He stares every man down with eyes that promise death if they try anything.

"Viona, come here, please." Callian's tone quickens my pulse. He continues his conversation with Samuel. "This was a slaughter." Callian runs his hand through his hair, pushing his long, dark strands to the back.

Samuel clears his throat. "My prince, there is a note addressed to Viona." My stomach turns. His eyes bounce between Callian and me as he holds a piece of paper in his hand. He looks absolutely exhausted. Thick bags hang heavy on his round, hooded eyes. His russet skin is flushed with the heat. Worry forms in his brows as he awaits Callian's next words on what to do with the information he holds. Samuel leans in and lowers his voice. "I was the first to arrive. I pulled it off the body before anyone else could read it." His hand begins to shake with anger. His hesitation tells me he already knows what's in it. All the muscles in my body tense.

Callian nods. "Thank you, brother. Give it to her."

I look down at the aged paper. Blood mars the corner of the note, and my eyes widen at the dark-red ink that was used. "It's written in blood." My teeth clench together. Flames burn under my skin. "Whose blood would this be?" I look up at Callian to see his lips pulled taut and brows narrowing down.

I turn my back to Samuel and walk a few paces forward, wanting to put space between him and me. I look over my shoulder. The worry in my eyes is enough to tell Callian I want him beside me when I read this. He comes to stand behind me, pressing his chest against my back, softly rubbing my shoulders.

"Once upon a time, there was a little bird.
I clipped all her wings and kept her in a cage so she could not fly.
Somehow, by the grace of the gods above, she grew her wings back and flew away.

Now, she hides with the enemy.

If you value the lives of the rest of your flock,
I suggest you surrender and return to me.
Besides, I made a promise to Solas
that he could take the virtue of our princess
before the entire kingdom.
He was much obliged.

Love, Daddy"

Callian's fingers press into my arm as all the air is knocked out of my lungs. I suddenly feel numb. What little energy I have drains from my body. I'm frozen in time as my father's betrayal cuts deeper than any pain I thought I could handle. The shame and disgust I feel makes me sick to my stomach. He would pass me off like I'm nothing. Another pawn in his game, having no respect for my body, my choices, or my true value. I'm just a vessel to him, nothing more. I try to speak, but my voice cracks.

"Let me see that," Callian grabs the paper. He reads it again. I turn around to face him while putting a hand over my mouth, trying to hold back a strangled sob. With each second that ticks by, his features grow darker. A part of me can sense him taking those words and creating a storm of boundless rage. All the muscles in his neck bulge. From behind, I notice Samuel walking back to the pile of bodies to give us space.

Callian's eyes stay frozen on the last two sentences. I know he's letting them sear into his mind. Before it makes both of us go insane, I extend my hand, willing the power inside me to burn the paper. I don't want to see it anymore. I don't want it to exist. Tears enshroud my vision as it ignites into flames. The wind picks up around it. Callian holds the paper between us as we watch it burn. Angered tears swell in his eyes as he watches me between the flames, seeing another type of pain cutting through my heart. We have shared so many different looks across a fire, but I never thought one would be like this. I begin to shake my head as if this isn't real. None of this can be real. His eyes are the only thing keeping me grounded right now. When the fire is about to burn the tips of his fingers, he releases the paper, willing his own powers to push it away from us until the wind finds it and sweeps it away. The embers glow against the early dawn, drifting in the sky until they blend with the stars.

He joins me at my side, pulling me into his arms.

All the embers have turned to ash. We're side by side, watching the stars fade against the rising sun. As they disappear from sight, so does the last piece of me that still loved my father. Today is the day another part of me died.

With a shaky breath, vengeance fills my voice.

"I will never shed another tear for a man who never loved me. I'm going to kill him," I vow.

"He cannot have you!" Callian growls, slamming his fist into the weathered wood of his father's desk. His voice thunders across the room, rattling the windows. "You aren't supposed to feel any more pain, not when you're with me." Guilt fills his voice.

"That's insane, Callian. You can't guarantee such a thing. It's inevitable that pain will be a part of our lives. We cannot control when it happens, but we can at least control *how* we deal with it," I reply, astonished that such calm words can flow through my lips at a time like this. Crystal stares at me with pride. She doesn't say much, following the king's lead, but her emotions are obvious.

I know Gareon already spoke to the king about our meeting, but I decided to tell the rest what he shared with me, all I discovered about who King Tarvas really is and what it could mean for me. A demi-god—a word foreign on my lips when it comes to my future. The possibility of longevity—something I can't fully understand or process right now. A part of me isn't sure if I believe it.

Callian and King Valor share a look, and the king rubs his thumb over the scars on his hands. He turns, his silhouette stark against the sunlight. A reflection peers back in the window. His stone-cold gaze stretches far beyond any of this. Perhaps he too is in disbelief? It is hard to discern.

I'm sitting by the fireplace watching Callian pace back and forth. Though he feels my pain, I've already processed my father's words and put them in the right place in my mind. There's a numbness that follows the truth, and though I can feel King Tarvas' death at the tips of my fingers, I know we have to stick to the plan. Patience has never been my thing, but that was something I had to accept quite some time ago.

I take a sip of my coffee. My mind flashes back to being in King Tarvas' throne room, seeing Solas sitting beside him. Both of them smiling as they looked in my direction. A chill rushes down my body picturing the gleaming stare Solas sent me from across a room of chaos.

"I know my father," I say, pulling myself back from the memory. Callian stops pacing and looks at me with his brows still furrowed. "I have a strong feeling he promised Solas something else to further his efforts and gain his alliance. I was just used to sweeten the deal. I've fought against Solas and his men before. There's no doubt in my mind he will take anything he can get. They won't stop coming for me."

King Valor turns around to face me with his hands still clasped behind his back. His embellished, dark-blue coat pulls taut against his muscular structure. "That is why we must go forward with the plan. We will host our annual ball for all the other kingdoms in Vendrelle. We need to strengthen our own alliances to see who will stand with us against Sao when the time comes. We will honor those from our kingdom who died in these attacks and invite any of our people who want to attend. We must unite all kingdoms to fight with us this possible war."

He turns to Callian, waiting for some sort of response, but Callian just nods in agreement with a darkness filling his eyes. It's obvious Crystal's concern is growing for Callian. It wears heavily in her violet eyes. She's reading his emotions with every move he makes.

Within a few strides, his father sits in the chair across from me and leans forward, clasping his hands around mine. Scars mar his flesh between his knuckles, thick and calloused. His emerald eyes warm with sympathy as he searches my face. A look that might be one a father would give their child when seeing they're troubled. A look I might have yearned for from my own flesh and blood, but now, seeing the truth to my father's words written on that note, that desire has died. I faintly smile at King Valor.

"My sweet child, with all you have endured, I find your strength inspiring." Hair dangles in front of one side of my face as I watch King Valor run his calloused thumb over my hands. Just like Callian. I have no words, a numbness just fills my eyes. "Remember the events of today, not to draw you back, but to encourage you to take a stand. Rise, rise against it. Remember who you are and who you are destined to be."

From the corner of my eye, Callian finally stops pacing. He listens to his father's words. I tighten my grip on King Valor's hands and give a curt nod. "Thank you, King Valor. Not just for your kind words, but for everything you have done for me without ever second-guessing. I see why your people love you just as much as your family does." I smile with sincerity warming my eyes. He squeezes my hand, his own eyes reflecting the same warmth.

"Shall we go to the throne room now? We have much to discuss with the council." A heavy sigh escapes King Valor as he stands. "We all know how interesting this will be."

WE LEAVE KING VALOR'S personal study and enter the throne room. A thick, blue carpet lines the way to the king's throne and the large, rectangular table with just enough seats for the council to sit. The smell of roses fills the air, reminding me of what's to come later. My heart sinks, each death weighing heavily on my shoulders.

A room full of eyes peers in our direction as King Valor is presented. Crystal, Callian, and I are at his side. The energy in the air is charged with anger, and it's all directed at me. Low chatter sweeps across the room, seeing the stance we are making to show unity, not separation.

Most of the elders and Ronan stare with disapproval. Whispers grow among the council, sitting and standing. It wouldn't be the first time a crowd scoffed at my presence. History has a way of repeating itself around me, but I lift my chin and pay them no attention. We reach the table, and Crystal sits beside the king. To my surprise, Gareon is here, standing behind the chairs, not far from Crystal. His face is hardened, and his chest is puffed out. He could stand anywhere, so why by her? Two guards flank his sides. He turns to look at me, lifting his brow. The dark, thick arch peeks between a strand of blond, moonlit hair that's braided and draped down his dark-blue coat. It almost feels like he is blocking me out. My brows pinch together in confusion. I blink back and quickly shift my attention elsewhere.

I search further down the table. Two empty chairs separate Iván from Crystal. Samuel stands behind his younger brother. At least there are some people in this room who don't wish me dead. Callian and I take those two seats. I sit beside Iván and faintly smile, but he's exhausted with a sullen look of death on his face. Callian sits beside Crystal.

When everyone has settled, King Valor stands.

"The ceremonies will begin at dusk by the northern shores. I expect everyone in this room to attend. Tomorrow, I will be extending the Royal Ball invitations to the families of those we lost. We will celebrate their memories. Extra preparations will be made." Low murmurs spread throughout the small crowd. I can only make out a few words here and there, but it's evident they aren't happy about it.

A man with short, salt-and-pepper hair and spectacles hanging down the bridge of his nose points his finger in the air. "We simply cannot have them dressing in their . . . everyday clothes attending such a prestigious event. What will the other two kingdoms say when they see commoners walking among them at the Royal Ball?" There are a few at the table who share his enthusiasm. I raise a brow. How could this asshole think he's better than anyone else? His imprudent behavior infuriates me. I keep my hands clasped together and pinch the inside of my palm to stop me from casting fire his way. King Valor shoots him a look of warning.

"Crystal plans to let Sydney know of these changes. If any of them do not have the proper attire, Sydney will be in charge of providing them with everything they need." Crystal nods as she laces her fingers together. King Valor looks back over to the older gentleman with a smug look on his face. The man uses his index finger to push his spectacles back in place and clears his throat.

King Valor continues, "There was a time, Salamir, when you were a commoner. I do remember I broke tradition when hiring you to be on my council. Though you have proven your defense to be as timid as a babe in cold water, it was your extraordinary eye for detail in combat strategy that placed you here. Over time, eyes grow weary. Being humble is a feat, and it's best not to forget from whence you came."

I snicker under my breath and glance over to Crystal who I know is struggling to keep her poise as well. Salamir gives King Valor a curt nod before sitting back into his seat, probably wanting to disappear from this very room.

"Your Majesty, the other two kingdoms have started to arrive. What will they say when they see we are having a pyre ceremony for seventeen people?" The woman who speaks has an accent I cannot place. Her light-blue eyes sweep over the room as a few others nod in agreement.

"I will be meeting with both queens, their consorts, and their representatives to bring them up to speed with our current situation. Though I suppose this is going to be quite the long discussion, I am well prepared." He reaches down, taking a sip of his coffee and glancing over to Callian. They exchange a look, one that tells me it's going to be a long night.

"Yes, my king," the woman replies.

"We will be doubling up on guards to survey the hills during the ceremony, and we will not leave any corner unlit. We have a week to prepare for the Royal Ball. Keep your eyes open. Once the event has ended and the queens and kings have settled from the festivities, we will discuss the next step to our plan. Only then will we see who will stand by our side. I have faith that, by the time this is over, we will be strengthening in numbers." Voices sweep over the room in agreement with their king.

He looks over to Callian who has remained silent. Callian looks like he's on the verge of expelling all his anger. "My son, you will stand beside me at the ceremony, and we—"

"I am requesting to stand in the crowd with the people of Callisto." Callian clips his father's words.

King Valor's eyes go wide at the sudden interruption. "That is not the tradition for our pyre ceremonies." His father's nostrils flare as he struggles to control his rage against his defiant son.

"When have I been known to follow tradition?" Callian icily responds, mocking his father's words from only moments ago.

"He is not worthy of your time, Your Grace, let this be seen as an act of rebellion against his king to all the people," Ronan retorts, stifling a grin as he plays with the handle of his mug. His upper lip twitches as he and Callian share a glare of hatred from across the table.

"And *you* are not worthy of bearing the family name!" Callian's seethe turns into a growl as his fist slams against the table. All the dinnerware rumbles against the wood. His teeth grit together as he points a finger at Ronan. "Let me ask you something, *cousin*. Do you mourn as my people do? Or will you sleep well tonight, tucked away in your silken sheets, not even giving these events any thought other than how they are an inconvenience to your day?"

Ronan scoffs, looking toward the king for validation, but King Valor's expression doesn't change. He only lifts a brow, waiting for Ronan's response. Ronan then turns to Callian with a look that tells me he is about to say anything but the truth.

"Of course I do. I'm sure I will not sleep tonight."

"The incredulity in your tone is comforting," I hiss. My hands tighten around my mug, so tempted to bash it against his head. He turns to meet my glare, eyes igniting with anger as tension flutters in his jaw. Clearly, just hearing my voice strikes a chord.

"You wound me, enemy," he retorts.

"Enemy . . . " I scoff, letting that word sing in the air. "A label you decided upon at first sight. A poison and judgment you unleashed upon me in front of a crowd in order to draw more alliances at your *own* back." I've kept my mouth shut as best I can out of respect for the king, but I can no longer hold my tongue. "Where do your loyalties lie,

Ronan? Are they with your king? It seems as though you do not have faith in his judgment of me. Maybe it is you who brings mistrust and lies to the table." Shock washes over the room. Ronan takes one good look around the table before he looks at me.

"Mistrust and lies . . . " He grins, running a long finger down a strand of his black hair before tossing it behind him. He leans in, meeting my glare. "You have lied to yourself every day since you arrived, thinking you can save us. All you have done is damn everything you touch." He goes to stand, shadowing over me with his knuckles pressing into the weathered table. He leans forward, a weak attempt to try to intimidate me.

I will not stand for it. I rise to my feet, challenging him with eyes that pierce through him like daggers. Callian stands up beside me, his chair grating against the stone floors, his chest heaving with rage. From my peripheral vision, I see Crystal tensing, creating a ricochet effect as Gareon's fists tighten at his sides. They both glare at Ronan. I don't trust him. Not a single fucking cell in my body trusts him. Every time I have to be in the same room as this piece of shit, I feel as though my senses must be on full fucking alert.

"That is enough!" King Valor's voice thunders across the room, shaking the ground beneath our feet. "This evening, we will bury the dead. I do not want to see such animosity displayed at this event. This meeting is adjourned."

CHAPTER 36

T HE OCEAN WAVES LICK the shoreline. We stand north, not too
far from where the bodies were discovered.

Everyone is in place. King Valor stands in the very center, Callian
and Crystal at his side. Other noblemen and members of the court
stand behind them. Ronan is among the elders who eye me like a
hawk. Sydney, Iván, and Samuel stand in a small crowd behind Crystal.
Guards are posted high on the outer rim of the service, their horses
moving briskly along the hilltops. Gareon is among them, astride his
horse, clad in black with his hand tightly wrapped around the reins,
wearing a look that says he's ready to kill if anything happens.

Callian's eyes find mine in the center of the crowd of families. He
whispers something in his father's ear. The king nods, though he still
doesn't seem fully pleased. Callian slips back. I can't bring myself to
stand among Callisto's royalty, not when I have brought death to their
kingdom. That is not a place where I belong, and I hold no title in the
kingdom of Callisto.

The families of all the deceased begin to seep through the crowd to
mourn their fallen. Between the stifled sobs and cries, I see some glaring
at me while comforting their loved ones—if any were to retaliate and
take a blade to my back, I wouldn't blame them. Others look at me
as if they're grateful for where I stand. Callian goes to each and every
member of their families, extending his condolences. When he joins
my side, an older woman reaches for him, kissing both of his cheeks
before moving back into step with her family.

Seventeen bodies are sewn in shrouds of cotton, the crest of Callisto
wrapped in the very center of their forms. Its gold embroidery glints
in the setting sun. Blue to match the color of the ocean. White roses to

shower the dead. Their bodies face the waves. The scent of sage drifts between the wind and the sea.

One member from each family stands before the pyre with a torch in their hands.

The air is somber and silent as King Valor steps forward also holding a torch, its flames roaring against the wind.

"The gods will carry them to the stars where they will shine bright in the night sky.

Let us not forget their names; may we speak of them fondly and remember all the good they brought to this world. Let us not forget there is always light in every darkness, and a fire lit for those who've lost their way."

One by one, each torch is set alight with its flames licking against the cool air. How many times did I have to look into the fires of a pyre? Wind whips my hair around my face. Sorrows of what will never be hanging on the hearts of those who have been lost. In a world where darkness hides, these people shouldn't have been sacrificed.

Crystal leaves the king's side and stands between the crowd of people and the royal court. She puts her arm around a weeping woman with black hair and a dark-cyan shawl wrapped around her shoulders. Her black dress drapes along the sand. The woman seems shocked at first, but then leans into her. Crystal looks to her other side and extends her hand to Iván. He joins her and Samuel follows, along with a few more from the royal court. She begins to sing in a language I have never heard. Her ethereal voice sweeps over the crowd. As people begin to follow her voice, both nobles and royalty gather on each end. Before too long, I can no longer see a division. We all stand, blended together and united. Tears enshroud my vision seeing Crystal standing there, stoic and brave, always holding all the answers when she finds people in the dark. She is special. I realize now that it's true what people say about her.

She is the heart and the light of this kingdom.

I WATCH AS THE BODIES BURN, each and every one, until they are nothing more than charred remains. Wind kicks up, taking their ashes to the stars. When I finally look up, I see the sky has turned to twilight. The high tide is drifting in. The incoming waves lick against my boots as a reminder that I can't stay for much longer, but grief still binds me here. I stifle a sob. I wasn't there to help them, I wasn't there to save them from their unjust slaughter.

"Viona," a warm voice exhales in a whisper. That firm hand I know all too well presses against the small of my back. Breathing in a shaky breath, I open my eyes again to the night sky and turn my head to look at Callian. His jaw ticks, grief tightening his features. Those emerald eyes look far beyond the sea. He's been struggling today with so many things. The heat emitting from the palm of his hand feels hotter than usual as he rubs circles on my back.

"Ronan is right. All I bring is chaos and death," my voice rasps as the anger runs hot within my veins. My fists clench at my sides, my fingernails dig into my palm because I'm afraid if I release my hands, they will scorch everything around me, including him. The chaos is whispering beneath my skin, calling to my darkness like a hand longing for a touch. "What I wouldn't do to know how it feels to wrap my hands around my father's neck. To feel every bone in his throat break as I wring his life from existence, but I know that won't be enough." I look at Callian, realizing something foreboding is blooming to existence. "Something is coming. I have to be ready for it. I need to be strong and harness what I've been given. He won't stop. He won't stop until he has me. That is the cutting truth."

"There is always loss of life in war, but please know that you are not the cause of this. Do not take the blame for those who seek harm against you." The moonlight glows, a silvery shimmer against the ocean's waves. He turns to me, eyes prowling, but he holds back with much resistance. "You will get your revenge." Callian brings me flush against his body and places a kiss atop my head. "Do not lose hope, Princess. I crave the day I get to see the look on your face when you end his life. It will come, and he will not be able to hurt you or anyone else anymore."

CHAPTER 37

I'M TETHERED TO AN *oceanside seen only in my dreams. Dark, ominous clouds drift above a raging sea. I'm standing on the ledge with my arms wrapped around my body, withdrawn and far from reach. My core shakes, reverberating in the center of my chest. My head tilts back with my eyes closed, listening to the whispers calling my name, letting them lead me in a dance I know all too well. An inescapable, divine force calls me to the deep end of my existence. I stare down at the waves as they mercilessly slam against the cliffs. My heart beats against my chest, like a low, heavy drum, synchronizing with the crimson glow beneath the murky water. The frigid air does nothing to soothe the torrid current swelling inside of me. I dig into my flesh, scratching the violent storm clawing at my insides, but it's not enough. It will never be enough. The harrowing truth coursing through my veins becomes too much.*

I am out of my depth and out of my mind, but fear is fleeting.

There is no escaping this hollow space where all my darkness hides. I take one step forward, watching the waves swell high and then crash down against the sea. My pulse begins to race against time. Each step is as freeing as the last. As my foot dangles over the ledge, the wind brushes against the soles, and the sheer, white gown flutters against my body. The urge is growing, as is the wind. I'm slipping away, drowning in the melody of a woman's voice saying, "Adnama." The shrill cries are everywhere, repeatedly screaming her name. Tears sting my eyes. The back of my throat burns. There's a tightness in my chest upon hearing their agony. My head turns in slow motion. Adnama stands beside me, long before she was oppressed by the undertones of the White Forest. In a time where air filled her lungs and her skin was a soft, glowing, tawny color. Life fills her eyes, a kindness that stretches beyond her faint smile. We both look toward the sea, her hand clasping mine, warm and welcoming. Inhaling a deep breath, the waves churn one last time, the wind whips through my hair.

One last inhale before I . . .

A big, calloused hand wraps tightly around my arm, pulling me out of what I think was a dream, though I am not in my bed.

Where the fuck am I?

My pulse races into a panic, looking side to side at my surroundings. There are four figures moving about like a blur. I try summoning my powers, but my body is frail, weak, as it always is when I have these episodes.

Fuck . . .

"This was way too easy," one murmurs. "Your prince isn't here to save you," he growls into my ear.

Chills rush down my spine, realizing what is happening. I'm unable to speak. Nothing but inaudible sounds break free as I'm being carried away down one of the hallways.

Callian . . . only a faint whisper in my head.

"The princess must like you, you've left her quite speechless." Another male with a deep husky voice bellows out a laugh.

"Keep your voices down, you idiots, or we will be heard!" Another man seethes under his breath.

"Fuck you," I retort in a raspy voice, the only words I can manage. My eyes roll to the back of my head. He laughs at me, tightening his grip.

"Save those words for later when I'm ready to fuck some respect into you." His words sound so hateful and threatening. I squint my eyes, trying to focus on the shadowed men, counting down the seconds until their features become more visible so I can see the faces of who I'm about to kill. The one in front of me is an older man, mid-forties, with brown hair tied back. The one carrying me has short, rusty-blond hair and . . .

Feeling my stare, he looks down at me. Those pale-blue eyes glare with searing hatred.

That scar above his brow. He turns his head ever so slightly. Just at the right moment when his pink flesh glints in the candlelight . . .

Another chill sweeps over my body knowing damn well who this is. *Rossburn.*

He's one of the guards who walks the palace. This prick has been patrolling my corridor outside our chambers since I arrived. He's not in his usual garb of armor. Tonight, he's cloaked in dark linen. His pale-blue eyes darken as he surmises my thoughts. With little shame, he grins maliciously.

"That's right, princess. I hear the way he pleasures you. I think I deserve a turn." Bile creeps its way up my throat.

"You wouldn't dare touch me." I seethe, my upper lip twitching into a snarl. He restrains my arms against his body. My strength is slowly starting to come back. I thrust around, trying to break free. Every attempt is met with his grip tightening. "Let me go, you fucking bastards," I snarl, looking around to see who the other guards are.

I can't believe the betrayal that will soon come to King Valor. One of them wears the royal armor of Callisto. It is quite possible the other two are his men as well.

All the little hairs on the back of my neck rise. An energy ignites, electrifying the air in one swooping motion as though it's being pulled in one direction. Darkness unfurls beneath my skin. That familiar tether returns, pulled taut as it moves as an unseen light, desperately searching for its other end. I know all too well exactly what I feel. It is coming for me, but something darker awaits Rossburn and his filthy men.

"Just wait until the king and the prince find out what you're doing." My voice grows in strength. I glare into his eyes, seeing his fate is now inevitable. I will be the last thing he sees.

"Your prince is nothing but an unhinged fuck. What does he have that I don't?" he growls into my ear.

Every second it draws closer, I know exactly what this is. Grimacing, my smile stretches wide. "He holds something you could never fathom...my demons," I whisper.

The ground shakes beneath my feet, and it feels as though all the air has been sucked out of the hall. A hand wraps around Rossburn's neck. He lets go, causing me to stumble back. As I gasp for air, Rossburn's throat is being restricted. He desperately thrashes about while Callian dangles him in the air. Callian slams him against the wall, and Rossburn falls to the ground, moaning in pain.

Like a raging beast, Callian eyes his next prey, the betrayal evident as he sees the male in his royal armor. Callian grabs him by the throat as well. The next thing I hear is armor being ripped off the man's body, uncaring of the limbs that go with it. An ear-shattering scream rips from the man's throat. In a blinded rage, Callian punches through the cavity of the man's chest and pulls out his heart. The guard's carcass drops to the ground.

The other two men stand frozen in horror, regret, and fear as they see their dark prince standing in a pool of their man's blood. Callian looks up at them. In a panic, the two men try escaping through a side door leading to one of the many rooms. A power emits off Callian as he thrusts his hand out, slamming every single escape shut.

Metal slices in the air. The two men panic. Their eyes grow wide, staring at Callian's sword. He strides forward, impaling one in the chest. A gurgling cry follows, the sound reverberates in my ears as he expels his last breath. Callian yanks out the sword, now slick with blood. The other man backs away, shaking his head.

"No, please, my prince." When he sees there will be no mercy, he spins on his heels and goes screaming down the hall. The end of a pointed blade catches him. One swift movement was all it took for his body to hit the floor.

Callian turns around, heaving with rage when his eyes lock on Rossburn. Callian stalks toward him as Rossburn remains seized by fear. His rusty-blond hair is slick with sweat against his face. He holds his hands up in surrender. Callian grabs him by his shirt, yanking him off the ground.

"Tell me why I shouldn't end your life right now," he growls. Rossburn's eyes bulge, red veins crest the corners, spreading like wildfire. Callian growls again at the betrayer's silence. "*Tell me!*"

Rossburn begins heaving. "Because I know who is behind this," he admits, legs trembling.

"Who?" Callian demands, eyes darkening. White teeth glint in the faint candlelight of these halls. I already know he's going to make this man suffer until he spills the truth, and I welcome every part of it.

"I—" Rossburn's eyes fill with tears as horror spreads across his face. "I cannot tell you who made me do this, or he will kill my whole family."

"You decided their fate the moment you agreed to this abduction," Callian counters.

"Please have mercy," he whispers as the words of his prince sink into his reality, fearful for the fate of his beloved.

A group of heavy footsteps scurry down the hall, and I turn my head to see more guards rushing to our aid. I quickly cross my arms over my chest, remembering I'm wearing my sheer, white nightgown. When they arrive, their eyes go wide, trying to assess the situation. Iván breaks through the wall of armored men. He immediately looks at me.

"Are you okay, Vi?"

I hold my chin up and give him a nod.

"Take this piece of shit down to the dungeons. He and I are going to have a little chat later on." Callian throws Rossburn toward Iván who catches him with pleasure.

Callian puts his arms around me.

"What happened?" His tone softens. He removes his dark, long-sleeve tunic and slips it over my body. The warmth of his fabric already begins to soothe me. I shake my head, unwilling to speak around any of these guards. I look down to the ground and begin rubbing the side of my temple. The pressure in my head is heavy, but at least my strength is returning.

Off to the side, I see Samuel arrive. His eyes skim over the massacre within the corridor. Callian must sense his presence.

"Leave the one who's missing his heart where he lies. Clean up the rest." His eyes never leave mine while he speaks. I can tell by the green tendrils of shadow and his ticking jaw, there is more rage to be had. I cup my hand to his face, running the pad of my thumb along his shadowed jawline.

"Let's go," I whisper, desperately wanting to retreat to my room.

I start walking down the hall. The fabric of my gown brushes against my bare feet, and I glance at the sheer material that barely gave me any cover. I will have to be embarrassed about that later. At least I have some of my dignity left hidden beneath his tunic. Still, I move my hair to the front and cross my arms over my chest. Callian's eyes are still sweeping over me to see if I am hurt.

"I said I'm fine," I sigh, picking up my pace, but he's so tall, he remains unaffected by it. I notice he is still wearing the clothing he wore to the pyre ceremony yesterday, and his hair is disheveled. The dark circles under his eyes tell me he most likely didn't sleep or possibly ever go to his chambers last night. I feel bad that I've caused him so much stress. If I'm being quite honest with myself, I shouldn't be here at all. I try not to fault myself. I should be saving my anger for Rossburn. The fucking bastard. With a deep, heavy sigh, I side glanced Callian. "I'm sorry." My voice softens.

He turns his head and looks down at me with worry pinching his brows. "For what?"

"For all of this." I wave my hands into the air.

"Please don't ever tell me you're sorry, Princess."

As we head back to my chambers, I see all the guards who stood post last night are on the ground, causing me to stop in my tracks. My heart drops to the pit of my stomach. Callian looks at me and sees the shock on my face. His head whips down the hall. I step forward, pressing my two fingers against the neck of the closest guard.

There is no pulse.

I look up at Callian, shaking my head.

"Fuck!" he growls, running a hand through his hair. He turns around and calls out for Samuel. It doesn't take long for him to rush to Callian's side.

"Bloody hell . . . " Samuel mumbles, his round eyes widening. "What's happening?"

"Who fucking knows." Callian exhales, checking every other guard's pulse. He then checks for injuries, but there are none. "No pulse, no wounds, I don't know what's going on."

Samuel stares at all the dead guards, rubbing his chin. His wavy, bronze hair bounces as he shakes his head. "This isn't good. What do you want me to do, brother?"

"Not a word to my father. I will inform him shortly," Callian instructs him. They both exchange a look with heavy features. Samuel nods. Before he leaves, he takes one final look at me with concern pinching his brows.

"Do you need anything, Viona?" Still in a daze, I faintly shake my head from side to side and step inside my chambers. Callian follows.

I rush toward the bathing chambers, removing the tunic and my gown, tossing it into a basket. I dip a cloth into a bucket of cool water and run it along my chest and arms. For the first time, I'm annoyed by my request to remove the mirrors when I first arrived. I want to see my reflection; I want to see what stares back at me. My mind starts reeling at the events. My vision, the attack. With each moment that ticks by, my pulse is rising. I feel his presence in the doorway, pulling me from thought.

"You aren't really going after his family, are you?" I ask gravely.

He scoffs, "You know I would never do such a thing. Instilling fear though..." He pauses, and I sense the smile in his voice. "It's my specialty."

My mind flashes back to the White Forest where it all started. Where we truly began. I recall how he made me feel as he pressed me up against the tree. How could I forget the way his eyes filled with darkness? With a voice that stilled the beat of my heart. The memory, though fresh, no longer frightens me now that I know who he is, but for someone like Rossburn, well, he brought it upon himself.

"That is where your true talent lies," I say between splashing water onto my face. He chuckles before retreating into the room. I look down at the palm of my hand, tracing the lines in the center with my thumb. "There will be no mercy for those who cross me."

CALLIAN BURSTS THROUGH THE doors of the throne room, and everyone's head whips in his direction. There's a stillness in the air, a numbing chill washing over the crowd as they see his hand wrapped around a guard's neck. Not just any guard, he wears the broken armor of the kingdom of Callisto.

"Callian, what is the meaning of this?" King Valor stands from his throne and descends the steps as he recognizes the face of the deceased. Two guards flank his side with their hands hovering over the hilts of their sheathed swords. The king searches his son's face for reasoning, trying to piece together what happened before Callian can speak.

Ronan has a black brow raised. His hands clasp together behind his back, taking in the scene that is unfolding. I walk in further behind Callian and stand off to the right, keeping my chin lifted. All eyes are on the prince of Callisto. I guess it takes a corpse to keep a room full of eyes off of me.

Callian's steps are hard and heavy, and rage still hasn't left his eyes. They flare like green flames licking the night sky. He skims the room, glaring at all who stand here. It isn't until then that I see some of the royals from other kingdoms have arrived. Their own guards already barricading them.

Callian releases the carcass. The sound sends gasps among the crowd, watching in horror as blood continues to spill out from the open cavity of the chest, staining the light-blue, royal carpet.

I swallow the lump in my throat as a chill rushes through my body.

Callian finally speaks. "*This* vile bastard and several others attempted to abduct this woman right here." He points a finger at me. My stomach turns as all eyes are on me but I keep my chin lifted and shoulders straight. "As you can see, they failed." Tension hangs in the air as Callian's chest heaves. Teeth gritting, jaw ticking, every breath is a growl. The man who stands before me is no prince, he is a beast protecting what's his.

King Valor looks in my direction with worry pinching his brows. I take a deep breath, keeping my head high.

Low murmurs simmer throughout the crowd as they exchange looks. King Valor extends his hand back, ordering for his guards to stand down. They remove their hands from the hilts of their swords and fall back. The guards from the other kingdoms remain with their weapons drawn. I search the crowd for Crystal. Her bright, velvety eyes are wide in shock. As she rushes to my side, I can already see her face is guilt-stricken for not being there for me. I quietly whisper to her that I'm okay.

"An attack on her, is an attack on me. It seems as though we have people working against us. *In my palace!*" Callians voice rattles all the stained-glass windows throughout the expansion of the room. He takes a few steps forward, walking down the line of people. "Some of you may still see her as an enemy. You are *fools* if you think such things. Let this be known: anyone who even thinks about putting her in harm's way will be killed on sight." He looks at me while he speaks, eyes flaring with so much heated rage that goosebumps shiver down my body. He turns back to the crowd.

"I am not one you want to cross. I will not restrain myself, no matter what title you hold, what crown sits upon your head. I will see your flesh only as a barrier to the blood I'd spill for her." His voice bounces off the walls. He points to me again. "She is *mine;* nobody fucking touches her. "

My cheeks flush at the intensity of his words, sending another wave down my body, but this time, it's pure heat. The finality of his promise settles deep within my core. I've never felt death and truth so promising until he spoke those words.

King Valor's nostrils flare as his eyes skim the room. "Viona Tarvas is under the protection of Callisto." Then he turns to me. "Viona, I guaranteed your safety here, and I have failed you. For that, I am sincerely sorry. We will find out who is behind this," the king promises then addresses the room. "Anyone who attempts to harm her will be charged with treason and tried as our *laws* command."

Silence fills the air while he and Callian exchange a look. One that suggests this will bring much division between them behind closed doors. Apparently, they seem to have different views on how treason is dealt with. The way he turns his back on his father and faces the crowd sends a clear message to everyone in the room. He will kill . . . for me. No trial necessary.

CRYSTAL AND I TRAIN IN A more private garden outside the palace today. This large, circular space feels more like a prison with its high, heavily guarded walls. Gareon stands on top of the parapet, pacing around. I'm certain he smirks a few times, intrigued by watching us train. I'm tempted to throw a fireball at him, but I wouldn't dare test his powers. Other guards are spread out along the walls. Iván is down below with us, guarding one of the entrances.

Crystal and I spar with weapons and our powers, a combination of moves as she orchestrates a combat symphony until I feel comfortable enough to move fluidly. I'm more aggressive today, unfocused, but it's nothing she can't handle. She insisted I take a day's rest, but I need to release the fire clawing at my insides. I'm starting to notice, as my powers grow stronger, so does the desire for release. Restraining my powers would cause them to begin to itch and spread like a rash. She told me that is normal, and when my body acclimates, it'll go away. I can't wait for that day to come.

It's nearing dinnertime before we stop. We rest on the ledge of a small wall that overlooks the wide-open space. It's ridiculous having so many prowling guards on full alert, but it was the only way Callian would confidently leave me while he tries to sort through this mess. He promised me he would wait for me to be done with training before he went to the dungeons to see Rossburn. I told him what happened in my vision, but seeing Adnama is something I kept to myself.

My eyes drift down to my hands. I stare at my palm with all its lines and small crevices, remembering the familiarity I felt through her touch. One I can't get out of my head.

Crystal clears her throat then tips her head back, taking a long pull of water from her flask. The swells of her breasts protrude from her tightly laced, cream-colored stays. When she's done, she sets it aside and unties her long, wavy hair. It cascades down around her body. I roll my eyes, seeing exactly what she's doing. My brows arch watching her put on a show.

"Who are you eye-fucking? Iván or Gareon?" I ask, mischievously grinning ear to ear. I swear I almost see her heart stop when I mention the other male. The one particularly handsome mystery man I've seen hovering around her.

"Whoever decides to take me first." She glances at me with her lips quirked to the side. "Lucky for you, your love interest seems to have no trouble deciding. The only issue is, when are *you* going to have sex with Callian?" she counters.

I playfully nudge her shoulder. "I'm not as giving as you, I suppose." We erupt in laughter that has most of the guards looking in our direction. Gareon's brow lifts so high, it might float away.

"It's not every day a man is willing to go against his morals and kill for the woman he loves. You should have seen some of the looks on those women's faces in that room. They might have taken his anger as a mating call."

"He doesn't love me." I huff out a shy laugh, tucking a strand of hair behind my ear.

"You can say that all you want, but that doesn't make it true, Vi," her voice goes an octave higher. "All you're doing is denying yourself happiness. Happiness that you deserve."

I lightly scoff, reaching over her to grab the flask. I jump off the wall and walk toward the entrance of the garden. I unravel the top and drink the remaining water. She catches up to me and wraps her arm around my shoulders.

"It's going to eventually happen. You'll see," she drawls.

"Trust me, the day that happens, you can put me in that awful, lilac, floral dress I almost put on before meeting King Valor," I reply.

Crystal laughs, looking at me with a wide smile. "It's a bet."

CHAPTER 38

Nighttime falls.

Callian leads me down a dingy flight of stairs to the dungeons, per my request. Only a few torches light the way. As we descend further, my eyes strain, fixed on my boots. The further we go, the thicker the staleness in the air grows. I walk behind him, the perfect place to be. If I misstep, he will likely catch me without my fall disrupting his stance. He reaches back, finds my hand, and laces his fingers with mine. The sudden touch stills my heart, leaving me breathless. My eyes trail up his arm. The candlelight maps out every thick vein and muscle in his triceps, making me want to explore all the other places the light doesn't touch.

When we reach the end of the stairs, I remind myself where we are. Two guards are stationed at the mouth of what I assume is the cave entrance leading to the cells. The hinges of the door are fastened to the stone wall. The guards are silent. Once they make eye contact with Callian, they step to the side.

I unclasp my hand from Callian's, refusing to let any of these pricks see it as a sign of weakness. I don't need to be on the arm of a man to be here. I move to the front, letting him know I'll enter first. He says nothing as we proceed forward.

As the door opens, it creaks, echoing through the space ahead. I hear sudden clanks of metal. It seems as though, even while locked behind steel bars, the prisoners are chained. A heaviness sits on my chest. I wonder about the crimes these men committed to be held in a place like this. It seems the palace of Callisto has dark parts after all.

One of the guards tells us Rossburn is in the last cell to the right. As I walk forward, whispers drift between the bars, but I try not to make eye contact. Rossburn is sitting in the corner of his cell on fresh hay and bound in chains. He looks up at me through a hooded glare, but as soon as Callian steps beside me, all the color in his face drains.

Water slowly drips off a wall somewhere. It's a sound that would drive me mad if I were held captive here.

Rossburn stands. As he walks over to the bars, he holds his hands up in surrender and speaks in a raspy voice. "We weren't supposed to do it so soon, we had a plan, but we had no choice. She came out of her chambers, dazed like she was caught in some dream." Horror fills his voice as the memory comes rushing in, remembering something I cannot fathom. My pulse speeds up, not wanting to hear what I have always felt could be true.

"Some of the guards . . . " He pauses, reaching for his cup of water and taking a long sip. He says nothing more for a short while. Those pale-blue eyes look up at Callian through the bars. "Some of the guards were in deep sleep. When others saw what she was doing to them, they only attacked her to defend their lives. She entered this idle state, as if she were moments from fainting, I took that as an opportunity to take her." While Rossburn speaks, Callian's features are stone-cold with a glare that only the stars themselves could truly surmise. "She had no weapon; her eyes were onyx, and it was as if she stole the souls right out of them. They dropped dead on sight."

This is impossible . . . Is he lying?

It can't be true. Was that the upheaval of my powers? I start shaking my head in disbelief. "She is evil, my prince. She is no savior. The prophecy says—"

Callian reaches into the cell, grips Rossburn by the throat, and slams his face so hard against the steel bars, the faint scar above his brow splits open.

"A prophecy that holds no meaning to me other than the fact that she is not the end-bringer." He seethes through gritted teeth.

Rossburn's eyes gloss over. His demeanor changes.

"You're nothing but a fool who keeps feeding the snake," he growls, looking over to me.

Callian hits his face against the steel bars once more. "Do not look at her," he yells. "Tell me who is behind this, or I will bleed it out of you."

Rossburn erupts in a cynical laugh.

Disgusted, Callian releases him with a thrust, causing Rossburn to fall onto his back. His laugh doesn't wane. "You think your kingdom is strong, but the longer she stays, the more fissures spread throughout the palace. You have no control over your people or their beliefs."

Then, his eyes narrow in on me. "He's coming for you. He will get to you before you reach your full potential."

The attention goes back to Callian. "Those who do not see her in the same light as you will step forth and let it be known." His eyes change. He begins blinking back the words he just spoke. In disbelief, his eyes trail up to find us on the other side of the bars.

An icy chill hits my chest, thawed by the flames coursing through my veins. Pausing at the entrance of the doorway, I give Rossburn one final look. "If you believe me to be such horrific things, just wait until the darkness takes hold of you. I can assure you, my demons await your arrival." Finding Callian's bold stare in the dim lighting, satisfaction blooms in my chest as we share a look that I voice.

"Kill him."

SYDNEY HAS BEEN KEEPING to herself lately. Over the last few days, she has even skipped our morning visits. A bit of insecurity blooms, wondering if she is upset with me. Or maybe she is tired of me bringing so much death into her home. The way she looks at me now with a half-warm smile makes me uneasy. Is she pulling back? I'm starting to like Sydney, and I hope this won't end in a similar way as my relationship with Alyce. I often think about her, hoping she's okay. I miss her more than she will ever know.

I sigh, blowing away the dark strand of hair dangling in front of my face.

"You know, it's not easy standing here naked," I finally say.

She looks up at me with an arched brow, giving me the same half-smile that doesn't quite reach her rich-green eyes.

"It's not easy being you at all these days," she scoffs. "Surely being naked in front of me should be the least of your worries." The long pause stretches on. She takes another look at me, this time looking less stern. "Don't worry, I'm almost done."

I roll my eyes and stare out the balcony windows, looking at the ocean in the distance. I'm still set on my idea of stealing one of their ships and sailing far away from Vendrelle.

Sydney double checks the measurements of my shoulders and arms, then she measures around my neck. As she rounds my front, she hands me a cloth.

"Here, you can cover your breasts while I measure your front."

I nod, bringing the soft fabric to my chest. My brows knit with unease, worrying about the Royal Ball. All the talk around it unsettles my stomach. She begins to write in her notebook, making sketches and small notes. I look over her shoulder to see what she's conjuring up.

"Is this where all your brilliant ideas come from?" I ask, watching her draw small gems off to the side.

"Yes. I've made so many sketches throughout my lifetime. I'm not sure how useful they will be to anyone once I'm long gone, but they mean the world to me for now."

"May I?" I ask, reaching for the notebook.

"If it will stop you from bothering me so much, then have at it."

I try ignoring her tone and begin flipping through the pages. Some of the clothing has been beautifully stroked with paint. I recognize some of the drawings as outfits I've seen on Callian's father and Crystal. When I stumble upon Ronan's, I scoff.

She looks over my shoulder and laughs. "Somehow, I knew you would find his outfits. Unfortunately, I am not in a position to choose who I design for."

"Apparently," I groan, quickly flipping to another page.

She chuckles under her breath, keeping a trained eye on the fabric samples she brought with her.

I hear Crystal walk into my chambers behind me, pushing in a cart filled with food—its sweet aroma fills the air. The fresh bread and pastries are already making my stomach rumble. I start thinking about which jellies I will choose to spread across them when my thoughts are interrupted.

"My gods, Vi, I didn't know you were hiding such an incredible ass. You put mine to shame."

My cheeks flush, turning redder than a cherry, as I forgot I'm naked. I quickly turn, shielding my ass from her sight, forgetting Sydney is behind me which sends me crashing into her. We both stumble back, but she catches my fall as she steadies herself against the table.

"When I agreed to get fitted for dresses together, that didn't mean you could look at me!" I reply, holding the cloth against my front even closer.

She responds with a laugh, holding her hands up in surrender. "I can't help it. I'm just trying to bring us some food peacefully. I didn't think you would be sticking it out so much," she teases.

I growl.

She picks up my apple from the table, but before she can sink her teeth into it, I extend my arm and push forth the energy building in the palm of my hand. The apple flies out from her grip, rolling under my bed.

"Stop eating my apples!" I yell.

She counters with a prideful grin. "Impressive."

"Are you two done?" Sydney snaps, causing me to turn. She wears a look that screams she's ready to murder us. Her hip is shifted to the side, arms crossed over her body as she holds a pencil in one hand.

"Ask her. She's the one with the big mouth," I retort, thrusting my arm back at Crystal.

"This may come as a shock, but the *both* of you have big mouths. I'm surprised they haven't got you two into more trouble." Sydney's voice grows louder the more she speaks. A loose strand of hair falls free from her bun as she scolds us. "Now shut up so I can finish fitting you girls for dresses. I only have a few hours left to put them together."

I glance over to Crystal, holding back the snicker that wants to break free. Crystal's lips are sealed and pressed thin. She turns around to hide her eye roll from Sydney and picks up a piece of bread.

"You always get this way before the ball," Crystal mumbles, spreading what looks to be apricot jam over the buttery slice.

"What way is that?" Sydney counters, placing the pencil down with emphasis, the sound echoing throughout the chambers.

"Reclusive, distant though present, crazed, easily set off—"

"Alright, I get it." Sydney glares at Crystal over my shoulder.

"And everything always turns out just fine too," Crystal reminds her. They both share a look, and their features soften. I guess that was their form of a truce. If this behavior is normal for Sydney, then I guess she hasn't been trying to avoid me.

It's hard to discern how people feel about me. Living my life without much outside contact, no friends, and minimal family, I've never been good at reading social cues. I always end up losing the ones I care about.

A few minutes of silence fill the air. Sydney sighs in satisfaction as she stares at her drawing. I put on fresh linen and walk over to the table full of the food my belly has been dying to devour. Crystal picks up a plate. Her violet eyes are full of mirth.

"Bread or a fresh pastry?" I skim over the array of foods and point to the blueberry muffin. She slides the plate over to me, and I sink my teeth into its moist texture, groaning against the flavors swirling in my mouth.

I can hear Sydney flipping through the pages of her notebook. "Ah, here it is. Luckily for you, Crystal, I only have a few things to double-check," she says, pulling out Crystal's dress.

While Crystal and Sydney fall into a quiet conversation about the specifications of her outfit, I fill my cup to the brim with coffee. I look around the table for my apple, then remember I flung it out of Crystal's hand moments ago. My eyes search the ground until I spot it under my bed—its shiny, red skin reflects the rays of sun beaming in from the balconies. As I reach for it, something else catches in the light. It's a dark stone. My arm extends further until I feel it in my grasp, and my hand presses against the bed as I take a seat. As my hand opens, my jaw drops.

"Labradorite," I whisper. My heart slams against my chest, and all the blood in my face drains. This is mine. The last time I saw it, it was on my side table in Sao. I had found this as a child while on the shores of my home. Why would it be here?

"Are you alright?" Crystal calls out, causing me to jump. My hand clasps shut.

"I'm fine. I was just retrieving my apple." I quickly slip the stone under my pillow.

It's not long before Sydney is done with Crystal. I keep to myself, quietly eating my apple and filling my head with thoughts that only drown me. I barely notice as they prepare to depart. Crystal asks if I am okay one more time before she makes her leave, and I assure her I am fine.

CHAPTER 39

I'M SITTING ON THE edge of the bed, dressed in the most beautiful gown I've ever been graced with, and I still can't rid these torrential waves swelling inside. Feeling sullen, I watch dusk settle into the sky, hoping it'll soothe my thoughts, but my anxiety is tightening with every breath. Occasionally, I lift the pillow to glance at the stone, worried about how it got here. It has to mean something, but what? There were no pockets in my clothing the night I was taken. With the events that have unfolded, is this a sign that someone from Sao is here? My senses heighten. Waves of heat have been churning inside me since I was attacked, lying low, coasting through my veins.

A loud knock pulls me from my thoughts. As if my heart couldn't sink any further, I know who stands on the other side. With a long, deep exhale, I try wiping the worry from my face and steady myself before swinging the door open. I've done this before. Hiding my emotions has become a way of survival, but I've never had to do it in a dress that steals all the air from my lungs.

But now, it isn't the indecency of my dress or my nerves that leave me breathless. It is him, Callian, dressed in the finest clothes I have ever seen him wear. He stands at my door, clad in black leather trousers and a matching vest. His long coat is adorned with embellishments that weave in intricate leafing made of threaded gold. His dark hair gently brushes his shoulders in soft, windswept waves.

For the first time since I've known him, he wears his golden crown upon his head.

For the first time, I see him in his entirety.

The Prince of Callisto.

Callian takes a step forward, eyeing me with lust—there's nothing chivalrous about it. The man who will one day rule this kingdom stares at me like he's seconds from ripping my dress apart and exploring me with his wicked tongue.

"Fuck," Callian grunts, taking a step forward. He, too, seems breathless, taking in the sight of my dress dripping with diamonds and blending into an onyx shade. No doubt he is enjoying the way it hugs my curves. We step back into my chambers. "You are devastatingly beautiful. I'm almost tempted to say you have fallen ill so I may rip those diamonds from your gown and have my way with you."

I smirk. "Touch me, and bear the wrath of Sydney." My brow lifts. His grin tells me my warning makes no difference to him. He closes the space between us, curving his arms around my waist, and pulls me flush against his body.

"I don't care," he says against my mouth. His scent of cedar and mint envelops me.

"Maybe I don't care either," I pant.

His smooth, soft kiss sends butterflies swirling in my stomach. The way he went so feral at the sight of me almost has me convinced to say I truly am ill. I'm utterly exposed from the front as the neckline dips down my chest, ending just below my sternum. He splays a hand across that empty space and tsks as if the diamonds covering all of my *indecent* parts are too much. With the other, he motions the door to slam shut behind us.

"Since neither of us care, I should just rip this dress off you right now." He slips his fingers between the thin fabric to caress my breast. I moan out a laugh and pull away.

"If one diamond falls loos—"

"I promise I'll be careful," he says with bated breath, kissing my neck. He cups the back of my head, bringing me closer to his face so his forehead rests against mine. "I have something for you," he whispers, struggling to continue. The slight tremor in his hand catches me off guard.

"Wait here."

He steps outside for a moment, then returns with two black boxes, the smaller one on top. He walks over to the fireplace and sits on the settee, and I join him on the other side. The crackling of the fireplace fills the silence. He takes me by the hand as his chest begins to rise and fall.

"When I took you, I assumed you had been treated as any other princess would have been—with the honor and respect you deserve. To know you suffered so much in silence angers me. How can people be so cruel to someone who has so much love to give? You opened your heart to me when I didn't deserve it. You continue to show me who you are. Tonight, I want you to know how much you mean to me."

He opens up the biggest box. My eyes widen, seeing a tiara made of silver to match the diamonds on my dress. A sizable, bold sapphire shines bright, perfectly placed in the center with smaller ones on each side. "I had this made just for you. Sapphire to match the boldness in your eyes. The silver reminds me of your soft skin glowing beneath the moon's luminescence."

I hold his gaze.

"There will never be a crown worthy of your head, and though we aren't one for titles, I wanted to give you the choice of wearing one tonight."

I place my hand over his and smile. "If I wear this crown, then you owe me a dance," I tease, eyes warming.

He places it upon my head. "I would dance with you until the stars descend from heaven."

My heart swells with emotion.

"That's not all." He takes a deep, shaky breath. "Close your eyes."

I arch a brow at him before my eyes sweep shut in one soft flutter. My heart won't stop racing while I hear him open the small box. A thin chain of cold metal drapes around my neck, and my body hums beneath the touch of the gem around it.

He clasps it, adjusting it perfectly. "You can open them now."

My eyes widen, seeing the small crescent moon made of silver. "This can't be." Tears swell in my eyes. I shake my head in disbelief, but seeing the blue silk cloth inside the small box sitting on his lap is all the affirmation I need. "How did you—" I'm at a loss for words.

He exhales with relief washing over him. He must have expected me to be angry with him, but I'm feeling quite the opposite. In fact, I don't know if I've ever been this happy.

"Before I left, I saw it glint in the moonlight." He pauses. When we spoke of him taking me, it must have still been a topic he felt he needed to tread lightly on. "I don't know what coaxed me to grab it for you, but I did. I took you with nothing but the clothes on your back. It's a guilt I will carry for the rest of my life, but taking this was the least I could do. I wanted to give it to you sooner, but it was being fixed—such delicate little chains had to be remade. Sydney measured the length of your neck so it would rest perfectly against your chest."

This is truly a surprise. "Thank you."

Callian brushes my cheek with the back of his hand. "At the time I took it, I didn't know how important it was until you spoke of it. There must have been something guiding me that night. The moon shone in at the perfect time, a simple glint, enough to draw me to it."

I realize I didn't want the beginning of our journey to be something we always have to parry around. Callian doesn't need to feel guilty about the early moments of us. I clasp onto the crescent moon and exhale, feeling another stone lift off my chest.

"I forgive you." My gaze meets his. He studies me for a moment with warming eyes. "I forgive you for taking me. I don't want you to look back and feel bad for doing what you felt was right. At the moment, things felt heavy, but I chose to come here. If I don't have guilt, neither should you."

A smile tips the corner of his perfect lips. He exhales a small breath as if I have released him from his own guilt. He leans in, lashes lowering to my eyes and lips before they flutter closed. He kisses me, softly and gently. The heat envelops us as we remain by the fireplace, crowned and dressed in the finest of clothes. How far we have come since. If it's true what the prophecy says about me, I'll hold on to this moment until the darkness claims me.

I AM OVERWHELMED BY THE grandeur of The Royal Ball. We make our way toward the foyer, a place I have yet to see, on the west side of the palace. The halls are packed with some of the lingering guests from Callisto and its allied kingdoms. Both floors are occupied by nobles and royalty, along with commoners from the families of Callisto whose presence is a constant reminder of all they have lost because of me. I can feel their glares searing down my back. My eyes skim over the crowd. These halls contrast the typical bright colors of Callisto. A much darker setting that might be frightening if walking alone in the middle of the night. Every carved pillar has intricate leafing and vines curling up to the ceiling. Each wooden sconce has an array of different expressions. I do a double take, thinking the light is casting an illusion of thorns, but it disappears. The statues lining the halls are so realistic, all wearing the same fierce look, frozen in time by war. As I stare into their eyes, I'm haunted by their allure.

Callian leans down, his lips barely brush against the shell of my ear. "Such curious eyes."

"This place is—"

"Eerie? I know. Every time I walk these halls, a chill runs down my spine," he says, nodding to one of his guards. I can't understand the sensations sweeping over me, but the history of this place is evident, stretching far beyond many generations, dripping onto every corner of the palace. Though broad smiles fill this room, I can't help but sense something unsettling about this place.

"This used to be the residence of Prince Neverell Valor, my uncle."

"Ronan's father?" Shock spreads across my face.

"Yes, he was the commander in chief, but we will save that history lesson for another time," he says. A heaviness blooms in my chest while Callian leads us through the crowd toward the entrance to the ballroom. As we draw near, banners embossed with different royal crests hang between each pillar, displaying the kingdoms in attendance. We walk up to the second level where royalty is announced upon entering the ballroom. Music echoes throughout the entire expansion of the space.

Two men dressed in lavish blues and whites stand at the top of the stairs and swing open the doors when we approach. My eyes widen at the height of the ceiling in the ballroom. Candles are lit to the top, reaching several floors high with a celestial, glass-stained window above. A wave of emotions comes flooding in as realization washes over me. We stand together among the sea of guests as the prince and princess of two kingdoms separated by a haze. This is more than a royal ball. This is a symbol of strength and unity, sealing my betrayal to the kingdom of Sao and its dark king.

Heads turn in our direction, waiting for one of the men to speak.

"Presenting Prince Callian Valor of Callisto, son of King Thoman Valor, and Princess Viona Tarvas of Sao,"—the man pauses as if he were receiving this news for the first time—"daughter of King Mal Tarvas."

All the air is sucked out of the room. An array of expressions stare back, the most obvious reminding me once again of how much separation my presence brings. Callian's chin lifts, and his shoulders widen. Our eyes meet under the candle-lit room that flickers like the stars. All I can see is him. Stoic, charming, and wicked in how his lips turn up into a grin, shameless in how he looks at me. He places his hand over mine, gently running the pad of his thumb across my skin. The simple gesture does far more than he realizes. We descend the stairs as everyone watches with curiosity. Not only because of who I am, but because who the prince has his eyes on.

"Seems like your presence is turning every woman's eye," I whisper. He softly chuckles, a deep rumble in his chest that moves me every time. He smiles, giving a nod to a gentleman he makes eye contact with.

"On the contrary, little flame, it seems as though the whole world is looking at you." My stomach takes a dip. He sends me a seductive smirk that has my heart fluttering. I swallow the lump in my throat, keeping my poise. My brows lift.

"Most hate me," I remind him with a mirthful smile that doesn't reach my eyes. He knows all too well, watching me as I skim over the crowd.

"Let them fear you, let them fear us both."

I suck in a shuddered breath, shocked that he would say such things and run the risk of being heard. "Wicked words for a prince."

"Just because I'm a prince doesn't mean I'm kind. I'm greedy when it comes to you."

I bite my lower lip, letting his words settle over me. We don't speak for several moments while we blend into the crowd. The cellos and violins create an enchanting ambiance with their slow, melodic tune. We find a place to stand off to the side. Already, a woman with a mission comes our way. Within a few strides, she's eyeing my prince. Callian leans toward me with a look all too knowing as she cuts her way through the crowd.

"Prince Valor, it's so nice to see you here." The woman smiles. With how she angled her body, she can ignore that I am standing beside him. Her full lips are painted red. Her hair is as bright as fire, and though she is breathtaking, her beauty doesn't mean anything to him.

He responds with a gruff sigh. "Well, it is my kingdom." He smirks, giving her a not-so-polite laugh. "It would be rather odd if I weren't here at my own event." He picks up two glasses of red wine from one of the nearby tables and hands me one. He looks past her with furrowed brows while he takes a sip.

She laughs nervously, pressing her hands down her lilac dress. I swivel the wine in my hand, watching her amp herself up for another failed attempt while refusing to acknowledge me. She bats her thick, lush lashes. I know she feels my glare by the way she fidgets. As she opens her mouth, Callian turns to me.

"Shall we?"

I nod.

We leave her with her mouth hanging open.

"Bold," I reply under my breath, side glancing at him with a smirk. He presses his hand against my lower back as he guides us through the crowd. The sudden touch sends warmth to my lower stomach.

"She always is."

I hum, but when I see Ronan peering at me from across the room, I almost stop in my tracks. His eyes immediately lock on mine, and he makes his way toward us. The sudden presence tightens my nerves.

"Ronan," Callian says in a scathing tone.

"Hello, cousin. Your father is requesting your presence. The queen of Corsal wants to meet your"—he pauses, sizing me up with a scowl—"guest." His lips curve into a grin, but he turns around before we can respond.

Callian sighs under his breath as we follow Ronan through the crowd. Within a few moments, King Valor comes into view, standing at the bottom of the dais and holding a giant goblet. I can tell he has been drinking steadily; his cheeks are flushed from the ale. I take a deep breath, noticing the queen of Corsal and her quaint smile. Her rich, dark skin accentuates her mahogany eyes.

I've only seen her once before, many years ago, when she met with my father at our castle. Memories seem to come and go so quickly, because it wasn't long afterward that I faced her son on the battlefield, a battle Sao won. Callian and I draw near, and her eyes drift toward me. Her thick lashes remind me of the night sky. Every so often, the light hits them so slightly that it makes them glimmer. I lift my chin, holding a faint smile as we approach them. She's mid-laugh, pressing her hand on her consort's shoulder. Her silky, cyan gown bellows around her tall frame.

She turns to me, nodding her head with grace, catching the attention of King Valor.

"Ah, there she is. Viona, this is Queen Josephine Lana and her consort, King Nerian Lana," King Valor says.

Sao's enemies from the southeast, but no longer mine, I remind myself as I nod, eyes bouncing between the two.

Queen Lana's consort equally matches her beauty with eyes so bold and blue, the gold circles around his irises almost leave me breathless.

"You've already met my son," she adds while her eyes skim over my dress. "It's nice to see you again under much better circumstances." A tight smile tips her full lips.

"Likewise," I reply, feeling the pressure under her stare. Back home, I was a royal guard; my job was to stand back and observe, but my role here is a stark contrast to that.

I glance at her king. "I must admit, I have never seen eyes your shade before. They are quite fascinating."

He responds with a wry smile, and his tan skin turns a few shades of red. The queen chuckles mockingly. My brows raise in response. Apparently, I need more practice socializing.

"I'm surprised; they are the same color as my son's," she says. Tension hangs in the air. I inhale through my nose as my mind flashes back to a time when my sword collided with Prince Marius'.

Callian takes a small step forward. "Where is he, by the way? I hear he is keeping busy as commander of your Royal Guard now?" he says, trying to lighten the topic.

King Valor chimes in. "Something our sons have in common. A duty that never lets you sleep."

The queen humors them with a smile before her eyes drift back to me. Her smile widens, raising her already high cheekbones. "Last I heard, you had similar duties in your kingdom. Am I right, Viona? I'm sure it wasn't easy betraying your king, especially since he is your father."

At this point, she's either being nosy or sinister. Most likely, the latter. I let her coax my darkness. She's baiting the wrong bitch.

I lightly scoff. "Betrayal is such an interesting choice of words, but it truly all depends."

"On what?" She sounds irritated.

My smile widens. "On your perspective."

"Yes. Yes indeed." Her words fade off as she studies me. "Seems as though your sharp tongue remains." Her voice lifts.

I hold her stare. Every muscle remains relaxed on my face as we engage in a silent face-off for what seems like an eternity. In my kingdom, we handled disagreements differently. From the corner of my eye, I watch as King Valor downs the rest of his drink.

"A sharp tongue and a sharp blade. I feel bad for those who aren't on my side." I remind her. A few extra listeners turn their heads. I could have sworn I heard a few gasps in response to what I said, but they were muffled by the slight ringing in my ears. Ronan stifles a chuckle—the first real emotion I've seen from him—as Callian's chest swells with pride.

Queen Lana takes a small sip of her wine, eyeing me from the brim of her glass. She curtly nods her head. Suddenly, I feel a mutual respect lift the tension in the air. She smiles.

"Indeed." She turns to King Valor and raises her glass. "The representatives from my kingdom have informed me of recent events. You have our alliance. My son and our army will stand by your side if needed." She looks behind me. The motion has me squaring my shoulders. Prince Marius joins us, standing between Ronan and King Nerian. He's tall, dark, and handsome. He turns his head to greet the rest of us, wearing... a warm smile. It catches me off guard.

"I am not one to hold grudges. I tend to look at the bigger picture." He turns to look at me. I'm taken back, seeing his hand reach out to shake mine. It's firm and calloused. He must have overheard our conversation as he approached. I finally see the kindness instilled behind those sea, blue-and-golden eyes.

"As do I," Callian says. The same firm handshake extends to Callian and Ronan, though Ronan doesn't quite share the same expression.

"Wonderful," Prince Marius says.

"There you are, Callian!" a man calls out. I can tell who it is by the way his voice carries over the crowd.

Callian turns to Queen Lana, her consort, and Prince Marius. "If you'll excuse us."

As we part ways with the royals, Callian leans down, speaking low enough so only I can hear.

"Fucking gods, Viona," he groans with arousal rumbling in his chest.

I gently laugh, my lips curving up. "What?"

"The way you stood your ground had me thinking about how many different ways I plan to rip that pretty little dress off you tonight." A brisk wave of heat sweeps down my body. I'll never get used to his straightforwardness. I glance at the sharp edge of his jaw and almost press up on my toes to kiss it.

"Samuel," Callian calls over the crowd, closing the distance. "Job well done, brother. I see all the extra guards are in place."

Samuel nods and playfully slaps him on the back. He looks dapper in his long, red coat and thick leather trousers. His wavy, bronze hair is tied back. "One would be a fool to attempt anything tonight."

"My thoughts exactly," Callian adds, skimming over the crowd.

It's nice seeing Samuel so relaxed with his arm linked around a petite woman, her beauty catching the eye of every man she walks past. She immediately looks at me with bright-hazel eyes. Her dark hair is braided and pulled into an elegant bun with gems matching her maroon gown, complementing her deep, rich skin.

"It's nice to see you here. I'm surprised you could make it, with the new babe and all," Callian says, but her eyes remain fixed on me. I can see her piecing together all the little bits of information Callian must have shared with Samuel.

A bright, white smile stretches across her face. She takes my hands in hers and pulls me into a hug. The sudden thrust makes me gasp.

"I'm Candace." Rich vanilla envelops me. My eyes go wide with the unexpected embrace, but my shoulders relax as I'm enveloped in her warmth. "It's nice to finally meet you, Viona. I've heard so much about you."

My cheeks flush. "Hopefully, all good things." I notice Iván lingering idly behind them, searching over the crowd. I know exactly who he's looking for, and I start wondering where Crystal is myself. She's probably speaking with the other representative. She would be a fun distraction, but I know as soon as she arrives, she will be looking for him as well.

Callian approaches Iván, squeezing his shoulder. "You look strapping tonight."

Iván nervously clears his throat. "Thanks."

He's clad in a sky-blue long coat with gold embellishments. His form-fitted, white breeches outline the muscles in his legs, and his attire shows off his broad shoulders. I know Crystal will be very pleased when she sees him. The damask-flocked, ivory vest matches one of the fabric pieces I saw on Crystal's dress. Interesting. She must have planned this out. He does look amazing; Crystal's really going to enjoy this. As he and Callian engage in light conversation, I notice they are almost the same stature, Callian only slightly bigger and taller.

Everyone falls into a steady conversation. The more I stand here, the more prying eyes I feel on me. The whispers never simmer, and the attention is overwhelming. I watch couples dance in the middle of the ballroom, trying to ignore everyone's stare, taking another sip of wine every so often. Samuel and Callian's voices carry over the crowd, but for me, they fade into the background as the gravity of this place remains in the front of my mind. My head begins to hurt. I look down to the floor, pressing my fingers to the sides of my temples.

"Well, I've heard enough of this boring banter," I interrupt. "Iván, will you accompany me to the drinks? Maybe we will find Crystal along the way." I can already feel the wine giving me that little spark of courage. Callian's features tighten. He still isn't comfortable with me leaving his sight, but he says nothing. "If you'll excuse us." I smirk before taking my leave.

Samuel bows humorously. "Madam."

Callian's jaw tenses. He changes his position in order to have a clear view of me as I walk away. I look over my shoulder, meeting his stare. Samuel continues talking, but Callian keeps me in his line of sight. I sense his worry, sending a wave of awareness over me, a feeling I can't quite place.

"Thank the gods." I pick up a glass of water, chugging it down, trying to even out all the wine I've had. "Are they always like that together?" I ask.

"Like what?"

"Loud," I reply, rubbing my fingers against my temples, hoping it will soothe the pain. Iván laughs, taking in another sip of wine.

"Always, ever since we were kids. As soon as they were in each other's presence, they'd become inseparable." He fidgets with his now-empty glass and sets it on the table, staring at the light-blue fabric. I smack his hand away playfully.

"You should focus on having some fun tonight. Enjoy the scenery and all this marvelous place has to offer you." I wave my hand around, mocking the people here as we began laughing like two children who snuck into the party. I glanced up from my drink to see Callian still watching us between his talk with Samuel. "How are things with you and Crystal?" This is a question I have no right to ask, but I do anyway.

"They're going." Doubt fills his voice. "She's present but distant. A lot has been on her mind since the attacks. I think it opened up a lot of old wounds." His eyes meet mine as we both remember what occurred that day far too well, and images of Crystal begin to flash in my mind. He cares for her, and I'm glad he wasn't there to see everything that day. It would have probably broken him. "I've been holding her through those moments, spending more time with her at night."

"Trauma has a way of sneaking itself back in at the least expected times," I admit. "Just continue to be your charming self and be there for her, even when she sits in the dark. It's all you can do until it passes." I press my hand over his arm, and he faintly smiles. We stand there, silent for a moment, appreciating each other's company in a room full of people while the air grows thicker by the minute. Envy, judgment, fear, gratitude. The prying eyes become too much. "I need some fresh air. Grab a drink, and let's head outside." I pick up a glass of wine.

"My thoughts exactly." Iván exhales, taking a glass for himself.

The cool, night air carries the sweet scent of jasmine on its breeze, and we head over to one of the benches overlooking a garden. "I worry this royal ball won't help our efforts," I admit, taking off my shoes.

"Why do you say that?"

"The one person who's supposed to help save the lands emerges from a kingdom known as the enemy. Sounds disastrous." I roll my eyes while massaging my feet.

Iván's laugh echoes throughout the garden. He leans down, resting his elbows on his thighs, and stares into the garden. "Your birthplace doesn't define who you are, and though you can't expect everyone to like you, you just have to focus on your goals. It shouldn't matter what everyone else thinks." He toys with his drink and exhales. I can tell by his demeanor that he is relieved to be outdoors as much as I am. Though he sits only a few feet away from me, his mind is miles away.

"So, when you aren't lost inside your head, where do you like to go?" I smirk, slipping on my shoes.

He coyly laughs. "My mind is always brimming with ideas for the next piece of art, my next series. It's like the phases in my life, always different depending on what's going on. When I'm not patrolling the outer walls or being thrown into bar fights, I'm traveling in my mind, inside my paintings."

I chuckle, staring at the moonlight gleaming off his freshly polished boots. He really did clean himself up for her. His words all make sense, and my mind reels back to when I first met him; he was lost looking at the iron rods and pillars.

"An artist's mind is never fully at rest, is it?"

"Never," he admits.

"Well, when your next series is done, you better show me, Iván. I'll hold you to it," I teasingly threaten him.

A female's voice breaks the conversation. "You know I don't do well with threats. Especially when it comes to him, Vi."

When I turn around, my jaw hangs open. My gods, Crystal is stunning. She's dripping with beauty from head to toe in her ivory down.

"Crystal." Iván exhales. Her breath seems to catch at the sound. He gets up quickly and rushes to her side, and her chest begins to softly rise and fall as he closes the distance. Moonlight shines through her blond hair with prisms of purple. Her lips slightly part. He takes her chin under his finger and presses his mouth to hers, catching the next words on his lips. In a shuttered breath, he says, "You must have fallen from the stars to be here." Desire churns in her eyes.

I decide to leave them be and walk back to the palace. As I ascend the stairs, Gareon comes into view, standing at the top step. I jump at his unexpected presence. He's stunning in his black attire with red accents, dressed in fine royal clothes. His amber eyes bore into mine. His hair is pulled back into a thick ponytail with two wavy locks dangling free, exposing his chiseled jawline. The blue markings on his body sprawl up, spanning the column of his neck. It's a sight that will take some time to get used to. If he and I are the same, I wonder if I too will get markings on my body. What colors will they be?

"Surely there are more frightening things lurking inside that ballroom than I," he says with a playful smile, catching me off guard.

He looks over my shoulder, down to where Crystal and Iván are. My brow lifts in suspicion, distracting me from all my other thoughts of what ifs.

"I believe it is you who is lurking, Gareon. You seem to be everywhere Crystal is lately. Is she aware of this?"

"Now it is you who is prying, Viona." He shoots me a look of warning. I take another step closer, challenging him, only a few strides from reaching the top step.

"I think it's only fair to ask," I say, meeting his stare, but he seems unfazed. Of course, he would be. He's seemingly more powerful than I could imagine. He turns his head to look my way with calm features.

"I am not one to spread business around, I suggest you keep to your own affairs. However, to soothe your curiosity, I am here to make sure she arrived at the gardens safely . . . and to ensure you make it back in as well."

"Thank you," I mock, "but I have enough eyes on me tonight."

He responds with an amused chuckle.

I ascend the rest of the stairs, but something stops me when I reach the top step. I turn to him before asking, "How old are you, Gareon?"

He smiles, taking a step closer. "I am centuries old, my curious friend."

My stomach takes a dive, and I can't help but suck in a sharp breath before my breathing stills.

"And when did you stop aging?"

Something flickers in his eyes. "When I came into my power, as will you when you get yours."

"*If,*" I bite back, unsure how to take this news or what it means for me.

"*When,*" he corrects me.

Before I can counter one last remark, I wince as the shooting pain returns to the sides of my temples.

"Judging by your headaches, you, too, feel something is off," he surmises.

My vision is slightly blurry. "What?"

"There are many eyes on you tonight, Viona. Not only because you are striding this ball as stunning as the rarest of gems, but because of who they think you are. Be on guard."

I blink back a few times. "Shocking, I didn't know you were one to give compliments," I say. I link my arm with his before we head back into the ballroom.

CHAPTER 40

A MBIENT MUSIC CONTINUES TO play, and Gareon heads back outside as I search for Callian, pressing up on my toes, trying to see over the crowd. His crown and the top of his head peek out. While making my way through the crowd, I pause midstep, seeing a woman sweep between two dancing partners toward him. She extends her hand out as if Callian is supposed to kiss it. My brows knit. I narrow my eyes on her as they rake up and down her body. She's a curvy, stunning woman wearing a golden dress that reminds me of a goddess. A matching crown sits on her head. Her back turns, but it doesn't take a fucking fool to figure out what she's trying to do. He half smiles at her. I can see it in his eyes, he hesitates, staring at her hand. His brows arch, unamused, but being polite. I lean against a pillar, crossing my arms and shifting my hip to the side, just waiting to see what he'll do. He turns around and picks up a glass of wine, offering it to her.

My brows lift. *Good boy.*

The tips of her fingers caress his hand as she takes the drink. Her greedy fingers are doing anything she can to touch him.

I can't keep my heart from beating faster than it should as I watch them. He looks over her shoulder, finding me glaring between two pillars under a floral arch. He nudges his head, gesturing for me to join him at his side. I roll my eyes, pushing off the pillar with my hip.

"Princess Ophelia Raya Alexandria, this is Princess Viona Tarvas," he says as I approach. Her eyes scale over me. Her upturned nose is perfectly shaped, and her cheeks are flushed from summer's heat. Soft, black hair falls around her bare shoulders in long, thick waves. She wears a smile that, I can assume, will never reach those piercing eyes.

Silence hangs in the air long enough for me to notice the topaz speckles shining like little diamonds in them.

She clears her throat. "So, this is the girl you were forced to take in? Such a benevolent thing to do," she says as her glare drifts in my direction.

I start, in an attempt to be civil, "If I may correct you, Princess Oph—"

"You may address me as Princess Alexandria. Only my friends call me by my first name," she cuts in with words already snipping at my patience.

I blink back, crossing my arms as a grin spreads across my face. I turn to Callian, making it known I'm not amused that he put me in this situation.

"She came here willingly, Princess Alexandria. I can assure you she was not forced."

"Oh, my apologies." A coy laugh slips out, showing she's not fully taking his word. "I thought you were doing one of your many charitable things." She takes a sip of her wine. "You know, Cal and I go way back." Thick lashes flutter at him.

Cal. How cute.

"Oh?" I faintly scoff.

"Yes, we have spent many, *many* summers together. If I may be so bold to say, I was surprised he hadn't written to me to tell me of your arrival."

"He's been busy." My voice lifts, taking a glass of wine off the table while keeping my glare, letting those few words settle in. "Very busy, actually. So busy that I'm sure less important things have slipped his mind." I observe her perfect frame—the way her golden dress hugs all her curves, the top mound of her breasts on full display. How can he not be interested in her? Those full lips are painted a soft, blush pink, and her sweet, floral scent is just as alluring. I begin to wonder how he spent his time with her, and with all the women he has been with before me. Or if he has lain with any while I've been here.

Anger simmers beneath the surface the more I think about her and him in those *many summers* together. I take a longer sip of wine, not taking my eyes off her.

"Princess Alexandria must be referring to when our parents made us walk the gardens. Such a long time ago, before I got into the affairs of being on the council."

The princess' features tighten. A hard, tight smile stretches across her face. She forces a laugh out. "Oh, it's okay, you don't need to be so formal in front of her. Please, call me Ophelia." Her eyes flutter, and those long, pointed fingers glide along the rim of her glass.

This bitch is persistent. Callian's brows go flat. His jaw ticks, but he continues wearing a smile.

"So tell me Princess Alexandria, were your travels well?" I ask.

"Well, as you can imagine, when you're royalty, traveling takes a little longer. Especially when accompanied by other guests and members of the council. Don't you agree?"

How am I supposed to know? I clear my throat. Every second she stands here, my sense of awareness goes on alert.

"I don't need an entourage to travel," I reply.

"Why not? Aren't you a princess?" She glances at the tiara Callian gave me. I'm annoyed that I have to explain why I don't feel as such to everyone.

Taking a deep breath, I maintain my composure. "Though I was born into royalty, I found my calling in the Royal Guard."

She laughs as if this is the funniest thing she's heard all day. Callian's brows remain flat, glaring at her with a humorless expression.

"So then, you're just here playing a pretty princess?" Her voice lifts an octave higher. The way she mocks me has a few heads turning our way. Callian's eyes give warning as he sees the anger flaring behind mine.

"No, Princess Alessia, while you find your power in the pretty little dresses you wear, I find mine wielding weapons and making use of my powers. To each their own," I reply. Though my features remain calm, every vein in my body is heated. She's trying so hard to snake her way under my skin.

"Alessia?" she laughs, pressing the tips of her fingers against her chest as her mouth gapes open.

"Isn't that your name?" I grin. A few heads turn our way. Some snicker under their gloved hands.

Insulted, her eyes bounce between Callian and me. Her neck and chest redden. "That's…not my name."

"Oh," I mock. "Must have slipped my mind." Tension chokes the air. She waits for me to apologize, but I refuse to.

Two women wearing crowns arrive arm in arm. Callian abruptly breaks the deadpan look I'm giving the princess.

"Your Majesties, it's good to see both of you," he says. I assume the one with similar features to Princess Alexandria is her mother. She has the same thick, wavy, black hair fanning around her gown, but her eyes are a soft, pale blue. The crown on her head is made of diamonds, pointed at the tips. Her consort has lovely, warm skin touched by the sun with a smaller crown. Callian approaches them with a knowing smile. His demeanor tells me they are nothing like their daughter.

"Callian, it's so good to see you." The queen clasps her hands around his. She gives me a quick once over.

"Viona, this is Queen Raya Alexandria and her consort Queen Elias Alexandria from the kingdom of Sebina," Callian says. I give a polite nod. She waves his hand away with a friendly scoff and reaches for my hands in the same soft manner.

"There are too many Alexandrias around here. Please call me Queen Raya, and you may call my wife Queen Elias."

My features warm. "It's lovely to meet both of you."

"We've heard so much about you, my dear. All good things," she continues, removing her hands from mine and placing one on Queen Elias' lower back. "I am very excited to get to know you."

I swallow the lump in my throat. After seeing the division I've caused, she might leave regretting that.

Queen Raya's eyes drift to her daughter. In an instant, they grow cold. "Ophelia please go get some air before you do something foolish."

My eyes widen with delight. I already like this woman. I stop the smirk from forming on my face and glance over to Callian who is equally humored. The princess leaves in a huffy fit. The sounds of music play while they wait for her to be out of sight.

"I apologize for our daughter's rude behavior. She gets quite envious of people as beautiful as you." With a flick of her wrist, a fan whips out, and she begins to fan away at her flushed cheeks.

"It's alright." I smile.

Queen Elias hands her a glass of water. "The weather here is far too warm for us. In the Sebina Mountains, we are used to cooler summer nights."

I chuckle. "It feels quite the opposite for me. In Sao, it's hot like the desert ruins during this time of year. This place feels cold at times." I lock my arm around Callian. The touch makes him go still, and he inhales a deep breath. The energy between us thrums. He cups his hand over mine, soothing the top with his thumb. "But it's something I could get used to." I look at Callian through a hooded gaze. He gently squeezes my hand in response.

"I'm glad you feel that way," he replies, speaking in a much softer tone.

Queen Elias sighs and leans her head against her wife's shoulders. "You two remind me of us, long ago." She runs her hand up her lover's arm.

"The beginning of us seems like it was just yesterday." Queen Raya smirks, admiring Queen Elias' smile. "We were their age when we met."

"Exactly. That was many lifetimes ago." They share a look. One that tells me they will explore that feeling tonight after the ball has ended.

I lean my head against Callian's arm, watching the way they love one another. I often wonder if my parents ever shared the same kind of affection. Memories of them together are so far from reach, they almost don't exist anymore. I exhale a deep sigh, still in awe at these two lovely queens.

The pianist ends his song and leaves the small stage off to the side. A violinist begins to play a piece that seems to speak to her soul. The woman sways her body, becoming one with her instrument. The candles gleam off her shimmering dress as the crowd watches. She reminds me of a woman dancing in the woods during the night. Bare and unbound, moving with each note that seems to be as freeing as the last. Couples make their way to the center of the ball room.

"May I have this dance . . . Princess?" That smooth, sultry voice calls to me in ways that wrap around my heart. My head turns the moment Callian slips his hand around my waist.

My cheeks flush. "But I don-"

"Just trust me." He pulls me against his body and slowly laces his fingers with mine, one by one, as if he is threading our souls together. As we begin to dance, he looks down at me with those piercing eyes, and a warmth rushes up my arm.

Though I'm breathless, I nod. We move through the center of the ball room with fluid grace as if we are one, moving with the stars, becoming that spark in the sky that turns everyone's head.

"Everyone is staring at us," I whisper under my breath with a smile.

He lowers his head slightly. "I know you've been wondering why some of the women here have been *persistent* tonight." He swings me under his arm, and I somehow spin back toward him.

"Humor me," I grin.

"It's because everyone knows the prince of Callisto doesn't dance with anyone. The last time I stepped foot in the middle of this ballroom was with my mother. I was young, and very protective. Every ball, I made sure none of the other men danced with her because I knew she hated it. I felt like if I stepped in to save her, she wouldn't have to deal with the nonsense of the politics they'd whisper into her ear. She despised hearing it." He takes a deep breath, jaw fluttering with emotion. "At her service, I vowed never to dance with anyone again, not until I found a woman worthy of my heart. I don't just give it away to anyone, Viona." His voice was so deep, so sincere. He rarely spoke about his mother, he rarely ever shared anything about her. I suddenly wish he were able to have one more dance with her.

I press up on my toes and kiss him. I kiss him so deep, I think I hold back a sob. "I think she would be so proud of the man you've become," I whisper, kissing him again.

This time, he moans into my mouth and smiles against my lips. "Look who's being shameless now, Princess."

My heart flutters against my chest, feeling the warmth emitting from his body as he holds me so close. The entire room has their eyes on us. All their faces become nothing but blurs as we continue to dance around the ballroom with our eyes locked on one another. Heat flickers in his irises, and I can somehow feel the way it ignites around me. He swings me once more and draws me back in. As the music stops, we are left with palpable lust coiling between us.

Everyone applauds. We hold each other's gazes for a few moments longer.

"For your first dance, that was pretty good." He smirks, pressing a kiss to my hand.

"May *I* have the next?"

That familiar voice grates down my flesh. My eyes flick to Princess Ophelia, who is now hovering near us like a parasite. Callian's eyes grow cold as we both shoot her a darting glare.

"Your persistence is amusing," I reply in a scathing tone.

She takes a step back. "Excuse me?"

"I think it's obvious Callian isn't interested. I suggest you kindly turn around and flutter away. You're beginning to pester us." I seethe.

Her eyes dart to his. "Are you going to let this untamed woman speak to me like that?"

Tension chokes the air as all eyes are on us, and whispers are circulating the room. From the look in Callian's cutting glare, it seems like he's about to rip her head off.

"It would be wise to walk away, *Ophelia*," I cut in. Fuck titles.

Tension flutters along her jaw. She's clearly not taking no for an answer. Her eyes skim down my frame again, this time in disgust, then they flick back to him. "Cal, surely you don't think she's anything lik–"

I catch her by the wrist before she can stroke his face, meeting her with a stone-cold sneer. "Don't you fucking touch him."

Suddenly, all the air gets sucked out of the room. The music stops.

"I know what you are. I see it in your eyes. You're not what this kingdom claims you to be. You must have tricked the prince into loving you," she replies in a loud tone that turns more heads. The more she speaks, the more raw heat unfurls under my skin until it begins scratching its way to the surface.

"You have no idea what you are talking about." I retort. The palm of my hand is growing rapidly hot. She squirms in my grip, but each tug only fuels me to tighten my hold.

"It's true!" She grunts, her brows knit together. "You're a demon, a monster, lurking out from the same hell your father crawled out of! Get your hands off me!" she yells.

My palms are glowing and scorching hot. The moment I smell her flesh, I let go. It is only then that I hear her screams as she stumbles back, wincing in pain while a few people rush past me to her side.

I take a few steps back and look down at my hands, watching fire churning rapidly in a tight ball of fury. I'm heaving, and my thoughts are spinning out of control.

What have I done? I have ruined everything.

CHAPTER 41

T IME SUDDENLY SLOWS, THE ticking of a stopwatch coming to
a painful halt as faces stare at me with fear. It all begins to blur.
Their gasps and screams tell me I have turned into the very thing I
have feared most; a monster. The ringing in my ears muffles every
other sound around me. I can't bear to look at Callian, fearful he will
share the same expression as everyone else or, even worse, to see the
disappointment on King Valor's face for ruining the plans. What will
he say? I need to leave before I find out.

I do the only thing I know how to do.

Run.

I leave the ballroom, letting my feet carry me as fast as they can and
removing myself from a position I should have *never* put myself in.

Being vulnerable.

Fuck, how could I have been so stupid and impulsive?

The echo of my footsteps are pulling me underwater. I can no longer
hear my thoughts. My heart pounds wildly against my chest. I don't
even know where I'm going, but I keep running.

Every darkened hall looks the same until I turn a corner and see a
long stretch of windows spanning one side with moonlight casting in.
I stick to the shadows until I reach the two large doors at the end of the
hall. I hope to the gods nobody is in here. Holding my breath, I turn
the knob and slip inside the dark room.

The door clicks shut behind me in an echo that tells me this room
is large and probably empty, which is another relief to me. I squint my
eyes, trying to find my way through. Since I haven't run into anything
yet, my next steps fill with confidence, hoping there's an exit in the
direction I'm going, but the rush quickly wanes.

I slam into a tall, large frame. A big, calloused hand wraps around my wrist, catching my fall.

"Did you forget, you cannot hide from me?" Callian's voice sweeps over me like a warm, soft blanket. He sounds calm, as if he's smiling. I pull back, trying to put distance between us, but his grip remains firm and dominating. The lines of his face are barely visible as my eyes adjust to the faint light streaming in. His head slightly tilts to the side, watching with such intensity, as if he can see me clearly in the dark.

"Yes, I can, and I will." I seethe. It dawns on me that he could very well punish me for what I've done, for ruining everything. "Let me go," I whisper. Tears sting my eyes. I glance toward the doors, fearful guards will be rushing in at any moment.

"No one is coming," he responds.

My head whips back in his direction. "What? Why not?" I rasp.

"No one will dare enter this room knowing I'm in it."

What does that mean for me? I don't want to stay here to find out.

"Let me go," I demand, trying to thrust out of his grip again, but he holds me in place, this time closer to his body. A faint shudder of emotions comes over him as he inhales my scent.

"Where are you going?" he asks.

"Far away from here. Callian, please, I cannot do this anymore. I cannot pretend to be something I'm not, and I cannot pretend that you and I can work. We could never be together, not in this lifetime." My words seem to pierce his heart just as deeply as they pierce mine. His pulse throbs against the column of his neck.

"Listen to me," he grits through his teeth. His ripple of frustration sends another chill down my spine. "I don't care about what's outside that room. I couldn't give *two fucks* about it or that fucking bitch. Or any other woman, as a matter of fact. Do you want to know why, Viona? For fuck's sake, if you can't see it, you're going to rip my fucking heart out." I turn my head to the side, refusing to listen, but he yanks me flush against his body again. It's not hard, but enough to grab my attention. "All I care about is *us*."

Us.

His breathing grows shallow. He runs his hand through my hair, cupping the back of my head. I faintly see the glow in his eyes, the intensity burning behind them with every ragged breath he takes.

"My mind goes to the most disastrous things if I cannot have you by my side." He slightly shakes his head at the unimaginable.

"No." I stifle a sob. "I can't . . . I don't want any of this. I don't want you." I begin shaking my head. He's too kind, and I am so undeserving of any of this.

He curves a finger under my chin and tilts my head up. "I can taste your lies before they ever reach your tongue. I can smell the irritation flowing in your veins, but the way your heart beats every time I'm near, every time I touch you, I know you feel the same. The way our eyes can still find each other from across a crowded room, the same way we can sense when each other is drawing near. Don't you ever wonder why, Viona? Why we feel this constant gravitational pull bringing us together? Please don't hide from me, stop running. Let me see you in all your beauty."

He exhales deeply. A minty scent brushes across my lips. He runs the pad of his thumb along my jaw. The touch sends a warmth down my body, traveling below my navel. It goes deeper, past every thickened wall, stretching further. Far more than I've ever allowed anyone to go. He reaches into my darkness with his bare hands. My body is thrumming alongside his magic that wraps itself around me. We are playing a dangerous game, not caring about the consequences as we get lost in our storm.

"We are fated." I can't seem to catch my breath as I say it, and yet, every emotion I have ever felt for him sparks the moment those words leave my lips. I close my eyes and softly exhale, releasing my powers to do what comes like second nature. My eyes flutter open, seeing the soft wave of light dispersing my embers into the air that his powers somehow seem to draw out. There is no chaos or rage in my release. My embers surround us, churning like stardust as they light every candle and chandelier in the room. Hundreds of them are flickering like the stars. Another shock sweeps down my body—mirrors cover the entire expansion of each wall from floor to ceiling. I expect to see my darkest form in the reflection, but all I see is me. I am no longer running from the shadows, from the monster I feared would stare back at me. Tears swell my eyes. I turn to Callian. His features are warm as every angle of his face illuminates in the candlelight.

"You are magnificent. Can you see it?" he whispers. "I would endure an eternity of suffering if it meant to be with you, to be inside your body and heart. You are the very blessing and sin of my soul. May the gods be damned with you in their presence."

My breathing stills as Callian cups the side of my face. An intense heat flickers in his irises, and the cutting edge of raw emotion brims his eyes.

"I love you, Viona Tarvas. I never want to miss the feeling of your touch, even if it's cast with fire and sharp edges. I love every part of you. You are my fated mate."

Callian drops to his knees. My chest rises and falls, watching him remove his crown and place it on the floor, exposing his fragility at my feet.

"I'm willing to throw it all away for you," he confesses with a heated gaze, trailing his hands up my leg and rubbing his cheek along the softest part of my inner thigh. His touch is warm and cool simultaneously, and my need for him intensifies. A wave of emotions brushes across my body. He sees the tears falling down my cheeks and takes my hands in his, kissing each finger to the tip. I exhale in a faint, soft breath. My heart is racing. Shifting my dress up, I lower myself onto the floor and cup his cheek, brushing his wavy, dark hair away from that beautiful, striking face. I remove my tiara and gently place it on the floor beside his. "You are mine, Viona. Now and forever."

"And you are mine," I whisper, pressing my lips to his. The warmth of his tears slip free. He smiles against my mouth, and in a bated breath, he deepens the kiss. "Take me, now," I gasp. With one thrust of his hand, the doors seal shut behind us and lock, turning this room into our world away from all that awaits us outside.

"You don't ever have to beg," he says. The growing heat between us unfurls. I swallow down my nerves, knowing what is to come.

There is fragility in my next thought because . . .

I am his.

Something tells me I always was. I want to explore all the reasons why. I want to know what it feels like to be claimed, to belong. With all that I have lost, I want the feeling of home within someone's heart. This invisible tether has been pulling me into his arms since I met him.

I hook my thumb under the fabric of my dress and slip it past my shoulders. It weightlessly falls to my hips, and my nipples pebble at the cool air. Callian takes his fill, cupping his mouth over my nipple, warming me with every lap of his tongue. I gasp. The sweet sound of pleasure makes his length throb. I lean into him. Callian pulls me flush against his body and presses his lips to mine, so hard and claiming that a deep groan rumbles in his chest.

I want more.

I move off his body and stand so he can watch me remove my clothes. My dress slips off my hips and pools around my legs. He watches me intensely as he removes his clothes. When he's done, he leans forward, curling an arm around my waist, and brings me back onto his lap, leaving me to gasp at the sudden thrust. He catches my gasp with his mouth. I straddle him, melting into the warmth of his naked body against mine. The need for him blooms between the apex of my thighs. I was a fool to deny it for this long; I know that now. Those big, strong hands move up my back as I wrap my arms around his neck.

In another swift motion, he brings me to the ground, laying me gently across his coat. Thankfully, the soft, fur rug is another layer of cushion for our bare bodies. I stare down to see his perfect body that is now all mine. His cock beads at the tip, full of desire. I gnaw on my lower lip. My gods, he is beautiful. My eyes flick to his, watching as he settles comfortably between my thighs. My legs make room for him. He rests his elbows on either side of my head, caging me in. I feel his entire length press against my very center. With hunger in his eyes, he studies me, taking my hand and placing it against his chest.

"Do you feel it?" he says in a deep, husky tone. I feel his heart pounding just as hard as mine.

"Yes," I say, "I feel it."

"Soon, we will *see* it. Are you ready for me, Princess?" he whispers, staring at me with a hooded gaze—the pad of his thumb trails along my cheek in one soft stroke. I nod, letting him feel my hunger as his length pulses against my very center. He groans, closing his eyes. "I want to explore everything the light doesn't touch, and I promise to be gentle."

Clasping my hands around his neck, I nod again, biting my lower lip as anticipation builds in my core. He lines the tip of his cock outside of my slit. Pressure builds at my entrance, and my heart flutters at the slight motion. His eyes flick to mine once more, but not because he thinks I'll hesitate. He wants to see the look on my face as he inches his way in.

With one gentle thrust, he pushes inside me for the first time, just the tip. My mouth gapes open as my fingers dig into his biceps, already feeling more than I had expected to feel.

"My gods," I moan. He barely has the tip in.

Pleasure and pain pierce through me. He kisses me through the process with such tenderness and precision, without moving while I adjust to his size. My lips part, gasping for another breath, feeling the moment he goes deeper. I exhale in desperation, gripping his arms, preparing to take more. My eyes drift down, seeing every divot and rugged line of his body. I thread my fingers through his hair, a small gesture to let him know I'm okay—another wave of pain courses through me as he goes further.

Desire flares in his eyes. "My little flame, I love the way you take me. Those sweet, soft moans make me so weak for you." He purrs, throbbing while he's inside of me, waiting patiently until I'm ready for more. With one last thrust, he slides his entire length inside me. A loud moan rips from my chest. He catches my moan, claiming me with not only his mouth but his cock. My entire body shudders with emotion. We stay in this position for a moment, kissing, letting our hunger for one another chase away my pain.

My body is thrumming against the steady pace he's now giving me. I greedily take it, rocking my hips with his as he gives me every part of his being. My soul is reaching for it, reaching for him. What felt like searching in the dark now appears before me as a light. That familiarity returns, the tethered pull is no longer invisible, it is seen. He sees the light reflecting in my eyes as I gaze upon its beauty.

"My heart will always call to yours, and yours to mine," he whispers into my ear. Those words ripple through time as my heart wraps around his. I feel a bond pushing to the surface.

Ours.

Ours, and it's beautiful. A powerful wave of energy disperses into the air. All the candles in the room flicker. I gasp, feeling myself fall through space in the embodiment of his magic. Two forces begin weaving together in an enigmatic light. I see the stars in his eyes and all the dark and light that make us who we are. I grab onto him, kissing the heated flesh on his shoulder and neck as he quickens his pace.

"I need you," I confess. I've always needed him.

"I will always need you. All of time and space couldn't keep us apart," he purrs, kissing a tear I had no idea slipped free. "I would rip the stars from the sky to find you." His words are spoken like a vow. I revel in the way he sounds, the way he moves. From how his hand tightly clasps onto my thigh to how he holds my heart, truly knowing what he has. Every part of him is coursing through me, ensuring I see everything the light doesn't touch. My body falls back, feeling the pleasure intensify. I'm chasing it, craving to reach the crest of the wave. My hands grip the rug as he drives deeper into me. He leans down, slides his tongue into my mouth, and splays a hand across the hollow of my chest. I open to him, letting his tongue fill me with greed.

Callian cups my breast and gently nibbles on my lower lip, then he kisses his way down to the crook of my neck where he rests his head.

"How many nights I've dreamt of having my soul buried inside you." His groans reverberate along my flesh, sending another wave of awareness down my body, making my nipples pebble again. "I began marking you as mine the moment I laid eyes on you. You have always been mine, Viona. And you always will be. Forever, until my last breath." He presses his lips onto mine, tugging at my heart.

My breathing hitches, hearing the raw truth of his words. Something primal blooms in the pit of my stomach. His thrusts become punishing, knowing I can handle it. Our bodies are in sync, chasing the feeling of ecstasy. That pulsating heat ignites. My spine arches into him as my head tilts back. My need for him sends me teetering on the edge.

"Fuck, Callian. Don't stop." A soft, demanding plea leaves my lips. My toes curl as my core tightens. The way I sound when I pant his name still shocks me. A man who was my captor, who was really a prince, knelt before me in a crowded room as my protector, and now he's my fated mate. Mine, and we're about to ascend our bond to the stars.

"I'll never stop. I love the way you feel, Princess. You're so fucking tight."

The boldness of his words leave me breathless. They always have, ever since we met.

I want more. My need for him grows. The desire churns into a fiery heat. His eyes have a glint, the intent to take me to ecstasy. I revel in it, feeling it with every motion as I meet his gaze. My body clamps down. A wave of heat flushes down my face and chest, unable to bear his tantalizing thrusts any longer.

"That's my girl," he groans, increasing his long and hard pace.

My fingers dig into his arms. They flex with every motion as he penetrates me to the very base of his cock. I cry out as my orgasm unfurls, moaning so loudly that my voice fills the expanse of the room. The bond, a newfound awareness, ripples through us. Wave after wave, my body spasms around him in tight flutters, sending him into his own orgasm. A loud and very powerful moan ruptures through him as he comes inside me. In hard, spasming shudders, I feel the warmth of his release. My eyes widen, still riding my own wave and seeing our bond pulse in a beautiful bright light around us. His forehead rests against my shoulder. Every heated groan and sheen of sweat seeps into me. I kiss his cheek, feeling his pace slow, his body trembling above. The scent of him, of us, is in the air. Closing my eyes once more, writhing beneath him as the last shudder of pleasure courses through me. Clearly feeling spent, his body relaxes on top of mine. A warm surrender and peace settles over us.

"I wish I could stay inside you forever." He exhales roughly. I comb my hand through his hair, placing another kiss on his forehead while my mind reels to the raw truth of his words, we are fated to be together. As I stare at him smiling, tucking a loose strand behind his ear, my heart is soaring with the stars. A low grunt rumbles in his chest as he pulls out and lies beside me. With a deep, and heavy exhale he says, "You are so perfect, Viona. You might be the death of me."

I huff out a faint laugh, staring up at the crown molded ceiling. I can't help but feel the tears swelling my eyes, not of sadness but of realization.

"Wherever you go, I will follow you."

We remain on our backs with my body nestled into his arm. My fingers move down his chest, tracing every hardened curve and edge. The magic around us slowly fades into the air. We both watch in silence until it is gone, and the candles' flames slow to a soft flicker.

CHAPTER 42

I WATCH CALLIAN EAT his breakfast from across the table as if my outburst at the Royal Ball never happened. I remain silent, wondering if I have truly fucked myself over despite his reassurances last night. I exhale a shaky breath, drumming my fingernails against the glass of water.

"What's wrong?" he asks.

I hold my tongue, which wants to say, *your health,* as he slides another six pieces of bacon onto his plate. I guess this is how a six foot two male is supposed to eat. Especially if they're using their body as a weapon every day. My eyes rake down his body. His rich, tan skin glows in the morning light.

"Not that I should care, but what happened to Princess Alexandria last night after I left?" I ask. A smile tips those perfect lips, but his eyes remain on the plate of food.

"She's fine. One of her healers was at the ball. Everyone knows how she gets. So, if you're worried that I may have to fight their army off, rest assured, her parents' anger is with *her* for making a scene."

I blink back a few times, shocked and somehow relieved. I don't press any further. I watch him eat his fill, even though there's something heavy looming here. I can't seem to grasp what it is. Unless . . .

"I was wondering, have you brought anything else of mine from the castle?" I ask, playing with the rim of my glass. I've kept the labradorite stone under my pillow. It's out of sight, but it still pushes to the front of my mind. Callian pauses midbite, his arm flexing as it remains frozen in place. Even as he sits across from me wearing nothing but breeches that offer no discretion as to the shape of his length, it's a nice, welcomed distraction.

"Well aren't you greedy," he hums, eager to get back to stuffing his face with bacon.

I roll my eyes playfully, resting my chin in my palm. "You know, you and Crystal eat the same way," I retort, fluttering my lashes. He chokes out a deep laugh.

"Really?" he drawls, cracking a side smile and exposing just a sliver of his pearly, white teeth.

"Yes, like damn starved animals."

He grunts with humor. "I burned a lot of calories last night."

My eyes dart to his. He flashes me a grin while forking a piece of potato. My cheeks flush, remembering what it said in that book about fated mates. Our bond will grow stronger by the day, especially every time we're intimate. Each time, our powers will start weaving together until they become one, shared. I wonder if that's what Gareon meant.

I clear my throat. "Anyway, how much longer do we have until we meet with the council?"

Callian wipes his mouth and places the napkin on the table. "Right after you finish eating your food."

He goes to stand. The morning light filters through his thin linen, displaying that massive length hanging between his thighs. He closes the distance between us, places a kiss on my brow, and strides into the bathing chambers. My head turns, eyeing him like he's my prey, gnawing at my lower lip because staring at him isn't enough. I explore his body from those broad shoulders, to every muscle on his back until he disappears. Smirking, I take one final bite of my apple before I abandon my breakfast.

Now, leaning against the doorway of the bathing chamber, I watch him slip his body into the water. He moves down until his long, dark hair hangs outside the edge. I can't help but stare at every corded muscle in his arms until my need for him becomes an ache. I remove my clothes, the action sends heat pooling between my thighs. Heat floods across my face and chest as I step up to the edge, bared, nipples pebbled from the slightly cool air. He stares intensely, eyes raking down my body as another part of him reaches out. Every breath becomes shallow as I feel the bond flutter along my skin, running up my thighs and exploring as a beam of light with the need to grow. I shudder.

"Come here, Viona," he says in a low, heated breath while he holds my gaze.

I step into the wide tub, eyeing his length that's already hard, peeking halfway out of the water and resting on his abdomen. His lips slightly part, sending another wave along my skin.

"So this is what it feels like to explore everything the light never touches," he whispers. There's a faint glow to his eyes as he watches me straddle him. I gnaw at my lower lip, positioning myself between his thighs while the warmth of the water rises between our bodies. A groan rumbles in his chest as he throbs beneath me.

"It's beautiful, everything about us is beautiful," I confess.

Those strong, calloused hands run up my back and along the slope of my shoulders until he has me wrapped in his arms. As I rest my head against his chest, I slightly move atop his length. "Why aren't you eating your breakfast?" he asks, working small circular motions on my back.

"Sometimes, I like having my dessert before the main course," I tease, softly whispering against the crook of his neck before kissing it. "Will the bond appear around us every time we're intimate?" I ask since I didn't get to finish that particular book.

"Now why would I ruin that surprise?" he replies. His voice reverberates against my chest. The beat of his heart is a slow and steady calm. I guess that will be another thing I get to explore with him. We spend the next hour in the water until it runs cold.

I use this time to clear my head, getting lost in him while he's inside me. Getting lost in the beauty of our visible bond. I know what I have to say when we meet with the council, but I pin all those thoughts while I discover this new part of us.

"Two weeks," King Valor confirms, standing at the end of a very large, rectangular table. Everyone seems to agree this is a reasonable timeframe. Enough for the kingdoms of Sebina and Corsal to travel home and organize their armies. King Valor explains how Sebina will be stationed in the southern territories of Callisto on standby, protecting the land that connects both their kingdoms. Corsal will be waiting south of Sao at the borders of the desert ruins. King Valor made it clear he does not want to throw them into war, their assistance will be used only as backup.

This room is dark, and the walls are thick, made of solid stone. Its structure reminds me of the Alora Archives, except we are still in the palace, just an older part of it—away from prying eyes and ears. The only light casting in is behind King Valor. Three arched windows fill the expansion of the wall from floor to ceiling. Each adorned with Callisto's, Corsal's, and Sebina's crest. I realize they must have kept their alliances for centuries.

Off to the side is a large, stone table with the entire map of the lands. Hundreds of little figures are carved from stone and wood.

"That's enough time for all of us to gather our men. It will take a few days for my army to leave the port and sail around the lands, docking at the northeast of Sao. We need to prevent King Mal Tarvas from making any more attempts to take Viona."

A chill washes down my body. I glance at Callian, pulling his attention in my direction. He sees my tightened features. My chair grates across the stone floor. I stand firm with my hands clasped behind my back.

"He will be expecting this," I say. All eyes turn to me.

"How so?" King Valor asks with his brows furrowing. He's clad in warrior armor. His salt-and-pepper hair is brushed back, exposing the strong angles of his jawline. The way he looks at me is almost like a mirror of Callian's features. By the way his jaw ticks, I can assume he doesn't like that I'm questioning his plan. He leans forward, pressing his knuckles into the weathered wood of the table. "Well, my dear? Please tell us why." There's an edge in his tone.

I walk over to the large table with all the figurines. "First of all, Sao's castle is inaccurate. There are three main towers overlooking the north, west, and south territories. They're occupied at all times. In your display, there is only one, and it's looking in the direction of the White Forest. If you advance by sea, he will see you coming. Halos

Mountain will not shield you for long. Your position will leave you vulnerable and exposed, putting your men in harm's way."

Low chatter fills the room. There is a piece of me buried deep inside that feels like a traitor, helping Sao's enemies in the attack of my home. I suck in a sharp breath, staring at the carved figure of my castle and the homes of my people, but it's not my home anymore. They remain trapped in a land ruled by an evil king. I swallow the lump wanting to form in my throat and turn around to find Queen Josephine Lana of Corsal sitting not too far from where I stand. Her consort is on her right while her representatives are standing behind them. Her rich-brown eyes meet mine.

"I thank you for your willingness to help me. Your forgiveness means more to me than you will ever know." I take a small step away from the display. "There will be people wanting to flee my lands. I would be grateful if you would take in any refugees from Sao and provide them with food and shelter. They . . . " I pause, coming to my own realization. "They have always been victims, and they deserve better treatment."

Queen Lana looks at me with warm eyes. "Viona, I know what it's like to run from the enemy with nothing but the clothes on your back. I had a long discussion with my representatives last night after the ball. From what they tell me, it is in our best interest to stop King Tarvas in any way we can. We refuse to allow his tyranny to stretch beyond the borders we share. You have my word, we will assist your people and make extra preparations to have them travel back to Corsal."

"Thank you. King Tarvas is ruthless. He's evil. He doesn't care if you are a woman or a child. If you stand in his way, he will kill you. There is no remorse for what he does. Losing lives is inevitable, but I want to prevent a flat-out war if I can. You all need to be well aware of what he is capable of."

Prince Marius clears his throat before speaking. "If I may be so forward, Viona is right. I have fought against Sao before. King Tarvas is known for his—" There is a pause. Something glints in his eyes, and everyone who has seen war knows what that is. Trauma kicking down the door. A pang of guilt and sorrow cuts through me, seeing firsthand what it's done to the other one holding the blade. "He's known for wielding dark magic to gain the upper hand. He does not fight cleanly or honorably." Prince Marius looks in my direction. "No offense to you, Viona."

My brows arch. I keep my chin lifted. "None taken. Prince Marius is right. I know how he fights, and I've heard whispers of what he has done. Though I am ashamed for ignoring it, I want to assure you all, his actions will never reflect who I am. He's after me. *He wants me.* I have seen what he has brought to the walls of Callisto. He will not stop, which is why I have devised a plan that will send me ahead of the army." I look directly at King Valor while everyone in the room erupts in chatter. Through the bond I sense Callian's concern, but he remains calm and leaned back in his chair.

"Everyone settle down," Queen Alexandria says. "She knows him better than any of us ever will. This was her home. She knows the ins and outs and every nook and cranny. I spoke with my representatives and my council this morning. I want to hear what she has to say." She curtly nods for me to continue.

"Corsal will remain on the borders of the desert ruins, and Sebina will stand guard in the southern territories of Callisto as you suggested. But Callisto's forces will enter through the White Forest," I say.

Half of the room erupts in shock and disagreement while the rest hushes them. I patiently wait for everyone to simmer down before continuing. This time, Callian's stare feels too penetrating, too observing as he rests his elbows on the table.

"I will look for the woman who guards it and ask for safe passage for Callisto's army." The room erupts again. I keep my chin lifted, raking my eyes over the crowd, waiting for them to be quiet, but the moments stretch on. Gareon beams with amusement, seeing the disruption on everyone's faces. He must know I'm right.

Callian looks at me with pride. "Viona is right," he says, lacing his fingers together. "I have faith she will succeed. She remained unharmed in the White Forest. Going there and coming back were two different experiences for me. With her, nothing happened." My eyes go wide. My lips slightly part. He never mentioned anything happening when he crossed it alone. It gives more affirmation to my plans.

"How can you guarantee you will be granted the safety of my men?" King Valor says, scratching his chin as his arms are crossed.

"I can't explain it, but I can almost feel it. If I close my eyes for long enough, I'm there. What I have inside of me is leading me to it. If I am the one prophesied to unite the lands, if I am the one who will end King Tarvas' life, I need your support in my efforts." My eyes carry over from King Valor to Crystal with the reality of this hitting me faster than I can grasp, to Iván, who already looks like he is planning. "And if anything were to happen to me. If . . . " My voice fades off as I'm moments from looking at Callian. Fear, I feel fear of what is to come, not knowing how this will end, when *we* have just begun. The fear of losing him if I fail.

Crystal abruptly stands. "No." She slams her fist onto the table. Tears threaten to slip free from her piercing, violet eyes. "Don't say it," she asserts, shaking her head as her two braids sway across her chest. "I won't accept that. You *will* bring balance to this land, and you *will* succeed. There are no *ifs*."

I exhale a sharp breath, seeing the intensity and love for me glowing in her eyes. My heart swells. I suck in a deep breath, and a smile curls up. My eyes skim across the table as, one by one, everyone raises a glass . . . to me. To my shock, even Ronan.

Callian stands. "We have you, Viona Tarvas."

"We always will," King Valor echoes and takes a drink.

We.

Time seems to slow as everyone stands with wide smiles stretching across their faces.

One by one, everyone at the table pledges their alliance. They stand beside me, all of them. I meet the eye of every king and queen in this room with a smile. I would have never thought this would happen. A chill sweeps down my body, wishing my mother were here to see this. To see me step out from the shadows and into the light where I have people around me. For the first time, I know where I belong. I am no longer the enemy standing in the middle of the room with glares searing down my back. I don't have to go through this alone.

I walk around the table, taking my seat next to Callian. He puts an arm over my shoulder and brings me against him. As the room fills with chatter, celebration, and more flowing wine, he pulls me in for a kiss. He is shameless in the way he claims me, wrapping his heart around mine, freeing me from the inner chains of my past, bold and searing. The kiss is hard and passionate, full of pride. I press my hand against his chest, fingers slightly slipping between the ties of his black tunic.

When we pull away, he brushes my cheek with the back of his hand. "And we will always have each other."

CALLIAN AND I RIDE CIRRUS to the harbor. My arms are wrapped around his waist.

Over the next week, the kingdom of Sebina parted ways, traveling in three groups with one hiding the royal family. I was glad to see Princess Alexandria leave, for many reasons, actually. Callian must have sensed it, being as I was pretty sure I could feel his amusement through our growing bond.

"I feel you're less tense now that Princess Alexandria is gone."

My head tips back in a laugh, knowing I was spot on. "She's lucky she left with all her fingers intact," I admit. He slightly turns his head with a side-glanced smirk. A loose strand of his hair bellows in the gust of warm wind.

"Were you jealous?" he drawls, already knowing the answer. I huff out a laugh. My chin remains lifted with brows arching as a smile of satisfaction spreads across my face.

"I refuse to stroke your ego." I huff out a scoff.

He tightens his hand around mine, caressing the soft part of my wrist. "I have something else you can stroke then," he purrs.

My cheeks flush.

Within a few moments, Cirrus stops outside the harbor.

"This is where we get off." He lets go of my hand so I can dismount.

I take a few steps back, looking up at the sign made of dark oak wood across the entrance.

"Elliam Harbor," I read aloud while shielding my eyes from the sun.

"Cirrus isn't a fan of trotting over large bodies of water. He will rest here while we say goodbye to Prince Marius."

I run my hand along Cirrus' neck, giving him scratches around his cheeks. "So it looks like you *are* afraid of something," I tease, giving him one more pat before leaving, but he nudges me in the back with his nose. A giggle bubbles out of me. "What?"

Callian sighs. "He wants you to do the head thing."

My eyes go wide with humor. I turn to Cirrus, smiling. "Is that true?"

He neighs, nudging me again. I press both hands on the sides of his face and lean in. Cirrus and I are silent as we listen to the faint bustle of life beyond the harbor. I hum, feeling the warmth and comfort he gives me. After a few moments, I step away and join Callian at his side.

"Traitor," Callian mumbles under his breath just loud enough for Cirrus to hear.

For the first time, I see the harbor of Callisto up close.

We watch the queen and king of Corsal leave on a large, full-rigged ship, leaving two barques still at the docks to follow, one of which, Prince Marius will be on.

Callian and I remain by the pier until the ships are out of sight.

There is an odd warmth in the thick air today, and the wind carries no relief. Callian takes a deep breath, tugging on the bottom of his already-thin, black, sleeveless tunic to allow the breeze to drift through. His hair is half tied back, but that one rebellious strand of hair dangles free again.

"Bloody hell, it's hot," Callian says, as we begin to leave.

"Don't be such a baby, it's not that bad," I tease, swatting him on his stomach. A deep grunt rumbles in his chest, catching him off guard, but his eyes are full of arousal.

"That's easy for you to say. Not everyone is used to Sao's heat."

My heart flutters, noticing he doesn't call it my home anymore.

I smile. "Yes. But if you're that hot, then I guess you should go shirtless when we get back," I hum, eyeing him from the side. Even though I'd love to stay and explore this harbor, I'll save it for a day where the heat isn't so bad for him.

We mount Cirrus. This time, I'm in front, encased in Callian's arms. As Cirrus takes us back to the palace, there's a sense of familiarity in the wind. I inhale deeply. As I expel the air from my lungs, something unsettling looms.

Sage and sea.

The smell of the shores back in Sao.

And it all comes crashing down on me as grief settles in. I ignore the tears prickling in my eyes and rest my head against his chest.

"Let's go home."

WE HEAD TOWARD OUR CHAMBERS, ascending up the never-ending flight of stairs. Something is still snagging at my throat. There's tension gripping, building up around every muscle in my body. This feeling is new and one I can't seem to place. As we reach the top of the stairs, all the hair on the back of my neck rises.

I pause.

"What do you sense?" Callian stops, lowering his voice. He grips my arm, firm and protective as if he feels it through the bond.

There's a searing pain growing in my temples.

"I'm fine. I probably just need some water." But when we enter the long hall leading to our rooms, it grows deathly still.

"Where are the guards?" I ask, pressing my fingers to my temple again. The sound of metal slowly cuts through the air as Callian's sword is unsheathed at his side.

"I don't know, but I'm going to fucking kill them for leaving their posts."

A deep, husky laugh echoing behind us has me spinning around on my heels. When I see who's at the end of the hall, a chill sweeps down my body. As a stone thrown into a bucket, my heart plummets to the ground.

Solas has his boot over a pile of dead guards. "Don't worry, prince. I took care of that for you," he grins maliciously, keeping his foot planted on the carcasses at his feet. "They refused to address *me* as their prince. As you can see, I'm quite sensitive." He steps on the bodies, crushing their bones beneath his boots.

Callian growls, moving me behind him in one swift, predatory movement. Solas cocks his head to the side, smirking at the notion as he widens his shoulders. The leather rubs together as the fabric is pulled taut. The sound stretches on, filling the silence until his eyes narrow in on me. I remain behind Callian, gritting my teeth. He pauses. Heat rushes through my veins and fire ignites in the palm of my hands as his eyes rake down my body.

"She's quite feisty," Solas says. The corner of his mouth twitches into a grin as he takes another step closer. "Please, allow me to take her off your hands." His posture is of a gentleman, moving with elegance and grace as he extends an arm out to me. My lips twitch into a snarl.

"I will fucking rip your soul from your body if you take another step," Callian warns in a predatory growl. His body thrums with power, rippling waves of energy thicken the air. A buildup rising in him, causing me to take another step back, unsure how the next few moments will pan out.

Solas cracks his knuckles, moving his head from side to side, and thrusts back his hands. His head rolls back in our direction. Shadows rise from the ground, curling around his body. His long, dark coat bellows in its wake.

"Such strong words coming from a man who thinks she belongs to him," he says. Green flames form in the palm of his hands, swirling in dark-emerald clouds. He looks around at the scenery, clicking his tongue. "Such a gorgeous home. I would hate to leave it in ruins." His eyes trail down the hall, admiring the structure. He tilts his head to the side again and looks at me. "Why don't you come here, pretty princess. I'll take you home to Daddy." His lips are slightly purse.

My heart continues to slam against my chest, time seems to slow. Within a second, I know his men are coming. I felt their darkness rolling in like a raging storm over a sea.

Solas releases his powers. He comes at us hard with two fiery flames shooting through the air, blowing past the statues and paintings, knocking down everything in its path. At the same time, his men breach the walls, shattering the stained-glass windows behind us. Callian uses a force of energy to shield us from the flames and shards of glass.

The barrier is large enough to cover the entrance of his room.

"Get inside! Now!" he growls over the humming sound.

We make it inside. All corners of the walls buzz with the same protective shield.

"There's a hidden entrance behind the bookshelf," he says while standing between the door and myself. "Go!"

I nod, spinning on my heels, running toward it. Lightning crackles in the air, cutting me off before I can reach it. The sound is almost ear-shattering. Solas appears in a cloud of smoke. Having no other choice, I slide under him. My boots skid across the floor. I jump to my feet, casting flames into his back, but he remains unfazed. My eyes widen as the fire spreads around him, staying inches from his body, unscathed. He turns toward me, looking amused.

"I never knew a power like this could feel so good. Compliments to your father for the little incentive of our alliance."

Tendrils of black smoke fill Callian's eyes; they're no longer churning with emerald haze. Fear rushes down my spine, feeling pieces of myself buried deep within him.

The bond. He's harnessing what he can to save me.

I see it now, as it all comes crashing down. I misinterpreted my vision.

I wasn't killing Callian. I was seeing through the eyes of my enemy.

Callian advances forward, rushing Solas with his sword raised. Solas swiftly turns around, countering Callian's attack with a shadowed blade appearing in his hands. They cross weapons. Solas grits his teeth, trying to hold his position, but Solas is no match for the darkness that lurks behind Callian's eyes. Solas has entered the den of a wolf, and now that wolf has been unleashed. He growls, pushing forward as Solas' feet begin dragging back. With one hard thrust, Callian sends a powerful force of magic, throwing Solas' body against the wall. Callian extends his hand, lifting him into the air, and slams him against the ground without touching him. The walls behind me open up. Shadowed pirates are on the other side in the hall with their eyes pinned on me. Darkness follows them in misted curls of smoke as they step into the room. Shards of glass and debris crunch beneath their boots.

I unsheathe my sword, moving into a defensive stance. The walls close up behind them. Suddenly, the energy in the room shifts. Callian's barrier dissipates as Solas rebuilds a forcefield of his own.

"I'm not leaving until I have her, and nobody is going to interfere this time." Solas licks his lips, stumbling to his feet. We're being surrounded.

Closed in.

Trapped.

My heart drops to the pit of my stomach. I'm now back to back with Callian, feet apart, willing to do whatever I have to to save us.

"Time is ticking, and so is the beat of your heart," Solas says. He disappears, leaving a trail of smoke behind him.

In a blaze of fury, I skim the room. "Where did he go?" I yell out.

"I don't fucking know," Callian replies, eyeing Solas' men who surround us like hungry sharks. They attack. A stream of fire emits from my hand. I spin around, cleaving one across the chest. All my rage begins to unfurl on them.

Callian and I continue to take down Solas' men one by one, catching them with our blades and magic as they disappear in and out of sight.

Suddenly, like a soft brush against my flesh, onyx fills my eyes, dark as night. I feel the ambience of the Shadow Realm as if I'm somehow in sync. My eyes bounce to Callian. We share a knowing look as he precisely cuts into another shadowed pirate who reappears directly behind him. We use our bond as we are guided by a source unseen. Like a small root sprouting in the freshly turned dirt, we are tethered. I allow my soul to dip further into the dark, reveling in the satisfaction of seeing the men writhe against the black fissures spreading across their chest, drawing on the power that is connecting me to this source of energy.

A mist of blood snags my attention. The aptitude of my senses rises, feeling another source come through. Another one of Solas' men disappears, but when he comes back, dark jagged roots protrude out of every orifice of his dead body. My brows knit, seeing a pool of blood left in its wake.

What the fuck?

More of his men funnel in through the wall, and more than half of them are being taken out, disappearing into the shroud of darkness, only to return dead with pieces of their body missing or strangled by more jagged roots. Each death creates another pool of blood.

The clamor of war slips through the opening. I hear a female yelling in the hall. My heart nearly stops beating.

"Crystal." My breath hitches. She's trying to break the wards to help us. I can hear her yelling alongside Callisto's guards as Solas' men rush them.

"Viona!" Callian yells. My head turns. Callian thrusts his arm out, stopping one of Solas' men from reaching me. The man's body goes flying and slams against the wall, ending in a fatal crack. Callian saved me, but as I turn to meet his stare, a dagger is lodged into his body.

Before I can take my next breath, Solas appears behind me, curling his arm around my waist like a snake who's finally caught its prey. He holds my head against his chest, making sure I see Callian on his knees with the hilt of the dagger deep in his heart. A sharp, fiery pain shoots up my body, feeling the tiny shards of glass slicing into every chord of my flesh. It burns through my veins, to my very core, conjuring the release of what I felt lodged in my throat. In a blind rage, a scream rips through me. All of Solas' men go flying into the air. I will their deaths, and it comes for every single one of them. The sounds around me begin to fade. The last thing I hear is a growl tearing through Callian—one full of fury, fear, and regret—before I feel myself slipping into the dark.

CHAPTER 43

CALLIAN

I FINALLY SEE IT.

A glimpse of the world coming to an end through the eyes of a power lost in time. The moment the blade pierces through my skin, it only takes a subtle flinch in her wrist to set my chambers aflame. An unforgiving scream wrenches from her throat, expressing the truth that she will rip this world apart for me. She tosses Solas' men aside without even touching them. One by one, she tears them to shreds, struggling in Solas' grip. Our eyes lock as the fire spreads throughout my room.

It's true what Gareon said—I have fallen in love with the sun. His voice comes back to haunt me as I stare into her eyes. Pieces of her that first came to me in dreams are now locked in place.

Viona reaches for me. Her gaze warms, but then it changes. Those beautiful, big, blue eyes widen with not only fear, but regret. Communicating words she wishes she spoke to me sooner. Her expression feels like a bolt of lightning coursing through my veins and striking my heart.

A long-forgotten blade forbidden by the gods, hidden away and never to be used. Here it is, protruding out of the waist of my true love. My fate, my destiny. She closes her eyes, and tears stream down her face. Her head falls back against the chest of our enemy. Solas stands behind her with his hand wrapped around her precious throat while the other holds the dagger embedded to the hilt against the soft skin beside her hip bone. A sadistic grin forms on his face as his eyes bore into my soul. A look of feral satisfaction.

Gods-dammit. I cannot bear this pain. Tears threaten to break free, and a thunderous growl rips from my throat. Rage courses through my veins with menacing chaos and destruction. I lurch forward, ready to rip his fucking spine from his body, but a portal opens up behind them.

Just like that, they are gone.

I'm left on my knees as something in me cracks. Darkness surrounds me in what I think is the remnants of the portal, but no. It's her, the darkest parts of her soul surging through my veins like sweet poison, weaving into the chords of my source of power. My head falls back as black shadows curl around my body. I welcome the touch, the embrace, the only part of her that becomes us as it soothes me into the dark.

"Viona!"

I cannot see, I can hardly breathe, and yet I continue to search blindly through the flames. Searching for the sun, that bright light, her radiant smile that hides a lifetime of pain. I would do anything to take all of it away. There's a searing pulse in my skull from the deep gash marring the side of my head, blurring my vision.

Under the tips of my fingers, I feel my healing powers start to work. I'm now able to take in air without my lungs feeling like they are on fire. Then the realization comes rushing back to me, hitting me like a relentless wave pulling me into an undertow.

The moment repeats itself over and over again. The look on her face. Fucking Solas. His hand wrapped around the dagger and the other on her throat. The gleam in his eyes. It tears through me every time I see it. A growl rips through me. Pushing myself to my feet, my knees buckle.

"Fuck." I grit my teeth, feeling the dagger deepen with every movement.

The clamor of armor grows, making its way down toward the corridor, and another portal opens up through the wall. Gareon stands on the other side as Crystal storms in with her own chaos, pushing her hands to the side to part the flames around me.

"Where is she?" she yells over the roaring inferno, shooting powerful blasts of ice and freezing the entire side of my wall. Words cannot form quick enough. My chest tightens. I'm broken. I'm not ready to say those words. I can't. All I can do is shake my head and beat my fist against the ground.

"No . . . " She chokes out a sob followed by a long-cursed cry that splits my heart in two.

My father rushes in with guards flanking his sides. He storms in not as a king nor as a warrior clad in armor, but as a father. On one knee, he wraps a firm hand around my arm. The guards fan out, searching the rooms around us.

"No one else is here," I exhale, jerking away from his grip. He reaches for me again. The stubborn fucking bastard won't let go. I'm carried away. The last thing I hear is Sydney's voice as she lulls me under compulsion to sleep.

SHADOWS UNVEILED

PART III

CHAPTER 44
VIONA

I'M FALLING.

Time evades the blissful surrender of my life somewhere between the sky and the stars.

There's a comfort in the remnants of the dark. The hollow spaces I once feared are no more.

A bright fissure spreads across my face. My eyes flutter open to its comfort. I'm surrounded by bold, shimmering twilight. In the masses of an expansive space, it's just me as my senses become a knowledge, curving through every line in my hands. I trail the pad of my finger along each one, enamored that I can somehow see I'm everywhere all at once, expanding across the plains, valleys, oceans, stars, and even the dark. Each one glows prominently.

But I'm not meant to live with the gods in this part of the stars. Not yet.

The brightest star hides amidst an enormous, ominous cloud of dust and cosmic gasses. In the complexity of this space, it's home.

Even now, between the earth and the sky, there is still us. Callian's voice echoes in my mind, soothing me into a calm and gravitating me to where I'm needed. As my soul descends back into my body, the gravity of the world shifts, pulling me into an undertow. Back into a world filled with so much betrayal, death, lies, and pain. My mind floods with every moment of my life, racing against torrential waves of memories, trying to catch a glimpse of my mother, father, endless war, the ocean, the friendships, Callisto, and him. Callian.

And it all hits me right in the face.

"WAKE UP, YOU FUCKING BITCH."

I gasp, eyes still closed, choking on a hard cough as water engulfs my lungs. Time seems to blend in a nauseating mass of nerves.

Another wave of frigid water hits my face. My eyes fling open, feeling as though I'm moments from drowning as I heave. Every attempt to chase away the burn in my lungs is met with a desperation for air. The beat of my heart pulsates in my ears as if my body has gone to war for survival, fighting for my power that now feels like it's scratching beneath the surface. It only takes a few seconds to register that I've been bound.

Where am I? I suck in another ragged breath, focusing on the blurred movements throughout the room.

"That's not how we treat our princess, Morel." Solas seethes, grabbing the bucket out of the man's hands.

I hear it hit a wall and tumble, confirming we are somewhere indoors, most likely hidden. My nails scrape against the sticky, weathered, wooden floor as I struggle to push myself up, but my arms buckle. The side of my face hits the ground, slamming back into a nasty puddle of water mixed with a lifetime of smells that make me want to hurl. A group of men break out into laughter. The pungent air is a familiar scent. My heart sinks into my stomach, knowing exactly where we are.

Back in Sao.

The faint clamor of drunken patrons tells me we are in one of the back rooms of the local tavern outside the castle walls.

"She isn't so powerful now," one of them says in a deep, husky tone. Hearing the slight wheeze in his pronunciation, I commit his voice to memory. The wheezing seems to carry over to his labored breathing. I think about cutting the vocal cords from his throat.

A firm hand grips my arm, rolling me onto my back. My head feels like jelly at the sudden motion. Feeling gravity shift, the searing, throbbing pain returns. Solas hovers above me, squinting his green eyes in a hooded glare.

Every time I cough, my chest aches, and the fire churns beneath, but I know no release is coming. My powers remain idle because of whatever fucking magic is cast in these shackles. My lips press thin, glaring at his stark silhouette as I think about all the ways I will end his life the moment I break free.

"Good, now that you're awake, you can eat," Solas says. His dirty-blond hair remains slicked back, secured at the nape of his neck, looking like he can't be bothered to lift a finger while I lie in a puddle of contaminated water and vomit.

"Eat?" I scoff. "Fuck you, you piece of shit."

I whip my head to the side, trying to move the hair away from my face so I can get a better look at my surroundings. Solas' jaw is tense with irritation. He steps over my body so that I'm now between his boots. His dark, leather trousers rub together as he leans down. His hand reaches toward me cautiously, removing the lock of hair slick against my face. I flinch at his touch.

"You, my dear, will take anything I put in your mouth." He shoves a piece of bread in my face with his other hand. I gag, feeling the soft loaf push in beyond my fill.

The men erupt in another wave of laughter, causing my anger to spike. I bite down into the loaf and spit it out. The contents land right on Solas' boot.

"You fucking stick anything more than a piece of bread in my mouth, and I promise you, I will *bite it off*," I growl, tasting the muck sweat from my lips. "You hear me, you fucking assholes? That goes for all of you! Touch me, and I'll strangle you by the cords of your balls!"

Solas blinks back, looking shocked and humored at the same time while his men fall into unrestrained laughter. "My my, you're so quick to go dark. Don't worry. None of these grotesque bastards will ever think of touching you as long as I'm around." He maliciously grins. I don't know if that is supposed to relieve me or remind me that he thinks I'm his. I let the next retort die on my tongue.

"You got your hands full with that one, Boss," Morel says. I can hear him eating, tearing into meat somewhere behind me, every chord of flesh he gnaws between his teeth. My eyes flutter to the back of my head. I can hear every sound around me increasing. My senses are overwhelmed, shaken with shock and probably hunger. It's all too much. My eyes flutter shut. I try speaking through my labored breathing, but inaudible words come out.

Solas whispers into my ear, "Sleep, pretty one. You're home now."

She stands beside me, a step ahead. Water gently laps against our bare feet, the outline of her body illuminated by the rising full moon. A blood moon.

Her long, brown hair wisps around her small frame.

"Mama," I whisper, letting the cool, night air steal my breath. Tears sting my eyes when I feel the warmth of her hand in mine. Is this real? She remains looking out to the sea. Though her touch is warm, I cannot feel her anymore.

The world is shifting beneath our feet. The waves recede, sinking us further into the sand, further into the depths of all her rage woven with sadness. The wind picks up with gale-force speeds, pushing me toward the sea. Every sudden gust of wind forces me to step further away from her and into the violent, raging waves to swim in her storm. Every loose rock and grain of sand flies past us into its depths. My hair whips around my face. I'm holding on, but my grip is slipping. The sheer glimmer of her silhouette begins to fade. She turns to look at me one more time.

My eyes slowly drift open, and I discover I'm on horseback, gagged with a thick, cotton cloth fastened tightly around my mouth. I suck in a strangled breath, heaving. The remnants of seeing my mother are etched into the back of my mind, but the sharp pain at my side pulls me from thought. The scent of sweat, leather, and pine assaults my nose, and I realize that Solas has me in his arms. I assess my current state. My legs are still bound. They dangle on one side of his horse. I move around, fighting against his hold. Every movement is met with more searing pain. My eyes trail down to where he stabbed me, and he takes notice.

Solas clears his throat, pulling me from thought. "My apologies. After seeing you wouldn't go willingly with me, I had to somehow stop you from potentially burning my favorite coat. That dagger is quite special," he says. My brows pinch into a scowl. The incredulity in his tone is scathing. "What did it do, you ask?" He casually waves at the villagers as we pass. The shock on their faces is evident as they watch me enter as a captive.

"The dagger I used on you possesses the ability to weaken all of your powers. It is forbidden by the gods, but since it was a gift from your father, he said I could use it. And since I have the power to wield shadow, I can create endless shadow blades, which is what I used on your dear lover. They all have a similar effect, though only the one I used on you channels the blades' full capacity," he says, resting a hand on my thigh as he holds onto the reins with the other. I jerk my body at the motion, trying to ignore the pain. He tsks, stealing a glance at my wound. "I can see it barely worked on you, though."

My eyes lower to said wound that looks like it's starting to weave itself back together. A gift through the bond and a small piece of hope that these shackles haven't suppressed all my powers. The restraints whisper the same dark magic that was in the blade. My stomach takes a dip thinking about Callian, and my mind flashes back to the last time I saw him. Fear. True fear in his eyes before I set his chambers aflame after seeing the hilt of a dagger sticking out of his chest.

"Seems you're quite special after all. Compliments to your . . . lover." His words clip.

Before he can see the tear slipping down my cheek, I look away, only to meet the green eyes of a young girl with matted, dirty-blonde hair. Another girl stands beside her, taller with short hair and eyes the color of a cold winter. The younger girl tugs on a women's dress, pointing in my direction. By the expressions on the villagers' faces, I know my arrival will be the talk of the town. As we continue to ride through the village, some of the villagers watch, while others seem to scurry away to spread the news that I have come back.

We approach the walls of Sao, and a knot forms in my chest as I see it in a new light. It used to be a place to rest my head and a chamber that housed my demons. I now return the same way I left, taken against my will. I knew coming back would be a battle I couldn't prevent, no matter how far I ran. I just didn't expect to return like this, shackled like an animal, like the weapon King Tarvas strived for me to be.

We come to an abrupt stop. The thick chains grind together as one of the guards pulls up the portcullis until the metal gate rises. Within a few moments, we continue, riding through the bailey of Sao. A row of Blood Moon Knights come into view. I expect to see a reaction, but the knights remain almost lifeless, until only two of them step out of formation.

"This is where you get off," Solas says, unsheathing a knife. He cuts the cotton gag and yanks it from my mouth. My head whips in his direction and I spit in his face. Before he can react, I'm pulled off the horse. I smile, watching him wipe off the symbol of my disdain.

Staggering to my feet, two men hook a hand under each of my arms and pull me up. It's the first time I've used my legs in I don't know how many days. One kneels down, unlocking the shackles on my ankles. As soon as my legs are free, I kick him in the chest. Before I can launch myself at him, I'm held back, surrounded by guards, and I have no other choice but to comply and walk forward toward the castle doors.

As they swing open, the air rushes in, causing everyone in the foyer to look our way. Nobles and members of the council clutter the halls. They remain frozen in place when they realize who just walked in. Shock spreads like wildfire in their wide-eyed expressions. I search for Alyce among the crowd, but she's nowhere to be found. Every single one of these assholes eyes me in disgust—I see nothing has changed. It gives me such satisfaction to know my presence causes them to revolt. My lips quirk up into a grin as I'm shoved forward.

I'm led through the never-ending halls toward the throne room.

For the first time, I really take a look at my surroundings, from the people to the vines carved into the tall, stone pillars. Secrets and lies lurk in every corner. The long, purple carpet no longer looks as bright and cheery as it once did. It is cold, dark, and unwelcoming. The glass-stained windows barely have any light coming in. It is as if the sun refuses to shine for the wicked. The truth now taints the walls of a place that once felt like an honor to walk through.

Cursed.

That's what this place was and always has been—a place where all my grief could thrive. I was foolish to let it hold me by the throat for so long. Sao festers with lies told by a man who is no longer my father. He is a dark lord. Disgust takes root in the pit of my stomach.

Guards line the halls, standing in unison, bearing the moon's crest. *The blood moon.*

My lips slightly part in a soft exhale, wondering how much time had passed. How long until the moon turns red?

I see the king is taking extra measures with the excessive number of knights today. He knows I'd set this fucking hellhole on fire and burn everything down if I wasn't worried they'd kill me first. My vision tunnels down the last hallway. Beyond those thick, heavy slabs of wood, I know who's on the other side.

I take a deep breath, watching the doors swing open. I'm pushed forward. The motion almost makes my knees buckle, but I bite through the pain. There's a sudden shift in the air, tightening the knot in my chest. The searing pain on the side of my head returns. My eyes close for a brief moment as I succumb to the pain. I'm thrown onto my knees at the bottom of the steps leading up to King Mal Tarvas' throne.

CHAPTER 45
CALLIAN

Tʜɪs ɪs ʀᴇᴀʟ. Tʜᴇ world's gravity is shifting again, knocking me off my fucking axis. These moments have been coming and going, hitting me harder in the chest each time I wake. Time has been bleeding into days and nights while I've been left to feel every ounce of her absence.

At one point, a part of me thought I was dead. Maybe I was for a moment because I saw Viona briefly while drifting in and out of consciousness. She was floating among the stars as every beam of light illuminated the curves of her body. She had the semblance of a goddess, draped in a white, silk cloth that so delicately flowed around her chest, hips, and ankles. Every prism of light filtered through. I longed to brush my lips across her soft skin. The sight brought me to my knees. I called her name, hoping she would respond, but she remained serene and idle.

Every time I open my eyes, I am reminded of the recurring nightmare of how she was taken. A memory I can't escape.

"Fuck," I growl, feeling Sydney rip the bandage off my chest, pulling me from thought. Her rich-green eyes flick in my direction, and her lips press thin as she mirrors my glare.

"Good morning," she softly says.

A ghost of a smile appears. I squeeze her hand in response and turn my head toward the door. Sydney has stayed by my side, despite my silence, tending to my wound and healing me in segments. I thought I felt Crystal sitting beside the bed, whispering to her. It has been hard to discern what is real while lying here. Now, feeling a little more awake, a little more balanced.

"You're nearly healed," Sydney observes, but her focus remains on inspecting my wound, gently pressing around the sensitive area while she wears a knit expression.

I hiss, jaw clenched, feeling her fingers work that tender spot.

She pauses, resting her hands in her lap, and studies me. Her mahogany hair isn't in its typical bun. She looks a lot younger with her hair down, but the dark circles under her eyes tell me she hasn't slept much, spent from the amount of healing she's done on me.

I turn to stare at the door as if Viona will walk through it.

"Care to share your thoughts this time?"

I huff out a faint laugh. "Are you taking advantage of my vulnerability since I have nowhere to go?" My voice sounds hoarse, and the back of my throat burns with my reality. A moment passes between us as I hold her gaze. She stands to leave, but I gently reach for her, and she pauses before sitting back down.

"I was imagining Viona walking through that door, laughing, pretending this never happened. I pictured a stack of books in her arms while she nestles herself into a chair by the fireplace, feeling safe. Safe from all those who seek to harm her, from those who want to use her to get what they want... I look at my father and then think about hers. How could anyone be this evil, so driven by greed that his daughter's life is so meaningless to him. I..." Sydney cups my cheek, wiping the tears I had no idea slipped free. "I just want to see her living in a world without her own flesh and blood trying to rip her apart for what makes her special."

For a moment, time seems to slow again as I feel the pain course through the bond from her being so far from reach, but I stop myself before my mind slips away. Sydney's touch pulls me out of thought again as she gently squeezes my arm.

"When I first met Viona, the first thing I noticed were her eyes. Not because of the color, but because of what I felt behind them. As I got her ready to meet your father, the moment we were face to face, I saw that inferno brewing behind a wall so thick, it should have been impenetrable to those outside it. I've watched that storm calm just enough to let us in. I've watched her blossom into a beautiful rose while keeping her thorns tipped with that power. He will know her wrath soon enough, and she will have that peace."

She pats my leg before walking over to the table. Her words settle over me, calming the beat of my heart, because she's right. I know everything Viona is capable of, I know how strong she is.

While Sydney gathers her things, I notice she's not in one of her typical buttoned-up dresses in various colors of cyan. She's in trousers with a long-sleeve tunic and a tight vest with little pockets for hidden daggers. I haven't seen her dress this way since I was a child. She is ready to fight if need be.

"How long have I been in this bed?" I ask the question I've been hesitant to get the answer to.

"Four days."

"Fuck," I reply.

"The dagger that was used on you was laced with dark magic, slowing your healing process."

"It was all a part of his plan." I seethe. My teeth grit together as my fists tighten. I've had enough time lying here to think about all the ways I would end her father's life and all the ways I would torture Solas for hurting her . . . even touching her.

"I know that look. I swear to the gods, Callian, if you get out of that bed and leave this room, I'll knock your ass out again. You need rest, one more day at least. If you care about her, you *will* let your body gather back its full strength."

She's right, but lying here trapped inside my head is far worse than any pain I've ever felt.

She turns toward the door and takes one more look at me. "Now rest. When you're fully healed, you will figure out how to bring her back to us."

Us. My chest tightens. Her eyes flutter, trying to hold back the tears. She isn't one to show them, but this is enough to sting my eyes. I will do everything I can to bring Viona back. I will not lose her. Every part of her was made for me. My lips press thin. I give Sydney a tight nod before she leaves. Once I hear her footsteps fade down the hall, my arm flops over Viona's side of the bed.

Viona is strong. She's so strong, I remind myself every moment that passes by. I bring her pillow to my face. She's gone, but her scent remains. Vanilla, rich cinnamon. I envision my face nestled into her soft, dark hair and my arm curved around her body. She isn't dead, I can feel her through our bond like a rope that's been pulled taut.

"Fuck." I exhale, a tear slipping free. This is torturous. I miss how my thumb trailed along the softest part of her hips. That little space between her hip bone and lower stomach. My eyes remain shut as I shift to the side. Being in her room, in her bed, is the only thing that soothes me right now. My hand moves across the soft, white sheets to where she once slept. Something cold and hard hits the tips of my fingers. My eyes fling open, feeling it thrum against my skin.

"What the . . . " I whisper.

Flashes of purple and pink glint in the sun. It's a stone, but not just any. No, it's labradorite. Where would she have gotten something like this? It isn't possible, but it is staring at me right in the face. I take a deep breath, clasping it in my palm and holding it against my chest. My mind drifts to so many places, it's hard to grasp anything with clarity. I do the only thing that I know could bring me the slightest bit of peace.

CHAPTER 46
VIONA

MY KNEES HIT THE ground so hard, I think the bones have shattered. The palms of my hands skid across the floor, slick with sweat. Pain shoots up my body like shards of heated glass, but I refrain from wincing. My head flips up, and I push off the floor, leaning back onto my heels as I glare at the man whose life I'd love to end. I take a deep breath before rising to my feet, never taking my eyes off him. My hands are clasped together with my feet spread apart, lifting my chin to show him being here has not broken me.

"My little warrior, how you've grown. Left a prisoner only to return as an enemy. It's interesting how things work out, isn't it?" King Tarvas remains seated with a glass of wine in his hand, his rings clanking against it. I notice his hair is slightly shorter, combed back to the nape of his neck. I'm satisfied to know those few strands of hair resting above his brow annoy him. I remain silent, watching him sip his wine while he tries to figure me out from behind the brim. Silence becomes potent in the air. When he sets the glass down, the sound bounces off the walls. Both our jaws tighten, holding onto many unspoken words.

"I sense a change in you, sweet daughter. I couldn't quite place what it was the last time I saw you. But now as you stand before me, I see it. You've been hiding many things from me." His tone falls flat as he adjusts the black cuffs of his sleeves. I continue glaring at him, saying nothing. "You lied to me," he drawls, his voice dipping an octave lower, growling in a deep whisper that rumbles in his chest—words laced with darkness sending chills down my spine. I swallow the lump forming in my throat, wondering what else he can sense besides the obvious growth of my powers. "What would your mother say about your betrayal?"

My eyes narrow in on him, and my chest begins heaving at the mention of her—a word that has not left his lips since the day she died. My fists tighten. My knuckles turn white. Heat scratches at the surface of my skin, begging for a release, pushing against the wall of dark magic cast in these fucking shackles. He notices the cracks in my wall. Being the snake he is, he rises to his feet, stalking down the dais. There's a heaviness blooming in my chest, and my heart is beating like a war drum.

Like a dark shadow, he sees all the ways he can slip in. "We all know she loved you most."

My pulse is rising with every step he takes. I feel as though I'm moments from bursting at the seams with no way of release. I need to keep my shit together. My jaw flutters with anger, and I'm clamping down so hard, it hurts.

"You betrayed us, little one." He rolls his sleeves up. Black tendrils of darkness fill his eyes.

Shock stills my breath, seeing a mirror of myself and the undying curse that seems to follow me. He reaches for me, a caress against my cheek before grabbing my face. I growl, biting back the pain.

"You know"—he pauses, jaw ticking—"as I get closer to you, something else is being revealed." His eyes rake up and down my face, and he inhales, closing his eyes in an angry flutter.

My nostrils flare at the notion. I try pulling back, but a knight comes up behind me, holding me in place. I can feel King Tarvas' dark power racing through my veins. His eyes fling open the moment he finds what he's searching for. His grip tightens, cutting the inside of my cheeks. The back of my throat swells as the taste of metal drips down my throat. I fight back the tears threatening to break free.

"What would your mother say if she knew you have been sleeping with Prince Valor like the filthy little whore you are?" He lets go, and my body lurches forward as I exhale the breath I've been holding. Suddenly, my head whips to the side as I feel his hand slap across my face, sending me stumbling back.

"How dare you!" I seethe, snapping my head in his direction—the taste of metal pools in my mouth. My core shakes, and something inside me begins to rupture as a wave of cold and hot chills reverberate

around me. "If my mother knew of all your lies, if she knew the truth of who you really are . . . " I take a step forward, feeling heat spread across my face and chest. "*You* have betrayed *us*!" I scream. More than a scream, it is a cry, a buildup of all the years of pain he has given me. Somehow, my voice shakes all the glass-stained windows above us. "Look at what you have done *to us*. To everyone you ever cared about. I was never your daughter, I was your asset. You were never going to put the crown on my head. You've been using me all along to take Vendrelle. You are a dark lord, cursed and damned by the gods above. You are nothing without me, and that makes you afraid. You have betrayed your *entire kingdom!* What would my mother think about *you?*" I step forward, spitting in his face. A mist of blood coats the white of his ruffled collar and parts of his jaw. Some of the knights look our way. Disgusted and outraged, King Tarvas steps back, eyes narrowing with malicious intent.

"Bring her in . . . " he growls.

Three words.

Three words is all it takes for my heart to cease.

Alyce.

My heart begins racing as I watch two knights leave. What has he done to her while I've been gone? A wave of panic washes over me like a cold chill. Within seconds, I hear the clamor of chains dragging against the ground. With every step, my heart sinks further into the pit of my stomach, into the depths of hell.

A silhouette of her frame comes into view with her head cloaked in a brown, burlap sack.

"No . . . " I whisper, dropping to my knees, my vision already blurred from the tears stinging my eyes. I shake my head back and forth, repeating the only word I can manage to speak. "No, no, no."

They nudge her forward and toss her to the ground. Her body slams against the cold, hard surface, causing me to flinch. The guard rips the sack from her head. A woman dressed in dark, ragged clothing lies at his feet with her head hanging between her shoulders. She's bound in chains that look to weigh more than her, but there are no hints of gray hidden between dark curls. There are no curls at all. What I see is long, unkempt, brown hair.

"Why don't you ask her yourself?" King Tarvas seethes. The woman lifts her head. Those eyes, upturned at the corners, stare at me between matted strands of hair.

Time slows as I crawl to her side on my hands and knees, sobs ripping from my throat.

"Mama . . ." Tears stream down my face. All this time, all this pain. *No, no no, it can't be.* I'm dreaming. I must be dreaming. My mother is dead, but she's here. I can't stop repeating it. "I saw you burn on the pyre." My voice is nothing but a cracked, faint whisper, and I'm unable to get ahold of my own reality.

She reaches for me, a small, frail hand that feels like bones cupping my cheek. "Viona," she says in a painfully hoarse tone that slices through me. I thought she was dead. But all this time, she's been here, hidden from the world, hidden from me. She has been kept away from me.

"Why?" I beg, narrowing my eyes on the monster who did this to her. My heart is ripping into millions of pieces.

He takes a deep breath, watching me struggle to pull my mother into a shackled embrace. Something glints in his eyes, but it's gone in a fleeting moment. He flicks the strand of hair away from his brow.

"Because in some twisted, fucked up way, you are right, Viona. I do need you, but I also need her. I've waited many lifetimes for our paths to align again. 'Love bound in darkness,' just as the prophecy says. The gods from the stars did me wrong. Not once, but *twice*," he seethes. "Killing my lover centuries ago because it was forbidden for me to fall in love with a mortal. Then they told me if I ever found her again, I would know great sorrow."

"What does that mean?" I demand.

"'Not too early, not too late, timing marks their fate,'" he recites another piece of the prophecy. "I began hearing whispers from the gods below of how to gain my powers back. A sacrifice needed to be made. I always thought love was everything, but it isn't." He sighs as if his soul hurts from the loss of his powers. "I made my choice," he says, growling.

"You disgust me." I seethe. He ignores my retort.

"Now that you're here together, when the blood moon rises, I will get back what has always been rightfully mine," he says, motioning for the knights to haul us away.

CHAPTER 47

CALLIAN

I KEEP MY GAZE on the chair Viona sat in the last time she was here. The labradorite is warm from my touch; I haven't let it go since I found it. My father quietly shuffles through papers, each turn of the pages jarring as the memory of her continues to slice through me. Between his occasional groans and my stubbornness, we let the silence comfort us. Oddly, his study is the best place for the both of us to think. When I was a boy, this would have been the last place I was allowed, but when my mother passed, he moved some furniture around to make room for me.

I remain partially slumped in the chair with my head leaned back. Since the attack, a chill has remained in my bones, one I can't rid unless I am in a scorching hot bath or, like this, close to a fireplace. I listen to the flames crackle and pop. The fresh strips of linen wrapped across my chest give an extra layer of warmth. My father clears his throat once more.

"I'm glad you're on the mend, Son. You gave us quite the scare."

My eyes remain fixed on the flames. A heaviness cuts through me, reeling back to the look on Viona's face when she was taken. I never truly understood fear until I saw the dagger in her flesh. Just like that, she disappeared into the hands of the enemy.

"You love her," he states—his way of saying it's okay to feel every bit of pain he sees cutting through me. My head rolls in his direction. My jaw tenses, holding back the raw emotion threatening to break free. My fists clench tighter around the stone.

"I do," I confess, sounding more like a fierce vow. The gods know I fucking do. "I haven't had the chance to thank you for coming to my aid."

My father gives a tight smile and nods. The creases in his eyes have become more prominent this week. It seems like he never sleeps anymore. The tiredness and grief consume him. He might hide it well around everyone else, but I see what lurks behind those eyes. Some nights, it worries me. I know if I ask, he'll only deny it or do what he does best and casually joke as he pours himself another drink—his remedy for pain. A drink doesn't seem so bad right now.

"You're scratching your chin again," he observes while picking up the stack of papers. I watch him squint his eyes, but now isn't the time to tell him he needs glasses.

"So? What does that mean?" I ask dryly while still rubbing the pad of my finger along the scruff of my jaw. I should shave, but I remember Viona likes it this way, so I keep it just for her. A tightness forms in my chest as her bright-blue eyes flash in the back of my mind. My head turns slightly in his direction as my brow lifts.

"It means you are far from here, only this time, your heart isn't on a ship far away in the middle of the ocean." He lets the last few words stretch as he flutters a hand in the air. "Your heart now goes wherever hers is."

My eyes remain fixed on the flames curling in the fireplace. It's been hard sorting through my emotions. The air always feels dry, and the never-ending pressure on my chest feels like a boulder. I stand to walk over to the window and pour myself a drink.

"You two completed the bond," he says in a way that sounds more like a request for confirmation, like he already knows.

I rest my forearm against the window, watching the distant port. My jaw ticks. He doesn't move or speak. We are left frozen in time with this game we're playing of who can hold out longer. I swivel the drink in my hand before taking a sip, welcoming the burn as it goes down my throat.

"Like I told Viona, I may be old, but I am not a fool. The moment I saw that book in the Alora Archives, I knew you had chosen her. It had only been a matter of time before it happened." My father sighs, lacing his fingers together and placing them over his stomach. "Does she know what happens when two are fated and bonded?"

"About the shared powers? Yes, she knows." My attention draws back to him. I watch his hands rise and fall. Long ago, I used to find comfort in listening to his long, steady breaths, but now, I know him sitting in that position is his way of prompting me to talk about my feelings. Something he learned from my mother.

"There are greater things at risk here, Callian. I'm sure you already feel your powers blending, but if she is a demi-god, you must consider what that means. Are you prepared to live a longer life? Can you handle the powers she's giving you? Look at what happened to Gareon and..."

"*Stop.*" I seethe, exhaling roughly. "I know you're trying to help, but please don't go there right now."

He lifts his hands in the air and leans back. "Alright. You've been resting for four days. What's our next move?"

My head dips back as I take another drink, fighting the anger rising in my blood. My teeth clench together. I place the piece of labradorite onto the desk. His brows knit with curiosity.

"Where in the gods' lands did you get this?" His eyes widen. "This isn't from Vendrelle." He holds it up to the light casting in from behind him.

"I know," I say, sitting across from him.

"Where did this come from, then?" he asks, handing it back to me.

"It was under Viona's pillow."

"Did she mention it to you?"

"No, but I have an idea," I confirm. He leans forward, waiting for me to speak. "I know King Tarvas has her somewhere in his castle. Though it's easy to say we can storm Sao, something tells me that won't work. I'm going to Halos Mountain to speak with Gareon. I know what I need to do. I can feel it through the bond. If my assumptions are right, then this labradorite is the key. Gareon will be able to read it."

"So you already know, and you won't tell me," he observes as tension knits his brows. He rests his elbows on the desk and leans forward with his fingers laced tightly together, waiting for me to speak, but I remain silent. He sighs, opening one of the drawers beneath the desk. The smell of his favorite whiskey hits the air as he pours some into his coffee. I smirk, taking this as my sign to leave.

"I'd appreciate it if you wouldn't drink your worries away while I'm gone, Father."

His laugh wanes into a soft sigh. He takes a sip. "You sound like your mother," he says under his breath. "And when you're angry, your eyes flare just like hers." He looks down at the ring on his finger and rolls it between his thumb. "If it makes you worry less, then water it is."

I scoff, "Liar," squeezing his arm and trying to forget he just mentioned my mother. I can't bear any more emotions right now. My other hand gently pats him on the side of the face, meeting his emerald stare. "We all know your cup has never seen a drop of water in its entire life." We break into a slight chuckle.

My mind drifts back to Viona. The love I feel for her burns inside my very core. She has set my soul aflame. I lower my gaze, staring at the faint scars that mar my father's hands. I hope to the stars I never have to know the pain my father lives with every day.

"True." He pauses, patting me on the hand. His rough, calloused fingers make a dry sound as he pulls away. "You will get her back," he says. "We can only imagine what Viona is going through right now. Once again, her world has been flipped upside down. Use your bond to connect to her. It will be a beacon."

My jaw ticks, feeling his words of encouragement overshadow the unsettling sense of foreboding spreading like thick curls of smoke into the darkest corners of my mind.

A MAN'S SCREAM ECHOES in the distance as snow gently falls from the night sky. It echoes somewhere throughout the valley until death claims him. My jaw ticks, hearing another life lost. I should have been there by now, and I would have if I were traveling alone.

"Who the fuck would think about traveling all the way up there?" Iván asks.

I look back to see his hand extended as he helps Crystal step over a fallen log. I knew they would slow me down. I'm surprised he can move under all those thick layers of fur and leather. That's probably the reason why it's taken us this long to get here. He doesn't seem to mind the fact that they're both matching, and I can only assume Crystal was behind that. I grunt in response before turning my attention up ahead.

Crystal has been so lost since Viona was taken, spending most of her days patrolling the palace's outer walls with Iván and Samuel. By night, she's been getting into bar fights. From what Samuel has told me, she's been dragging Iván along with her, too. I reminded him his little brother is quite capable of making decisions for himself; he has just as much hair on his balls as Samuel. We both had a good laugh at that one. And for a moment, the constant pain in my heart flutters because I know Viona would have been proud to hear me stick up for Iván.

Going up the mountain and back down is only a day's travel. The first part of this trip was full of Crystal and Iván trying to talk to me, presumably to keep my head distracted, but it only made my irritation grow. Now that night has fallen, they finally murmur among one another—if only they'd gotten the hint hours ago. I should have left alone, but Crystal needed to feel like she was helping. Even if I had to be annoyed with her constant questions for a day, as her brother, it is a small sacrifice I could make.

Something moves within the shadows, and I raise my hand to get their attention. We all go silent.

The scent of blood fills the air, setting us on guard. My breathing slows. As my senses open up, I can hear a faint, fast-paced heartbeat thrumming up ahead. I hold a finger up, then point again. A trail of blood mars the fresh snow. I kneel down cautiously, ensuring my leather boots don't rub together. With an ungloved hand, I drag my finger across a puddle of blood. It's still slightly warm to the touch. My eyes skim the ground. Judging by the deep handprints left in the snow, the body was dragged. Whoever this human was, they put up a fight.

We keep moving up the cliff's side. The temperature suddenly drops, and a gust of wind bristles between the pines. We wait for it to pass. It would only take one hard gale to throw anyone off. Looking ahead, the trail splits into two. We ascend the mountain, following the path hollowed out into a long tunnel.

"Fuck," I grunt, seeing a carcass lying up ahead. There's no need to check the man's pulse; I already know he's dead. I turn around and slowly shake my head at them. Crystal and Iván give a tight nod. My lips curve into a snarl when I notice remains of the man's heart lying not too far from his body. Disgusted, I stop in my tracks.

Crystal comes up beside me. "Those little bastards."

"What?" Iván pants as he catches up. His warm-russet skin is flushed from the uphill hike.

"Rose eaters," I groan, annoyed that these little fuckers are already awake for their nightly feeding. This is the exact reason I wanted to leave right after talking to my father.

Crystal sees the confusion and shock on Iván's face. "They are small, vile creatures who only kill for the heart, and unfortunately we can't kill them," she confirms.

Iván blinks back in disgust. "Why not?"

"Because you cannot kill what has been protected for centuries." Gareon stands at the end of the tunnel, responding to Iván though his amber gaze is locked on Crystal. His long, blue coat flaps in the sudden gust of wind funneling through. The three of us approach him. There's a glint in his eyes, but I'm distracted by the hairy little fucker nestled against his arm. Its golden, cat-like eyes widen as its small, sharp canines peek out. Gareon strokes its mismatched black-and-orange fur. The two of them seem unbothered by the dead body and remnants of a heart only feet away.

"You're safe now. I've let them know not to harm you," Gareon says.

My lips contort in disgust.

"I don't think he was talking to us," Iván drawls.

"I don't think so either." We both share a look. I find Gareon's communication with these *rose eaters* very peculiar.

"Ugh," Crystal grunts, stepping over the body to stand on the other side of him. "I still can't believe you like to pet those hairy things."

Gareon smirks. "Maybe you can think of other things you'd like to stroke if it helps ease your mind."

Crystal freezes. I can't see the expression on her face but I assume he made her cheeks flush by how fast she walks past him and out of the tunnel as Iván follows her.

My eyes bounce between the two of them. If any other man said that to her, their ass would be knocked to the ground within seconds. So why does this asshole get a pass? As soon as she leaves, my eyes flick to his, and I step into Gareon's personal space. He meets my glare with a grin, but I have a few inches of height on this bastard. She might be okay with what he said, but I am sure as shit not.

"You know why I named these little holy creatures 'rose eaters?'" Gareon smiles wide enough that the tips of his canines stick out. He strokes the hairy furball under its chin. It's now nudging its face between the locks of his hair.

"Why?" I snap.

"Because a rose and a heart are very similar. Both have many layers until you get to the center. Once you spend so much time peeling back all those layers, you seem to know every curve of its veins or every soft stroke of its petals."

Silence fills the air. I envision pulling out his heart to see if he is right.

"These *creatures* and I like to eat in the same manner. We take our time." He grins, knowing all too damn well what he's doing.

The creature in his hands purrs louder as the tension between us rises. I press a finger into his chest. The fire in his eyes ignites to that fiery blue, and every ancient marking on his body glows.

"You better be careful which roses you pick. You better be *damn* sure before you decide to peel back any of those layers," I warn, knowing all Crystal has endured in her lifetime.

"Not that I care what you think, Callian, but I'm nothing like you. I don't use the words driven from my loins to lure a woman, I use my heart." He sets the rose eater down. The creature begins purring and rubbing itself against his leg. "But," he drawls, "I consider myself a fair man, so I'll give credit where it's due. I've seen the change in you since Viona's arrival. It's good to see you using your heart more. She's training you well."

"Are you guys coming or what?" Iván calls out.

Gareon smiles. "Shall we?" He steps to the side, gesturing down the path. "It's not safe to travel here at night. Judging by the piece of labradorite in your pocket, your journey was worth the risk."

CHAPTER 48
CALLIAN

"**I**F YOU MAKE ME float, I'll kill you," I warn, remembering that sometimes people float in Gareon's mystical sphere. I need to keep my shit in check, though, because the last thing I should do is piss off the only person who can help me. Crystal and Iván saunter over to the kitchen area while Gareon stares at me from across the slab of stone, smirking.

"Oh, but pushing your buttons is so much fun," he drawls.

I scoff, extending my arm. A blue needle forms between his thumb and middle finger, allowing him to draw a few drops of blood from my fingertip. While he prepares, I adjust myself on a cushion, legs crossed, wondering how he can sit like this all the time. Especially when he spends hours in this position meditating.

Glancing over at Iván, I see he's making tea, navigating his way around Gareon's kitchen as if he already knows where everything is as Crystal casually discusses the new posts being set up outside the fortified walls of Callisto. The two have already made themselves comfortable. I adjust once more.

Though the kitchen area seems to be well kept, Gareon's tables and shelves mirror the same set up as his study at the palace. Organized chaos is what my father calls it. As my eyes skim over the endless scrolls and books, I'd have to agree.

I tend to forget how mesmerizing Gareon's home is; it's been quite some time since I've been here. The hearth is more of a visual comfort, as rare crystals and stones are the primary source of light. They illuminate each room with soft hues of blues, purples, and greens, reminding me of Callisto's skies in the winter. Despite being in the high altitude of Halos Mountain, it is quite warm inside thanks to the hidden hot spring. I, unfortunately, had to find this out the hard way while venturing through the tunnels. The memory of him bathing naked is forever etched into my mind. I blink back, wishing I could unsee the moment he rose from the water, uncaring that he was on full display.

"Are you done thinking about me naked, or do you need more time?" Gareon says, amused by my scowl. His face is half-illuminated by a blue aura casting off the crystals in the wall. The swirls on his body faintly glow against his skin. Fancy fuck.

"Let's begin," I reply.

"The labradorite," he requests. Long, moonlight-tipped fingernails drag across the back of my hand as he takes it. Together, my blood and the stone ignite. Violet flames lick the air, causing Crystal and Iván's conversation to cease as they watch the smoke curl to the ceiling. Gareon raises his hands. The swirls on his body grow brighter, and his eyes flare like sapphire flames. Crystal's mouth slightly parts in awe. I'll give it to him, he is impressive when you put aside the arrogant, demi-god complex. The sphere forms around us in a churning, blue-and-white light.

"It's been centuries since one of these was last seen. Only the gods above were known to possess labradorite. While it's found its way here, this stone carries the weight of darkness," Gareons observes. "This stone has its own capabilities. It holds not only magic, but strengthens the intuition of those who possess it—spiritual enlightenment and protection. It is another eye into the realms both above and below."

"When I touch the stone, it feels tainted somehow. As if remnants from the underworld lurk within," I reply, resting my chin on my knuckles.

He nods. "Also known as the Shadow Realm. I see that you've been reading. Good to know you're not just muscle and a pretty face." He smirks.

"Thanks for the backhanded compliment." I huff out a laugh.

Then, something glints in his eyes. "She has never mentioned Adnama to you." He holds my stare as he observes my reaction, as if he senses the sudden chill sweeping down my spine. As if he knows the name sends my heart racing. I lower my arm to my thigh.

"Not that she knows of," I admit. "I've heard her say that name before, while she slept." I comb a hand through my hair as the knot in my chest returns. I didn't think anything of it the first time, but it is a name I have seared to memory. I never mentioned I heard her, never once brought it up in case that name was tied to a bad memory. The nights where I held her in my arms as she cried in her sleep. I wish I could have done more for her. Jaw tensing, my fists tighten. I look to the side as my chest begins heaving.

"She didn't want you to know." Gareon cuts through the silence with a softer tone.

"How can you tell?" I reply. The words draw out like a punch to the gut, knowing she took on another silent burden—one she didn't have to face alone.

"People who have had a lifetime of pain do not always know how to share that with others. Sometimes they can't. It varies per person," Gareon says as if speaking from the heart. I nod in response.

"There is a reason you feel connected to this stone. The same reason people are connected to other things. There is energy everywhere we go. From the air we breathe, to the plants and trees, to the souls we meet and objects they possess."

His words hit me like ice. Gareon wills the stone to rise. With a gentle thrust of his palm, it floats gracefully back into my hand. Still warm from being lit by magic.

"This stone has so much of Viona inside it, and since you two have sealed your fate and completed the bond, you already know where to go," he drawls.

We stare at one other for a few moments. As the sphere begins to fall in a shimmering light, his blue eyes return to their usual fiery-amber hue. Simultaneously, a portal opens up behind me. My gaze flicks to my cloak hanging over a chair off to the side. A chilling gust of air hits my back, eyes still remaining on the cloak billowing in the wind.

I know what I have to do. I feel it in my bones. My fate has been calling to me since Viona was taken. There has always been that tethered pull since the day I met her. One I tried to ignore at first, thinking there must have been some mistake because she was just so fucking difficult. Now, it's as clear to me as the color of her eyes. Clear as the words Gareon spoke moments after he rushed into my room one night, watching the remnants of my dream drift on a light gust of wind out the window. The trail of shadows my vision left behind is the same one I have felt following me since. I knew there was always more beyond the two of us.

I glance over to Crystal, feeling guilt slice through me. Her head tips back in laughter with that bright smile stretching across her face as she talks to Iván.

"Watch over her for me," I say to Gareon. He turns toward her, hands clasped behind his back, catching that radiant smile of hers. I know that look. The way he studies every curve of her face. The same look I give Viona. For some reason, that gives me comfort.

"I will," he says, chest rising as he takes in a deep breath.

I gather my things, knowing he has extended his wards to conceal what I'm about to do. I fasten my cloak, secure my weapons, and slip the labradorite into a hidden pocket by my chest.

"Thank you for this, for everything. If she knew where I was going, she wouldn't let me leave without her." I meet his stare.

"I know," he replies, extending his hand for a firm shake. He then pulls me in for a hug. I tense for a moment, then my shoulders relax. When we pull away, his eyes flare with warning. "Be careful, be strong, and let your instincts guide you. Say her name when you arrive. She will find you."

A FRESH LAYER OF SNOW coats the ground of the White Forest. The silence is almost as chilling. As I pull the hood over my head, I'm reminded of how dangerous it can be. It beckons the beat of my heart, the blood in my veins, calling me to this place so many fear. What I fear most, though, is never seeing Viona again. Every breath I have taken, every decision I've made has been for her. I'd do it all over again just to see her smile, to see those rare moments where she finds peace. I long to see her dancing in the light again, as she had in the tavern. The freedom she seemed to feel while the music moved through her body as her soul ascended to the beat. Every sway of her hips drove me to madness that night. That is where I strive to find her. Not locked up in some fucking dungeon her father placed her in. I can sense through the bond that is where he has her.

I tread deeper into the woods, working my way through the twisted, uprooted limbs, searching for the woman who roams this place. The terrain is thick at first, but then the birch trees fan out to surround a clearing. The sound of metal cuts clean through the air as I unsheathe my sword. The labradorite hums against my chest as the faint sound of music begins to play—the same melody Viona and I danced to at the ball. Chills sweep down my body. I'm caught in a cataclysmic daydream of inner longing for her while fighting back the bitter cold against my face. The memory dances across my mind as the violin strings hum, spiraling me into a melodic twister. I am lost in her, with thoughts of being inside her that night. Candlelight illuminates the silhouette of her body and her beautiful face. Those bright-blue eyes upturned at the corners are heated with lust. I'm swimming in her serenity while our rawest selves move together. My hands grip her thighs, a nice handful, as her nipple falls into my mouth, surrounded by the sweetness of her skin.

The ringing in my ears pulls me from thought, away from Viona and her decadent smell of vanilla and roses. I blink back, trying to keep my shit together while looking into the distance. The thick haze has returned, and beyond it, a silhouette appears. It's her.

"Viona." My breath hits the air in a frothy mist.

It's her. Standing in the middle of the forest, shrouded in white, her jet-black hair blowing wildly across her face as a hard gust of wind funnels behind her.

"Viona!" My voice thunders across the way, but she remains in place. I continue calling her name against the roaring winds, shielding my eyes from the snow. I can barely see her. Another strong gale of wind pushes me forward, coaxing me to run. I move as fast as I can through every step; every second is just as freeing as the last.

When I reach her, just moments from touching her, she disappears. My fists clench together. Anger flows through my veins.

An illusion. This was all just a fucking illusion. This forest is cursed. It's messing with my head.

"Fuck!" I yell, kicking the ground while rage rips through my throat, creating deep, thickest vines through my heart.

Then it hits me like a cold sheet of ice. I know.

I know it's her.

She is fucking with my head—taking the weakest part of me and throwing it in my face. I remove the stone from my pocket, clenching it in my hands.

"ADNAMA!" My voice thunders throughout the woods, causing snow to fall from some of the branches.

I turn around, looking in all directions.

"I know you're here!" I growl, combing a hand through my hair. "This place is a fucking *tomb*."

The ground stirs beneath my feet. Before I can step out of their path, roots protrude through the ground, breaking the frozen layer of ice.

"What the . . . "

Vines snake up my sides, wrapping around my arms until I'm suspended in the air. I've seen these before. The day Viona was taken.

My eyes narrow in on their dark color. They were helping us as Solas' men disappeared into the Shadow Realm.

"There aren't many people who know me by name. Yet, here you are, yelling it as if you've come to harm me." Adnama says as the wind flows through her sheer, ivory gown.

My head whips up. She moves with fluid grace as if she is swimming beneath waves. Her eyes black as the night sky. One might throw themselves into her storm; it is beautiful and horrifying at the same time. The gravitational pull, undeniable.

Adnama stands twenty feet away. A chill sweeps down my back, feeling the sheen of sweat above my brow. The way she smiles squeezes all the air out of my lungs.

"Quite the brave prince. A woman might kill for a man like you," Adnama drawls.

Within a blink of an eye, she's in front of me.

"Put me down," I sneer. The vines, *her vines*, stroke the column of my neck as those obsidian eyes rake over my body, watching the rise and fall of my chest, studying the pulse in my veins. She walks around me, all while my heart is pounding against my rib cage. For some reason, I cannot take my eyes off of her.

She smirks. "Your persistence is very alluring. The devotion, the lust, the rage, the *revenge*," she whispers, her brows slightly arching while she speaks. "I can feel it deep within your roots, the bond." She holds my stare watching me try to navigate through these feelings of familiarity with her, this connection. "Give me the stone," Adnama demands.

I give a tight nod, hoping to the stars I won't fuck this up. The vines around my arms loosen enough for me to retrieve it from my pocket. The palm of my hand opens, and she takes it. The moment she glances at the stone, the vines withdraw, settling me back onto the ground. This confirms my suspicion that the stone would give me safe passage this time. When she looks up at me, a pair of deep-mahogany eyes stare back.

The subtle changes to her features remind me that, once upon a time, she was alive. Before she was this, her skin might have been a soft, light brown. She must sense my prying eyes, but says nothing as a gust of wind drifts between us.

"Where is she?" she asks. There's a soft shudder in her next breath.

Another chill rushes up my body. "She was taken to her father," I confirm.

"King Mal Tarvas." She seethes, looking at the ground. Moments pass without any words. Then, she looks up at me again. "He has what he wants. You are not strong enough to help her. If he kills her, this is it. It is all over, and everything she worked for and everyone she loves will be destroyed. We are teetering on a ledge and cannot let the prophecy be on his side."

"You're connected with her, aren't you?" I observe, nostrils flaring, teeth gritting as moments stretch on. The feeling grows the more I watch her movements, the more she continues to stare at me in a way that makes me feel like she can see inside my soul. I have no other fucking clue to how I know this other than it could be the bond I share with Viona.

"In many ways, more than the both of you know." She smirks.

"What are you saying?" I don't care for the games this woman keeps playing.

She walks around me, dragging her long fingernail across my back to the front of my shoulder. "How far are you willing to dip your hands into the dark?" she whispers into my ear. I close my eyes. The knot in my chest returns, squeezing all the air in my lungs. Hidden beneath her smooth, ethereal voice is Viona's, lulling me into the depths of my mind. "Would you do anything for her?"

My pulse slows to a calm. "Anything." I exhale. "I would do anything for her." The words leave my lips like a vow.

Without hesitation, Adnama rises above the ground. The wind blows the hood away from my face, and she presses her hands on my head. A searing pain bolts through my body like lightning. She opens my mind, infusing all her visions into me, spreading like a fissure of light across my eyes and down my body.

Truth.

The truth is unveiled. I see it now—her connection with Viona. Adnama's voice drips into the cracks of my mind as black tendrils of smoke fill my eyes. Every part of Viona is raging inside me like an inferno. Viona is a flame under the moon of fire and sea; Adnama floods the gates with earth and wind. Two demi-gods, two sisters, twins, always turned toward each other, separated by realms.

My head tilts up toward the sky as a scream rips from my throat. I ascend into the air with Adnama. An illuminating light surrounds us. I see it all: the prophecy, the blood moon, their birth, King Mal Tarvas, the sacrifice. Tears brim my eyes.

"No," I shudder, seeing Adnama's sacrifice. This is all too much. "No!" My voice thunders across the forest, knowing I can't do anything about it. I see her rebirth, the protection spell that bound her to this forest. Cursed. This was all a curse. Their pain burns through my body like acid rain because of their father—a dark lord, a deceiver.

"Find her," Adnama says. "Tell me where she is."

I search through the bond, reaching out to Viona, calling to her from the depths of my mind. My soul searches past the White Forest, through the darkened valleys of Sao, and through the walls of her broken kingdom. I harness every ounce of our connection to see exactly where she is. The wind in the White Forest picks up, spinning in an unwavering force around us.

I see her, Viona, hidden in a secret part of the castle. I see her exact location. Her wrists are bound in chains cast with something ancient to weaken her powers. My heart plummets. The fucking bastard has her chained.

"No . . . " I growl, discovering more to what has always been hidden beyond the veil. It cuts through me like a blade. Seeing what is to come, and all she will have to do.

I yell, and the ground shakes. Light emits from my chest, sending a powerful blast across the frozen woods. Trees snap like twigs, crashing violently onto the ground.

"Do you see why you were brought here? Why you are fated to her?"

"I see it." The light in my eyes dim as the two of us descend. Dropping to my knees, all I can do is shake my head, trying to come to terms with... with fucking everything.

"I've been living in these woods for as long as I can remember. I didn't understand it at first, why I was here. Until I had a vision when I was small. I saw a woman, my mother. That's when I tried to leave, but I couldn't." She stares off as if lost in memory. "Then, one day, it all hit me. Visions of how I was sacrificed and remade—bound to the White Forest. To this day, I hear whispers of what the people of these lands think of me. It's true, I am the one who guards this place, but there is far more than what meets the eye here."

Silence hangs in the air for a moment, with only the sounds of the wind drifting between us. Then she continues. "The closer we get to the Blood Moon, the more my connection to Viona grows. Your vision confirms my suspicions of her whereabouts. Our connection has been blocked since she's been taken, and I can't—" She pauses, and it's the first time she's shown any kind of emotion. Distress. "I can't see my mother in my visions." Her words strain, but she looks up at me. "Those chains are cast with a power you cannot break. I'm the only one who can save her, but I cannot leave unless someone who is connected to Viona takes my place . . . "

My chin lifts as I wear a knit expression, fists clenched. I know where this is headed.

"The wind you carry in your soul will allow me to travel faster. That bond you share will be the guiding light to find her. She will be free to harness her powers and stop King Tarvas. In exchange for her freedom, you will live between worlds for eternity."

"She is going to endure *so much pain*," I whisper, unable to stop my mind from reeling. "But, I know what must be done," I state.

Adnama appears ten feet away. A black pool of liquid forms between us—boiling and popping in thick bubbles of tar. Black shadows curl up, churning into many faces that fade into a smoked blur.

My love for Viona will move through the stars and carry me onto my next journey. I take in a deep breath, exhaling the heat I feel swarming in my chest, ready to explode.

I unsheathe their mother's dagger that I kept fastened to my side and hand it to Adnama.

"Do it," I growl, determination and loss hitting my veins like ice and burning them with wrath.

She drags a deep cut along both my forearms. Blood drips off my flesh and into the shadows.

White, it's all I see, dropping to my knees at the blinding pain. A growing chasm courses through my body. My hand dips further into the pool of darkness, and I feel it—the bond, the connection with Viona—being tethered to Adnama. What was once filtered through a golden light now runs thick and all-consuming, shooting up my veins like fire and ash. Adnama takes the dagger and drives it into my heart. A roar tears through me as my body writhes. Obsidian tendrils vein up my forearms.

Adnama takes a piece of me. The part that belonged to Viona. The winds that promised to take her on that adventure, the one we will never get to see. It's fleeting as I succumb to the depths of my mind.

I open my eyes, seeing snow gently falling around us.

Ash, it's all turning into ash.

This place is already shifting as I teeter between worlds. Adnama takes my sword and knights me in her place. The labradorite, Viona's piece of labradorite, was welded by the chasm's shadows into the hilt. Black smoke curls around the blade.

I'm slipping further into the dark.

"I need you to tell her something." I swallow the lump forming in my throat. "Tell her I love her, to keep going. Tell her I said, 'Do not stop, do not yield, and live.'"

I can feel my soul leaving my body, and my eyes flutter to the back of my head. Our bond now blinding, as fissures of shadows drag across every tethered cord and pull me apart from the inside.

"Go." My chest heaves. "Save her."

Adnama takes my love for Viona, and under the guise of wind, she disappears.

Everything begins to fade. The White Forest is changing. Or is it I who is leaving this realm?

I would become what people fear. I would become anything Viona needs me to be. All-consuming, I let the darkness fill my eyes.

I become the shadow.

I become death.

For my love, I transform into the darkest force the Shadow Realm will ever see.

CHAPTER 49
VIONA

T HIS ALL FEELS LIKE an illusion. One big, fucked-up nightmare I can't seem to shake. I close my eyes, focusing on the sound of waves crashing against the cliffs. I've spent my whole life listening to the same waters with a piece of my heart missing. All this time, my mother was right here. I shudder as guilt pierces my heart.

There's a dark storm looming over Sao. Glimpses of my mother in the cell next to mine flash with the lightning. Somewhere between the weight of my eyelids drifting shut and the thunder rattling the ground, the pounding in my head remains constant. It's maddening. My head is foggy. The back of my eyes fucking burn.

When was the last time I truly slept? I exhale sharply.

It was with Callian.

I searched for him twice through the bond, the thread that held us together. Somehow, thank the gods above, I caught a glimpse of him. However, both times I soul searched, they were only flashes of a picture. The first time, he was in bed, healing. The second was of him going up Halos Mountain with Crystal and Iván. I wondered where they were going.

My mother's dry, delicate hand sticks halfway into my cell. She can't quite make the reach. Her dainty, little wrists are frail enough to snap. My lips quiver. I shift my body closer, angling myself on the pile of hay until my head is resting against the iron bars. They're cold to the touch, but I welcome it. The tips of her fingers brush my knee. When she wakes, I'll be a little closer for her.

She hasn't said much since I arrived. She's weak. I fear a part of her was always dying. My last memories of her being alive—rosy cheeks and soft hair—marred by turmoil as if I'm locked away with the ghost of her.

We are almost completely in the dark, save for the small window in each of our cells that seem to have been carved by madness and desperation. I need to rest and get control of myself, but I'm afraid if I close my eyes, she might disappear, and I'll wake up in this cell alone without her on the other side of the bars. Every time I close my eyes, I'm reminded of the black, murky haze of all my memories here.

The only way to protect myself is by locking up all these thoughts, pushing them so far from reach that the temptation will cease to exist. No matter what I do, having nothing but time on my hands, all I see is my mother. She's alive. While my prison was in my mind, hers was here. I shudder at the thought.

Nausea eases its way back up my stomach. Even if I do hurl, there's not much to expel. I've barely eaten, and the food they did send down was fucking trash. If I sit here and allow myself to think too much about it, about everything, the heavy swells of fear will rise.

I can't lose myself. Not now.

I try to think of the moments when I felt whole. Most of those memories are with Callian. A smile tips my lips, thinking of us in the White Forest. The look on Callian's face when I called his home a dungeon. I stifle a laugh, looking at the conditions I'm currently in as a tear streams down my face. My gods, I was so wrong. It was a mindless insult he didn't deserve, and now... Now, I'd do anything to say I'm sorry. But I know him, he would remind me I never have to say that, followed by an inappropriate comment of how I could make it up to him if I truly felt that bad. The moment I allowed myself to escape is fleeting as the pain in my wrists returns. The magic cast in these chains is suffocating, and my restraints pull taut against every fiber of my powers. The flames flowing through my veins remain idle, churning like hot lava while my body begs for a release. Air burns as it moves through my lungs. I rub my hands together, massaging my palm with my thumb to smooth out the itching pain that wants to ignite.

My eyes drift to my mother again. Her breath, light and steady. She's dreaming. I hope her mind is at peace and she's far away from here. My throat swells, wishing I could join her wherever she is in her dreams.

In a place where she can swim and extend her arms out into the light, where her skin is warm from too much sun and her belly is full of all the rich foods she can eat. Somewhere between thinking of her on the beach and being safe in Callian's arms, I'm lulled to sleep.

"Viona. Viona, wake up." Someone is shaking my leg. The familiarity in the woman's sharp, pointy fingers sends my heart racing. My eyes fling open, blinded by the sun beaming through the windows, casting small prisms of light in the woman's wild curls. The headache returns, and hunger gnaws at my stomach.

"Alyce?" I whisper, taking a moment to realize this is real, and somehow in my cell with the door wide open. Finding my strength, I rise to my feet. "Alyce!" My voice shakes. I reach out to her, chains and all, but she pushes her hands out to stop me.

"Shhh! Quiet girl, or you will have me as a new roommate," she shoots back in warning, a tone so cold and scathing that I pause and withdraw my hand to my chest. My brows slam together in reaction to her tight and tense expression.

Then, it hits me.

Emotions spill over, wanting to sever all kind thoughts I've ever had for her.

"How could you allow this to happen?" I snap, hearing the dryness in my voice. I'm parched, and my lips are so dry and cracked that little needles prickle along them as I talk. I quickly draw them in to dampen them. Then my attention shifts to my mother who is now awake from the commotion. She's slowly trying to sit up.

In an instant, Alyce's eyes grow hazy. "I didn't know, Viona. I swear, I never knew she was here. I never knew." She takes a step forward, reaching for me as she repeats herself.

My chin lifts. All the warmth I'd normally have for her turns into a cold glare. "Are you here to set us free?" I hiss, taking a step back.

She begins rubbing her hands. "I'm working on it," she says, stealing another glance at my mother.

"Why can't it be now?" I demand. "The door is wide open."

"There are too many guarding the area. Solas' men are everywhere."

I remain silent, studying the expression on Alyce's face, looking for any cracks in her façade.

Fuck.

I exhale, realizing I don't have a gods-damn choice but to trust her word.

"The only comfort I can give the both of you right now is to move you into her cell. The guards who bring you your food gave me their word they won't say anything. At least the two of you will be closer together while I try to figure something out."

I let her words hang in the air as I try to do some sorting of my own. It isn't good enough, but it's all we have.

"Alright." My lips press thin.

Alyce peeks her head down the small walkway before jerking her head for me to follow. The guard opens my mother's cell. I stand outside the door, looking down the darkened hall, feeling the light breeze hit my face.

"Viona," Alyce calls.

I walk into my mother's cell, relieved we can be together without cast-iron bars between us.

"My daughter," she says, wrapping her arms around my waist. Chains clank between us.

Alyce shuffles behind me. A big pile of hay is thrown next to my mother's. Alyce dusts herself off and steps further inside. I can feel her eyes sweeping over us, and soon, another pair of arms wrap around us.

"I'm so sorry, girls." Alyce stifles a sob. "I have failed you both." I close my eyes, embracing the family I thought I had lost—a godsend in the middle of a nightmare.

My mother shakes her head. "No, no you didn't. He failed us. He failed us all."

As always, Alyce's visit was short-lived. Not too long after she left, the guard brought down extra food. I never knew coffee and an apple could bring me so much comfort. My mother and I eat in silence, a strange peace settling over me. Though her hands shake, she is equally enjoying the extra food. I watch her shove it into her mouth. Her nails are overgrown, some broken off. Her hair hangs in long knots around her face. It's so painful to see her this way, but I'm happy I have her.

"I can't explain it," I say, shaking my head as I set the cup down onto the floor.

She flinches, drawing her eyes to my mouth and every hand movement I make. For a moment, I question her coherency. I repeat myself. My head turns slightly, observing her. Her eyes find mine again as the confusion fades and she meets my stare with a smile.

"Explain what, my love?"

I revel again in the sight of her chest rising and falling. *Alive, she's alive.*

"The shock I feel because you're alive." A tight smile quirks my lips.

Her expression suddenly changes again.

"What is it, Mama?"

She softly exhales. "He wasn't always like this," she says, struggling to swallow the lump in her throat as she stares at a small streak of water dripping down the wall.

"My father?"

"Yes."

We let the faint sound of the ocean beyond our cell fill the silence—a growing comfort I find solace in. I take another bite of my apple.

"Long ago, when I was younger, I believed he did love me. Once upon a time." Her voice trails off as the memories come flooding in. "He told me he'd searched many lifetimes for me. At first, I thought it was romantic. I believed it. For a time, I truly felt it. Until one day, it all started to shift. I was pregnant, and something gleamed in his eyes.

Then he changed. That's when I started having more dreams, the same ones I told you about as a child."

"Yes, I remember. You told me you felt your time here would be short," I say, scooting closer to her as I try to mask the pain behind those memories.

She looks at me wide-eyed. Her breathing stills, causing me to stop eating. I set my apple onto my lap. She looks as though she's afraid to let her next words escape. She reaches for me. Though her bones look brittle, her touch is firm, reminding me a piece of her might still be inside. My hands clasp around hers.

"I wish I could have told you, Viona. I'm so sorry I couldn't." She pauses as if searing my face to memory and cups my cheek, shaking her head. "I'm so sorry."

My chest tightens, closing my eyes at her touch, one I've longed for ever since the day she died. A tear slips free, dropping onto her hand.

"You don't have to be sorry, Mama."

She shakes her head. "No." Her voice is nothing but a soft whisper. "There is so much more, my beautiful girl. I just hope by the end of my story, you won't grow to hate me."

CHAPTER 50

VIONA

"**I** DON'T UNDERSTAND." I shake my head, confused.

"In my dreams, I saw both of you—one with eyes as bright as the sky, and the other with eyes as dark as the soil of Vendrelle. Glimpses of your destiny flashed before me, but I never really understood how or why."

A cold chill sweeps down my spine only to rise back up with nausea. "What do you mean by *both?*" I ask, feeling my pulse rise as my breathing deepens. The slight tremor in my hands has returned, so I clasp them together.

"Two heartbeats were growing inside of me. People said you would arrive early." She smiles, rubbing the phantom swell of her belly, but the light in her eyes quickly dims. "I knew in my soul that you would be born on the blood moon. One of my dreams told me a sacrifice would be made to regain what was once lost. One of you was chosen for life, the other for death, but I couldn't wrap my head around it, no matter how hard I tried."

I squeeze her hands, trying to remain calm while she gathers her strength, but my hands can't stop shaking after hearing that word.

Both.

The anticipation grows agonizing as she slowly takes a sip of her water.

"I couldn't face the possibility of losing a child. In my desperation, I used dark magic forbidden by the gods above. The one chosen for death would become the guardian of the White Forest. This was better than being gone forever. She would be bound between two worlds, ours and the Shadow Realm. I put this protection spell on you both while you were growing inside me, not knowing which one it would be. The night I went into labor, I was so out of it and in so much pain from the delivery. Then, my worst fear came true. I was told one of you had died. The pain I had to endure, thinking, 'Why was I sent that warning if I couldn't do anything about it?' When I saw you for the first time, the one with azure eyes, my heart tore in two. I told no one about my dreams or the prophecies surrounding your birth. They were only words to me, because all I wanted to do was be a mother and the queen of Sao. To your father's disappointment, no powers awakened. I often questioned my sanity, wondering if all of this was an illusion because something was still looming over me. Then, on the night of your tenth birthday, *she* came to me in my dreams to warn me."

A flutter of energy prickles my skin. My mother runs a hand down her arm, soothing the same chill.

"Who, Mama?" I stifle a sob.

Her brows knit as she continues without acknowledging my question. "I saw her standing in the White Forest. The same age as you, growing as you did, but bound by the haze. My protection spell worked, but she'd never be able to leave."

My chest began heaving. "Adnama . . . " My voice cracks, connecting why I felt that familiarity when I looked into her eyes, why she follows me and continues to guide and protect me from those who seek harm. My stomach turns as I begin reeling back to the dark silhouette that stood behind me in the vision with Gareon.

His words echo. *A shared power.*

My sister.

"Your other half. Twins, but not identical," she clarifies, tucking a strand of hair behind my ear. "The closer we get to the blood moon, the stronger your powers and connection with her will grow," she confirms while studying me.

My mind flashes back to Rossburn and his men. Every one of those guards' lives slipped into Adnama's vengeful grip. She took their souls while trying to save me, just like every single time she'd appeared in warning.

"In that first dream, Adnama showed me what your father did the day you were born. The sacrifice. He walked away thinking she was dead. There was something different, and I . . . " She takes a pause. Tears are streaming down my face, now knowing all that she has been through. "Since then, I have only been able to see her in my dreams and only glimpses of you.

"That night, I woke up screaming, crying, rejoicing, and feeling the skies and the depths of the underworld crashing down on me all at once because I saw her. That's when everything became clear, as if an ancient part of myself had been unlocked, freed. That looming feeling came to light, flooding into me like crashing waves of knowledge about who your father truly is. The fallen god who was made into a dark lord. I went after him as soon as I awoke, searching through the castle late that night. When our eyes finally locked, I knew we were star-crossed, never destined to be together other than to live to watch our world fall apart. That's when he knew he not only needed you, he needed me too."

"If I ever found her again, I would know great sorrow." King Tarvas' words echo in the back of my mind, haunting me, forcing me to recall the moment I lay in the throne room with my mother at his feet.

My heart pounds as hard as a war drum.

"There are consequences for love bound in darkness," my mother says as if she can hear my thoughts. "The first blood moon after your twentieth birthday is when he can reclaim what was his. Which is why he kept me alive all this time."

"How?" I ask, voice trembling. "How can he get his powers back?" This can't be real.

"He has to kill us before the blood moon rises. The gods from above spread your father's powers within us all—you, me, and Adnama—but you were chosen to take it back. In order for you to get your full powers, it is you who has to kill me. I am the last piece for you to claim what is yours so you can stop him. The gods have blessed you to save Vendrelle."

Cursed, is this what we have always been? Anger gnaws at my guts and moves through my veins. My palms are slick with sweat. The inferno brewing inside me needs to be released. A searing pain follows, feeling the shackles react to my powers.

"No," I sob, staring down at the ground before I meet her bright eyes. "No," I bite back. "I won't do it." I pull my hands away from hers, unwilling to grasp the reality of what she's saying.

She takes my hand and places it over her chest. Her body is so frail to the touch.

"Listen," she whispers, her heart thrumming against my fingertips. With an enigmatic force, her soul calls me like the sea caught between two worlds. I suck in a sharp breath, feeling the connection, one that shackles cannot seize. My gaze flicks to hers.

"It was you," I gasp, reeling back to all my visions and dreams of the crimson glow floating idly beneath the waves. The veil has always been waiting to be pulled back, but I never knew it was waiting for the touch of my hands. I close my eyes. My mind opens up the chasm of time. This place, the ocean, it's what she's longed for. She meets my stare, wiping the tears off my cheek. I understand what must be done, but my heart doesn't want to comply. This is all too much for me to bear.

Suddenly, the air shifts. All the little hairs on the nape of my neck rise.

Adnama.

Her voice is everywhere and all around me, whispering in every corner of this cell and my mind, *"Viona . . . "*

"Do you hear her?" my mother says, closing her eyes—succumbing to the serenity of her daughter's voice. "She's here." She smiles, becoming lost somewhere inside her head. I can only assume it's the only place they could truly be together all this time. I become still, drawing in every sound.

"What the...Who the fuck are—" a guard says. His body drops to the ground. Dead on sight.

Another guard unsheathes his weapon. Bones crack, and the clamor of his blade reverberates throughout the hall, followed by a deep, guttural sound that expels out of him as if his soul has been taken. I find satisfaction in the melody of their demise—hearing each one fall for what they have done, not only to me but to my mother.

All this time, she's been here.

Rising to my feet, the tremor in my core grows with anticipation of feeling the connection with Adnama. As it's pushing against the shackles of these chains, she carries something with her . . . wind.

"Callian," I whisper. *Is he here, too?* My heart begins to race.

One of the men who guards the cells draws his sword. "I'd stay the fuck away if I were you, dead witch," he calls out. An aura illuminates his body as he casts himself in a sapphire glow. The light filters in, stopping at the tip of my boots. A protection spell?

Adnama laughs. "I believe that belongs to me."

"What does?" he sneers.

"Your life." His magic turns against him into a thousand shards of glass. His eyes grow wide in horror as every pointed tip is directed at him. One second. That's all it takes for them to pierce into every pore of his flesh. Blood mists the air. She steps over the mangled pieces of what made him whole and sends a powerful force of wind to break the entryway of the iron cell.

There's a faint humming in the air. A scaffolding truth as Adnama steps into our cell and meets my stare straight on with brown penetrating eyes. Our father's eyes, except there are no speckles of amber to count, just a boundless dark looming. I step forward, studying her. From the curves of her face, to the shape of her eyes—upturned at the corners—to her brows, seeing pieces of me, in her. Her jet-black hair looks as thick as mine. Her white dress shrouds her frame, billowing in the slight breeze. We have the same shape, though I'm slightly thicker and her breasts are larger. Without thinking, I reach for her cheek as if who stands before me is an illusion. Her skin gives off a slight warmth that affirms this is reality. I sense the ashes in her veins, but she's further from death and closer to life now, based on the coloring of her skin, a part of her that belongs to our father.

"Adnama, my . . . " My voice trails off. The shackles clang together, a bitter reminder, swaying between us.

"Sister," she finishes my sentence. Lavender fills the air with a soft caress against my senses.

"All this time, it was you, wanting to help me," I say, still not believing what's unfolding.

"In the only way I could." Her voice is soft, almost as quiet as the silence that hung over the White Forest.

Adnama holds my stare as if a piece of her has returned from being lost between the realms. A small glimpse of humanity, one that quickly fades when she wraps her hands around my wrists. Something foreign glints in her eyes as if she recognizes the magic. With a gentle hush of wind, the shackles crack open, falling onto the floor. A faint smile curves her lips. I feel the rush of my powers surging through me in a smooth, decadent release. My strength is slowly returning. I wrap my arms around her. She goes rigid against the sudden contact, but as moments pass, the tension eases in her shoulders, and she returns my embrace. We are reunited. So much time was lost between us and separated by realms, a curse, living in a haze at the expense of greed.

Our father's lies kept us apart, but there's something else inside my sister—something nearly tangible in the faint scent of cedar, and . . . my breathing stills.

"Where's Callian? Why isn't he here?" I take a step back, desperately searching her eyes for an immediate answer, but her smile fades. Fear gnaws at my gut.

"This belongs to you," she says. My mother's dagger appears in the palm of her hand.

"No." I stumble back, unable to breathe, hesitant to take it. I can't seem to catch my breath as my eyes bounce between her and the dagger. My stomach turns. I slowly reach out and grip it in my hand. A wave of chilled panic shudders down my spine.

I can't breathe.

Callian's voice echoes in a faint whisper, a memory from when we were in the Alora Archives as he leaned over me, eyes warm as he whispered, *"Love that cuts like knives."*

A vision rushes through me in a clouded haze: Adnama using my mothers dagger, slicing down his forearms. Blood spilling out in pulsating waves into a pool of darkness.

"No!" I suck in a sharp breath, seeing the moment she stabs him in the heart.

"Tell her I love her . . . " His silhouette fades into a mist of shadows.

"The prophecy." My voice cracks as my words expel the truth my mind refuses to believe. I fucking know this is exactly what he would do. I clench my chest, feeling all the pent-up power returning with nothing but scorching rage. Fire ignites in my hands, and I feel the torrential winds of an inferno swelling beneath my skin. Blind with rage, every moment feels like a whip across my back, tearing open my insides.

The clamor of chains dropping to the ground pulls me from thought. My head whips around to find my mother and Adnama embracing in a hug. One that they must have been longing for their entire lives. While their world is coming together, mine is falling apart before my eyes.

Adnama turns to me and says, "He sacrificed himself to save you and Mother. It was the only way."

I let Adnama's voice fade into the background.

"I loved him," I whisper, staring down at the dagger as a small, filtered beam of light glints against the blade.

My mother looks over Adnama's shoulder, and I can already see the color returning to her face. Her light skin is flushed with the same rose undertones I remember from my childhood.

"I'm sorry, Viona." Our mother walks over to me, embracing me in that firm hug. "I'm so sorry. But our window of time is fleeting. We have to go. Callian would've died for nothing if we don't leave now." She grabs my wrists, somehow unaffected by the flames in my palms, and stares into my eyes intensely. "Save your chaos for your father."

The inevitable returns like a slap in the face, knowing what is to come. Reality burns through my mind quicker than I can grasp. The calm in her face is clear.

She's tired. I know her next words before she says them.

My mothers eyes warm as she says, "The blood moon will rise tonight. Take me to the shores of Sao, and set me free."

WE SPEND THE LAST FEW hours of daylight hidden inside an alcove offshore, waiting for dusk so we can slip out into the shadows and make our way to the ocean. We speak softly to one another. The guilt-stricken expression behind my mother's eyes shudders my core. I'm slipping, seeing she already grieves for us. The gleam in her eyes holds stories I won't ever get to hear. She will leave us. Again. My heart strains against the truth, but as I sit here awaiting her fate and giving her faint smiles, I know what's coming. I clasp my hands together, trying to conceal the slight tremor of dread that has been coming in constant waves.

While we share a few quiet laughs, the pressure rises faster than the tide. Adnama is devoid of emotion, but I can sense her foundation cracking. Beneath the rage, she waits. Vengeance fills her eyes . . . and may the gods help us all when she releases it.

My mother looks at the both of us, eyes lowering. "It's time, my girls." She reaches for us, just as she did in the vision I had while she stood at the sea. My heart plummets to the ground as we rise. My world is shifting upside down. I've lost and gained so much in my short lifetime. *So much, just to lose it all again. I fear, this time, I will lose myself.*

The countdown begins. My mother holds our hands as we walk out of the alcove. Her ragged, beige dress flows behind her. I'm stuck in an hourglass—every grain of sand pelts against my beating heart.

Our mother squeezes our hand, a firm grip as she smiles back at us. The creases in her eyes pinch. "Be strong for me one last time," she says. I swallow the lump lodged in my throat and give her a tight nod.

The waves are calm, and a faint haze settles above the sea. Death is waiting, but our mother is ready to go home. The air hums as every beat of my heart remains weighted. There's still a burn in every breath I take, an inferno building inside, waiting for its release. In the stillness, I feel the connection to our mother growing. The beat of her heart synchronizes with mine, and I look at Adnama who can't keep her eyes off her. We both stare in waiting. I don't know what this will mean for Adnama or her fate beyond this, but I would love to somehow freeze what little time we have, store it in the back of my mind, and save it for a rainy day.

Our mother faces the sea. The three of us stand in formation—a triangle in the water. As the waves lap against our ankles, the tide is rising. She squeezes our hand once more.

"Time was never on our side," our mother says as she closes her eyes briefly, listening to the crashing waves. When her eyes flutter open, they sing with so much love and pride as she looks at us.

My mind is underwater. I fear I might learn to breathe beneath the waves if I am forced to keep swimming. There is no wind, just a faint breeze of cedar brushing my skin like a kiss. It's soft and delicate enough to remind me to breathe, soothing me just enough to get through this.

My mother hands me the dagger. The knot in my chest thickens, sinking me further into the darkest parts of my mind.

"I can't do this." I drop to my knees, unscathed by the water's frigid temperature as it swirls around my legs. "I can't do this!" I bite down on each word, sobbing. "I can't lose you again. I won't. I've lost so much already."

But we know there was never a tomorrow for us. Nothing will stretch beyond this moment but more scars.

She hands me the blade. "Take what has always been yours. As strong as you are right now, you cannot fight him and win. You need to come into your full powers." she reminds me, her eyes beg for that release. "This world was never meant for me. It was meant for you. You are destined to rise, so do it. Do it for me."

I feel the dagger turning hot in my hands. I can't stop the tears from falling, and I'm afraid our last moments will become a blur. I rise to my feet, gripping the hilt so tightly, the cracks on my knuckles split. I feel the air hit my dry flesh in stinging waves.

She grasps my hand, holding the blade to her stomach. My breaths become heavy. My eyes bounce between Adnama and her. I give a tight nod.

"I love you both. There is nowhere to go but onward," she says. Words spoken like a true warrior. Her jaw flexes with the rising anticipation. Through this all, she has shown stoicism and strength. She is not only my mother but a fighter, the queen of Sao. I see the bravery in her eyes, the unwavering dedication, like a beam of light that I will search for to guide me.

I strangle a sob, feeling the blade cut cleanly into her flesh. A guttural sound escapes as her eyes light up. The warmth of her blood spills over the top of my hand, cascading in pulsating waves. A cry rips from Adnama's throat, seeing our mother's body fall back. The black tendrils along Adnama's skin darken. She catches our mother before she falls, and we hold her up above the waves as water laps against her back. An aura illuminates around her, shimmering in a silver light spreading throughout her body.

She was never meant to be ours, and I will no longer keep her hidden in the back of my mind. I have to let her go, and so we do, as the gravitational pull of the moon moves her through the water.

I look at Adnama, her eyes are brimming with tears. Even the darkest of souls have somebody they love, and for Adnama, that was her, our mother. There is a calm and peace as we feel her take her final breath. It disperses in faint speckles of light, casting all around her body. The semblance of her fades, rising above the water and ascending into the air, sweeping the remnants of her soul across the ocean. The wind carries her to the moon, where her spirit will remain our guiding light. Our mother took our love and turned it into the stars that surround us.

I take a few steps back with my chest heaving, looking at my sister. Her dark eyes widen as she presses her hands against her chest and stumbles back against the receding waves. The weight of our world has shifted once more. There's no escaping what's to come.

I pull myself to shore, the water weighing down each step. When I reach the sand, my knees buckle, and my body lunges forward. All I can do is cover my face and scream. I'm screaming at the top of my lungs, sounds I would have never thought I could make as grief rips apart every chord of my throat. I'm trapped in this chasm of consuming rage. Everything I have been through comes crashing down.

My soul cracks, letting my mother's death seep into its foundation. The ground beneath our feet rumbles. Boulders crash down the cliff-side as my father's betrayal rattles both our souls. The fire courses through my veins. I see flashes of Callian's eyes. He found me in the dark and didn't try to pull me to the surface. He stood by my side. Even as my mind was slipping, we danced on the balcony, as the rain pelt against our bodies, moving through a somber night. He was with me until the very end, and now he remains in the darkness I drew him to. I wail, feeling my throat burn with my cries until my entire body ignites into a fiery rage.

A powerful blast of energy releases the inferno inside me. I become the fire beneath the rising blood moon, unburying the truth—what has always lurked beneath my skin.

My destiny.

Not a curse, nor a monster.

There will be no more battle against this ancient power awakening. There's acceptance, a knowing, a growing knowledge as every second sweeps by. My hands release all my love and all the rage that makes me who I am.

I am the embodiment of a power lost in time, reborn through the shadows of pain and suffering. I call to the dark and serene waves of the ocean, hearing whispers from thousands of years before. I revel in the sight of the waters rising from the sea, rushing inland. Fire and water surround me in a twisted inferno. Two powers weave themselves into every fiber of my being, creating a balance within me until they are one. My heart beats at a staggering rate. Adnama and I ascend into the air, encompassed by a blinding light, but I can still see her. She is the earth and wind. The sands of Sao surround her body in a powerful cyclone. Separated by realms no more—we are united.

As we both descend, a powerful blast rattles through the shores. A moment passes between us as we stare at one another. I run until I collide with Adnama, wrapping my arms around her. She's warm to the touch, and I feel her coming back as more time passes, losing her connection to the Shadow Realm.

"'Souls of a triangle unite,'" she recites the prophecy as if saying it for the first time. Her words leave in a soft, warm whisper. We look at the moon in all its beaming glory, seeing the remnants of our mother across an onyx sky. "The penumbra will soon rise over the lands," she says. Her dark hair wisps around her face. Though loss is hidden in her eyes, she holds her chin up.

The sound of a war drum fills the air, horns blaring. Our heads whip in the direction of flames scorching the sky, igniting throughout the outskirts of town where all the townspeople live.

We quickly rise to our feet and share a look.

Our bond was severed to hide a secret, but there is one thing our father never realized: you can cut and hack away at a thorned vine, shredding it down to the nub, but you can't miss the most important thing—the roots.

Determination fills my eyes. I turn to look at Adnama who wears the same look of malice. Darting a glare at the burning town, my palms ignite with flames.

"Let's go find our father."

CHAPTER 51
VIONA

PLUMES OF SMOKE BELLOW into the sky. Adnama and I run south down the shores until we crest the hill that leads up toward the screams. When we crest the top, I almost stop breathing. Solas' men have set the towns of Sao on fire.

The clamor of fighting between Solas' men and villagers has begun. A knot forms in my chest, pulling taut against the sight of dead bodies already littering the ground. King Tarvas left his people defenseless to these ruthless killers. The ones he so easily brought into his castle. Now, they're here, reigning aimless hatred on the innocent. Women and children run barefoot in the streets, screaming as they try to avoid the heat of the flames. Some of the villagers are garbed in mismatched armor, anything they could find to protect their families, *their home*, but they are no match for these shadow fuckers. Anger and sorrow tears at my insides. These people are ruled by a king who would kill in an instant just to prove a point. He uses their cries as a beacon because he knows this is where I'd be.

Unscathed by the flames' heat, Adnama rushes to the closest home, calling to the wind to put one of the fires out. A shadowed pirate comes up from behind her. She must feel his steps against the soil—the connection palpable beneath the soles of her feet. She stops in place. The hem of her dress bellows in the wind as her back remains to the enemy. Roots protrude from the ground. Each vine encases him in a tomb, slithering along his body, tearing and piercing through his flesh with a malicious grip. A scream ruptures from his throat until he explodes into a mist of blood. His weapon clangs against the gravel. Without turning to see the damage she just inflicted, she keeps walking. I dart forward to retrieve his weapon. From the corner of my eye, I see a man with nothing but a broomstick. He remains in place, flattened against the wall, seized by the sight of Adnama. I step toward him.

"Please! Don't hurt me!" he cries in a tone riddled with fear when he realizes I'm with her.

I shake my head. "We're here to help," I assure him, handing over the blood-slicked sword. His hand trembles as he takes it. His stance tells me he's never held one a day in his life. Something we will have to change for the people of Sao once all this is over. I show him a few quick moves. He nods. It isn't nearly enough, but the sword will give him a better chance at surviving.

"I need you to tell the others to head south toward the desert ruins. The kingdom of Corsal will have stations ready to aid our people."

His lips press with worry.

"You can do this. Now go!" I give him a gentle nudge.

He gives another tight nod before disappearing into the smoke-filled town.

"Princess Tarvas!" A shrill woman's cry whips my head to the side. Her stark silhouette is in the doorway of her home. Her fingers press against its frame before someone pulls her in. Whoever her attacker was, they kicked the door shut. Flames engulf the roof. I think back to when Crystal was training me, how she pulled from the elements around her; There is water in the earth. I feel it thrumming against my fingertips as it rises through the soil and into the air. My hands raise, willing it over the roof. When enough has gathered, with a flick of my wrist, the water descends onto the flames. I kick down the door searching for the woman. She remains in the corner without her assailant.

"Where did they go?" I ask.

"They're pulling us into the fires, one-by-one, and leaving us to die," her voice rasped. I check her over for injuries, but she has none. I help her outside. To my surprise, people are fleeing south.

"Go with them," I order. She nods and then disappears into the crowd.

Adnama and I put out more fires. Some of the villagers remain behind, trying to save what is left of their burning homes. I pull water from the surrounding elements, but it's not enough. Through the threads of my power I summon the ocean, willing it to form in my hands. I put out the fire in the surrounding homes.

In the distance, Adnama descends her rage upon Solas' men, ravaging through them as her vines tear them apart. A controlled gale of wind surrounds her. That boundless darkness gleams with hunger from many years of pent-up rage. She is the missing piece to my other half, my reflection. I look to the night sky, letting the same inky tendrils of onyx fill my eyes. Vengeance courses through my veins like wildfire, igniting fire in my hands. There's a break in the crowd as we advance forward. People are fleeing by the hundreds, if not thousands as their voices fill the air. While they run past us, I can only make out a few words at a time.

"She has returned."

"Our savior."

"Our princess."

More of Solas' men appear from the shrouds of smoke. We stand parallel to them as more of Sao's villagers flank our side, wielding what they can, ready to fight for a failed kingdom they had no other choice but to call their home.

One of Solas' men with jet-black hair stalks forward. He laughs. "Such a pathetic little army."

"It's pathetic for you to prey on the defenseless," I retort, seething as anger scorches through my body, knowing while chaos has erupted here, the Blood Moon Knights take a back seat beyond the walls. I vow to kill every one of them as soon as we breach the rise.

Adnama takes one step forward with her foot gently pressing against the soil.

"You're sort of cute," she says, slightly cocking her head to the side, looking at the bastard who just spoke. "I'd love to see what your shadows can do wrapped around my body."

The pirate's eyes set deep with lust as they rake over her frame shroud in white. He licks his lips, tempted by her beauty. He steps forward—ego buoyant by the ether of her call. Within a blink of an eye, she stands before him, trailing her white fingernails along his jawline. His breathing hitches. A smile ticks the corner of his mouth, but somehow, I feel the beat of his heart pulsing throughout the ground the longer he stares into the abyss of her eyes.

She cups the back of his head and brings him to her open mouth. She does the unexpected, kissing him passionately. My face twists into disgust.

His eyes close, succumbing to her ecstasy. Suddenly they flick back open. Horror spreads across his face. Dark, rotted roots burst through the back of his skull, penetrating through the hearts of several of his men who flank his sides. Their bodies writhe as fissures spread across their chests. All at once, they drop to the ground. They disappear in a shroud of smoke, leaving nothing but a pool of blood in their wake.

Adnama cracks her neck, moving it from side to side as she narrows in on the rest of them. "Who's next?" She smiles, licking a drop of blood from the corner of her mouth.

A kiss of malice.

That was fucking brutal.

Solas' men exchange a look before revenge fuels their next move. They storm us, attacking from all angles. They begin disappearing in and out of sight. The innate ability felt through my body draws me to every single place they appear. With my dagger in hand and flames in the other, we begin the dance of death. Adnama moves with a haunting grace as tremors rattle the ground, willing vines to weave through each pirate. A fissure cracks open, widening with her will. With a push of my palm, a group of them plummet into their shallow grave. The earth reclaims them until they're no more.

Another pirate advances toward me from my side. A ring of fire ignites around his neck. My fist clenched, constricting his airway. The smell of burning flesh scorches the air. His sword drops to the ground. In the corner of my eye, I see one of the villagers surrounded. I thrust my palm out, willing the blade to her feet. She picks it up and fends them off, parrying their moves and cuts diagonally in a sweeping motion.

A wail whips my focus back to the one I had in my fiery grip. I jab my dagger up behind his ribcage. Blood sprays the air, running like a hot stream against the side of my face. The taste of metal hits my mouth. I feel the hollowness in my chest fill.

The taste of revenge.

I swing my sword, the blade cleaving across the chest of another, and another. One by one, they drop to the ground, disappearing in plumes of smoke. Adnama and I make our way toward the outer bailey of the castle.

Solas appears in a plume of smoke between his men. As it clears, I find his deep-set glare fixed on me.

"There you are, lover. My, my. Your father is quite angry with you." He runs a hand through his dirty-blond hair and takes another step.

Smoke curls around his boots and up his legs while his coat flaps in the wind, revealing the forbidden dagger sheathed at his side. My stomach takes a dip at the sight. His hands are extended out, giving the sign of truce.

My eyes narrow in on him.

"There will be no truce between us, you bastard." My nostrils flare.

"We are to be married, sweet one. There has to be a truce," he mocks, but his eyes soon drift to Adnama who has a steel expression on her death-stricken face. He tucks a loose strand of hair behind his ears and straightens the cuffs of his sleeves, lured by her beauty.

Solas exhales a breath, forgetting the mockery of vows he just expressed to me. "Who is this lovely, dark angel?"

My head cocks to the side as I grin. "Have you met my sister? She's fucking crazy."

Within a blink of an eye, Adnama wraps her hand around his throat. A gasp leaves his lips as his eyes bulge out of his skull. He starts to make inaudible sounds while his arms flail around. His men advance forward in wild swirls of smoke. I forge a ring of fire around us, shielding the three of us in.

"So, this is Solas," she whispers, studying all the sharp angles of his face. "I heard your voice through the echoes of the wind. You wanted to claim my sister's virtue in front of the entire kingdom?" More sounds leave his mouth as he tries to speak. His face reddens from the lack of air. "It's time to make a lasting impression. Watch what I do in front of *your entire army*," she seethes. Adnama turns her head. "Release the shield," she demands in her soft, ethereal voice. Wind whips around our faces inside the forged shield surrounding us.

My eyes dart to hers. "What? Are you fucking crazy?"

She smirks.

I nod, releasing the shield as the ring of fire disintegrates into the air.

Adnama looks at Solas' men. "You follow a leader who is weak. One who preys on the innocent. Where is the power in that? Look at him. He serves under a king, but cannot be one himself unless he charts a barren sea. He can wield dark magic, but where is it now?"

Solas' men look at one another, dumbfounded. "Do you want to serve the one who plays with dark magic like he does his cock, or do you want to serve *the one who owns it?*" Adnama's voice dips into a low sinister growl.

She releases Solas, but he remains suspended in the air, floating idly above his men. Thorny vines tear from the ground, weaving into a pike against his back. They wrap around him, tearing his clothes and across his flesh until his pants rip off, exposing his genitals. My face contorts into disgust. Solas begins screaming, begging for his life. She lets his cowardly words hang in the air for all his men to hear.

"Let his death remind you what happens when you harm our people." Her chin lifts. In the background, the remaining villagers laugh at Solas' humiliating display and cheer her on.

"What? No! No!" Solas screams.

Vines curve around his thighs and at the base of his genitals. They begin pulling on the flesh. A cry rips from his throat—a sound that gives me chills.

With one motion of her hand, the vines castrate him at the very root. Chords and pieces of his testicles rip from the base, raining down onto his men in splatters of blood. The vines pull the rest of his body apart, limb by limb until there's nothing but a disfigured carcass falling from the pike onto the ground. I never thought I'd see fear in the faces of these shadowed pirates, but there it is. A look of horror before they spin on their heels and flee.

A smile curves my lips, giving chase to their fear. With a flick of my wrist, they're surrounded in a cage of fire. Their bodies ignite, writhing as their weapons wield into their flesh. My rage bleeds into the tendrils of heat until the men are nothing but piles of ash.

Adnama and I skim over the massacre. I pick up the forbidden dagger from the carcass that was once Solas. The power it holds begins thrumming against my palm. I sheathe it into my boot. When I stand, something catches in the corner of my eye. That gravitational pull is tethered to another darkness, but one I wish to expel, one that carries all my vengeance, so much, that my core shakes. As the blood moon rises high into the sky, peeking between a few dark, ominous clouds, there stands my father in one of the highest spires of the castle.

CHAPTER 52
VIONA

THERE'S A SENSE OF satisfaction when Adnama and I storm into the castle of Sao. Anger flutters my jaw as I meet the eyes of my enemies. I crack my neck, teeth bared at the nobles and members of the court who become seized by fear, shocked at what they thought would be unobtainable—my freedom, with a power they now dread as fire churns in the palm of my hand. Adnama stands by my side like a siren who has been unleashed from the depths of their own nightmares.

My mind flashes back to the moment the dagger pierced my mothers flesh. Forged in fire and water, it carries her blood.

Pain. Pain is what they will know soon enough.

I charge forward, eyes narrowing in on a man who has already unsheathed his sword.

My gaze darkens.

In one movement, the dagger cuts cleanly across his throat. His weapon falls to the ground as a mist of blood sprays the air. He clutches his throat. Ruby waves pulse from the cracks of his fingers, and this nameless prick drops to the ground. He turned his head every time I stood there suffering in silence as a child. I now revel in the sight of him bleeding out.

With my powers humming, I see everyone as they truly are. Nearly every member of this court is vile in some way. I can smell the heinous crimes they have enacted upon the people, some hiding unspeakable things behind closed doors.

The full moon bleeds for a purge to cleanse all the filth from this castle.

Death. Their death is coming. I go after them, reigning hell on them all.

In the corner of my eye, I see a woman with a pastel-yellow dress standing between two pillars. It's the woman who was in the company of the young man I decapitated some time ago. All the color in her face drains as she watches the stream of fire shooting past her. Our eyes lock. She presses a hand to her chest seized with fear.

"Get out of here!" I yell. "Seek shelter in the South," I shout over the flames. The woman backs further into the pillars. Before I turn my head, one of the members of the council rushes her, grabbing her by the arm. With my abilities, I sense he has done more to her than buy her that pretty dress. I lower my hand and stalk toward him. I grab him by the coat, seething with rage.

"Keep your fucking hands off her," I growl, tossing his useless body against a pillar. His spine wraps around the post, going lifeless on contact.

My eyes skim the foyer, turning my attention back to the crowd trying to escape.

"We need to find the Blood Moon Knights." I call over to Adnama who is taunting someone in the corner like a cat playing with its food. After she ends their life, she turns to me.

"I have a feeling they are protecting King Tarvas."

Of course. Why would he use them to protect the lives of the people in the castle?

"I know where he is," I say, rushing out of the foyer.

The cries and screams fade into the background the further away we get. Our footsteps fill the empty halls until Adnama and I hear another pair of footsteps up ahead.

A man enters from our left. He's the same one Alyce trusted while I was shoved into a cell. He gave us extra food and did what he could to make us comfortable while my mother and I lived through hell. His eyes go wide when he sees me.

"Princess Viona." He takes a step back. "You escaped." His fear is palpable as I narrow in on him.

"You've stated the obvious," I mock, not stopping in my tracks until we're face to face. I pause, glaring into his eyes even though I have to look up to see them. Beneath the crown he serves, there is good inside him. "But you were kind to me in moments when my mother and I needed it. I will let you live for now."

"Thank you." He exhales a deep sigh of relief.

"Where's Alyce?" I demand, still displaying an icy tone.

"I'm right here."

I spin around on my heels. Alyce is walking arm in arm with two women aiding her. My shoulders relax seeing the stern look on her face which tells me she's okay. I walk toward her. Suddenly her eyes soften as she searches behind me, looking past Adnama as if she's looking for someone else.

"Where's your mother?"

A knot forms in my chest as my breathing stills. It's a kick to my fucking gut as tears break down the walls I've constructed around my heart to get me through these next moments.

"She's . . . " Words evade me. Will Alyce forgive me for what I've done?

Alyce takes a few steps away from the women, closing the distance between us. Her frail hand reaches for me. This time, I don't pull back as I did in the cell. When she touches my face, a tear slips free. Her eyes warm, taking us back to that place we once were where there were no barriers between us.

"I had to ki—"

"I know you, and I know your heart." Alyce's lips quiver. "You did what you had to for the better good. Do not *dare* waste a day of your life blaming yourself. Do you hear me? I won't have it." Her voice shakes as emotion lodges in her throat. "And my gods, dear child, what you have to do next... How you still stand on two feet is beyond me."

I inhale a shaky breath. "He has made so many suffer," I whisper so low only she can hear.

Alyce's attention is drawn to Adnama, and curiosity fills her eyes as they bounce between us. She smiles.

"I have lots of questions, but I have a feeling I already know who you might be. Let's go, girls." She pats my face before reaching for the guard. "Jordan," she says. He locks his arm with hers. Alyce turns to the two women who remain uncomfortable in our presence. "You may go."

They curtly nod before spinning on their heels. Alyce starts walking in the same direction we're headed.

"Alyce, what are you doing?" I raise a brow and shift my weight to one side.

She turns, annoyed and already spent from making it this far. Her tight, wild curls bounce with the slight movement. "He has put me through enough, and knowing your mother was here all this time . . . " There's a pause as grief fills her tone. "You two were born to rip his soul apart, and I want to be there to see it."

THE FOUR OF US WALK through the last corridor. I know beyond these thick, wooden doors sits my father on his throne of lies. Sensing the energy in the air, I also know Adnama was right: the Blood Moon Knights are going to stand between us.

I turn around, to look at Alyce. "I need you to stay out of the way, please. I can't lose you too."

"Girly, you don't need to worry about this old broad. I dare any of them to touch me."

I huff out a soft laugh. Hearing that fire in her warms my heart.

"You know, I can see where I got my strength from." I lean down, giving her a kiss on the cheek. "Maybe we can play a game of chess after all this is over?" I ask, tears stinging my eyes once more.

"My fierce girl, I would love to."

I embrace her in my arms and hold back the sob wanting to break free.

"I will make sure no one harms her," Jordan vows.

"Honey, I don't need a man to protect me. You're only here for looks," Alyce snaps, wearing that sly, mischievous smile I love. Jordan's warm skin brightens to a soft blush.

I turn around, facing the doors to the throne room. Adnama looks at me with a smirk on her face and eagerness burning in her eyes.

We storm in. The Blood Moon Knights fill the space, putting distance between King Tarvas and where we stand. He sits on his throne, devoid of all emotion, with eyes narrowing on me. Silence hangs in the air, and I hear the soft footsteps of Alyce behind me as she takes a quiet place in the background.

"I see betrayal runs deep within our castle. Alyce, you traitorous bitch," King Tarvas replies with a slack expression. "And *you*," he says, casting a glare at me with a malicious grin spreading across his face. "The forgotten princess has returned in a fiery rage, and she brought a friend." Silence hangs in the air. As he plays with one of the rings on his fingers, he studies the woman who stands beside me. The more he stares at her, the more his jaw ticks with recognition.

"FUCK!!! *FUCK!*" he yells, slamming his fist onto the arm of his throne. His hair flies out from the clasped tie.

Adnama laughs. "Hello, Father." Stepping forward, a grin tips the corner of her mouth. Her eyes narrow in on him like he's prey. Clearly feeling threatened by our presence, he stands with fists clenched at his sides.

"Attack them! Kill them all!"

I grit my teeth, keeping my focus on the Blood Moon Knights who I stood with all these years. Just as I'm about to claim the lives of every one, they do the unexpected. They shift to the side, making a straight clearing between where we stand and King Tarvas' throne. His brows slam together at the defiance.

"What are you doing you fucking idiots? *Get them!*" His eyes dart to us. I take a step forward. My eyes lower to the ground as dark tendrils of smoke wisp around their feet. Simultaneously, they all turn their heads toward Adnama and me, and they kneel.

They are bowing . . . to us.

"Seems like they don't think you're in charge anymore," I retort, grinning in satisfaction. I play with the possibility, keeping my unease at bay.

King Tarvas takes a few steps off the dais.

"You think because Adnama stands beside you that all is well? Look at your half-dead sister. She appears to you as a savior of light, but deep down, that boundless chaos is waiting to take you out. You are not safe.

Nobody is as long as she roams free. Whoever switched places with her was a fucking *fool*."

Callian.

My teeth clench. Stealing a sideways glance at Adnama, her eyes widen. For the first time, I see worry plague her. "He lies to you, Viona. Can't you see? He's trying to get inside your head."

I blink back a few times trying to gather any reasoning I feel slipping from my grip. My eyes bounce between King Tarvas and my sister. Both my blood.

"If you kill me, Viona, you will be giving her the last part of her powers she will need to end these lands. Did you think the prophecy was about you? You've always been a worthless, little, fucking brat. Always thinking everything was about you."

Fire ignites in my hands as I stare in a clouded daze at the ground.

"Sister," Adnama softly says, reaching for me, but I take a step back, unsure what to believe as more of my reality begins to shift. "Do not believe the lies he feeds you," she pleads.

King Tarvas laughs. "Now I see it. That look on your face," he surmises. "She took your lover away from you. She convinced him to take her place. Your prince was so eager, *so willing* to hand over his life to save yours." With a sneering growl, he stabs his finger at Adnama. "*She* took advantage of you and those you care about."

I take a step forward, my mind spiraling out of control with a quarrel of emotions. I can't see what's real anymore. I'm tired of feeling like I can't trust anyone. Tired of everyone using me as a fucking pawn in their game. Though I do not trust King Tarvas, is there truth to his words? Now, standing between Adnama and him, I don't know what to do. As Adnama's voice feeds the tension, I turn to her as heat churns in my palms.

"Is it true? Did you trick Callian into switching places with you just to be set free?" I cut my gaze to her.

She shakes her head. "Remember what I told you. You are giving your trust to the wrong people."

"And what if that's *you*?" I counter, cutting her off as anger stings my eyes.

"I came here to save you, to free our mother. I've been guiding you this whole time, the best I could while I was bound to the White Forest. Follow your heart and it will show you the truth." She tries to calm me, but I can no longer hear her words. Time has slowed, and I am slipping into a place I am afraid to be. Chaos—enough to tear these lands apart if the prophecy ends on the wrong side of my wrath.

My mind is reeling through a lifetime of memories. Running down the shores of Sao with my mother trailing behind me. All I can see is her smile as the wind whips across her face, her laugh, how it now echoes in the shadows of my heart. To all those moments I stood on the balcony, looking out to the ocean, never knowing she was here all this time, barely being kept alive. Then, running into the arms of my captor, my destiny, my fate.

The air is charged, causing the little hairs on my arm to rise. Tendrils of my hair rise above my shoulders, floating idly as if I roam the stars.

Before I can think through my next move, Adnama's eyes widen as she looks over my shoulder.

It is fear—death-stricken fear spreading across her face.

The onyx in her eyes dissipates into a rich brown. My mind flashes to the bond we share, the two figures on an ominous beach—one garbed in ivory, the other in ebony.

Then she disappears from sight, reappearing directly behind me. I turn to find King Tarvas blasting a stream of lightning into Adnama's chest. My heart ceases feeling the moment he strikes hers.

"No!" My voice cracks watching her body drop to the ground. I drop to my knees next to her.

"Such a pity. Looks like she was telling the truth after all." He mocks.

I run my hand along her cheek, brushing a raven lock from her face.

"It's funny what love can do to you. It makes you weak, foolish, and blind," King Tarvas says.

Time remains as a slow-flowing wave.

"*Love*," I whisper.

My mind reels back to the memory of being on the outskirts of Callisto sitting across from Crystal. Her bright, ivory smile glinting in the sunlight. Her braids swaying against her as she spoke. So carefree, full of kindness, as patience gleamed in her eyes every time she was with me.

I remember what she taught me: *Love weaves itself into magic.*

If Adnama carries a piece of Callian with her, then through our bond, she *will* heal. I press my hand against her chest, feeling a faint heartbeat beneath my palm. I'll let King Tarvas think she's dead for now.

I rise to my feet.

"I was a warrior long before I had these powers. Before the prophecy, I was a girl who lived for the sharp sound of my blade being drawn. I yearned for the battle, for the adrenaline rush when weapons crossed. I did as you asked, even when I didn't want to. Back then, I didn't think I would ever meet your glare on the other end of the blade." I unsheathe my mother's dagger from my hip. "And now, I crave to see *your* blood spilled on it." My fist tightens around its hilt.

"Where did you get that dagge–"

I stalk closer, letting the invisible force of my powers wrap around his neck. His eyes go wide, and his crown hits the floor, rolling into the foot of a Blood Moon Knight.

"Do you feel that, Father?" I mock, willing the grip to tighten. "That struggle for air, that desperation racing through your veins . . . the panic?" Extending my arm out, the invisible tether raises his body inches off the ground and drifts him toward me. The leather of my boots rub together, filling the silence as I close the distance between us. A sheen of sweat forms above his brow as his face reddens.

"All this time, my mother was here. You stole her life." I pierce my mother's blade into his flesh, feeling every muscle tear beneath my grip. He gurgles words I don't care to hear, I only find solace in his inaudible sounds. "You threw your children to the depths of your greed where wolves thrived. You left us in the dark, and we made it our home, and now you're just pissed because we reign in it. You sealed your fate the moment you placed us there."

A powerful force ignites in my palm. The swelling heat intensifies as my mind reels back to the moment I drove this dagger into our mother's body. I shove the blade deeper. All this time I've longed to see him suffer, I crave more even as a tormented scream rips from his throat. He wraps his hands around the dagger's hilt. I can feel his mind racing against time. I will my magic to slam his body against the ground.

Darkness ignites the flame, love controls the chaos.

I look into King Tarvas' eyes. "You took *everything* from me, from us, from your people. I refuse to let you take Vendrelle too." The ground shakes beneath us. "You are done ruining lives. You are *done*."

I extend my other hand and will the forbidden blade to rise from my boot. When I feel the hilt in my palm, I stab it into his heart. His body writhes as he bites down the searing pain. The forbidden shadow blade begins to slowly melt into his flesh. With my mother's dagger still protruding from his body, I relish in the duo. One was for me and the other for Adnama.

"There is nothing left for me to fear," I whisper, watching as boils appear all over his body. He is burning alive, slowly, because I am the source of the heat. "I will stain the ground with your blood and revel in the sight of where I placed you. There will be nothing left but your ashes."

His body writhes as fissures of darkness spread throughout his body. The forbidden blade disintegrates into his flesh. I feel the moment his heart takes its final beat, as if time has frozen long enough for me to whisper, "There is no one left to claim you." His heart implodes in the cavity of his chest. I feel it, just like I felt my mothers.

His body slumps down. There's a sudden calm as an unseen chasm lifts. The darkness in his eyes fades, staring lifelessly into nothing.

I exhale deeply and rise to my feet, watching him burn until he is a carcass with unrecognizable remains. A few rogue tears slip free, but they aren't for him. I'm taking back the pieces of me I allowed him to hold. His death will be the remedy and release of everything our souls have been longing for.

Adnama's groan pulls me from his body. I quickly rush to her side, sitting on my knees as she collects herself.

"I'm sorry," I admit, taking her hand in mine while I help her rise to her feet. I couldn't see it until now, but it's hard to see the truth when someone has been fed lies their entire life. Feeling the hollow of her chest, she exhales. She finds me amidst my thoughts as I continue to stare at her.

"I'm sorry too," she replies in a warm, forgiving tone. "When I first met you, I couldn't tell you who I was. I couldn't interfere with your destiny. I—"

Before she can continue, half of the Blood Moon Knights disappear beneath their armor, one by one, dropping to the ground. Their souls ascend in dark clouds of smoke out the window until they disintegrate into the air. The others who remain stagger and wobble on their feet. The hold King Tarvas had on them is no more. Beneath the armor are men and women who look insanely confused. When their eyes find Adnama and me still in an embrace, they drop to one knee.

Before I can even begin to put everything together, a pang of sadness strikes my heart. I'm happy Adnama remains by my side, knowing she is free, but I'm reminded of who remains left behind in the White Forest.

"Callian," I whisper, looking into her eyes. The knot in my chest returns. It feels as though my heart has been set aflame, knowing there can be no more us.

Alyce stands between Adnama and me, placing her hands on our backs. "I will take it from here, girls." She turns to me. "Go. Go to him and say your goodbyes. All of this can wait."

Before she can say anything more, I turn to Adnama looking at the palm of her hand as she extends it out. I glance at her as she says, "I will take you to him."

I step into her space as unease prickles my spine, not knowing our means of travel. A ghost of a smile appears. She takes hold of my other hand and stares into my eyes. Before I can discern what's happening, the world around us vanishes.

CHAPTER 53
VIONA

DARKNESS.

There is nothing but a boundless dark before our feet touch the ground. I exhale my next breath, landing smoothly and effortlessly, but my stomach still turns. We just *appear* in the White Forest. The way Adnama teleported us looked a lot different than how I'd seen Gareon do it, and it makes me wonder what else is hiding up his sleeve. Does he see the same black abyss, or something more?

I ignore the nausea rolling in my stomach and straighten my shoulders. The moment we appeared, an eerie dread began to flutter along my skin like a cold, winter's embrace. The desolate existence of this place is a reminder of all that has been lost within, sending another wave of pain and sadness into the hollow of my chest. There's no comfort as I step foot into the forest, but still, I look for Callian, searching for the essence of what I feel still remains, like a faint prism of light after a storm. I swallow the lump in my throat, knowing what I must overcome. A part of me will always hold onto him and all he's given me.

The light in my dark.

My mind flashes back to his smile, the way the sun filtered through his hair, to how he looked at me the first time I woke upon a fresh layer of snow. His eyes bored into mine through the flames. He knew. He knew we were destined, fated to one another. I fought him every step of the way, until I didn't. He began unveiling every layer of my soul while also giving me time to feel it for myself, never pushing. He set the world at my feet with his sacrifice. Vendrelle is saved, but this might ruin me, all of us.

Now . . . Now I'd do anything to get him back.

I turn to Adnama who moves throughout the only place she's ever known. My sister—words so foreign on my tongue, ones I thought I'd never get to say—whose face still reminds me of a darker part of myself. A place I've only seen through shadows and dreams. Her eyes are to the ground as if she's sensing something. She slowly looks in my direction, eyes widening at something over my shoulder. When I see her hardened gaze soften, I spin around on my heels.

Across the haze is a tall, dark silhouette. I squint my eyes at the shadowed figure until the wind brushes once more against my skin like a soft, winter's kiss.

My pulse quickens.

"Callian?" I whisper in a soft frothy exhale. I can feel him. That insatiable, tethered pull is wrapping around me. "Callian!" I stifle a sob and run. I let my fire for him flow through my veins, no longer feeling the brunt of the cold stinging my cheeks.

"Viona!" The sound of his voice sends my heart fluttering.

It's him. It's him, it's him. My love, my light. I desperately repeat it like a mantra, like a prayer to the gods above to hear me. His arms extend to his sides as the ground trembles beneath my feet, but I keep running. I run as the haze recedes as if it fears him.

"Callian!" I cry out, quickening my speed. His stark silhouette stands in the middle of a clearing. As I close the distance, his green eyes glow within the shroud of his hooded cloak. Shadows emerge from his body, whisking around in an onyx-hued, torrential wind as they rush toward me. My powers reach for them, *for him*. His shadows wrap around my waist, like a soft caress against my skin. A shadow-kissed embrace, as though he's touching me for the first time. My heart flutters in anticipation as I'm lifted off the ground and into the air. My gaze flicks to him. The intensity in his eyes flares like bright, burning emeralds. The force of his powers pulls me toward him, and I stare in wonder at his transformation—pieces of me have been reborn, woven from the stars into his shadows. They pull me through the clearing until I'm in his arms.

There's so much tenderness in the way they set me down, pressing my body against his. He stares into my eyes with shock as if he's dreaming, searing this moment to memory. My hands slide up his chest until I'm cupping the side of his face. The rich-tan skin that was once full of warmth is now cold to the touch. It hits me like ice, causing me to shudder as our reality slices through me, stealing my next breath. A tear slips down his face as he watches me fall apart.

"I'm—"

I push up onto my toes, pressing my lips to his before he can finish speaking. The beat of my heart quickens, becoming entwined with his as he wraps his arms around me.

Cold.

He's so cold, and he smells of lavender, not of cedar with his fresh, floral scent I love. His cold embrace unleashes the tears to stream down my face. My lips quiver, but I deepen the kiss, desperate to pull him closer, using the warmth emitting from my chest to heat his body. So desperate to warm him, as though it will change things. He moans into my mouth, threading his fingers through my hair until he's gently cupping the back of my head. He kisses the trail of tears streaming down my face. The ground rumbles as the chaos begins to rise from every breath I take. My arms wrap tighter around him, remembering everything I did in Sao and what I fear I'll lose again as soon as I walk out of this gods-forsaken, cursed forest.

The wind picks up around us, swirling violently as we become the eye of the storm—a beam of light emits from my chest, pulsating in waves as it spreads throughout the forest.

"I love you, Callian. I did even before I knew it. Somehow, my heart always called to you, and you found me. You came for me. You've carried me through the dark, and I'm afraid to let you go." The rawest of truths expel from my heart as it shatters. "I won't let you go. I won't."

"Don't be afraid," he reassures me, curving a finger under my chin to meet his gaze. The gale of wind continues to swirl around us. Those eyes, so penetrating as he stares back between the strands of hair whipping around our faces.

"You saved the lands. Now there will be peace."

"But I will spend the rest of my life without you." I lean my head against his chest, searing the sound of his voice to memory. The light around us begins to fade, and I turn to see the remnants settling along the ground. Callian's hair brushes along the top of my head as he sharply turns in alert.

"The haze," I whisper, taking a step back to observe what's happening.

"It's . . . disappearing," he adds, looking around in disbelief, watching it recede further into the woods like a wounded snake. The skies open up to an early dawn. "The blood moon has passed." Our eyes fix on the first glimpse of light that begins to chase away the stars. All the snow in the White Forest is starting to melt with lush, green foliage taking its place.

"What is happening?" I exhale, rushing to his side, afraid of what will come next, afraid he'll disappear like my mother did before I can touch him again. When he takes me in his arms, I jump back at the heat emitting from his body.

"You're . . . warm," I rasp, heaving.

"What?" he replies.

"When I first touched you, you were cold as ice, like Adnama, but now, you're . . . "

He runs a hand down his arm, not feeling the difference.

"'Rebirth between the trees,'" Adnama observes as she looks up at the crowns of the now-evergreen trees. "The curse over the White Forest must have been lifted when you fulfilled the prophecy. The darkness that looms here is no more."

My heart swells seeing she no longer looks like she walks among the dead. Her golden-tawny skin resembles our father's. Slowly, I walk toward her, reaching out until my fingertips brush her cheek.

"Warm to the touch." My voice lifts in a soft whisper.

While I'm piecing things together, my body thrums in response to the connection I feel between Adnama and Callian, both in different ways. Her powers simmer beneath the surface as my own, while pieces of me swirl within Callian's in dark shadow. I turn to Adnama, my eyes radiating with hope.

"This means—" I stifle a sob, and turn. Within a few strides I'm jumping into Callian's arms, wrapping my legs around his waist. The familiarity of his body returns as he emits more heat. "It means you're free too." I thread my hand along the nape of his neck and through his hair, something I've been dreaming of doing since we've been apart. "Kiss me," I plead.

He pauses for a moment, staring into my eyes, still not believing what's unfolding. Then he smiles. "You never have to beg me, Princess. The moment I laid eyes on you, I knew you were mine." Leaning in, his eyes close in a soft flutter. Those soft, *warm* lips caress mine, kissing me so deep and claiming as the stroke of his tongue slips in. Once again, he sets my heart aflame. Through every gentle stroke, I am savoring this moment. A moment I thought I'd never get to feel again, yet somehow, for some reason, the gods have given him back to me.

Thank you. I am in debt to you.

Though his shadows remain, this is part of the evolution of us, the evolution of these lands. I feel our bond stronger than I ever have before.

I remain in his arms with my legs wrapped around his waist. I turn my head to the side, watching Adnama explore the forest in awe. A smile perks my lips seeing the rise and fall of her chest while simultaneously feeling his against mine.

We will be okay.

Adnama looks around, wandering the forest, running her hand along the bark of each tree she passes while occasionally wiggling her toes beneath the rich, dark soil. As the light filters in through the treetops, I know our mother is smiling, seeing Adnama is free, no longer bound to this place. Both she and Callian can take each breath with gratitude. This was her hell hole for so long, but now she stands in the middle of a flourishing landscape.

"I *haven't* lost it all. I have everything I need right here."

"As do I, little flame," he hums, stroking my hair. I kiss him one more time before sliding off his body to stand.

"So, what now?" Callian asks as a warm gust of wind sweeps a few strands across his face.

"We live the life we've always wanted to live," I remind him. We share a knowing look.

Adnama casually strolls back toward us, pulling her long, dark hair to the front.

"What life is that?" she asks. The side of her mouth quirks up as she speaks.

"We can set sail and let the wind carry us to our next adventure," I reply, lacing my fingers with his. He squeezes back gently in affirmation.

"What about Sao?" he questions, glancing over to Adnama.

She blinks back a few times, holding out her hands in protest with eyes widening. "I sure as fuck don't want it," she blurts.

Callian laughs. He laughs so loud, his voice echoes through the forest. My chest tightens, realizing how I longed to hear that laugh. So freeing.

"You sound just like your sister."

Adnama stands on the other side of me and takes my hand in hers. *Warm. She's warm and free.*

Her eyes have so much life in them now. I blink back my tears, take a deep breath, and smile.

"That doesn't surprise me one bit."

THE THREE OF US WALK through the forest. One would never know this was a place where darkness thrived, where secrets were held. Already, life is reclaiming all it lost. Wildlife is already springing back to life. Birds fly to the canopy of the trees. The sun filters through the leaves, beaming down on us with its warmth against our backs.

Across the clearing, Crystal's violet hair sparkles in the light. She's astride her white mare with about a dozen guards flanking her side. Two of them being Gareon and Iván. My heart leaps out of my chest. I start running through the clearing, and her smile widens when she sees me. She throws the reins to Gareon, jumps off her horse, and runs. Iván follows, calling out to me. Hearing their voices sends my heart racing even faster. I take her in my arms, and we stumble onto the ground, crying and laughing.

"You guys are a little late," I scoff jokingly. After a few more tight hugs and more laughter, we rise to our feet. Iván appears behind her, those deep-set eyes glossing over when he sees me walking toward him. Crystal steps to the side, and he opens his arms to me. "I'm so happy to see you two again," I whisper.

"Us too, Vi. Us too," he says, hugging me so tight, I can't breathe. The old me would have pushed anyone away who dared to show me any sort of comfort. But I let him. Soon, Crystal joins us. Another weighted body surrounds us, and I know it's Callian's.

My friends. They remind me of all I was fighting for. Thank the gods we are together again.

Crystal begins to survey the terrain and then looks at Adnama.

"Clearly, we have some catching up to do," she says, studying the condition of my sister. Her prying eyes bounce between the both of us. Then it clicks. "Is she . . . " Her mouth gapes open.

"My sister, yes," I confirm.

Gareon and the rest of the guards arrive on their horses. He smiles down at me, eyes churning like galaxies as he looks between Adnama and me. He nods in her direction. "It's nice to finally see you in the flesh."

"Likewise," she responds with a smile.

The sunlight filters in behind her, casting a soft glow along her tawny skin. I realize now that her dress is so sheer, the guards behind Gareon are trying not to look. A few vines descend from the trees, simultaneously whipping the nosy guards across their arms. They all jump at the sudden pain as she cuts them a glaring smirk.

Crystal shoots me a look as I try to hold in the chuckle wanting to break free, and she rushes to her horse, grabbing a small, ivory shawl to drape over Adnama's shoulders.

"What is this called?" Adnama's fingers run along its soft fabric. A chuckle rumbles in Gareon's chest, finding humor in Adnama's response.

Iván runs a hand through his hair. "Well, this is going to get interesting."

We ride back to find there's a small army stationed along the outskirts of what used to be the White Forest. Callian sees Samuel and embraces him in such a tight hug, Samuel stumbles back with a smile. As Callian explains what happened, he leaves out the details of being left in the forest. I suppose he has a lot of things he needs to sort through before he shares those moments with anyone. Callian orders Samuel and a few other trusted guards to send word that this is all over. I see the relief in Samuel's face as he glances at me while I stand outside the carriage. With a knowing smile, he nods before taking off on horseback.

I bring the cold tea that Iván prepared to my lips while Gareon stands guard over us. I heat the cup in my palm until the liquid runs warm—another perk to my ability. Crystal leads Adnama into the carriage and sits next to her. Gareon follows, taking the seat next to Crystal. Callian and I sit across from them. When Callian joins me at my side, my chest tightens as my mind reels back to almost losing him. I guess I, too, will have a lot of things to sort through. I have gained and lost so much in such a short amount of time. But I know we will work through this darkness together. As we ride back to Callisto, Iván rides along the carriage with some other sentries.

Callian wraps an arm around my shoulders, pulling me against his chest. I lean into his warm embrace, exhaling a sigh of relief.

"What are you going to do about Sao?" Crystal asks as the carriage bounces us around.

All eyes are on me, except for Adnama's, who continues to stare out the window. My eyes glance between Gareon and Crystal. Callian begins running the pad of his thumb in a soft motion along my arm.

I take a deep breath.

"Being the queen of Sao isn't how I want my story to end. I've spent far too long walking those halls, being a ghost and the shell of someone I couldn't recognize anymore. It wasn't until I made a deal with my captor that I realized how dead I was inside." A ghost of a smile appears. *My captor, my fated mate.* Callian squeezes my arm and pulls me closer to his body. A loving caress flutters along the bond.

"Crystal, you are well-respected throughout Vendrelle. You have a light inside you, an ability to lead, a balance, and grace. The day of the pyre, there was no division, there were no sides. Your presence sent a message to all those who stood hand in hand with you. Sao has been missing someone who has that compassion. The people of Sao deserve a life they were never given the opportunity to have. I was never meant to be a queen, but *you* were."

Crystal's breathing stills as her eyes swell. A soft, humble smile curves her lips as those violet-hued eyes glimmer with delight. The rise and fall of her chest almost sends me over the edge to cry myself, and I return the smile.

"A crown would look quite lovely on your head," Gareon purrs. His gaze narrows in on her before his eyes drift down to her lips.

"It would be my honor to bring back the life I know the people of Sao deserve," she replies. "There would be a lot of paperwork to do, if you don't mind staying in Callisto for a bit before you two go off on your next adventure. We would need to ask a few members of the court from each kingdom to step in and offer their services to help rebuild Sao. The prince of Corsal is known for his generosity. I have no doubt he will assist with the immediate support your—*our* people need right now before we can get back."

"Being from the kingdom of Sebina, you have a good relationship with the queens. I know they will be honored to assist you in any way they can." Callian nods with approval.

"Alyce can help you navigate the castle, show you the ins and outs, and introduce you to the important people," I add.

What's left of them. Adnama and I share a look before she diverts her attention back out the window.

Crystal looks up at Gareon, gently moving a moonlit lock away from his face. The back of her knuckles brush up against his smooth skin. Her eyes warm when she finds his gaze as she says, "Once the documents are settled, would you mind teleporting the messenger to notify the surrounding kingdoms of these plans?"

He smiles, drawing in a long look from her as the golden embers in his eyes flare. "I'm sure I can be convinced."

She smiles.

"Then it's settled," I add.

Adnama is silent, her eyes fluttering open for a brief moment, staring at the rolling hills as she peacefully leans against the seat. After a few moments, she closes them again. Her hair drapes across her shawl and body like a silk blanket. Crystal's chin slightly raised as a look of content spreads across her face.

For the rest of the ride, most of us remain silent, save for the light murmurs and conversations between those we sit next to.

CHAPTER 54
CALLIAN

WE RIDE THROUGH THE rough terrain back to Callisto. Judging by Viona's slanted brows and distant stare, she's far away from here, perhaps back in that cell with her mother. I sense the new scars marring her soul, and it pains me to think about all she will have to work through. Grief can be an open door back into the dark. If she happens to find herself there, I'll be by her side with open arms, waiting and ready to fight any demons that surface. I can only imagine the torment she will feel, but thank the gods above that I can help her through it. And she can help me.

My eyes drift to Crystal whose eyelids look heavy as she tries to keep them open. She leans her head into the crook of Gareon's body as he wraps an arm around her.

"You know, I could use your assistance in Sao," she says through a hooded gaze. "I'm sure there are many things you could assist me with once things are settled."

The corner of Gareon's mouth quirks up. The blue markings sprawling up his arm and neck appear to be more prominent, almost glowing in response. I'm trying not to eavesdrop, but it's difficult in such small quarters.

"Would that *please* you, Crystal?" he replies.

She takes in a shuddered breath. "I would not be the only one who would be *pleased*," she muses in a feline expression as she looks out the window toward Iván.

I keep my eyes fixed out the other window. Adnama has fallen asleep. Though I don't truly know her, I somehow do through the darkness of my short time spent in the White Forest. She and her sister have both suffered immensely, but both have found each other and have risen from the ashes. She has much to learn about this world, but I know my father will welcome her with open arms. My head dips down, looking at Viona as her head leans slightly to the side. She looks up through thick lashes.

"You're beautiful," I confess, admiring every curve of her face. The way her eyes upturn at the outer corners, reminding me of a wild cat. Eyes that can cut like steel and bury me with one look. My gaze trails over the fullness of her lips. Leaning in, I press my lips to hers. She takes me, no second guessing or hesitating, even though we aren't entirely alone. I smile against her mouth at the eagerness in her kiss. I slightly pull away, angling my upper torso toward her, and lean forward, brushing her cheek with the back of my hand. "You taste divine." My voice dips lower, causing her to react by pressing her hand against my thigh, showing no restraint for her need. It makes my heart skip a beat. Her gaze softens as she smiles, still not fully believing the beauty I see in her. I will spend the rest of my life worshiping every inch of her body and soul. My heart leaps once more. I think I might fucking die by that look alone as it sweeps me up into to the stars.

"You're shameless, Callian," she says in a gentle tease. I press my lips to hers while my mind encourages me to do not-so-gentle things. I have to keep myself in check.

"When we get back home, I'm going to show you how shameless I can be, and I couldn't give two fucks who hears us."

"My gods, I hope somewhere between now and then, crows pick my eardrums out," Crystal scoffs, keeping her eyes fixed out of the carriage windows. A humorous laugh rumbles in Gareon's chest as he smirks, his eyes bouncing between myself and Viona. He turns his attention toward Crystal.

"I could put up a ward. No sounds would come in *or out* of your room," he drawls in that mysterious accent no one can place. Her cheeks instantly flush. Now I think *I'm* going to be sick, but the smile and excitement in my sister's eyes is enough to tell me that maybe I should give him a chance, as I did with Iván. They both bring her so much happiness.

I chuckle, watching the sun shining above the clouds, casting beams of golden light onto the open fields. Viona yawns, nestling herself into the crook of my body, and closes her eyes. Once again, it's just us, between the earth and the stars. Nothing will ever keep us apart again.

THE END

AFTERWORD

Thank you for reading A Flame Under the Moon! For updates on Book 2, please join the newsletter on my website for all updates, give-aways, merch and more.

www.authormonicaamore.com

Did you enjoy the book? Please consider leaving a review on Amazon (https://a.co/d/85yVjwn) and/or

Goodreads (https://www.goodreads.com/book/show/19632179 1-a-flame-under-the-moon).

Reviews help authors reach their audience and give other readers the chance to read their book!

ACKNOWLEDGEMENTS

My husband—my real shadow daddy. You believed in me way before I ever saw it. You created a barrier and protected my heart every step of the way, especially during the last portion of this book. YOU are my safe place. YOU are my hiding place. When the world around us gets too loud, you hold it back so the three of us may breathe. In many ways, you saved me, my warrior, my protector.

My daughter—my little rock and powerhouse. You make my world full of color. Seeing you read and write every day since you were small, inspired me to follow my heart. You opened up my eyes and reminded me to reclaim a passion that I had long forgotten. You are the light in all our lives. I'm so thankful for your reminders to have fun and let loose.

My grandparents—You gave me the freedom to express myself. Now as an adult, I cannot fathom living any other way. You listened to hours of me trying to process this self publishing journey and always reminded me to fill my cup. Though I don't know if you'll ever read this book, I know you will proudly display it on the dresser.

Mama Donna—the powerhouse, the one who always told me to 'do whatever the fuck you want,' and 'don't let anyone stand in your way' kind of woman, you are quite the storm. Not everyone is blessed to have someone like you. Thank you for always reminding me of who I am and to keep my wits. Papa, thank you for keeping your son company while I spent a year writing this book.

My sister—my twin even though we are years apart, in many ways we are the same. You bring so much laughter into our world. Your drawings are so inspiring, and you are beyond talented. Never stop being who you are.

My Mother—the creator of my imagination as a child. Growing up, you always painted a world for me that was bright and cheery. Thank you for being my cheerleader and for keeping my writings safe.

My uncle and aunt—Thank you for your wisdom.
My step dad—you are a warrior and deserve a mention because I can easily see you battling one of these larkin dudes, no sweat. Easy.

My niece Alyssa—I am always rooting for you.
My nephew Blake—your desire to dream big is inspirational.
Brother Ken—you tapped in and I listened. I didn't kill that character off.

My moon sister Mandi—my dark angel, may you rest in peace. You were such a beautiful and talented soul. The brightest star that fell from the sky. The world shattered when you left, but I know you were meant for bigger things far more than what was here on earth. In another life, we will have our time, in a world where there are three moons, caves full of crystals and endless fields of wildflowers.

My editor Rachel—We did it! Every time I think about this, it brings tears to my eyes. You took on this big project and worked with me literally every day for months. You went above and beyond with your developmental and copyline edits. I am so grateful for all your time and dedication to my debut novel. Thank you from the bottom of my heart for everything you have done for me.

To all my alpha and beta readers, you are all so magnificent. Each and every one of you brought something unique to the table, and I enjoyed reading all your unhinged commentary. Thank you for the amount of time you put into my book. Special thanks to Annika, Brittany, Chelsey, Jasmine, Karrie and Salina!

Thank you @clintcreates for doing the character artwork for me. You made my characters come alive for not only me but for the readers! I'm so grateful for the hundreds of hours you put into this project for me.

Thank you @miblart for creating such a beautiful cover for me.

To the book community,
You help indie authors like me get seen. I am so thankful for every comment, like and share you sent my way whenever I posted about this book. I appreciate your enthusiasm, it pushed me to the finish line. When this debut drops, we will be even louder! I'm very proud to be a part of such an amazing community. For someone who never felt like I belonged, I found my place.

As you see, it takes a village to make a book happen.
I am grateful for those who have followed my journey and for those I will pick up along the way.

ABOUT THE AUTHOR

Monica Amore is a self-publishing indie author who has west coast roots, born and raised in the City of Angels. She now lives in a hidden forest with her husband, daughter and cats somewhere in the Midwest. When she was young, she wanted the hero, but now she wants the villains. When she's not writing fantasy romance novels, she's somewhere barefoot in the woods or tucked away in her haunted little library reading more books. She loves iced coffee, spending time with her family, and loves being outdoors.

Website: www.authormonicaamore.com